Praise for

"Through v̶... a work of art. From first to final page this original fantasy is sure to draw readers in. *Auralia's Colors* sparkles."

> —JANET LEE CAREY, award-winning author of *The Beast of Noor* and *Dragon's Keep*

"Jeffrey Overstreet's first fantasy, *Auralia's Colors*, and its heroine's cloak of wonders take their power from a vision of art that is auroral, looking to the return of beauty, and that intends to restore spirit and mystery to the world. The book achieves its ends by the creation of a rich, complex universe and a series of dramatic, explosive events."

> —MARLY YOUMANS, author of *Ingledove* and *The Curse of the Raven Mocker*

"In *Auralia's Colors*, Overstreet masterfully extends the borders of imagination. Whereas so many writers sacrifice characterization for plot or substitute weirdness for substance, Overstreet does neither. His characters are richly crafted but still recognizably human and, therefore, inhabitable. This is a wild and intricate tale, a high-octane, full-throttle fantasy. Fasten your seat belts."

> —GINA OCHSNER, author of *The Necessary Grace to Fall* and *People I Wanted to Be*

"The late John Gardner said that a good story should unfold like a vivid and continuous dream. With *Auralia's Colors*, Jeffrey Overstreet has crafted just such a story, one that will leave readers ready to dream with him again."

> —JOHN WILSON, editor, *Books & Culture*

"Jeffrey Overstreet weaves myth and reality, hope and loss into his tapestry, and he ties off *The Red Strand* with a cataclysmic flourish."

—KATHY TYERS, author of *The Firebird Trilogy* and *Shivering World*

"Welcome to the land of the fangbear, the muckmoth, and the Midnight Swindler. To a story brimming with lovely literary rewards and a cast of characters by turns loathsome and hilarious, winsome and mysterious. It's not often one gets to be present at the birth of a classic, but *Auralia's Colors* is that kind of storytelling. A true delight on so many levels."

—CLINT KELLY, author of the *Sensations Series: Scent, Echo,* and *Delicacy*

"In this new fantasy novel, *Auralia's Colors,* Jeff Overstreet weaves together a wide cast of compelling characters and an intriguing story in the setting of a world both imaginative and arresting—a world *phantastic* in both old and new meanings of that word. Readers will care what happens both to the characters of the tale (all of them) and to the realm of Abascar itself and will not want to put this book down."

—MATTHEW DICKERSON, coauthor of *From Homer to Harry Potter: A Handbook on Myth and Fantasy* and *Ents, Elves, and Eriador: The Environmental Vision of J. R. R. Tolkien*

AURALIA'S
COLORS

A NOVEL

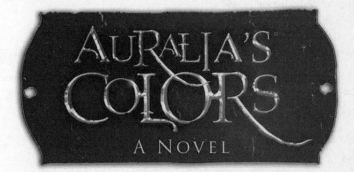

AURALIA'S COLORS

A NOVEL

JEFFREY OVERSTREET

WATERBROOK
PRESS

AURALIA'S COLORS
PUBLISHED BY WATERBROOK PRESS
12265 Oracle Boulevard, Suite 200
Colorado Springs, Colorado 80921
A division of Random House Inc.

ISBN: 978-1-4000-7252-1

Copyright © 2007 by Jeffrey Overstreet
Map copyright © 2007 by Rachel Beatty

Published in association with the literary agency of Alive Communications Inc., 7680
Goddard Street, Suite 200, Colorado Springs, CO 80920, www.alivecommunications.com.

Library of Congress Cataloging-in-Publication Data
Overstreet, Jeffrey.
   Auralia's colors : the red strand of the Auralia thread / Jeffrey Overstreet. — 1st ed.
      p. cm.
   ISBN 978-1-4000-7252-1
   I. Title.
   PS3615.V474A95 2007
   813'.6—dc22

                              2007017881

Printed in the United States of America
2007—First Edition

10 9 8 7 6 5 4 3 2 1

For Anne

whose poetry awakens the ears of my ears
and opens the eyes of my eyes

CONTENTS

ACKNOWLEDGMENTS

So many people contributed to this, the fulfillment of my lifelong dream. If I thanked them all in print, that would be a volume in itself.

Above all, I thank Anne, my best listener, my favorite editor, and a poet whose journal entries enchant me.

I thank my parents, Larry and Lois Overstreet, for investing time, prayer, and resources in my writing. And I thank my brother Jason, who patiently listened to me read my first storytelling attempts when we were very young.

I owe a great debt of gratitude to the many teachers and professors who gave me encouragement and showed such patience, especially Michael Demkowicz, David Robinson, Luke Reinsma, and Rose Reynoldson.

I am also grateful to Linda Wagner and to the members of her sci-fi/ fantasy writing circle—Beth Harris, John and Margaret Sampson Edgell, and Peyton Burkhart—who critiqued the earliest drafts of this story; to my co-workers at Seattle Pacific who endured my zombielike state during the final months; to Wayne Proctor and Fritz Liedtke, who offered suggestions along the way; and especially to Danny Walter, whose insightful questions inspired several years of revisions.

As I wrote, I thought of this project as a personal thank-you note to J. R. R. Tolkien for *The Lord of the Rings*, Richard Adams for *Watership Down*, Stephen R. Lawhead for The Pendragon Cycle, Michael Ende for *Momo*, Mervyn Peake for the Gormenghast novels, Mark Helprin for *Winter's Tale*, Guy Gavriel Kay for The Sarantine Mosaic, and Patricia McKillip for *The Book of Atrix Wolfe*. I hope to personally thank each writer, here or beyond.

And finally, thanks to those who gave Auralia a chance to find an audience: Marsha Marks and her magic telephone; my agents, Don Pape, who believed in Auralia, and Lee Hough, who gave such dependable counsel; Shannon Hill,

Carol Bartley, and the WaterBrook team, who devoted themselves to the project with insight and meticulous attention; and to Kristopher Orr, whose cover art takes my breath away.

Of course, all these were woven into the design by a Grand Artist, and I hope I have captured a glimmer of his glory in these pages for his praise.

THE EXPANSE

(AS PERCEIVED BY THE REMNANT OF ABASCAR)

OLD THIEVES MAKE A DISCOVERY

A uralia lay still as death, like a discarded doll, in a burgundy tangle of rushes and spineweed on the bank of a bend in the River Throanscall, when she was discovered by an old man who did not know her name.

She bore no scars, no broken bones, just the stain of inkblack soil. Contentedly, she cooed, whispered, and babbled, learning the river's language, and focused her gaze on the stormy dance of evening sky—roiling purple clouds edged with blood red. The old man surmised she was waiting and listening for whoever, or whatever, had forsaken her there.

Those fevered moments of his discovery burnt into the old man's memory. In the years that followed, he would hold and turn them in his mind the way an explorer ponders relics he has found in the midst of ruin. But the mystery remained stubbornly opaque. No matter how often he exaggerated the story to impress his fireside listeners—"I dove into that ragin' river and caught her by the toe!" "I fought off that hungry river wyrm with my picker-staff just in time!"—he found no clue to her origins, no answers to questions of why or how.

The Gatherers, House Abascar, the Expanse—the whole world might have been different had he left her there with riverwater running from her hair. "The River Girl"—that was what the Gatherers came to call her until she grew old enough to set them straight. Without the River Girl, the four houses of the Expanse might have perished in their troubles. But then again, some say that without the River Girl those troubles might never have come at all.

This is how the spark was struck.

A ruckus of crows caught Krawg's attention as he groped for berries deep in a bramble. He and Warney, the conspirator with whom he had been caught thieving so many years ago, were laboring to pay their societal debts to House Abascar. The day had been long, but Krawg's spirits were high. No officers had come to reckon their work and berate them. Not yet. Tired of straining for late-summer apples high in the boughs of ancient trees, they had put down their picker-staffs and turned to plucking sourjuice and jewelweed bushes an apple-core's throw from the Throanscall.

Warney was preoccupied, trying to free his thorn-snagged sleeves and leggings. So Krawg smiled, dropped his harvesting sack, and crept away to investigate the cause of the birds' cacophony. He hoped to find them eying an injured animal, maybe a broad-antlered buck he could finish off and present to the duty officers. That would be a prize grand enough to deserve preparation in King Cal-marcus's kitchens. Such a discovery might bring Krawg closer to the king's grace and a pardon.

"Aw, will you look at that?" Krawg flexed his bony fingers. The feathered curmudgeons flapped at the air over the riverbank, their gaze fixed on a disturbance in the grass.

"Now, hold on!" called his even bonier friend. "Whatcha got there? Wait for me!" Twigs snapped and fabric ripped, but Warney made no progress. "Speak up now, what're them flappers squawkin' over? Are beastmen coming to kill us?"

"Stop spookin', fraidy-brain," Krawg growled, and then he gusted air through his nostrils. "There won't be no beastman savages out here in the afternoon."

"What is it then? Merchants?"

"No merchants."

"Is it a swarm of stingers?"

"Nope."

"A fangbear? River wyrms? Bramblepigs?"

"Don't think so."

"Some young buster sneakin' up behind us? Come on now. What's got them birds so bothered?"

According to his nature, Krawg tossed back a lie. "They're just fightin' over a mess of reekin' twister fish they snatched out of the shallows." Groundwater closed over his feet as he made his way through the reeds on the riverbank. Increasingly perturbed by the way Krawg was stalking their target, the crows descended to the branch of a stooping cottonbeard tree and pelted him with insults.

As Krawg combed the grasses for an answer, Warney at last emerged from the trees with worry in his one good eye, gripping as if it were a hunting spear the long, clawed picker-staff he had used all day to drag down the higher apple-boughs. Warney seemed barely more than a skeleton wrapped in loose flesh and a rough burlap cloak. "What are they fussin' about now if they've gone and eaten their fill?"

Krawg's vulturebeak nose twitched in the middle of the few undisciplined whiskers that grew where a mustache did not. He leaned forward, apprehensive, and saw not a pile of fish bones but two tiny pink hands reaching into the air.

"One of the fish has got hands!" gasped Warney.

"Shush now! It isn't a pile of fish." Krawg took hold of the appleknife in his pocket. "Whatever it is, it's harmless, I'm sure."

Warney glanced back at the woods. "Don't forget to watch for you-know-who. Duty officers'll haul us in, bottom 'n' blockhead, if they catch us messin' with anything other than them berries. They'll ride their stinkin' lizards right through here soon. Come on now…there's a nice bramble just back here. You don't want the duty to string us up in the hangers, do ya?"

"Good creepin' Cragavar forest, of all the bloody wonders I ever seen… Looky!" The braver Gatherer flipped his black hood back from his hairless head and bent to examine the child.

Warney remained where he was. "Krawg, you're givin' me the shut-mouth again. What is it, old boy?"

"Just a creepin', crawlin' baby, it is." Krawg massaged the flab beneath his chin. "Mercy, Warney, look at her."

"It's a her? How do you know?"

"Well, howdaya think I know?" Krawg reached for the child, then thought better of it. "Warney, this must mean somethin'. You and me...findin' this." He scanned the spaces between trees on both sides of the mist-shrouded river and confirmed that the only witnesses were crows and a tailtwitcher that clung upside down to the trunk of a birch.

Warney splashed into the river shallows and prodded the submerged ground with his picker-staff before each step. The weeds around his ankles whispered *hushhh...hushhh...hushhh.*

The child convulsed twice. She coughed up droplets of water. And then she made a sound that might have been a laugh.

"Now that's odd." Krawg gestured to the child's tiny head. "She got brown and silver hairs. She's seen at least two seasons, I'd say. Probably born before that hard freeze we had awhile back."

"Yeah, gotta 'gree with ya there." Warney's eye was white as a sparrow's egg in the shadows of his hood.

"And she's not the spawn of those beastmen. Everything about her seems like a good baby girl, not some accursed cross between person and critter. Looks like she's been fed and looked after too...well, until she got tossed into the river, I suppose."

"Gotta 'gree with ya there." Warney now leaned over the child, swaying like a scarecrow in the wind. "She's better fed than any of us Gatherers...or crows, for that matter."

The crows were quiet, watching, picking at their sharp toes.

Krawg knelt and took to picking at his toes as well, poking at yellow places, which meant he was thinking hard. "We're too far east of House Bel Amica for her to belong to them proud and greedy folk. But how could she be from our good House Abascar? Folk from Abascar only step out of the house walls if King Cal-marcus tells 'em to. Too scared of beastmen, they are...these days."

"Gotta 'gree with ya there."

"Do you always gotta 'gree with me there?!" Krawg snatched the picker-staff from Warney's hands and clubbed his hooded head. Warney jumped away, growled, and bared his teeth. Krawg tossed the staff aside and rose up like a bear answering the challenge of a rat. Warney, like a rat realizing he has awakened a bear, fled back toward the quiet woods.

"Now don't you get it in your head to leave me here with this orphan," Krawg called, "or I'll rip that patch off your dead eye!"

"Have ya thought..." Warney paused, turned, and clasped his head with both hands, as if trying to stretch his mind to accommodate a significant thought. "Has it occurred to ya that... Do ya think..."

"Speak, you rangy crook!"

"Oh ballyworms, Krawg! What if she's a Northchild?"

Krawg stumbled back a step and narrowed his eyes at the infant.

The tailtwitcher, the crows, and even the river seemed to quiet at Warney's question.

But Krawg at last shook off worry. "Don't shovel that vawn pile my way, Warney. You been eatin' too much of Yawny's stew, and your dreams are gettin' to you. Only crazies think Northchildren are actual. There's no such thing."

They watched the baby's hands sculpt shapes in the air.

"And anyway," Krawg continued, glancing northward at the sky purpling over the jagged mountains of the Forbidding Wall, "everybody knows Northchildren are taller, and they drape blankets over themselves."

Nearby, branches broke with sharp echoes as something moved in the woods.

"Grab for a weapon," hissed Warney, "because I smell prowling beastmen!"

"Doubtful," said Krawg, but he bent his knees and sank into the grass.

"Duty officers then!"

In case their overseers were, in fact, looking for them, Krawg shouted, "We better get back to the patches, Warney! I sure don't see any berries out here." He lifted Warney's picker-staff and marched to join his friend in the trees.

But Warney seemed stuck, as though the girl had tossed a rope and snared his ankle. "You know what they say. If a man leaves a good deed undone, North-children will come creepin' at night and drag him off into the curse of the——"

"I'm not scared of you, butt-guster," Krawg whispered. "Now hush before anybody hears you!"

The girl, aware that she was alone again, began to murmur as if talking with someone they could not see. The Gatherers watched her clap her tiny hands.

A crow took wing from the cottonbeard tree and made a wide circle over the child's bed.

"They want that fresh meat," Krawg observed.

Warney nodded. "Gotta 'gree with ya…" His mouth snapped shut, and he winced.

Krawg loosed a weary sigh, waved a scornful gesture at the birds, and returned to kneel beside the baby.

Warney hopped back to peer over Krawg's shoulder. "What's that she's lyin' in? That isn't a sinkhole."

"No, somebody carved out this hole with their hands."

"Not with their hands, no. Look, Krawg…*toes.* This Northchild's lyin' in a footprint!" Warney's grin signified a victory. "Gotta *disagree* with ya there!"

The child had gone quiet and still. And that was what Krawg would remember for the rest of his troubled life—the moment when her eyes gathered sunset's burning hues and flickered with some element he had never seen; the way she rested, as though commanded to surrender by some voice only she could hear; the way he clenched his jaw, made his decision.

A wave of wind carried a few slow leaves, a shower of twirling seedpods from the violet trees, spiders on newly flung strands, and a hint of distant music—the Early Evening Verse sung by the watchman of House Abascar to mark the dusk of the day.

"Oh, our backs are strapped now. They'll string us upside down for certain. It's late, and we're bound to be found missin'." Warney's eye rolled to fix on the sun's fading beacons. "Let's turn the baby over to the first officer we see, and maybe——"

"What do you think a duty officer sees when he looks at us, Warney? I'm the Midnight Swindler, and you're the One-Eyed Bandit! They'll say we swiped this baby from somewhere. We already been punished for our thievin'. They made us live outside the walls as Gatherers, and there's only one shelf in the pantry lower than that: *the dungeons.*" Krawg threw the picker-staff down—*splack!*—against the wet ground. "I can't hand her over, but I can't leave her either. If I do, some officer'll ride through here and stomp her into the ground. We've got to take her. And hide her."

"Ballyworms!" Warney shuddered. "You 'n' me 'n a Northchild 'n' all!"

A commotion erupted just south of the marsh. First came a three-toned bellow, which the Gatherers recognized as the complaint of a vawn, one of the duty officers' reptilian steeds. Then came the din of crushed bracken and shaken trees. It was certainly an officer come to measure their progress.

Krawg bent low and lifted the naked child by the arms. "She's harmless. Didn't cast no spell on me. Didn't drag me off into darkness. She isn't a Northchild! There's no such thing."

"Well, let's hurry it up then," said Warney, grinning in spite of his fear.

A few minutes later Krawg and Warney reached the shelter of thatched grass roofs and crooked mud walls in the woods just outside House Abascar's boundary. There, the kinder sort among the Gatherers would tend to the River Girl's needs and protect her from the dangerous sort.

Warney clapped a hand over his mouth, muffling a laugh. "Don't it bring back memories, Krawg? Sneakin' off with treasure like this?"

"Warney," Krawg replied, "we've never, never lifted treasure like this."

Krawg and Warney weren't punished for carrying back the child. But they were "strung up in the hangers" and dangled from their ankles there a full day, scraping the filthy gutters of their vocabulary, when it was discovered they had returned without their designated picker-staffs.

Meanwhile, at the river's edge, water seeped from the soil into the footprint, turned to mud, and solidified. A mist rose, hovered over the place, then wisped away without wind to carry it. It would remain a mystery and a memory to the three men who had found it there—the two troubled Gatherers and one other.

Just after Krawg and Warney had absconded with the child, a solitary rider emerged from the trees and sighted that damp impression in the grass.

The young rider, small and eager, dismounted and studied the outline even as it began to fade. He pulled from the earth a riverstone and touched the face of it with his fingertips, where a dull magic blurred. The stone's color warmed, and it softened to clay under his touch.

Sensing the magic, the crows on the cottonbeard branch shrieked and scattered.

The boy etched a mark in the stone as similar to the contours of the footprint as he could—a sculpture, an equivalent.

Then he walked up and down the banks awhile, surveying the soil. When the vawn snorted impatiently, he returned and climbed back into his ornate saddle. The two-legged steed stomped off, happy to head away from the water and into the trees.

No one knew of the rider's visit to the river. No one saw the record of his discovery, which he kept like a clue to a riddle. And he locked his questions up tight for fear of troubling the volatile storms within the heart of his father, the king.

The Concert of Stitching

T he child became twigs and burnt autumn leaves, thin and fisty fingers clutching acorns and seeds as though they were stolen jewels. Her hair hung in tangles, silver and brown like the bark of apple trees. Her smile sealed off secrets. Each day she made a hurried journey to see as much of the world as she could bear and to harvest a small gallery of souvenirs.

The Gatherers saw her travels in her eyes, for wherever she went, they absorbed colors. She drank in the forest's full spectrum—green pheasant feathers, wild purple lilacs, red fur of lurkdashers, and dandelions both sun yellow and wisp white. When she appeared among the grumbling, half-awake workers in the morning, her eyes glinted emerald, ringed with red, remnants of the sunrise. Sometimes they reflected that light late into the afternoon.

At day's end, when all others were failing, she remained industrious, browsing through gifts the forest had bestowed, noting perfumes and patterns. With her fingertips, she traced the veins of autumn's fiery fan leaves—her favorite trophies. Once she scattered before her, like pieces in a game of fortune, a menagerie of chalk white bones, one perfect purple plum, a beastman's broken black tooth, and an abandoned nest full of rare glowing greenbird feathers.

"How do you know where to find all these things?" excitable orphans would ask.

She'd shrug and share their bafflement, saying she stumbled upon her surprises while following something she could never seem to catch.

Just as she collected souvenirs others would miss, she gathered into memory the details of all she experienced. A nest high in the crook of a coil-tree branch would catch her eager eye; fragments of eggshell glittering on the roots a few days later would provoke her to ponderous silence. On a canvas of stone, she could sketch a map of the trees that encroached on House Abascar from the north, west, and south—the magnificent Cragavar forest. Her map's exquisite detail proved useful to the Gatherers, such that when Yawny the cook lost his spoon or Meddles the weaver misplaced a needle, they made sure to discuss it when she was close enough to hear.

Intimate knowledge of brush-tunnels, stone stairways, ivy tree-ladders, concealed creeks, and buried reservoirs helped her stay lost when she wearied of company. The Gatherers' finest trackers eventually refused to search for her. She'd return laughing, dashing through the camps and discouraging their reprimands with simple surprises that made them marvel and covet her presence even more.

She was elusive and spontaneous like a bird, now chasing a crittercat cub up a tree, now clambering through a stranger's window to bother him with a riddle, now rummaging through a pile of leaves in search of the best one, and now suddenly escaping through some gateway in the brambles only she could see. But a crackling fire and a story—that would convince her to stay for a while.

On rare occasions when she spoke—she had that rough-edged speech common among those Gatherers who spurned education and lacked the patience for eloquence—questions tumbled over one another, unguarded. Gatherers tried to satisfy each inquiry. But at night they rose from their blankets and paced, repeating her questions quietly, until they grew suspicious of her reasons for asking. "She doesn't really want to learn anything," they'd say. "She just wants to remind us of all we don't know."

Some questions she repeated often: "Where'd I come from before I got found?" "What's up past the dark mountains in the North?" "That big, big shadow in my dreams... Why can't I find it when I'm awake?" "Why do I call it *the Keeper*?" "How come other children dream of the Keeper too?" And "Why don't grownups dream of the Keeper?"

As she puzzled in the Gatherers' midst, one would glance at another and mutter, "Them're the troublesome questions, girl. Nobody knows those answers." When she asked again, as though hoping for a different answer, they would shoo her away. And as she trudged off to her next mischief, she'd murmur a different sort of question, something that anyone could answer but no one felt comfortable saying—"Why do the four houses have to have walls?" "Why don't people from all the four houses visit each other?" "Why is House Abascar's palace so beautiful while the rest of the house is dull?"

As Gatherer women explained how crucial it was for the River Girl to "find her feet," draw a man's attention, and make her worth clear to those watching, she thrust out her chin. "Why's it *that* way, and who made it so?"

When the men explained the Rites of the Privilege, the ritual testing through which an orphan or a Gatherer might be granted a new life inside Abascar's mighty walls, she asked, "How come it's *that* way, and who made it so?"

"Why's it *that* way?" she sulked when they described the rules that would govern her once she passed those ceremonial tests. When they recommended she lavish her gifts on favored Gatherers to buy their affections and earn mention to the guards, she would reply, "Why's it gotta be *that* way, and who made it so?" She scowled at the answers that failed to please her, but she heard them all the same. If her elders answered with a *humph* or sharp retort, they'd soon find pebbles in their soup, thorny twigs tucked under their blankets, or snail shells in their stewpots.

Still, the River Girl learned from closely observing the Gatherers. She developed new skills quickly, from weaving to building to catching birds and fish, just by watching from the boughs above or from the edge of a clearing. Sometimes she shadowed them down forest paths, mimicked them like a tiny clown, and seemed to be searching for a sign to show her the role she should play.

That search continued as she listened to daily lessons from women with opinions as abrasive as their chapped and weathered faces, with theories as varied as the crimes that had cost them.

They spoke to her of the elements. Of the animals. Of the myriad hills, valleys, streams. And especially of the woods and their colorful trees, some safe and some fraught with danger. Of the peoples that populated the great Expanse. Of the wide River Throanscall that poured summer's mountain meltings southward from the Forbidding Wall, down, down into the Cragavar forest. Of the forest's broken heart—the ruins of the poisoned House Cent Regus.

Did she know that water from the Throanscall's source was said to make a mind go mad? That in winter, weighty drifts of ice would coast along its currents like fog-robed ships? That flowers grew in the deep woods that, if consumed, could paint nightmares into one's vision? That there were underground rivers, rushing and roaring through night black tunnels where dark creatures groaned and hid from the light?

They told her of the four houses. House Bel Amica on the western coast, where the Throanscall spilled into an inlet and the sea, where the people lived in opulence and strange ways, with ceremonies honoring moon-spirits. House Cent Regus, once a sophisticated culture in a sprawling, hivelike labyrinth made of clay and stone, where respectable people had meddled with magic and devolved into ravenous beastmen that preyed upon anything that moved. House Jenta of the hot and barren lands to the south, where quiet cave dwellings hid the simple rituals of robed and hooded inhabitants.

And their own House Abascar, its history of mining and harvesting, its brave kings and formidable queens. Abascar, they told her, gave strength and safety to those who obeyed King Cal-marcus's laws and lived within its stone walls. House Abascar, the finest house in all the land, they said. House Abascar, from which they had been cast for their crimes, cursed to work in peril and hard weather in hopes of earning their privileges again.

In return, the River Girl told them fantastic dreams—most often the dream of that shadow, the Keeper, who stalked her through the trees.

"Beware of shadows, River Girl!" they warned her. "Beastmen are hunting you, with claws out and ready!"

"No, no, no, I never dream of monsters," she insisted. "The creature is gentle and keeps me safe down beside the River Throanscall or at the edge of Deep Lake."

They patted her silverbrown head and explained that all children dream of such a creature. That she would outgrow foolish nightmares someday, just as they had. That all this nonsense about the Keeper would fade.

But the River Girl denied that her dreams were nightmares or foolish. "How can I see somethin' in my sleep I've never seen awake?" she asked. "And how come others have seen it there too?"

When their backs were turned, she drew outlines of the Keeper on their walls.

Through these first few years, the child had been called River Girl, thanks to Krawg and Warney, who doted on her like proud grandfathers. But one evening Old Lady Wenjee, whose talk was as rough as her temper, decided to announce a proper name for the Gatherers' most unusual orphan.

The River Girl sat in a circle with women inside a thatched hut. As a modest fire warmed their stitches, needles, balls of string, and gossip, she set about to patching two grey, threadbare stockings that Wenjee had bestowed upon her as if they were some precious inheritance. Walls of tightly woven toughstalk held in the sound of their whispers.

But Wenjee knew nothing of whispers. Her voice was suited to her voluminous mass.

"You know, child," said Wenjee, squeezing the River Girl's round face between her chubby hands, "you must get tired of hearin' a hundred different nicknames. It's time you were given a name proper. So, since you love me best, I'm the nearest thing to your mama." She grinned a collection of teeth gone wrong and declared, "So I'm gonna call ya...*Prinny!*"

The River Girl's eyes drained of color. Her jaw might have dropped open if Wenjee hadn't held it fast in a crushing grip.

"Why, y'ask? Because my mama called me 'Princess' when I was little."

"Little?" another voice scoffed. "Wenjee was never *actually* little, in truth."

"This was back in the days when Har-baron, Cal-marcus's one-armed father, was king. Mama figured I'd grow up and meet the prince and get married into the palace real good. Same smarts as a sheep's bottom, Mama had. If there wasn't six layers of dirt between me 'n' her today, I'd smack her for her yakkin'. Because young Prince Cal-marcus never chose me. Nope. He took somebody else."

"He *found* somebody else!" sneered Lezeeka from the corner, sitting outside the circle because she liked to sulk. "Prince Cal-marcus found Jaralaine, that waresellers' daughter. Only survivor of a beastman attack, she was. Father and mother hacked to pieces. Brother and sisters shot full of arrows. An angry child Jaralaine became. A wicked orphan!"

"Shh!" came a sharp whisper from Mulla Gee, who stripped strands of dry grass into narrower threads. "It's Wenjee's story for the tellin'."

"Anyways," bellowed the barrel-shaped storyteller, "Prince Cal-marcus ker Har-baron was all anxious to pick his bride."

The women began stitching faster, staring dazedly into the flames.

"What a day when Cal-marcus rode through on his vawn in all his splendid colors, surrounded by his handsome young busters. He went right up... He went right up...to..." Wenjee's voice faltered to a squeak. Her eyes leaked. She sagged back slowly, and her grip loosened. The River Girl pried her head free of the woman's hand, opened and closed her mouth to make sure its hinges still held. "Cal-marcus went up to this orphan rascal. A girl with hair like fire 'n' gold. A girl who'd never said a word to me, good 'r bad!"

"We all knew Jaralaine had been chasing Cal-marcus," muttered Lezeeka. "Muck-headed beast, that girl! Never trust a wareseller. Maybe it wasn't beastmen that killed her family. Maybe she grew so ashamed of mum and pappy that one dark day she let 'em have it."

The River Girl mouthed the name *Jaralaine*, absorbing the narrative cautiously. It was always a puzzle, discerning true history in the mess of tangled, tainted Gatherer memories. This story caught her attention. She recognized it, somehow, as true. "Hair like fire 'n' gold," she whispered, twisting a strand of her own hair between thumb and forefinger, wondering why it was both brown as earth and silver as the hair of an old woman.

"Yes, yes, Jaralaine," Mulla Gee muttered through the grass strands she held between clenched teeth. "Jaralaine wanted to be queen from the day she was found. Found in the wild, like Prinny here."

The River Girl scowled at the name, turned her eyes back to the flames. She picked up the stockings and knotted them together.

"Her mum and pappy never sold much," Lezeeka murmured from her dark corner. "Half-starved and wretched people they were, dealin' Abascar wares to folk from other houses and bringin' their purchases back to the king."

Wenjee seemed unaware of all those who joined in the telling. While they believed it was a chorus, she was in a solo performance, reliving the scenes of the story somewhere in the vacuous core of her colossal head. "Cal-marcus took Jaralaine's hand. He breathed somethin' in her ear, and I..." Now her voice had forgotten itself and was swaying and soaring like wind through a pinched space. "If it ever turned out she was still livin', I'd seek her out, and I'd..."

"You'd smack her?" asked Mulla Gee.

"To the mountains and back! She was a witch, I tell ya! Always runnin' off in secret, always hidin' things. Plotting how she'd outshine us all. You should've heard the outrage inside the walls. Prince Cal-marcus had claimed a wild forest orphan for a bride! Not a maid of the Housefolk. Not a courtgirl. Not a daughter of Sir This or Officer That. But a daughter of dead waresellers. And a mischief-maker, at that." Wenjee took in a great breath that drew the fire's smoke toward her, and then a sigh declaring immeasurable grief sent it streaming against the far wall. "But he chose *her*. That was that. And into the castle Jaralaine went. Never spoke to me again."

"Wenjee, now," said Mulla Gee, "you just said Jaralaine never spoke to you *at all.*"

The storyteller moved on without pause. "Now, this was long before Cal-marcus became our king and went all sour on Jaralaine. First she bewitched him into making her wishes into law. Then she disappeared. And well, that was it. The king got smart and claimed he'd made a whoppin' mistake. He put his ring on the table—that's what kings do, Prinny, when they make a procla-mation—and he decreed that all mothers and fathers in House Abascar would choose brides for their sons, because the sons just don't rightly know what they're gettin' into, and they can't choose any good for themselves. If y'ask me, old Cal-marcus got what he deserved, that old cock-a-doodle marryin' a huff-bucket like her."

"It was her hair," sighed Hildy the Sad One. "All fire 'n' gold."

"No, that figure of hers. She starved herself, she did," snarled Lezeeka.

"Ballyworms," muttered Mulla Gee. "Secrets were Jaralaine's bargaining tools. She bewitched him, I say. He never did seem quite the same person after he took her from the forest."

The talk—"cracker-squawking" it was called by the Gatherer men—had begun. Every old woman yammered at once while nobody listened to a word. Except the River Girl.

"House Bel Amica, out west. That's where Jaralaine wandered from. Them's weird folk, Bel Amicans."

"Some say that Northchildren dragged the bodies of Jaralaine's parents away to the North. And when they did, they took her heart along with them and left her half-mad in the woods."

"There's no such thing as Northchildren! It's all just lies and stories!"

"*True* stories! Northchildren have been howlin' in the dark since our grand-mothers' grandmothers first lost their baby teeth."

"That's not my point!" shouted Wenjee, panicking as she felt their atten-tion slip from her grasp. "Quit talkin' 'bout rumors and whatnot. This is his-tory! I'm tryin' to explain somethin' to Prinny here."

The cracker-squawking stopped, but the feverish stitching continued.

After her raging glare made its full round of reprimand, Wenjee turned back to the girl and sharpened her grief to steely intent. "Little Prinny, I want you to meet the son of King Cal-marcus ker Har-baron—the one they call Prince Cal-raven ker Cal-marcus—and get married just like Mama wanted for me. If the son follows the father, Cal-raven will take a liking to a wild forest girl. But when you catch the prince's eye, remember who named you. Remember who predicted you would be queen. Then perhaps I'll get my room in the palace after all. Everybody knows I deserve it."

The River Girl bowed her head to avoid Wenjee's gaze. Her fists tightened around the stockings.

"You're young, but you got a spark, you do, and spirit. I want you to earn your way inside the walls. When you're old enough for the Rites of the Privilege, pass those tests. Learn to be like obedient Housefolk. And impress King Cal-marcus's scouts. I want you to grow up good 'n' useful. Not like those orphans who spoil their chances. And surely not like those of us who were foolish in our younger days and now have to work to pay it all back. You're better than to be just a babymaker for some rogue or ruffian. So I named ya Prinny, cuz a princess is what you're gonna be, or I'll spit in the drink!"

Wenjee was so proud of her nearly unintelligible speech, she swelled a little larger, which frightened the women close by.

The stitchers quieted for a while, each one imagining things from the dark land of rumor, dreaming of days beyond reach. The stitching concert was over.

The River Girl stood up, brushed scraps of thread from her skirt, and opened her hands. The stockings fell to the floor, and those who noticed were stunned by how they had changed.

"I already got a name," she said flatly. "And it's Auralia."

To punctuate her declaration, she snatched up the vibrant stockings and waved them around in the air over her head like flags, streamers of red and gold, colors they might have absorbed from the fire.

Wenjee's fingers curled into fists. "But...but who ever named you that?"

"And how," whispered Mulla Gee, "did you change the color of them socks?"

"Auralia's my name," she said resolutely.

"But...what does *Auralia* mean?" sneered Lezeeka.

Auralia laughed. "Nobody knows, not yet already!"

Lezeeka rose and stuck her crooked snout into the firelight. "Nobody gets to make their own name."

"I didn't."

"Well, who'd you get it from then?"

"And how did you change the color of them socks?" demanded Mulla Gee, getting to her feet.

Auralia smiled a secretive smile. "Don't need to marry no prince of anything. Don't need to bother with the king's folk. I got things to do. Tracks to follow. And so much I still gotta see." Her eyes were dark, sparkling. She skipped through the dust, set the canvas doors to flapping, and danced into the night. It was as though she'd found her feet, and so she ran, and there was no more mothering.

After that, Wenjee tried to persuade the others to accept her chosen name for the girl: Prinny. But everyone called her Auralia. Auralia was her true name. That they all knew, as if it were a secret they had only just remembered.

3

A BASKET OF BLUE STONES

This was an hour for stealth. The evening sun, peering through an array of passing clouds, beamed ever-changing patterns of light and shade through the trees. When the wind rushed in from a vast and frozen lake, bare branches scraped against one another as if for warmth; ice fell in a clatter and snow in a chorus of whispers and splashes. A rider could pass ghostlike through this wilderness.

Captain Ark-robin had waited for this opportunity. He and his armored vawn were motionless, silent, hidden in brambles, listening.

Tap.

The captain's grip tightened on the reins.

Tap.

Perhaps pieces of shell were splintering under blows of a crackerjaw's beak. But it might also be a beastman's claws, anxious, wherever it lay in wait.

Here, an hour's ride from the outermost Gatherer huts, Ark-robin had found a trail of unfamiliar footprints through the snow beneath the old coil tree. The small tracks were still sharply defined. Recent. Strangely, the erratic prints of a massive fangbear wound along the same path. Perhaps the stillness meant the bear had caught its prey.

Ark-robin smiled, remembering how when he was just a boy he had practiced tracking—first his mother during her errand runs, then a vawn down Abascar roads, and later a wild viscorcat at the edge of the Gatherers' camp. As his hunting skills grew, he dreamt of serving in King Har-baron's ranks.

The world had changed when House Abascar's kingship passed from Har-baron's father to Har-baron and then to his son Cal-marcus. The soldiers Ark-robin adored in his youth, whose adventures filled the scrolls of the king's libraries, had fought battles across the Expanse, resisting the poisonous, powerful magic of House Cent Regus. Today, Abascar soldiers traded the vigorous discipline of war for a routine of tedious surveillance. Cal-marcus ruled a kingdom well defended, with soldiers to patrol the borders, secure the trade routes to Houses Bel Amica and Jenta, protect the harvests, and monitor the Gatherers' work. Ensnaring and killing the predatory beastmen, the deranged and ravenous remnants of House Cent Regus, were the closest things to war Ark-robin had ever enjoyed as a soldier.

What will the world become when King Cal-marcus passes his power to Prince Cal-raven? Ark-robin swatted a skeeter-fly from his ear. *What pathetic duties will dull the lives of future Abascar soldiers?*

Tap. A falling blue star flashed past him. A stone or a gem dropped from high in the tentacles of the tree. It landed in a basket strung up shoulder high with a twistvine.

Ark-robin's scout had whispered when she told him of a meddlesome trespasser. She had whispered because no House Abascar scout wanted to admit she had been outwitted, especially by a child. A young girl. A troublemaker who eluded duty officers by leading them deep into the woods. "I suspect," the scout had said, "that she is the source of the contraband we recently seized from the Gatherers. A thief, perhaps, robbing from House Bel Amica's vanity, making deals with her stolen wares."

Ark-robin vowed he would find her himself, this girl the Gatherers protected, and decide how best to deal with her. It was nothing like the adventures of King Har-baron's famous house defenders, but it was more interesting than his daily inventory of guard towers and spies.

A gorrel sniffed beneath a bush, then emitted a happy, full-bellied sigh. Ark-robin relaxed. Gorrels fled at the signs of fiercer creatures—wyrms, bears, or beastmen—and they left behind a scent that could throw a town into turmoil. But here the air was pure enough to make an old man young again.

He removed his helmet, polished it with his cuff until his blurred reflection cleared, then combed his beard with his fingers and practiced a scowl of authority and intimidation. Securing the helmet again, he dug his heels into the vawn's sides.

The armored mount burst through the brush and shook off the thorny strands that snagged it, wheezing and coughing in a flurry of snow. Ark-robin swept past the coil tree, putting on the pretense of a hot pursuit, then pulled up short and circled back to where the basket hung.

"Wild wyrms of Promontory Hill!" he shouted. With a quick stab of his sword, he snapped the cord that held the basket and caught it with his open hand. "What a fortune I've found!" he said for the benefit of whoever might be—and probably was—listening. He did not risk a glance upward. "Where do such stones come from? I have stumbled into an enchantment."

At that he heard distant laughter, like the fluttering cries of a shrillow.

"My daughter will be so pleased. Unless, perhaps"—now he looked left and right in an exaggerated gesture—"these stones might already belong to someone."

More laughter. Falling clumps of snow and drifting, dead wet leaves. He looked up.

Perched atop a high branch, there she was, squinting, smiling, but cautious.

"I'm so sorry, but I am afraid I cut your basket's tether!" He beckoned to her, taking off his helmet again so he could appear friendlier. "Come down here. I'll give it back."

She began to descend the way a hungry tailtwitcher approaches a man with bread, testing each branch, pausing, reconsidering.

"You have nothing to fear. It's my duty to protect those who live in these woods, for the Cragavar forest belongs to King Cal-marcus. I am captain of the Abascar guard and chief strategist for the king's armies. And I must say, I've never seen you among the orphans that the Gatherers have been commanded to shelter." He lifted up the basket like a tray of sweets. "You seem a fairer, friendlier sort than they. You remind me of my own daughter."

It was a lie but a strategic one. He wanted to seem safe and assuring, to lure her closer. He could now see her clearly, a strange and worried waif, ragged as a finch after a fight with crows, garments tattered and muddied, silverbrown hair glimmering like soft hanging lichen. Young, perhaps eight years, but her features were already striking, bright, inquisitive.

Equally transfixed, the girl studied his elaborate uniform and the vawn, its scales gleaming yellow green, eyes small as coins, and a tail that ended with a heavy, spiked club.

"I'm gonna surprise some Gatherers with those stones," she said. "I'm gonna hide them in their boots." She drew one from her pocket and tossed it into his glove—*clap*. "But take this one to your lady."

He turned it slowly. It cast tiny spots of light like diamonds all around the clearing. He was as bewildered by its beauty as by its sprightly collector.

"Cwauba birds, Captain. They carry the stones from somewhere far off. North, I think. Cwauba birds are lonely, and they get tired of shoutin' for others to join them. So they stick a stone in the crook of a branch where the sun'll make it sparkle. The color does their shoutin'. It's sorta like the way the Gatherer ladies dress up to tease the men or the way the men prance around to impress the ladies. It's like makin' some kinda promise. Do you like to climb trees?"

"I suppose you'll use some of these to bait a handsome young Gatherer boy... Am I right? If I had a son, would I have to warn him to watch out for you?"

She wrinkled her nose. "No, no, no. Crazy old man. I'm too little, too loud. Gatherer ladies say boys want good daughters of Housefolk from inside the walls."

"They say that, do they? I'm sure there are Gatherer boys who would like to marry my daughter, Stricia, if it meant they could live within House Abascar's protection once again. Stricia's beautiful, and she's earning all kinds of honor stitches because she takes instruction so well. She'll have suitors lining up at the door in just a few years. You could enjoy the same attention if you were to earn your way into House Abascar. How long have you been in our woods?"

"Eight summers, they say."

Ark-robin frowned. "You said cwauba birds carry these stones from the North. You've been there? The North? You can tell me a thing or two about it?" He spurred his vawn around the tree, trying to keep her in sight as she clambered about.

"I don't remember being there. But I can see it when I'm sleeping. Perhaps I was there when I was too small to remember..."

"You've heard the histories, no doubt—that the peoples of the four houses came into the Expanse to escape a life of nightmares in the North. I've seen some of the wild and untamed regions there. No one can survive on those mountains. It's a frozen world. Dangers of every sort. You should be glad to live near House Abascar. Duty officers are always on patrol." Ark-robin slid off the vawn, began to walk slowly around the base of the coil tree.

"Duty officers don't take care of orphans." The girl sounded sad. "They just call 'em nasty names. It's Gatherers that feed and clean up and teach the orphans."

"Gatherers care for orphans because they want to earn a pardon, not because they're decent. You think they make good teachers? Is that why you take your little treasures to them? You feel safe among thieves and bullies and liars, do you?"

She cocked her head. "Never met nobody who wasn't a thief or a liar once in a while. The Gatherers are just the folks who got caught."

Ark-robin began to lose his friendly tone. "You talk as if they're just ordinary folk, but the Gatherers are gross offenders of Abascar law—kicked out for spreading dissension, brawling, burglary. Some defy the Proclamation of the Colors, wearing colors that are forbidden to all but the people of highest rank. They disrespect the royalty. And so do you when you give those crooks such beautiful baubles. Treasures like that should be given to the king."

He had found a way to make his point at last. "Cwauba birds may leave bright stones in the trees, but they don't leave extravagant garments like those we have found hidden under Gatherer huts. If we catch the person responsible for giving the Gatherers treasures like those, there will be a reprimand."

He reached up to the lower branches and knocked on the trunk of the tree. "Why don't you just drop that handful into this basket, and I'll tell the king you're sending him a gift. Who knows? He may decide to show you some grati-tude. There might be a place and a task for you within Abascar's walls. I'll make sure he remembers your kindness when the time comes for you to be tested at the Rites of the Privilege."

"Get out of my woods!" Spry as a treecat, the girl bounded up three branches until she was just an outline through the boughs. "Get out of my woods. I'm not gonna be no Housefolk."

"Oh, of course you will...*Auralia!*" When Ark-robin spoke the girl's name, her mouth dropped open, and he laughed a hard, proud laugh. "You will join us in a few short years. These things we're finding in the camps—some Gath-erers say they came from you. 'It's Auralia's fault,' they say. Haven't they told you about the Rites?"

"Oh yes." Auralia reached around the back of the tree and lifted another basket full of stones. "Gatherers who have been good get pardoned. And orphans, when they're sixteen years old, are invited to live inside the walls if they show the king what they can do."

"Not just the king! You'll stand in front of all House Abascar, Auralia, for the people risk much by letting someone like you inside. You will demonstrate for them what use you will be, and the king will decide your value to the house."

"I know lotsa Gatherers who aren't useful to the king, but they're still worthsome, no matter what he says. And why does he think we gotta be inside the walls to be happy? Housefolk're always scowlin' and grumblin' when I see them. Prob'ly cuz things're so much more colorful *outside.*"

"Are you telling me you do not wish to return to the place you came from?"

"Ha!" Auralia bent her knees, dropped backward, and swung upside down from the branch. Her eyes flashed with wild secrets. "Didn't come from Abascar."

Seeing her face more clearly, Ark-robin held back a gasp. She was, certainly, from somewhere far away. It was not just her skin, although she was darker than even the Gatherers with their reddened, weathertough skin. It was her concentration, a fierce apprehension of everything. She was reading him.

He recognized his discomfort, something he'd experienced only twice before. Once he had felt it while standing in the presence of Abascar's queen. The second time, he had run through a burning house, and he had seen things lurking on the threshold of death—things he would never mention to anyone.

"You did come from Abascar. You just don't want to play by its rules." He knew his smile was unconvincing. "Tell me how you came to be an orphan."

Still upside down, Auralia grabbed a lower branch, unlocked her legs, and swung closer to him. Her toes hung just above the captain's head, and she tapped them lightly on the top of his helmet. Then she let go and, light as air, leapt and landed, again out of reach, on another contorted black branch. Dislodged by her stunt, red-green leaves, a remnant from autumn, spun slowly down around the disgruntled giant. "Did they tell you I'm an orphan?"

"If you're not an orphan, then you must have a family. And if your family lives beyond Abascar, then you are a trespasser. And if you are a trespasser, it is my duty to prevent you from trespassing further. You shall either quit these woods or live openly among Gatherers and come into our house at sixteen. During the next eight summers you might consider becoming a mosaicist. Or a roofpatcher. But I would recommend you consider weaving for the king. Those things we confiscate from the Gatherer huts show that you have a particular gift. And when you do come in for the Rites, bring the king some sign of your pledge, an exaltation of Abascar. He will put you to work. Maybe you'll meet my daughter. Stricia could teach you a thing or two about what it means to be respectable."

"I'm not gonna join the Housefolk. Don't want to give up paths for roads. And woods for walls. And caves for Housefolk huts. And colors for...for *that*." She gestured in the direction of the house. "The Gatherers blame that nasty queen who disappeared. She took away all the Housefolk colors."

"They told you that story? Thieves and meddlers cannot be trusted."

"You mean the Gatherers? Or the queen?"

Ark-robin's eyes narrowed. "It was a royal proclamation, not a whim, that designated colors for the privileged. We'll see how much you care about your colorful woods when that fangbear finally catches up to you." The captain climbed back into his saddle. "Then perhaps you'll wish you had followed my advice."

Auralia's brow wrinkled. "There's no fangbear chasing me."

"I'm a tracker, Auralia," the captain boasted, pointing to the bear tracks along the ground. "But surely you're not so blind."

"Oh, *that* fangbear. We were only just playing. *I* was chasing *him*. He got tired and needed a rest. So I thought I'd climb the tree." She gestured to the trees just over his shoulder. "Looks like he's got his strength back."

Across the snow between the tree and the captain, the tall narrow shadow of Ark-robin upon his mount was suddenly eclipsed by a deeper darkness.

Ark-robin turned and saw the red blur of fangbear fur just as his vawn reared in terror. A moment later he was facedown with a mouthful of muddy snow, blue stones scattered all around his head. Auralia's voice rang out in surprise and then—it would seem to him later as he reconstructed the memory—perhaps even a scolding. Pain seared through his shoulder. His fall had reopened an old wound. He heard a whistle and a furious roar and braced himself for the strike of razor claws.

Instead, the clearing quieted.

His vawn, grunting nervously, paced about the base of the coil tree. The bear was gone, and so was Auralia.

On a long and meandering route to the front gates, Captain Ark-robin found himself groping for excuses. He would have to explain the scratches on his face and the injury that would—he knew from experience—take weeks to heal.

As his vawn carried him through a clearing, a flock of starlings appeared, arcing up from the east, threading their way to the walls, where they massed and clamored at dusk. Thousands of small black birds gathered every sundown, a great winged tide as sure as the rising moon. Some called them "night-steeds," for it was as though they drew the night up over the forest, pulling it on invisible tethers.

Ark-robin watched their migration until they disappeared over the last stand of woods between him and Abascar's gates. With one hand he held the reins, and with the other he held the basket of Auralia's stones, which, he marveled, still glowed with daylight.

An Abascar watchman sounded the Evening Verse, adding an extra strain to wish the Housefolk a slumber undisturbed by approaching rain. Ark-robin raised his voice to sing along, hoping to ward off memories Auralia had loosed. Memories of another mischievous wilderness girl. Memories of a midnight when House Abascar had been deceived. His voice failed as he recalled there had been a storm song that night too, long ago.

The king's tower loomed, a silhouette now, the thin curve of the moon like a gleaming helm above it.

Ark-robin shivered. Memories of Queen Jaralaine seized him.

4

THE MERCHANTS' DAUGHTER

Snagged by a riptide of memory, Captain Ark-robin recalled how that momentous night, so many years ago, changed everything in Abascar.

It had begun with someone rattling the door while he lay watching his wife, Say-ressa. Hours like these, when this weary healer could turn away from the sick and the suffering and find a spell of peace, were rare. He would have ignored the visitor just to let Say-ressa sleep. But this was not just a visitor. This—the wall shaking, the latch breaking loose from the doorframe—would have to be a royal summoner.

Reluctantly he met the summoner's haughty gaze and learned that his presence was required in the king's tower.

He joined Tar-brona at the end of the avenue outside Ark-robin's living quarters. In those days, Tar-brona was captain of the guard, silver-haired and small but tough as gristle, unwavering in his obedience to Cal-marcus and strangely prescient when it came to the king's endeavors. Thus it unsettled Ark-robin to learn that Tar-brona knew nothing about the reason for their summons.

They proceeded together quietly, with haste, arriving at precisely the moment the house watchmen sang out the haunting Midnight Verse. An additional lyric—a storm warning—only increased his feeling of dread.

Inside the palace, at the entrance to the king's fireside library, a doubled guard let them in and then closed the doors firmly behind.

It was not Cal-marcus they found there.

A shaft of moonlight fell through the tall window at one end of the narrow chamber. A hiss of wind crept in and slithered along the floorboards.

No one stood at the map table, and no one was pacing and pondering scrolls from the voluminous library. There was only little Cal-raven in his white nightshirt sitting on the floor before a wall of shelves, talking quietly to himself. Beneath him, uncurling, was a great map of the Expanse. Cal-raven's small hands moved stone figures across parchment as though playing a game of strategy. He glanced up once at the defender and captain, blinked. "One of the pieces is missing. Do you know where it is?"

The men shared a troubled glance, then shook their heads and shrugged. "My apologies, young prince," said Tar-brona.

This seemed to earn them his disregard, for he solemnly sighed and said, with his father's familiar melancholy, "I suppose it's my mystery to solve."

Captain Tar-brona cleared his throat. "The prince is never awake so late. And where are the attendants assigned to him while his mother is away?"

Abascar's gates had opened for Queen Jaralaine's departure eight days earlier, while the courtyards resounded with the pomp and parade she arranged to celebrate her every decision. Jaralaine had surprised even the king with her announcement—she wished to see another house, Bel Amica, for herself.

This was not out of character. From the time Cal-marcus first discovered Jaralaine wandering in the wilderness, her mind had been fixed upon all she did not possess. As the daughter of merchants, she had been poor, powerless. As queen, with no one in Abascar to refuse her a request, she worried herself with Abascar's reputation elsewhere in the Expanse, concerned that her people and power might not compare to another's.

Aggravated by reports that House Bel Amica had become a place of wonder and invention, Jaralaine locked herself in her chambers until her husband consented to this journey. Bel Amica's decadence was famous. And it was no secret that the Bel Amicans had accomplished much by sea—Ark-robin had heard witnesses describe ships returning from Bel Amican settlements established on faraway islands. When the king surrendered to Jaralaine's demands, she sent messengers to Bel Amica announcing her visit. Then she ran off with Abascar ambassadors, bearing gifts of precious stones, determined to measure Bel Amica's wealth and ambition and to flaunt the best of Abascar.

King Cal-marcus had remained behind, a sleepless, nervous man.

Ark-robin had come to the palace expecting to find the king wearing out the library rugs, busying his mind with visions of Abascar's storied past. Summonses that came this late in the night were usually harbingers of trouble. The only trouble here was the young prince's search for a missing toy.

In the fireplace light, the king's high-backed chair cast a trembling shadow across the room. An open bottle of hajka rested on the floor. Ark-robin winced. Hajka was a threat to the king's health against which no soldier could defend. He knew Tar-brona would come to the same conclusion—that a foul temper had seized the weary king.

The queen, Ark-robin thought. *Has something befallen Jaralaine in Bel Amica?*

And then came the second surprise of the evening. It was not King Cal-marcus who rose from the chair, but Queen Jaralaine.

She gave the men an exquisite fright. There they stood, burdened with layers of skins, leather, and metal—duty's costume, not the armor of war—while Jaralaine wore a silken nightgown. Barefoot, she approached them as she always did—gingerly, the way someone wary of snakes tiptoes through tall grass. Cascades of golden curls, wild as willowstrands, fell about her shoulders. This was not formal attire, nor was it fitting for her to appear thus before any man but her husband. Ark-robin feared he would not be able to tear his gaze away from Jaralaine, that he would not be able to hide his enchantment or control his thoughts.

Were the king to suddenly appear, conversation would be awkward indeed.

Tar-brona knelt in flustered obeisance, expressing astonishment to find her here, already returned from Bel Amica, and wondering aloud why there had been no announcement or reception.

Jaralaine reassured them warmly. Word had reached her by messenger hawk that Cal-marcus was sick and she should return home. The king had retired to bed, assisted by a nurse.

Her words were rehearsed, tainted with that somewhat sour accent of forest folk. And she moved so swiftly from one subject to the next, they did not think to wonder who might have sent out a messenger hawk to recall her without their knowledge or consent.

But he thought of it now, in retrospect, and viewing her from this distance, he could see her far more clearly.

Rumors of Jaralaine's origins ranged between outrageous and impossible. In the king's version of the tale, he had found her while traveling. As a young prince, he preferred riding horseback fast over open ground to taking vawns through dense, dark woods. Vawns were for laborers and soldiers; horses were for adventurers and men of fortune. On one solitary venture, he had followed his curiosity northward. His discovery enchanted him, and for hours he had concealed himself to watch her washing a basket of apples in the River Throanscall, until she slipped into the water to bathe, singing songs that broke his heart.

When he approached her, she told him she was the daughter of waresellers unsworn to any house. She had been wandering for days, struggling to stay alive, moving slowly southward toward Abascar. Her thoughts were unfocused, meandering between the truth, which was bloody and awful, and a delusion, in which she was certain her family had merely gone on a journey and forgotten about her. Surely they would return, she told Cal-marcus, but she would welcome someone to watch over her while she waited there in the wilderness.

She welcomed his close attention to her account, his haste in helping her find food, and his knowledge of healing herbs. He won her trust.

When night arrived and her family had not returned, Cal-marcus brought Jaralaine to stay among the orphans who had been assigned to the Gatherers' care. No one came to claim her, but she seemed so delighted by the prince's frequent visits that she never fell into grieving. He visited her often, foolishly assuming he could do so unobserved.

One day Cal-marcus had taken her riding on his father's finest horse to revisit the site of their first conversation. When she saw the place again, she leaned into his embrace and wept. The memories she had shut away broke down the door. And so he learned the truth.

She had been gathering fruit high in some apple trees and had later returned to find the wagon stolen, the bodies of her family scattered in pieces beside the river. Alone at the desolate scene, she had tried to drown herself but failed, awakening on the Throanscall's shores, far south of the bloody ground. Her father, mother, brother, even the older sisters who had tormented her in childhood, and all the meager resources they had stashed in their skin-covered wagon—all of it was gone.

Filled with adolescent zeal, Cal-marcus vowed to drag the killers in to be tortured to death in Abascar's dungeons, vows that brought a hungry fire to Jaralaine's eyes. In those years, beastmen had not yet darkened lands north of Abascar. The blood of these merchants had been spilled by human hands. The waresellers' greatest concerns in the north, beyond the threat of disease or the trouble of weather, had been wild animals, river wyrms…and one other danger. Cal-marcus aimed his revenge toward the raiders from the clans of woodland thieves.

He would mount a campaign, with the blessing of his father, to comb the woods north of Abascar and eliminate those marauding clans. Then he would ask Jaralaine to marry him. When she became his Promised, she would be ensured a new life of honor and respect. She would want for nothing. He sealed this promise with a ring, one sculpted by his good friend Scharr ben Fray, an aging mage with unmatched stonecrafting talents. The ring would make it clear to all that she was to be treated with favor.

Two years later, despite the displeasure of King Har-brona, Cal-marcus wed Jaralaine.

Cal-marcus was welcomed as a hero sure to transform the house when he inherited the crown. The romance of his story endeared Jaralaine to the people. New songs were written for strings, and a new epic tale joined Abascar's legends. At least for a while.

While Jaralaine was hard, reclusive, and hollowed out with grief, the people seemed to share Cal-marcus's zeal to bring her a new start. Some Housefolk saw in her a reflection of the losses they had suffered during the wars with the Cent Regus savages. In devoting themselves to her delight, they could restore their own scarred spirits.

But House Abascar's love for the queen would not last. The people had seen what they hoped to see, not the vengeful spirit sulking through the days and tiptoeing suspiciously through the palace corridors by night.

Waresellers were known for their sharp-edged tongues, and Jaralaine's words left scars. Traveling merchants of the sort that had raised her bound themselves to no house. Their lives beyond the walls hardened them, changed them, and they fought bitterly for every scrap of profit, rarely earning respect. For merchants, the art of deceptive eloquence was a matter of survival, and they could, for a fee, establish complicated contracts and cultivate trade between houses. Jaralaine, it was clear, had learned how to bargain, how to make a robbery seem reasonable. Inside the house, a crown in her curls, she had seized the power her prince offered and, with a poetry of persuasion, taken more besides.

When Cal-marcus took the throne, Jaralaine ensured that he dismissed all his father's advisors who had looked at her with ill favor. She insisted that her husband needed no counsel but her own. He came to agree, and some guessed she had bewitched him with potions from a garden she cultivated in the castle's private courtyard.

Growing roots like a weed, she stole the resources that once fed everything around her, and yet she remained ravenous.

On the night of Jaralaine's return from such a short visit to House Bel Amica, it struck Ark-robin as unlikely that she had rushed home merely to monitor the king's nurses. The queen did not seem worried about Cal-marcus at all. She was as spirited as ever, dazzling them speechless.

Behind her, the murmuring flickers of what had been a grand blaze retreated into the blackened wood to glower and spit, irritable and weakening. *Like the king,* Ark-robin thought.

"How may we ease our lord's suffering?" There was a note of trepidation in Captain Tar-brona's tone, assuring Ark-robin he was not the only one suspecting trouble.

"You may ease his suffering by trusting his queen to convey his wishes." Jaralaine stepped to the oak table, a section from the trunk of a tree two thousand years strong before it had been toppled by lightning. "The road has made me weary—haste, worry, beastmen. And I am distraught by all I have seen. So I will not keep you long."

When she spoke again, her voice was lower, and she exhorted them to swear secrecy. "I assure you," she whispered, "these words are for those who can see past the burden of a heavy task to the harvest it will yield."

"We have never flinched at the king's ambition," Tar-brona assured her. "If it's a harvest he wants, put our shoulders to the plow."

She surprised him with a slow, secretive smile.

The events that followed would soon blur in the currents of time and rumor. But that smile and what Jaralaine had done to set those events in motion remained indelible in Ark-robin's mind.

"Abascar," she began, "is not as it should be. That's what I learned in my visit to Bel Amica. Cal-marcus's illness came in the nick of time, for I was desperate to be free of their condescension."

She lamented that the Bel Amicans held Abascar in contempt, that they questioned why such a small and pitiable house should command control of so much harvestland and such deep, rewarding mines. She gestured to a map spread across the table and explained how Bel Amica meant to grow and encompass islands in the western sea, and how they also meant to go north, troubling the dangers there, and south toward House Jenta. Of course, Bel Amicans would never speak of plans to advance eastward. But who would dare deny that this could become a tangible threat? Eastward expansion would give Bel Amica control of many trade routes and encroach on Abascar's borders.

Ark-robin felt a surge of ardor at the idea that war might be brewing. Would the day come at last for Abascar warriors to ride again in force? Would his men test their training against something other than beastmen? Would the promise of Captain Tar-brona's talents as a strategist finally be fulfilled?

Tar-brona objected. "Bel Amica bears us no malice. They owe us gratitude still for all we have done, for the way Cal-marcus cleansed the wild lands of the raiders."

"Captain, how do you know they're not training a host of soldiers on those islands? Why are Bel Amica's forges burning while a few inexperienced soldiers decorate their walls? I tell you, the day is coming when we will no longer know our neighbors to the west or what they are plotting. But there is more I must report."

She placed her hand on the map of the vast Cragavar forest between Abascar and the western shores. "Another threat. And this one is not about swords or spears. It's about seduction and treachery. As you know, we've had soldiers go missing from signal towers in the forest. And Gatherers have been deserting their posts, never to return. I heard familiar names in Bel Amica's streets. I saw strangely familiar faces. Some of them laughed when my back was turned. Abascar deserters are running into Bel Amica's gloating embrace, drawn by rumors of a glorious life at the edge of the sea."

"You know this?" Tar-brona's eyes narrowed.

"I was the daughter of waresellers," Jaralaine hissed. "I recognized their tone: disdain, disregard, derision. Queen Thesere's gluttonous tribe believes itself vastly superior. And how could I argue, with all that I saw? We are humiliated, Captain. Instead of feeling safe, our Housefolk have come to feel cheated and deprived. If Abascar's people begin to dream of House Bel Amica, they will come to resent us. If Bel Amica flourishes, surely their shameless exhibitions for invisible moon-spirits must be more than a charade! That's what our people will decide. Abascar has not been free of foolish superstitions for long, and the tide could easily turn. Tell me, do you want the ceremonies, the bizarre costumes, the sacrifices, the flesh-painting rituals that come with such madness?"

She strode past her son to snatch scrolls from the shelves with both hands. "I've read Abascar's histories. It's always been small, the stuff of jokes in Bel Amica and Jenta. But the proudest days of House Abascar were those when the people united to overcome a threat. What is it my husband boasts about? The days of discipline, when the people labored to follow a king's instruction in order to survive the Cent Regus threat. That is how Abascar resisted the spread of the beastman perversion. But since the Cent Regus decline, Abascar's people have become lazy. Nothing threatens them, so their unity and focus is weakening. They're tempted to wander."

The queen tossed the scrolls onto the floor. "They take the safety of these walls for granted. But new threats are rising, and it is time for Abascar to unite and grow strong again. We must give our people a dream. We'll make all things in Abascar new."

The young prince, distracted from his play, looked up at the shelves thoughtfully while the wind teased the ribbons that bound the scrolls.

Any plan to revolutionize a house would require difficult sacrifices. Jaralaine emphasized this point. But to neglect Abascar's weakness—that would cost much more.

She came and stood between them, hands alighting like gentle birds on their shoulders. The Housefolk, she explained, would need leaders who inspired them, a palace radiating glory, and motivation to stoke Abascar's fire.

Tar-brona began to suggest that the rumors of deserters were unfounded and that beastmen were still known to drag victims away. But Jaralaine's stare snapped his mouth shut.

Face reddening, she walked back around the table. "I want to hear about Bel Amicans deserting that bloated Queen Thesere to seek the splendor of House Abascar. I want House Jenta's philosophers to speak of Abascar's future in reverent whispers and bring us gifts to win favor. If the four houses all split from one great source, as our histories tell us, Abascar has every right to claim itself equal to the rest. We could be the jewel of the Expanse. The wars against the Cent Regus are over. Bel Amica has yet to advance. And Jenta is preoccupied with its quiet meditation. House Abascar will seize this chance to flourish. We'll transform what we have to become the envy of the land."

"How will this transformation be accomplished?" asked Ark-robin, for Tar-brona seemed dumbfounded by the queen's words. "We are a smaller house than Bel Amica. To increase the way they have, we would need to—"

"It's not a matter of population," she sighed. "It's a matter of distinction. Of glory. When people speak of a House, what do they speak of first? The palace. That is where we start. The people will refashion the palace until it is the envy of the land."

"The Housefolk will renovate the palace?" Tar-brona seemed profoundly suspicious.

"They will make this place a wonder," said the queen with a smile that told them much was already decided. "You want to know how we achieve such dedication? Motivation."

And then she announced the unthinkable.

"The king has asked me to oversee a period of celebration and change in which the Housefolk will unite for the transformation of the house. We will call the first chapter of this grand story 'the Wintering of Abascar.'"

During this period of Wintering, she explained, the people would redirect all their work, devote all their talents, to tasks set for them by the palace designers. They would build a better palace, beautify it.

But why "the Wintering of Abascar"? Her secret courtyard garden had inspired her. It was speaking to her every day, revealing a plan.

As a sign of commitment and unity, all people of Abascar dwelling between the palace and the walls would wear common garments—a wardrobe of black, brown, grey, and white, the colors of the Expanse in winter. "Abascar's people will give up their colors, their craft, their weaving, their bounty, the treasures that sit unseen within their homes...all to enhance the corridors of the palace."

And what of the soldiers? Abascar's officers would police the streets, visit homes, inventory belongings, and monitor the efforts. They would note those who served without complaint and promise rewards to those who dedicated themselves openly to the queen's plan.

Tar-brona and Ark-robin were to lead the counting of Abascar's riches, from garments to livestock, from structures to combs and pillows. Then the king and queen would invite the people to offer their best belongings as tribute. Anyone who gave willingly would win recognition, receive badges of various colors to signify the strength of their devotion, and collect an appropriate measure of precious stones from Abascar's abundant mines. These they could trade for increased privileges during the second season of Abascar's transformation.

Abascar's armies would carry this collection of the people's finest to the Underkeep in a celebratory procession. Anything judged beautiful and excellent would adorn the palace and serve to glorify the king. Others items would be stripped down to raw material and recrafted into finer inventions.

"In this way, the palace will belong as much to the Housefolk as to their king and queen," said Jaralaine.

"And...when the palace draws attention from across the Expanse?" Ark-robin heard himself whisper. "When it shines like the sun, what then?" Envisioning the change, the assembly of color like a bonfire at Abascar's center, he was distracted from asking the questions that would plague him later, questions about what this would cost the Housefolk.

When this was accomplished, Jaralaine continued, the king would declare the beginning of the second season, which they would call "Abascar's Spring." On the commencement of this Spring, the Housefolk would be charged to fashion a new world for themselves, with design and invention surpassing anything known. "During Abascar's Spring, color and splendor will return to Abascar's streets, as if spilling from the palace," Jaralaine rejoiced.

The freedom of colors would be restored to Abascar's Housefolk according to the contributions they had made. Mantles would distinguish their rank. Such visible honor would compel devotion to their House.

The captain of the guard was not easily convinced. He inquired how the people would be persuaded to give up what they had. The queen insisted that Abascar's people were proud and loyal. Those who set themselves against the Proclamation of the Colors would be revealed as troublesome dissenters responsible for so much of Abascar's lapse into irrelevance.

When Tar-brona tried to disguise an indignant laugh as a cough, Jaralaine answered without amusement. "Do you challenge your king's authority?" The queen of Abascar dropped the king's heavy, square-faced ring onto the center of the table. "Or are you accusing me of stealing this ring to use while my husband is too sick to stop me?"

Immediately all laughter—indeed, all color—drained from Tar-brona's complexion.

"Consider other possibilities, Captain. Perhaps I am a good wife, delivering a message for her beloved lord."

"So," Tar-brona sighed, "King Cal-marcus plans to make a royal proclamation."

"It is why you have been summoned. You are the witnesses, and I now speak for Cal-marcus."

Jaralaine stood straight and tall, one hand raised, the glow from the fire filling her garment with light so that she seemed to emanate supernal power. *"By proclamation of the king...I declare the rising of tomorrow's sun the first day of Abascar's Wintering."*

That was when the shelves of scrolls had fallen, casting the histories across the floor.

Cal-raven, quietly climbing the shelves like a ladder, certain that the missing figurine had been placed out of reach, had toppled them, and he fell in a cavalcade of journals.

Jaralaine ran to his side, gushing words of comfort, but the boy did not cry. He stood, kicking aside the scrolls, furious, holding up a figurine. "Look, Mama," he shouted. "Look! Someone's tried to hide the Keeper!" He marched to the map table and, imitating his mother's presentation of the ring, set down the stone figurine. It was crafted like a large beast with a horse's head, wings, and a gator's tail. "Someone's tried to take it away."

The queen flashed her effervescent smile in apology to the soldiers. "The little prince is that age, you know. Phantoms, monsters, adventures everywhere." She knelt down and put an arm around her son. "Cal-raven, you recognize Captain Tar-brona, don't you? He's been organizing patrols for many years, from the Cliffs of Barnashum to Deep Lake, all the way to the Forbidding Wall. And do you know? He has *never seen the Keeper.*"

Tar-brona was not listening. His eyes were fixed on the map of Abascar. Ark-robin could see that the captain already wandered its avenues in his mind, imagining the chaos that would ensue.

"And here also is Ark-robin, our house defender, who is charged with training soldiers to protect us from danger. Do you think such a large and dangerous animal could hide from him?"

Ark-robin met the boy's inquisitive gaze. Cal-raven was now fully returned from his imaginary journeys, realizing the strange company of this midnight meeting. Ark-robin sensed the prince was sifting him, judging him.

"They've never seen the Keeper," the boy concluded, "because they've never really looked for him."

Ark-robin promised himself, and not for the first time, that he would never let any son of his develop such fantasies. That is, if Say-ressa ever gave him a son.

The child suddenly shrieked, distracted by a muffled voice from the corridor. He broke loose from his mother, running to the chamber's closed doors. Before the queen could rebuke him, he opened them to reveal Scharr ben Fray, the king's old friend, the stonecrafter, clad in the heavy robes of a House Jenta philosopher. The old man entered as though pursuing a burglar.

"I've just come from the bedside of the king. And I must—" He stopped, surveying the spectacular sight of the scroll-strewn floor, and then pointed in disbelief at the table where the ring lay upon the map like the triumphant remaining piece after a strategy game. *"I see there is a ring upon the table."* Scharr ben Fray kept his face concealed in his deep hood, so no one could see his expression, but his voice was weary and laced with bitterness. "I crafted that ring for the king. It represents discernment, not rash decisions and folly. Do not betray him, Jaralaine. Do not rob the ring of its meaning, or you will ruin the one you wear as well."

"This is a private matter between the king, myself, the captain, and the defender," the queen hissed.

The mage's shoulders sank. "The hunger driving this affair will not be satiated, Jaralaine. Ask any of the thieves in Abascar's dungeons. The more you feed such appetites, the greater the pit becomes, until you collapse into it yourself."

The old man then departed and closed the doors behind him, taking Calraven with him.

From that day on, Ark-robin's life would be divided in two, forever *before* and *after* the Proclamation of the Colors.

It sickened him to remember that he had been convinced, and worse, moved by Queen Jaralaine's promise that Abascar's people would benefit from the tide of grandeur and extravagance. Her voice had been like that of a fortuneteller, spinning enchantment, conjuring possibilities. He was breathless from the enormity of the vision.

And later he felt robbed, distraught to find how deeply ran her lies. The queen slipped through hidden doors and tunnels in every statement, springing traps on any who protested. What was presented as an endeavor to glorify House Abascar had been a maneuver to satiate Jaralaine's immeasurable jealousy and greed.

For favor and advantage, volunteers carted away family treasures. They unhinged ornamental doors. They battered hand-painted shutters off their hinges and swept them into wheelbarrows. They rolled and shouldered exquisite handmade rugs like fallen trees. They strapped colorful garments into bundles and replaced them with uniforms of stifling dullness.

Ark-robin stood by while his soldiers followed instructions. The defender frowned like one of the victims, even as he acted as the king's—the *queen's*—hand against his neighbors, his own family. His bed would suffer a winter indeed.

Most of the Housefolk begrudgingly cooperated, for the king and queen had offered assurance of gratitude and repayment.

But not everyone. An old weaver, refusing to weave for the palace, collapsed dead as soldiers tore open a wall to extract the giant loom he had built inside. Another, an outspoken mosaicist, barred entrance to her workshop for the inventory; when they disciplined her by removing her works from the walls, informing her that thereafter she would craft what they prescribed, she grabbed a stone-breaking implement and cast herself forward, the sharp point of the device completing the breaking of her heart in full view of her horrified neighbors and the angry enforcers. (Furious, King Cal-marcus, with the queen standing beside him, banished the mosaicist's young brother to the Gatherers, to be raised with the other orphans.) Parents forced children loose from prized horses, favorite hounds, even a sizable hog, as the best livestock was marched to the royal stables, kennels, and pens.

Diggers and builders expanded the Underkeep to swallow a thousand cartloads of gilt and glitter, silks and satins. Workers labored under soldier supervision to construct, weave, and replace colorful things with dutifully dull and simple equivalents.

The palace loomed above it all, trumpeters lining its walls and Abascar's flag flying from every window, every watchtower, and every spire. To some the sights and sounds were festive. But others, especially those who gave up what little they had to offer, murmured that the palace resembled nothing so much as a gloating thief.

Spring never came. Housefolk accustomed themselves to their plain garments, sacrificing color and invention to their king, hoping for the day when such sacrifices would earn them lasting glory. A community of cooperation became a house of contention, one family against another in the struggle to earn honors and opportunities.

Once the queen had cultivated a vast garden of garments, jewelry, and wares, her devotion to management of the house disappeared. She spent days wandering the palace corridors, dreaming up new ideas, from murals for the great halls to furniture for Cal-raven's chamber. At night, she rose, restless, and explored the Underkeep's corridors, talking to herself (or, some said, boasting to her murdered sisters), touching all that had been collected, selecting what she liked to carry with her. She scribbled lists to catalog her treasures, and a year later, she did it again, until eventually even that became uninteresting to her.

When the queen's health began to fail, the inventory quietly cloaked itself in dust. The contents of the Underkeep lay abandoned, entombed, but never forgotten. When Jaralaine voiced further wishes for the house and was refused by the beleaguered king, she began to withdraw from him.

What transpired between them in those final days together was a tale the king would never tell. But everyone knew its penultimate chapter. The queen deserted her treasures one night, even her precious garden. She ran into the woods and disappeared, inspiring a hundred stories about what sort of terrible end awaited her there.

She left the king in ruins.

And young Cal-raven motherless.

Ark-robin ran his fingers through the blue stones in Auralia's basket. As he did, he wondered at the strange sieve of memory, how it caught and preserved so few days of significance. Yesterday was already fading. But he could still remember intimate details from the day he'd married the Lady Say-ressa—clouds patterned like cobblestones, the burning of new tattoos on the backs of his hands, the heaviness of the wedding tent curtain. He could even remember the day he first saw her, years earlier, when she mended his wounded shoulder. The death of Tar-brona—that, too, lived bold in his memory, for some had suspected him of playing a part in the captain's demise, even though the king saw no reason to investigate. Later that same day, Ark-robin's sudden promotion to become the new captain of the guard—he remembered the king placing the helm upon his head but little more.

And yet, of all these vivid memories, it was Jaralaine's summons he could recall most clearly. He remembered the intricate detail of the heavy ring on the king's table as the queen proclaimed the Wintering. Her seductive perfume still lingered. And for all his anger at her wicked machinations, he still felt the pulse of a thrill to recall her striding around the library in a gown only her husband should have seen.

"What's wrong, Captain?"

The voice smashed his reverie. He jerked at the reins, brought the vawn up short, and shouted as the sudden movement strained the wounded muscle in his shoulder. The basket tumbled from his grasp again, blue stones spilling into the grass.

Prince Cal-raven, now sixteen years old, fair-haired, was dressed in a royal advisor's robe. As always, he was unnervingly quiet. He stood between two moonbeam trees to the left of the trail, calmly chewing a sweetreed. "You look like you're sitting on an arrowhead."

"I was merely noting the lateness of things, my lord." *Such a foolish boy*, Ark-robin thought. *Still creeping about outside the walls while others prepare to sleep? I would teach my own son differently. If I had a son.*

"Indeed. It's late...for tree-climbers anyway." Cal-raven knelt and lifted a handful of stones. "There aren't many who know about cwauba bird treasure, Captain. Mother taught me how to find stones like these. Haven't seen anything like them in years. Father will be so surprised."

Ark-robin surrendered them immediately with a wave of his hand. His wife would never see these exquisite stones. It would do no good to argue with the prince.

"Yes, of course, you don't even need to ask. I'll deliver them for you, Captain. Perhaps they will give my father a moment's distraction from his foul mood."

Ark-robin never contradicted the prince, although each time they encountered each other, his dislike of the boy increased. "I'll let you in on a secret," he replied, momentarily inspired by his anger. He could strike back at Jaralaine even in her absence. He could punish her son. "I took these stones from a strange girl who lives free in the forest."

"A strange girl who lives free?"

"The Gatherers call her Auralia. She claims she isn't from Abascar. She refuses to accept the protection of the house. It will take some doing to catch her and bring her in for proper training."

"Where can I find her?"

Ark-robin smiled. "Oh, you won't find her...not unless she allows it." There was something sweet about this. The bait was set. And Cal-raven, mirroring his mother's arrogance and his father's curiosity, would take it. What would the king think of this, watching his own errors played out before him? "Do not trouble yourself with a wild one like her, Cal-raven," he continued, knowing the warning would only stoke the fires of intrigue. "Free folk in the woods can lead you on quite a chase."

"You'll alert your patrols, of course," Cal-raven smirked. "If she's smart enough to find a secret cwauba nest, oh what danger we're in!"

"After my reprimand, she'll likely move to trouble some other house. A shame really. She'll be quite a beauty someday." Ark-robin's grip tightened around the reins. This talk was risky, rash, and driven by a grudge Cal-raven had not inspired. The consequences of such meddling might well outweigh the shallow satisfaction it could bring.

Would the boy follow in his father's footsteps and fall under the enchantment of a meddlesome wood sprite? "May the king be heartened by the gems I've brought him. I'm sure they'll be kept safe...where no one else can see them." He risked an ultimatum by refusing an appropriate salute, then spurred his vawn on, cursing his impulsive temper.

He glanced back over his shoulder once more, hoping to see the prince brushing off the exchange and moving on. But Cal-raven stood still, lost in thought, staring into the woods, blue light in his hands, as the starlings drew darkness over Abascar.

5

THE ALE BOY

Seven winters spread and deepened the cracks in House Abascar's walls, and the king set workers to mending them with mortar and new stone. Inside, the people grumbled to see such effort invested in a facade when so little attention was paid to their domestic complaints. A wall could not defend their homes against snow, rain, and wind.

To make the people understand, King Cal-marcus encouraged his officers to share details of their patrols with Housefolk. Evidence of beastman activity quite near the house was easy to find, and fearful people were obedient people, striving to ensure that the king cared to protect them.

And if the people did not like to see him giving attention to the walls, surely they would disapprove if they learned of his latest endeavor. The king had commanded the Underkeep's miners to embark on an ambitious new mission—to open a tunnel northward all the way to the River Throanscall. This tunnel would divert water to the Underkeep, power new engines of industry, accelerate their mining, and much more. It was a grand idea, and it was his own. It was a way to begin a new era in Abascar, one that would turn the people's attention away from memories of Queen Jaralaine.

But he knew that the Housefolk were so intent on whatever disrupted their immediate comfort that they had no vision, no grasp of what House Abascar could become. No, the truth would not serve them just yet. The familiar threat of beastmen remained his best persuasion to silence their complaints.

Beastmen were not the only frights haunting conversations and furrowing brows in Abascar. As visiting traders spread out their spices, cheeses, dried meats, windup toys, cutlery, potions, powders, soaps, and dull weavings, they also spread reports that something mysterious and large had been troubling the waters of Deep Lake. One tale claimed the phantom had stormed down from the north by night, as if a piece of the mountainous Forbidding Wall had sprouted legs and come hunting with a rabble of Northchildren.

Sons and daughters gasped and asked, Could it be not a danger at all, but perhaps the Keeper, the protector in their dreams, come to their waking world at last? Parents scoffed and said if anything had crawled out of those mountains, it certainly wasn't a friend. A resurgence of superstitions long suppressed disgruntled them. This included an age-old rumor that if a traveler spoke of Northchildren, soon afterward someone near at hand would disappear without a trace.

As the fallen leaves darkened and decayed, the blood of the Expanse began to freeze. Gatherers bustled about more intently beneath the branches of vinewound trees, clearing plumspider webs and snatching hoards of winter fruit the spiders had stored.

Their thievery did little harm. Plumspiders spent summers digging storehouses for food, and after they prodded fruit and nuts into those burrows, they guarded them with venomous teeth in the autumn. But winter dulled their memories, and they spent the colder months sluggishly creeping about the forest floor, mindlessly searching for their hard-earned feasts. They would hardly miss what the Gatherers had taken.

And so it was one afternoon, as the laborers felt the lateness of the hour in the aching of their backs, Ersela, the Gatherer appointed to watch for beastmen, recognized the staggering gait of someone approaching. She exclaimed in relief, "Somebody better hold Radegan down, 'cuz here comes the ale boy!"

The walking barrel—it seemed a wooden keg with legs—trudged awkwardly into their midst and sat down with the *thrum* of a hollow drum. The small boy who carried the barrel appeared, a bashful, red-cheeked face under his tousled mop of gold brown hair. He thrust his arms all the way to his elbows into the pockets of a heavy cloak that would have comfortably fit a boy twice his height.

Rakes landed in clanging piles, and shovels were sheathed in the mud as the Gatherers huddled, smacking their lips, grinning the grins of children about to make mischief.

"What've you got for us this time, boy? Hope there's rum or apple brandy!"

"Blackberry wine would do me well. Takes the chill out of the air."

"Surely it is the season for pear cider!"

The boy looked down at the length of cloak that concealed his feet. "Fill the barrel, please," he murmured meekly.

"We'll get to putting apples in that bucket when I say so," said Radegan, a muscular, stubble-bearded brute who worked shirtless and brash in any weather. He elbowed the giant who was working alongside him like a bodyguard—Haggard, the Broad-Shouldered, whose crazed and wide eyes peeked through a mask of yellow hair.

"First," Radegan continued, "you can hand over your stash, or we'll take it ourselves!" He and Haggard mustered all powers of intimidation. They were a formidable pair, this young, notorious thief and the silent behemoth who followed him everywhere. Radegan's thieving had won him a nickname—"the Fox"—and ten years of hard labor besides. Haggard's temper had burdened him with six years of the same. Setting roots down in the hard soil of Gatherer life, Radegan and Haggard had only grown more thorns.

"Radegan, you know the order of things." The patient, maternal Gatherer who helped keep tempers calm, Nella Bye was elegant, educated, and better mannered than most. "Just because the boy once risked his job to bless us with a drink does not mean he'll do so every time. Don't go abusing him."

"I myself don't got no gripe with the boy," blurted Krawg. "But Haggard's right. While the stuff we gathered yesterday is warmin' the guts of Cal-marcus's fat and happy Housefolk, my belly wants some fire."

There was hearty agreement from the mob, and the ale boy shuffled closer to the barrel as if he might dive inside for refuge. "Fill the barrel, please," he murmured. "Ya got so many apples there. Won't take but a minute. Duty officers will come and cart it away soon."

Grabbing him by the cloak collar, Haggard brought the boy's tiny nose up to his own bristling beard.

"Try and scare us with talk of the duty officers?" Radegan sneered. "Haggard will put somethin' in the bucket, all right. Somethin' about the size of a boy."

As Haggard gripped the boy's cloak, that small, frightened face vanished. The boy slipped free of his oversized garment and landed in a heap, wearing only a rumpled brown tunic. Haggard blinked at the empty cloak in his grasp. Radegan stepped in quickly to search the pockets for the little bottles of relief they had hoped the boy would bring.

As surprising as a new stream running down a dry path, a song coursed through the trees. Singing was not strange among the Gatherers. But this was the wrong song for the moment, and it stilled the riot over the ale boy's belongings. Radegan backed away from the cloak, nearly stumbling over the boy.

"That's the Deep Night Verse," said Krawg, annoyed. "But...it's only early evening! Who's singing that?"

All eyes turned to a pair of birch trees that stood arched like a gate. At the base of one of the trees, there was a bramble of thistle and vines that unfolded and stood. The leaves shifted and rustled, and suddenly the onlookers discerned a gown of strange and awkward angles, papery with translucent leaves deep green and purple, sewn together with fronds of broadweed pulled from the river nearby. The edges of this figure blurred, like smudged paint, merging with the colors of the forest's wild backdrop.

The Gatherers recognized the figure's clever face, and murmurs of laughter and discomfort spread. But the ale boy looked as if he'd seen a ghost.

Auralia was still small, although she had been among them fifteen years now. Against the rich colors of her gown, her silverbrown hair glistened like the edge of a storm cloud trying to quench the sun.

Krawg, who usually greeted Auralia with a shout and an embrace, was flustered to have spoken harshly within earshot of the girl. He covered the redness that was rising to his cheeks and edged behind others in the mob.

Auralia looked about silently, then smiled as though solving a puzzle. She picked up the rope tie at the top of a lumpish harvest bag, which was twice her size, dragged it to the barrel, loosed its strand, and lifted out a handful of green apples and purple plums. She stood on tiptoe, prodded them over the barrel's edge, and they fell with soft thuds onto the bed of straw at the bottom.

Nella Bye glared at Radegan, her icy blue stare the only force devastating enough to freeze the roguish burglar where he stood. Then she moved to help Auralia.

The season's first snowflakes crept timidly down through the branches while Auralia and Nella Bye whispered together and filled the barrel; while the ale boy sat hypnotized by this strange apparition clad in purple and green; while raven calls echoed from the east, rang overhead, and faded into the west.

From the moment she arrived, the ale boy was fumbling for his wits. When Auralia spoke, her voice whispered in his ear no matter where she stood.

So when she approached him, he felt vulnerable and ashamed. He pulled on his heavy cloak, wishing he could disappear within it.

"The last apples of the year are always the sweetest. Don't you agree, ale boy? Hard to be patient and let them ripen so purple, but if you do... Look at how many they've picked!" She drew in air through her nose as if breathing pungent incense. "They've stirred 'em up, and now the whole woods smells like wine. The king'll be pleased with how hard everybody worked, won't he?"

"Yes!" the boy agreed in spite of himself.

"The Gatherers keep the whole house going."

"Uh-huh."

Even Haggard and Radegan began helping. Radegan dragged a bag of apples to the barrel and eyed Auralia suspiciously, as though she were taunting him. But it was clear to the ale boy that she was as innocent as she looked.

She sat down on the ground next to him. Through the growing white of the falling snow, he saw her eyes sparkle with affection for this crew of bedraggled souls.

"Ya see, that there's Krawg." She pointed out the old man passing in front of them with an armful of wild pears. "He found me by the river. I love him so. And I made that yellow scarf he's wearin'. Krawg! Ya better tuck that scarf into your cloak before any duty officers come along and strangle ya with it!"

Krawg ducked behind Big Yawny, then glanced back around the massive man and broke into his famous grin of brown and sideways teeth.

Auralia's eyes were as wide as they would go when she leaned close to the boy, smiled brightly, and winked like a conspirator. "Wish I could sneak all of you away and start another house. These folks are buckets of fun compared to the Housefolk, don't you think?"

The ale boy nodded. When she said something, he found himself wanting to agree.

He reached into his coat and produced from a secret fold a small and clear vial of drink as blue as a summer sky. "The king's favorite sweet ale," he whispered. "Don't tell anybody I gave you this. He calls it Mountaincapper. And believe me…you don't want to swallow it all at once."

She accepted the vial with fingers so cautious and steady it might have been a precious jewel. "Like someone melted a cwauba bird stone." She looked at him with renewed interest. "Not from among the Housefolk, are ya? You're too kindly mannered to be one of them!"

He felt her fingertips on his forehead, the very place where the mouse scar rested above his right eye. "Your eyes have no lashes. And you have no brows…" She lowered her voice. "Were you in a fire?"

He turned away. "I really should get back."

But she did not laugh as others did. "It's a beautiful color, your scar," she said. "Like plum wine. Like your name written right where all can see."

His mouth made a round O, and he stood up, clutching his cloak. "My name?" He did not understand what was happening to him, why his heart broke open in that moment, why tears stung his eyes. She had unlocked something inside him. Questions rose like water in a well, and he knew if he did not escape, they would pour out of him.

So he was quite startled when Auralia stood up, fast and straight, her head tilted askew, birdlike. She became perfectly still, staring through the busyness of the Gatherers.

When her brow crumpled and she gasped, he felt a sensation like tiny pins pressed against his neck. He started to ask what was wrong, but his breath caught in his throat. She raised her hand. "Hush."

Nella Bye noticed Auralia's sudden change. She, too, turned, surveying the trees, wincing in apprehension. Like a gorrel after a winged predator passes across the sky, she sniffed the air twice. "Why isn't Ersela back on the watch?"

"Beastmen!" Auralia shouted. "They're coming! Get back to the huts!"

"Aw, come now, 'Ralia. Why do ya think—" Warney stopped his protest and spun on his heel, his one good eye gazing to the southwest, tracking the shrill and jagged noise of someone in abrupt and terrible pain.

"Beastmen!" roared Haggard, the first word he had spoken all day. He grasped a heavy bough from the tall trunk of a storm-broken tree.

"They've got Groaney!" growled Radegan. "That sheepskull wandered too far from the harvesting site!"

Haggard tore the branch free and wielded it as a weapon. "Go back home! Go back!" he roared bearlike at the other Gatherers. "Back, scum eaters! Back to your holes! Hasty, now! Haggard's gonna teach the beastie a lesson!"

The ale boy could not move, paralyzed by a surge of memory.

He had once been caught up in a mass of Housefolk driven like a herd of sheep. That company of woodcutters had abandoned their stand of pillar trees at the sound of distant warning horns. He had seen no beastmen. But that night, deep in his small den near the Underkeep breweries, had been a dark and sleepless one. The nearness of such savagery had made his world seem more fragile. He had never been more thankful to dwell among the privileged within Abascar's high stone walls.

But now he was unhidden, far from safety. There was no one to organize the scattering Gatherers, no one to point them down the best paths, no one to arm them. The threat was close, and the killing—he could hear the death sounds that had sent Auralia to scurry about the clearing. Abascar's walls were a good hour's travel away.

Auralia shoved the Gatherers. "Go, go, go now!"

Some reached for their tools. Others leapt like rabbits—and a few like far less graceful creatures—into the brush in hopes they were headed in the right direction. Haggard's courage had burnt up like a dry leaf, and now he was running pell-mell. Krawg and Warney paused to fuss over Auralia. But with both hands she picked up the abandoned tree-branch club and threatened to give the old men a Haggard-sized beating.

When she turned to see the ale boy transfixed with fear, Auralia dropped the club and dashed to him. "You're too small and slow. You're gonna need some help." She crouched, lifted her strange green outer cloak over her head, and quickly cast it over the ale boy. "If they come close, hide in the bushes under this cloak. They'll go right by you."

"But..." He pushed his head up into the hood, it settled around his shoulders, and he could see again. It was light as air, if a bit too large. But he was not looking at his new disguise. He was staring at Auralia.

Shed of her camouflage, Auralia was clad in a cacophonous jumble of colors. She had stitched together gold and greens so bold and bright that it seemed the air had split its seams and burst open, summer reaching into winter. Her shoes were heavy pondpads stitched around her feet with red reeds.

He would have kept on staring, but another searing shriek—one that ended with a chilling note—sent his heart thumping. He was sure it would now be too late to meet the one Haggard had called Groaney.

"Are you sure I'll be safe?" he asked Auralia.

"It's how I watch beastmen without being seen. Now, get down low in them bushes. Don't let your feet show. Pull the hood over your face." Auralia pressed down on his head and shoulders and kicked him to send him scrambling. The frost had settled into his bones, and it was hard to run. He thrust out his hands and clambered into a depression where rain had run beneath a fallen tree, and then he lay still.

At first he thought he heard a heavy boulder rolling across jagged stones. Then he knew—it was the snarl of a beastman. He chanced a glance from under the fold of his hood.

Engulfed in heavy snowfall, Auralia stood in the clearing as defenseless and resplendent as a sunflower.

A hulking darkness stood at the clearing's edge. Steam rose from its bristling shoulders, which were as broad as a bull's. Its eyes were those of a man in a rage, but its bearded jaw, lined with yellow teeth, was that of a rodent. Blue and bulging veins pulsed along its smooth pink scalp and yellow throat. From shoulders to waist, it resembled a brown fangbear, save for those massive human hands. In one clawed fist it clutched a club with two sharp metal prongs that dripped gore into the patchy snow.

The boy had heard tales of the beastmen, heard that each manifested unique disfigurements from a corruption that confused their bodies into the natures of differing beasts. So it was true. The image would return to him in nightmares—his own nails would turn to blackened claws, feet spreading into black hooves, teeth sharpening, skin thinning into translucence, body slowly hunching forward.

The beast seemed momentarily bewildered by the dazzling costume of its prey. Then its pink lips drew back from a wall of fangs. It laughed a spluttering guffaw and dug two ruts in the ground with the prongs of its weapon.

Auralia stared back at the monster and spoke something like a quiet incantation.

A cough, like a question, burst from its lips. It dropped the club, patted its head, closing its fingers around the shaft of an arrow now buried deep between its eyes.

The creature's jaw sagged open. It looked left and right. And then its knees buckled. It crumpled into a heap upon the spiked club, which burst its lungs with a gurgling wheeze.

Shaking the earth, six giant vawns leapt over the fallen tree and the concealed boy. They hissed and stamped at the snow-dampened soil, and their armored riders shouted with confidence, circling the steaming beastman corpse. One of the soldiers, red-bearded and tall, fired another arrow from a caster into the beastman's back. The creature rocked with a spasm and then was still.

The ale boy felt a surge of relief when he recognized one of them by his stature and his unsheathed sword—Captain Ark-robin—but he did not call out or lift his hood. Despite the captain's famous strength, his mercurial demeanor always unsettled the boy.

The men exchanged hushed words, their attention drawn by the brightly costumed young woman in their midst. His fear did not leave, but it changed. Would Auralia survive a beastman attack only to be beaten by soldiers from Abascar?

Ark-robin laughed suddenly and spurred his vawn to approach her. "You again. So is this what you do when you stir up a nest of beastmen? You lead them here, to kill Abascar's Gatherers? I should drag you in for questioning."

Auralia did not flinch when the vawn's snout shoved at her.

"Who is this?" asked the red-bearded archer, who had already strapped another arrow to his caster in case of another threat.

Ark-robin hesitated. "A trespasser. Someone I should have stuffed in a sack and tossed in the Throanscall when I found her stealing from our woods." The captain narrowed his eyes and addressed Auralia. "Do you want to introduce yourself to Tabor Jan? He might know your name. He's heard about the impudent little weaver who brings the Gatherers forbidden things. And he'll be seeing you again, soon enough. If my count is correct, you're about a hundred days from your test at the Rites of the Privilege."

Another rider drew up between Ark-robin and Tabor Jan. The ale boy gasped, recognizing the yellow sign emblazoned on the soldier's shield.

"Ride back home, Cal-raven," said Ark-robin. "This isn't proper work for a prince. We'll check around for more beastmen. That dying Gatherer made such a noise he might have attracted others."

"Is this the girl?" Prince Cal-raven whispered. "Is this the one I've tried for so long to catch?"

Auralia faced them with the same readiness she had shown the beastman.

"I've looked for you, young woman," Cal-raven continued, much to Ark-robin's annoyance. "Why do you always run from me?"

Auralia looked at her toes, which were reddening on the freezing ground.

"It's extraordinary—what you're wearing," said the prince. "Illegal, but beautiful. How do you make such fantastic colors?"

"I don't make 'em," she said, and the ale boy wondered if the prince could hear her. "And they're not hard to find."

The prince nodded. "Ark-robin told me you would be difficult. But I'm not finished with you yet. I'll find you again, when this ugly business with beastmen is finished." He turned his vawn, reached to deliver a congratulatory clap to the archer's shoulder, and all the riders but Ark-robin charged off into the trees.

Auralia stepped back to avoid the beastman's blood, which spread like syrup across the frozen ground.

Ark-robin wagged his finger like a disgruntled teacher. "How do you feel about coming to live with us inside the walls now? Think you could give up this foolishness in order to enjoy some protection? We don't always come to rescue."

"There's worse dangers than beastmen," she quietly replied. "Besides, I woulda been safe. I already called for help of my own."

"Ha! Your friend the fangbear, I suppose." Ark-robin prompted his vawn to prance around her, kicking up a storm of dirt and slush. "Spoken like a true child of the North, the country from which nothing good can come."

"Never said I was a Northchild," she replied with menace in her voice. "I just told you I remembered being there."

"You cast a shadow like the rest of us, sure. But you've walked where trouble comes from, and so you bring it with you. Take it back, I say." He pointed his sword northward. "Get yourself gone."

"You talk like you've seen a Northchild," Auralia said with sudden intensity.

Ark-robin scowled, spat, and surrendered, departing in a rush, a few swinging branches the only evidence of his passage.

Auralia knelt before the fallen beastman. She combed tangles of its deep brown beard, then sharply jerked free a few strands and tucked them into a pocket. Prying the beastman's massive prong-club free with both hands, she then turned, smiled in the ale boy's direction, and stepped back into the birch gate through which she had come.

The ale boy thought to call after her, to remind her of her cloak, but something between his mind and voice remained paralyzed. His strewn thoughts realigned in the weary quiet of the clearing. His hands, which had been pressed against the fever in his face, came free and caught a stream of sliding snowflakes. The snow melted there into a small mirror. He watched the faint and wavering reflection of his scar. She had called it beautiful.

A tremor. A rain of snowy leaves. Even the earth, it seemed, was shuddering at what had taken place.

Then it shook again.

The ale boy looked intently into the trees. "Help of her own," he said to his quivering reflection. "She called for help of her own."

As the third thunderous footfall shook the ground, he fled, unable to make room for yet another mystery. Not today.

6

Summoner and Stranger

A vawn emerged from the mist, head high like a conqueror. Each resonant step left its signature print on the ground—three reptilian toes in front and one wide claw in back. A rumble of displeasure rose from the gold-armored belly, up the blue green arc of its throat, to blast in three voices from its nostrils. When it stumbled into a patch of muck, the creature dipped its mouthless muzzle into muddy soup and rested there, face half-buried, drawing ground-slime into its head. Teeth and tongues deep within worked noisily, separating leaf, water, soil, stone.

Meanwhile its rider sat proud as a jay and just as regal blue in her long uniform jacket. The outfit announced that the wearer was of a certain importance, but not a soldier—the high-collared design was certainly impractical. It took some effort for her to survey the woods around her.

She pulled back the elaborate black-tattooed mask and sniffed the air, then shielded her face again from the cold. Like all royal summoners, she depended on that striking, stern mask—a relic from the days of King Gere-baron—for a strong first impression.

At the sweet pang of burning applewood, she turned sharply southward. Her spurs jabbed the soft seam between the vawn's natural gold belly armor and the tough green flesh of its back. The mount's head lurched up. Nostrils blasted streams of mud to clear the way for whining voices. A lash of its tail overturned a tree to the right, smashed a bush to the left. Then it resigned itself to the weighty march forward and pushed its way out of the thick patch of trees to enter a well-hidden clearing.

A low murmur of voices rose, fell, and stopped altogether. A bonfire had settled into a mountain of smoky red and black so hot that the circle of Gatherers around it kept their distance to avoid scorching their ragged cloaks.

The summoner scanned the downcast faces, frowned on the bowing and the nodding and the strange spontaneous salutes, ridiculous attempts to appear well-mannered and cooperative.

In no mood for prolonging her task, she cleared her throat, drew the skin-mask back from her lips, and pulled from within her cloak a white scroll tied with a crimson ribbon. She snapped the red strand with a flick of her curled thumbnail and read quickly and colorlessly.

"Krawg. Brown Jelter. Ambaul. Warney. Echo-hawk. Joshoram. Nella Bye. These are recognized by their appointed duty officers. For their admirable efforts in daily assignments. And they are recommended to the king. For restored residence and favor in the house." She spoke in a mechanical, halting way, breaking each statement into fragments. "To claim this opportunity, they must appear. Before the king six days hence. Bearing a sign of their pledge of service. And the nature of their qualifications for labor. The king will hear each criminal's case. And judge fairly whether they remain inside the wall's protection. Or return to the wild for another season."

"What?!" came an urgent voice. A glowering, broad-chested young man stepped forward. "You did say my name, yes? Surely you said 'Radegan' in them there names."

The officer smiled. "There is no such name on this list. Stand back."

Radegan's face—even in the vermilion glow of the ember mountain—paled to ashen white. "But you said that I..."

The officer went on. She stared at the space above each individual's head, as though looking down at such people would cause her to lose her train of thought. "And those orphans. Children of age. To be reviewed...include...*Auralia*."

The gathering unanimously gasped. Krawg swung his hand around to stop up Warney's sob. "Summoner," he said, "there is no Auralia. Not for the Rites of the Privilege."

"Her name. It's on the list. She will attend."

Krawg shook his head. "She's disappeared, good officer."

"Find her."

"We haven't seen her in many days. Probably snatched by a beastman. Or stumbled into a hole. Or a tree fell on her. Or she got carried off by a devil wind. Or stole away to try to get into some other house."

"No one who knows House Abascar," snarled the summoner, "would think of living at any other house."

"True," Krawg added. She could see him thinking as fast as he could. "But Auralia's never known what Abascar's like *inside* the walls. She doesn't know what she's missing. And you wouldn't want her shut inside anyway." He flicked himself in the temple with his thumb. "She's not well in the head, you know. It's a sign of her affliction, that she's run away like this."

The Gatherers kept their heads bowed, visibly colluding in Krawg's desperate fiction. The summoner had never seen such a concerted effort to defy her. She might as well have come bearing news of a death sentence. "We shall send an inquisitor. To investigate Auralia's disappearance. Be ready for him when he comes. He will expect answers."

She went on to name the rest of the orphans who would be called before the king. But the Gatherers appeared distracted, uncomfortable.

Who was this girl they so revered? Where was she? And how did she elude all duty officers' attempts to apprehend her?

Radegan, meanwhile, persisted in his pleas. "My name is on the list, and you know it is!" he snarled. He stepped between the Gatherers and the vawn, speaking in a hushed and personal address. "Don't pretend you've forgotten what I've done to earn it either. It was all your idea, the things I've done to get this chance. I've...I've helped you out. Just like you asked. And you promised me you'd request an early pardon. You owe this to me."

"We cannot deny, thief, that your...your help...was most enthusiastic and rewarding for us," she laughed. "But you have served us so well, it seems we will require your contributions awhile longer before we are willing to send you back into Abascar."

"How do you know I won't lose my patience and—"

The summoner tugged at the reins, but the vawn's head had sunk completely beneath the mire in search of sustenance. The rider felt her grip on composure and civility slipping. She jerked at the leather restraints, and the vawn yanked its head out of the dirt, flinging sand and stones and painting both Radegan and the officer from head to toe in dripping sludge. At any other time, this would have resulted in the desperate sounds of Gatherers trying to stifle laughter at seeing such a figure so offended. But deathly silence remained as they stared into bonfire embers.

The vawn's three voices complained, dissonant, and it trudged off into the trees, while its muddied rider plotted punishments for the obnoxious beast.

The wet ground had only just closed the vawn's deep prints when the first currents of the cold night wind chased ashes into whirling dances above the bonfire coals. The Gatherers all took one step closer to the embers, tightened their circle, and began to utter their frustrations. While it was as close to a Gatherer tradition as anything might be—to follow an officer's visit with self-interested complaint—this time there was only one name on their lips.

"Auralia's not made for Housefolk."

"She'd never last inside. Why, today she sang the Morning Verse from the top of the Stone Tooth within view of the watchtower. Even before the watchman took his place to sing it! If he could have reached her, he'd have smacked her!"

Warney dabbed at his eyes (tears still fell from the empty socket behind his patch). "Krawg sometimes spies her asleep at the top of one of them giant evergreens by the lake. She likes to climb. Says she dreams about lookin' down and seein' the whole Expanse spread out before her. What'll she get into inside the walls? I bite my nails all night wonderin'! They'll be pullin' her off the palace spires."

Krawg nodded, tugged at the loose flesh of his neck. "Found her with a yellowbadger curled in her lap, I did. She was combing out its falling winter fur and stuffin' it in her pockets. It coulda killed her with a bite!"

"She wanted the yellow off its fur."

Krawg took one end of the scarf he wore concealed under his heavy woods-cloak and withdrew it before their eyes. "I'm a liar if I'm not the only one in these here woods to have a yellowbadger scarf! There's no Housefolk, or I'd venture to say, no magistrate neither, ever had one so bright and——"

"Shh, put that cloth away!" Lezeeka snorted so violently that things came out of her nose. "If the summoner'd seen that, she woulda taken you in for a good whippin'!"

"It's Auralia that's gonna get whipped!" grumbled Yawny, his face as white as if he slept among his flour sacks. "They threw me out here because they caught me wearing my favorite red hat in my own bed. I just wanted to keep my head warm. What I mean to say is…Auralia's not gonna live long before she starts cookin' up colors *inside* Abascar's walls. We'd better hope she gets in trouble right away and tossed back out like a hunk of gristle. Because she's the sort who might get sent to the dungeons if she has the time to stir up something serious."

"You've all seen what she messes with," grumbled Hildy the Sad One. "But me… I up and followed her one night when she was runnin' away. I know what she does when nobody finds her."

Warney's eye found Krawg, and there was an unspoken question between them. Then Krawg scowled. "Aw, Hildy, you're full of vawn pooey. Last year you told us you woke up on the floor because Northchildren had come for you. You said they pulled you from your bed and tried to drag you into the woods. Turned out you were just sleepwalkin' and ended up steppin' in a nest of stingers. So don't go expectin' us to——"

"No, I'd like to hear Hildy's story."

Krawg turned, and the assembly of nervous Gatherers shifted away from the man who had spoken, for he was strange to them.

He was small, in a simple green shift with a deep hood that shadowed a face like a pale moon. The firelight revealed his scowl. "If Auralia is to come inside House Abascar, we should properly examine her. We should find out where she comes from and what she intends to do." He opened his hands in a sort of shrug. "The more you can tell me what you know, the less I shall have to ask."

That the summoner could have sent an inquisitor so swiftly—well, it astonished them all. Their eyes shifted between their visitor and Hildy, who was shaking as though the puddle she stood in had turned to ice.

"So, Hildy. Tell me what you can. I have a meticulous memory, and my words within Abascar's walls do not go unnoticed. But I warn you, if a single word rings false, you will have a second inquisitor who is not nearly so kind as I am."

The poor woman had never been the focus of so much attention, and she stammered as she spoke. "At night, at night, Auralia goes to the caves, the caves, along the side of Deep Lake. Down in them cracks and crevices, down in them clefts and holes, she hides, she hides. She empties her pockets of seeds and leaves and roots and things. And seeds. And roots. And leaves. And things. Drops 'em into pots of water she boils over a fire." Hildy's gnarled hands tugged at her long white hair and twisted it as she spoke. "Over a fire."

"Can somebody else tell this story?" lamented little Abeldawn, pulling on his father's three-fingered hand. "She don't talk so good." His father shushed him by pinching his ear.

Wenjee tried to take the story away from Hildy and carry it herself, but no one understood her, for she was swallowing a bun.

Hildy continued. "Auralia breathes in strange vapor from those concoctions, she does. Her eyes light up. Her fingers wiggle. She dances around like a witch."

"And she chants!" burst Wenjee, bun finished. "She chants like a Northchild and probably throws curses on our dreams!"

The robed stranger had begun to smile, more amused than interested. Noticing this, Krawg barked, "Close that mouth, Wenjee! You have to lie down and rest just from walkin' fifty paces. You've never been as far as the lake!"

"There were misty ghosts, though, misty ghosts," said Hildy in a hush. "Misty ghosts blowin' like a wind from the water. She lies down, her eyes stare at the dark sky, and the stones around her shine and make a most alarming sound, a most alarming sound, breaking and cracking. And then she rises and grabs her brushes. And then she rises and grabs—"

"Her brushes!" shouted Abeldawn, whose father swiftly cuffed him on his shoulder.

Hildy glared at the child and went on. "She dips the brushes into the paints, and then she gets to coloring the stones all the way up and all the way down, all the way out to the edge of the water. Those stones're stained, I tell ya, stained as red as blood."

"Maybe it *is* blood!" murmured Mulla Gee under her breath.

Krawg scoffed. "My little Auralia would never hurt nothin' that lives."

Warney's response was no surprise. "Gotta 'gree with ya there!"

The visitor suddenly turned to Krawg. "You were the one who discovered her." The moon-faced stranger spoke so slowly, and with such gravity, that the words seemed new and magnificent as he voiced them. "Tell me about that day."

As the gathering groaned, weary of Krawg's favorite tale, the old thief cleared his throat and spread his arms as if presenting a stage for a drama. "It was by the river."

"The Throanscall. Take me there."

Warney gave a whimper, which Krawg quickly translated. "We're only Gatherers, sir. We're not supposed to leave the camps at night!"

"Who do you think you're talking to?" The stranger smiled again, this time with teeth. Crooked teeth like a weasel's. "You were once the Midnight Swindler. You're the kind of man who pays attention, who remembers things.

Show me where you found her, and tell me every detail. I will reward you with… Hmm, what does a convicted thief desire? A pardon? Does he want me to recommend him to Abascar's king as a helpful and cooperative man?"

Krawg dropped to his knees and reached out as if to determine whether or not the visitor was real. Warney stepped between them and grabbed the stranger's shoulders. "As you can see, Krawg's old and sore of leg. But I was there to see it all, and I'll take you straight to the spot where we found Auralia. I'll tell you the whole story and about every day with 'Ralia since then!"

Krawg rose to his feet with a roar and grabbed Warney by the throat. At the same moment, everyone began talking about Auralia and pressing in closer to the stranger, who raised his hands, laughing. "I can also spread word of an unruly and disrespectful mob!"

This had its desired effect, and a few moments later, it was Krawg who led the nervous procession into the trees.

At the river's edge in the tall reeds where the muckmoths flutter, Krawg and Warney bickered over the details of how they found the child.

The stranger listened but paced anxiously, examining the ground, dipping his fingers into the river, even tasting the water. When Krawg paused in mid-story, enthralled by the vivid memories, the stranger said, "Tell me about the footprint."

Sweat began to stream down Krawg's face. He cast a pleading glance at his questioner, who ignored him and stared instead up the dark flowing line of the Throanscall.

Housefolk did not smile upon talk of mysterious creatures, and if Krawg even referred to the Keeper, he might wake up in a dungeon cell. Warney began to edge away from the conversation, quite prepared to run.

"Sir," Krawg murmured, each word a cautious step, "there's some who'd say things unlawful, things untrue. But I'm the king's good man, and I make no claim 'bout the mark in which Auralia lay. But it was a humblin' sight. A footprint, or a hole dug to appear as such. And no creature had stepped upon her as she lay in the ground, no sir. The ground was broken first. And she was put down in it, nice and easy, still wet from the river."

"Some folks would say more? Tell me, Krawg—if the Keeper were more than a figure in children's dreams, might this have been a sign of its emergence from the river?" The stranger stepped into the water and tilted his head, listening to it rush around his legs.

Warney had seen enough. He turned to head for the trees and found himself face to face with an Abascar duty officer, who seized him by the ear. The old burglar's yelp interrupted the hushed conference by the river and startled the sleeping bushbirds, which clambered up the air and into the treetops.

The officer—no doubt patrolling for beastman activity—wore full battle armor and cut a gleaming figure in the bough-broken moonbeams. His helm covered his face, muffling his outrage. "Who wants to be first to invent some wild explanation for why a bunch of criminals are whispering down by the river after the Evening Verse?"

Warney whimpered an unintelligible excuse, and Nella Bye interpreted. "It was the inquisitor who brought us here, sir. As you can see, we're only answering questions."

"Show me this man you're talking about," said the officer.

The wet grass around Krawg's feet seemed to close its icy fingers around his ankles, binding him to the spot. Somehow he knew, even without looking, even as the others detailed frantic descriptions of the moon-faced stranger who had suddenly vanished, that he had been tricked, that the curious visitor had not been any royal official at all.

There was someone else in the woods tonight who wanted to find Auralia. Someone unattached and dangerous.

At the performance of the Morning Verse, a company of riders arrived escorting a true inquisitor. There would be no debate—this one was, as the stranger had promised, lacking in kindness.

When the inquisitor returned to the king, he did not bring news of Auralia, for she remained invisible, lost without a trace. Instead, he returned with news of a meddler among the Gatherers, a man full of questions and eloquent deceit. And the king put the watchmen on alert, inspiring whispered reports that Scharr ben Fray, the man who had taught Cal-raven tales of the Keeper, the troublemaker who had been exiled for his beliefs, had been seen among the Gatherers.

7

NIGHT ON THE LAKE

Two moons shone on the night the ale boy received his unusual orders. One rang out in the black sky, sharp and clear as an owl's cry. The other, an echo of the first, rested uneasily on the glassy surface of the lake. The forest held its breath, so that any ripple on the water indicated a presence, a movement, evidence of something—a gator, a rat, an eel, a fish—in a dive or on the rise.

The ale boy pushed the last crate of bottles off the edge of the dock and onto the rocking raft. Sweat ran cold down his back. He pulled on his heavy winter cloak, and when his head came up through it, he saw that the dock's duty officer had come to watch him. The guard frowned his trained suspicion, but his scowl had no effect on the boy, who had yet to see a smile from anyone on this day of endless errands.

You could have helped me, the boy thought, but did not say.

The guard scowled deeper as though he had heard the words anyway, or perhaps it just looked that way in the wavering torchlight. He wore a blue stripe; he answered directly to the captain of the guard.

The ale boy glanced around to see if Ark-robin was near. He was beginning to wonder why it was so hard for him to stray beyond the watch of the captain or his officers. Was he under suspicion? Had he been observed collecting ale from the leaking slats of neglected barrels? Had someone witnessed him slipping samples to Gatherers?

"I'm to remind you—show some caution on the water. And report anything suspicious."

"Suspicious, sir?" He wished he had not heard the warning. "Is there somethin' wrong on the lake?"

The guard watched the moon's reflection and slowly shook his head. "Personally, I'd give you a different warning: pay no heed to rumors. But Captain Ark-robin is particularly interested that you stick to your duties."

"Did he say why?"

Smirking, the guard gestured to the array of bottles on the raft. "More information will cost you, ale boy. One bottle, and your sworn secrecy. Do you know how hard it is for soldiers to earn king's brew?"

Where the dock met the shadowing land, a vawn slurped at the shoreline sand. The guard groaned. "No, don't go swallowing that shell-littered sludge, you bucket-head!" He stormed back toward the animal. The vawnwhip came free of his belt and—*whack!* It was clear to the ale boy that he and his business had been forgotten.

He unwound the rope from the anchorpost and stepped onto the raft. With the single oar, he pushed off. The sound of water lapping at the underside of the dock grew quieter as the raft cut a silver V through reflections of constellations. For a few moments, silence swelled until he heard only the occasional slice of his oar, the quiet tapping of bottles in the crate, and the faint squeals of bats zigzagging across the water. He lifted the oar and stood still, banishing all thoughts of the guard's warning. This moment, here, this span between the dock and the destination, was too fragile, too precious.

He knew they would come. They always did in moments like this. Without invitation, without explanation. Tears. Tears wavering and blurring the stars. Under the unblinking stare of the two white eyes, the moon in the sky and the moon in the water, no one could command him or expect anything of him. No blue-striped officer could spy on his activity. No one could hurt him or ridicule him for his smallness, his weakness. No one's shared laughter could remind him of his loneliness. No one's stature or success could tell him what he might have been if only his life had begun differently.

The raft moved like a long, slow sigh, careless, unobserved.

The stillness did not last.

A placid patch of stars lying on the lake quivered, sending a shudder through the field of lights.

From the size of the disturbance, it was clear that something approached, purposeful, aware. He had heard rumors of enormous creatures sighted from the walls of House Bel Amica, the smooth, gleaming arch of a leathery back breaking the surface of the western sea. Behemoths, they called them. But no such creatures lurked beneath this quiet lake. He fought the fear that froze him, jumped behind some ale crates, crouched low. The loudest sound in the darkness was his frantic, beating heart.

Just moments later, the stars stilled their crazy dance, drew together again, held their places. The slight rocking of the raft slowed.

He huddled mouselike on the edge of the raft as it slowly turned. He eyed the obsidian water. Pale points of reflected starlight might instead be eyes. A spiky tree branch breaking the surface might not be a branch at all.

Soon there were other sounds. Distant voices of the young women on the royal float in the middle of the lake. Though he could not discern the reason for their laughter, he felt they laughed at him, laughed for how he cowered before the slightest disturbance.

The royal float was a broad wooden platform on a tether fastened to a far-off dock. Kept by the king for special, private night occasions or for entertaining privileged guests and visitors, it rested within arrowshot of a duty guard in a solitary floating watchtower. The guard crouched like a watchful cliffhawk protecting a nest, just far enough out to be kept from overhearing the conversations of the favored company. The float was decorated with whiteflame torches, lined by a brass rail, and covered by a canvas to catch untimely rain. The ale boy hated the float, for no one went out on it for an evening without requesting more drink than was appropriate.

Tonight the float's honored passengers would receive these bottles of royal appletwist and raise glasses in honor of the Promised. The king had selected the town's most celebrated young woman to marry Prince Cal-raven: Stricia, daughter of Captain Ark-robin. She had made great show of admiration for the prince. She earned honors by turning in lawbreakers, including palace servant women she caught exchanging a share of their best colored linens rather than delivering them to the king as required.

Stricia's beauty was unmatched—narrow and sparkling iceblue eyes, wide lips framing a generous smile, and a river of golden hair braided elaborately about her head and down her back. In a realm where subjects were uniformly bound in grey and brown, the gleam of a person's hair could be an arresting distinction. Stricia's tresses looked as though they were spun from sunlight. Her beauty was not unknown to the ale boy, but neither was her laugh—a proud jay's cackle that clamored across the lake.

Stricia's chosen attendants passed around a stretch of fabric from the looms where her wedding gown was even now being prepared, a train of gold that shimmered under the moonlight as though it should burn their hands. The ale boy could see their wide eyes and gaping mouths as they adored the fabric. He could see envy in their eyes, wistfulness, as though they were suddenly remembering something precious they had lost.

"The only thing better than the touch of this gown against your skin," sighed one of the ladies, "will be the feel of Prince Cal-raven's arms around you as you wear it."

The ale boy winced. Of all the intolerable talk, the cursing of the Gatherers, the bickering of soldiers, nothing soured his stomach faster than the empty, predictable chatter of young Housefolk.

"Oh, stop your gushing, Dynei," Stricia whispered unconvincingly. "Have you thought about the burdensome stones I'll have to wear around my neck? How I'll have to eat with ridiculous manners while wearing rings on each of my fingers?" She gasped. "Imagine, walking down the street, so visible and so...so distracting. I'll long to go back to being one of the common. And it'll be even worse when I'm queen."

"It's been so long since the train of a queen's dress has trailed along the palace corridors," sighed another attendant. "I used to know when Queen

Jaralaine was passing our quarters by the sound of silky fringe brushing the floor."

The attendants gave a collective shudder of lust and envy, whether more for the thought of the throne, the prince, or the gown, the ale boy was uncertain. Their excitement unsettled the float, spreading ripples that rocked his raft as he coasted to a stop against the platform.

"The ale boy!" they chorused.

"There'll be pear cider with your breakfast," Dynei laughed. "White wine with your midday meal. Red wine with your supper. Perhaps even hajka."

"The king never shares his hajka," Stricia sighed.

"You had best gain Cal-raven's word that he won't be so stingy," another interjected, kneeling to be closest to the raft.

The ale boy wondered how much strength it would require to tip the float and send the women sliding into the lake.

He reached into a bag and withdrew three bottles of appletwist, set them in a glittering row on the edge of the float. Then he reached in again, found a rack of five clay sipping cups. He ignored the continuing gossip, uncorked the first bottle with a metal hook, let the sighing rush rise, tipped the bottle over the line of cups, then stopped. Stricia stood over him, laughing, holding another bottle, demanding the opener. He started to argue, but she snatched it from him and, as if by accident, kicked the tray of cups back into his boat.

"We will drink from the bottles, thank you. You can row on back and do...whatever boys like you do at night."

"You'll have to stop dreaming about Stricia though," said Dynei, who was enfolding the guest of honor in her arms as if to protect her. "She's been *promised*, you know."

"And that means the rest of these magnificent girls will win the love of soldiers," Stricia announced, overjoyed, and the ensuing gleeful outcry could surely be heard on all sides of the lake, as the women argued over their potential pairings.

The maidens drained the bottle and opened the next before the ale boy could untie his raft from the float's edge. Their mirth and gossip increased, and he scowled. A precious vintage gulped down the way laborers guzzled ale in the drinking huts after harvest was done. The royal brewer Obsidia Dram came to mind, a round and dusty woman, like a beer keg with leathery gloves for hands. He remembered the brewer roaring to any who would listen, "Royal appletwist should be held awhile so the chill goes off…then sniffed and lightly sipped to let its flavor explore the tongue and the crannies…and then…" There would be broken glass in the brewery if Obsidia caught wind of this evening's reckless waste.

He trained his gaze on the dark shore, wondered if a bottle of appletwist would be payment enough to hire a thief from among the Gatherers to steal this exquisite cloth so he could bring it to a different kind of young woman, one who knew to savor the color of the king's ales.

He had thought of Auralia often since that day a season past, when her fingers had brushed his brow.

The light of the float faded behind him; the torchless shadow of the guard's tower loomed close. The silhouette of the standing guard leaned over him.

"Shouldn't you be serving the ladies?"

"Pardon, sir, but the ladies…would not be served. Took the bottles and told me to go."

The guard grunted his disgust, which the ale boy presumed was directed at the Promised and her company. He held the oar in the water to keep from departing until dismissed.

"Well then. It must be nice, having a bottle in hand to make these long nights easier. Makes me thirsty…just thinking about it."

The ale boy could be punished for delivering his cargo to anyone but the assigned party. The trap being set for him was all too familiar—to go one way ensured a good bruising, but to go the other would ensure another good bruising. "Well, there is…erm…another crate of appletwist bottles that I was unable to deliver."

"I can't imagine they've all survived the ride without a crack. Let me take one of those casualties off your hands. And not a word about it, understand? If it's found missing, for all you know the party knocked an empty bottle overboard."

The ale boy thought it best to give no more words to this exchange. He quietly lifted a bottle and stepped to the edge of the raft.

In that moment several things happened at once. The guard climbed down the iron ladder, holding a higher rung with one hand while reaching out to the ale boy with the other. The tower tipped ever so slightly with the shift of the weight. The ale boy held the neck of a bottle out to the groping shadow. A great wave swelled abruptly behind the raft and raised it as lightly as if it were a leaf. The tower, a much heavier obstacle, lurched in the disturbance, casting the guard, bottle in hand, smack into the upward swell, and he disappeared without a cry. The ale boy managed an "Oh!" before the raft slid down the back of the wave and sent him tumbling off the edge.

The raft spun off into the darkness, away from the tower, away from the float, and away from the shore, bottles rolling and clinking against each other like alarm bells.

The ale boy had nearly burnt to death in a fire. The scar on his forehead was his souvenir—a reminder of that agony. He was surprised how similar it felt to drown in the cold lake. Water filled his ears, turning him deaf to the sound of his struggle. It poured in through his nose, and he choked cries that became undulating balloons of air rising up toward the surface. His cloak seemed made of chains, sinking him. Something like a tight fist had closed around his left ankle, pulling. He went still from fear, for there was something in the water with him, and it was not the duty guard.

He could hear something—a voice, a low humming, a rumble, a deep song. He opened his eyes, expecting to see nothing but the moon's pale impression like a shining coin floating above him, but there was something else…an immense shadow passing between him and the surface.

He felt compelled to call out. But he had no strength.

A strong current sent him spinning upward, and he found himself drawing in lungfuls of night air. Something bumped against his head, driftwood perhaps, and his feet kicked against rising ground.

He splashed forward three steps before falling, his legs half-dead. He lunged onto a shore of smooth, slippery stones. The waves washed in and around and over him and then receded, and he was left there, soaking in the shallows, icy lakewater running out of his head through his nose and ears, his heavy coat holding him down.

Soon, I will be able to feel again, he thought, watching his desperate breaths puff away in the breeze. *That will hurt.*

His body felt like that of an old, enormous man. One foot was still held fast. With quivering fingers, he untangled a rope from his ankle and realized it was the tie to the bag that held the clay sipping cups and some flasks of ale. They rattled together like shells as he felt around inside; they were all there, two of fourteen cups were broken, but at least the disaster was not a total loss.

He tried again to stand, but made it only to his knees. He blinked and made sense of the high shadow wall. Cliffs, with caves gouged in the base. The moonlight they reflected was full of soft colors. He looked back and saw nothing but the quieting waters and the lights of the royal float so far in the distance they might have been fireflies clustered on a lily pad.

And then the trembling took over. Water trickled off his skin, and yet he felt colder. He clutched the bag against him, evidence that he was still alive, still the ale boy, still a person of some responsibility. But nothing could ever be the same, for now he knew with certainty that something hid beneath those waters.

His face was wet with tears as he shook from the impact of betrayal—the adults had lied, and he had been punished a time or two for suspecting what was indeed true—and of hope: in his dreams, the creature had been gentle and sheltering.

A warmth encircled him, heavy, soft, like a blanket. It *was* a blanket. And there was that voice of welcome.

"I hoped you would visit me."

She was saving him again, wrapping him in warmth. She crouched beside him, a hunched figure in a hooded robe woven with all kinds of darkness.

"But you coulda come by land, you know. I'm not so hard to find."

She was already busy, collecting wet, sharp-edged shells that the waves had given the shore. "Really," she laughed, "the Keeper should be more careful."

8

THE UNGUARDED GALLERY

Roots like carrots bled orange dye. Taters from the house-kitchen rot bins could be mashed into pastes of brown, white, and grey. When fading summer brought the water level down from the doors of the caves, wide plates of slate lay safe for Auralia's painting. Colors rivered and washed in tides in her head, and she swept them accordingly across stone canvases. The moonlight was enough, and when it was not, she worked with shimmering hues that danced up the cliffs to light the tree trunks and illuminate the outstretched, wind-shaped boughs.

Ever since she could crawl, she had collected the colors of the Expanse, discerning the secrets of their making, and she had not been idle with the secrets fifteen years had taught her.

All this she shared with the ale boy, walking through the caves with torch in hand as though discovering the colors for the first time. Many experiments had collapsed, and many inspirations had come to preposterous conclusions. But sometimes the work had revealed itself and become a thing of beauty or a device she had never imagined. She laughed, embarrassed by some of the garish displays she had made.

He laughed too, because such passion seemed so dangerous—and sure to be stolen or destroyed. The walls were pockmarked with hand-carved indentations, each housing an exquisite invention. A small pillow of white feathers loosely bound by yellow grass and fringed with burgundy moss. Walking sticks, gnarled and smooth, stained in a spectrum of colors from regal blue to burnished gold. Autumn leaves spread into fans, sun dried, glazed with amber, ready to be brandished against summer's stifling heat. A stonecutter with a bone white grip and a bold red sheath. And bowls, bowls of all shapes and colors. "I like to make things that can hold other things," she said. As she ran her fingertips along the wall, she murmured reminders about what needed "work," what was "good enough," and the ale boy even caught her arguing with herself over the proper recipient for each gift.

Gifts. Hundreds of them. Not showy gallery exhibits. Auralia had stored up ready remedies and surprises for the Gatherers. The fan—"Poor Wenjee is always too warm." And the pillow—"Rishella's gonna birth her baby soon."

Impossible that such a menagerie glittered unguarded within Abascar's reach, and yet the king had not found and buried these things in the Under-keep. "Nobody bothers with this end of the lake," she explained. "Sometimes traders or soldiers'll pass by, but it's like they're blind. They don't look closely, or they're looking for the wrong things. They come out with a mind for conflict, not for savoring. The farther from Abascar, the more they sharpen their swords and move all hasty-like."

"But isn't it dangerous, living out here alone?"

"Of *course* it's dangerous," she snapped bitterly. "More dangerous every day. But aren't there dangers inside Abascar's walls? And really, what do they expect? The woods wouldn't be so dangerous if they hadn't left it to run so wild. Now they're afraid of it and probably ashamed."

"Ashamed?"

"Ashamed they've forgotten how to live here. They're too busy making piles of things they think they need and then buildin' walls around 'em. Makes 'em think there's nothin' out here they need. But out here they'd remember that they're small and that they need help."

The ale boy nodded as though he'd thought of this before. He was, after all, painfully aware of his smallness and his constant need for help.

Auralia stopped to whistle at a cavebird, with its oily feathers and bulging lidless eyes. "Why should the forest care what becomes of Abascar, when they've left it in such a state?"

"Why do you stay then?"

She shrugged. "How could I leave the Gatherers? They found me. Took care of me until I could walk. Gave me a place. They didn't have to help me. And I wanted them to know..."

"But they know," he interrupted. "They've known a long, long time. Whenever I visit the Gatherers, they're talkin' about you. They worry about you. You've repaid them, I think, Auralia. You don't have to stay. You can get away before something happens. Before officers start tellin' you what kinda colors you can't use."

"Perhaps. What do *you* want me to do?"

"Stay." He blushed.

She blinked at him. "You're a funny thing, ale boy."

Feeling very small indeed, the ale boy watched the waves of light splashing across the waiting gifts. He was tempted to ask if he could stay here in this heart of craft and care, a place so different from the Underkeep's corridors with their unsettling, transient winds, their mysterious groans, their tangled and knotted labyrinths.

He had caught a glimpse at last of what made Auralia skirt Abascar's borders and resist the pull of its gravity. Auralia's way was to bless the undeserving, not reward those who gave her what she wanted. What hope could she have when Abascar punished orphans who did not learn to follow instructions? Unless...

He returned to questions that grew stronger every day. Why was he an exception? He had never been cast out. He had never been awarded badges or subjected to the tests. What had he done that Abascar favored him? What had set him apart from orphans who were given over to the Gatherers' insufficient care?

Fear kept him from voicing such questions, lest the matter had simply been overlooked, lest officers should investigate, mutter their regret, and toss him into the wilderness. But now he wondered if there was some secret bargain that could be struck that would allow Auralia to dwell freely within the palace as he did. What was this third path, this life beyond the two extremes—the tedious exchange of labor for protection within Abascar's enclosure, and the scramble for survival on the perilous side of Abascar's walls?

He began to wonder which of Auralia's inventions might be useful to bribe an official or win a special pardon.

"Not even the palace stuff's good like this," he told her, picking up two discs of polished seaglass in a small rectangular frame of twigs.

"Try holding 'em up to your eyes."

He propped the frame on the bridge of his nose and peered through the discs. Auralia and the torch loomed larger, a bit blurry but unmistakable.

"You know old Radish? His eyes're so bad he can't see what's in his spoon before he lifts it to his mouth." She hushed her voice as if the old Gatherer might be nearby.

As they wandered through the ascending passage, the ale boy saw more and more and more—things pieced together so perfectly it was hard to imagine why no one had done so before. What did a tree cone have to do with an array of butterfly wings? When fitted together just so and then tossed skyward, they became a spinning, gliding top. What did honeycombs have to do with the spines of husktree leaves? In her hands, they became slow-burning candles with brilliant gold flames.

"I never knew there were so many colors. How do you find so many?"

"I put two colors together just to see what they'll do with each other. This one'll swallow that one. This one, mixed with that one, disappears, but it makes this one weaker at the same time. Sometimes they join." She clapped her hands. Echoes of applause sounded round about them, as though a hundred other children answered from a hundred different caves. "And *woosh!* You see something new and amazing."

The ale boy thought of Obsidia Dram mixing her wines and tasting them.

"I just know there's got to be *more* of 'em." Auralia's pale brow was crumpled in concentration. She walked faster, her finger tracing a yellow spiral painted along the wall in a line like that of a windblown leaf that never settles. "I know there's some colors missing. I can feel it...*here.*" She paused before a heavy vine-weave curtain that veiled another cave, closed her fists and pressed them to her temples. "It's like I used to see other colors, and now something's keeping them out of my head. Without them, everything seems unfinished. Everything." She spread her arms wide. "It's all imperfect. And I don't know how I know."

Everything here is perfect, he thought. *Isn't it?* "If he saw this, King Cal-marcus would ask you to paint the walls of his house." He reached absently for the curtain.

"*Paint* the walls? They should let me rip 'em down." Auralia grabbed his arm and drew him forward to the first bend in the tunnel. The torch grazed the wall, showering sparks and ash. "Used to be the walls were there to keep out the beastmen. But now they keep out everything."

She drew in a sharp breath and looked back. Then she clutched his collar, pulled him forward, and cast the torch down into a pile of stones. "Cover the flame! Put it out!" she whispered.

The quavering light dimmed. They huddled together against the wall. Smoke flowered from the stones before them, then dissipated on the low-moaning wind. Their heartbeats thundered. The ale boy, still wet with grimy lakewater, pressed against Auralia's heat.

He heard it now—heavy, wet, uncertain steps. A gurgling wheeze choked with lakewater. The visitor advanced, one step, another, up the long stretch, until he stopped a few steps from the corner. The passage was suddenly illuminated by a warm glow.

Auralia peered around the corner, toward the entrance. A moment of stillness, and she gestured for the boy to share the view.

The corridor was empty. Light touched the wall opposite the curtain, which had been drawn back to release streams of shimmering color. The ale boy could see the shadow of their visitor, a crooked figure outlined on the wall, one massive hand pressed against its head as if to an injury.

"It's the stranger," Auralia said in his ear. "He's come back."

"What stranger? From Abascar?"

"No."

A chill ran through him, and he began to crawl backward, but Auralia grabbed him by the sleeve and shook her head. "Don't be scared. He's not a normal beastman. He's different. This one, he comes for the colors. He stays. He sleeps. Sometimes I think he cries. Eventually he goes. I don't bother him; he doesn't bother me. I think the colors are helping him."

The shadow vanished as the visitor let the curtain close behind him.

"Are we safe?"

"For now."

The ale boy felt a scorch of envy for the visitor, who had immersed himself in the light. "The colors." He stood up and stepped back around the corner, drawn toward the music of the hues. "They move."

Auralia pulled the sputtering remnant of the torch from the stones and followed on tiptoes. "I know." There was awe in her voice and fear as well. "They're changing. Can't say how I made that happen." She put her lips to his ear. "We shouldn't stay. As long as he's here, it's not safe."

"But you said..."

"I said he hasn't bothered *me*. He hasn't seen you. Let's not test him."

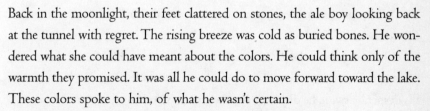

Back in the moonlight, their feet clattered on stones, the ale boy looking back at the tunnel with regret. The rising breeze was cold as buried bones. He wondered what she could have meant about the colors. He could think only of the warmth they promised. It was all he could do to move forward toward the lake. These colors spoke to him, of what he wasn't certain.

"I want to come back again. I want to see those colors."

"No," she said flatly. "They're too dangerous."

"How?"

"They're wild and moving when they're stitched just so. They put that beastman in a trance. No tellin' what they'll do to you. Don't want you to get burnt."

"Fire doesn't scare me." He touched the mark on his brow. "Remember?"

"It isn't a fire. It's just threads. I just started weavin' them together. They're pieces of something, but I can't see what. Not yet. Something's still missing."

He found Auralia watching him, as if she hoped to find some answer in his troubled face. "Don'tcha ever get that feeling," she said with the weariness of someone much older, "when you run up a new path in the woods that you'll find something at the end of it…something you've never seen?"

Yes, he did not say aloud.

"Or maybe you see something move in the lake," she said, "and you want to swim to it just to find out what it is?"

The ale boy glanced quickly, nervously, toward the water. "The officers don't want me askin' about things that aren't my business. It's best I stay away from mysteries. They get me into trouble."

He imagined himself resting from daily errands, lying on a cot in his humble cave deep beneath the palace in the Underkeep, staring across the bridge-laced abyss of a thousand torches, watching sparks from lanterns in the brewers' caverns spring out of their glass enclosures and gleam along the floor. A stray spark would sometimes tumble into a spill of ale. In its final hiss and glow, the color would change, swell, blaze, and suddenly fade, leaving a mark in his vision that stayed even when he slept.

"There are no Abascar guards watching us, ale boy," she said. "You don't have to be afraid."

He took her hand, led her down close to the water, and found them a dry place to sit on a large, twisted driftwood tree. Taking the bag that had survived his desperate swim, he drew out the ale cups and lined them up on the tree. She remained close, curious. He took the four flasks made of skins, uncorked them, and smiled up at her with a glint in his eye that was more than just the moon.

"Watch."

He filled four cups with ales of brown, amber, gold, and red. With the confidence of a juggler, he mixed different combinations in the remaining eight cups. There was purpose in his work. Auralia pounded her knuckles together while she watched. Occasionally she glanced back at her caves and then wrung the edge of her cloak. He could not repress his smile.

And then he sat back, pulled his knees up to his chin, and grinned. "Ready? Take the torch. There's still an ember there. Touch it to the edge of each cup."

She took the hissing branch, held it out to the cups, and *rush!* A flame leapt from the lip of the first. The next erupted in fire. She did not need the torch for the rest. The nearness of flame brought answering bursts right down the line, until there was a row of straight and steady lights between Auralia and the ale boy, each a different hue. One colder than blue, one bolder than red, and one a sort of rust she had seen only in leaves that clung to trees in defiance of winter. One burnt three colors at once, and where they joined at the base of the flame was a searing white gold. They laughed, his happiness rekindled by hers.

"Fire patrols watch the breweries. A brewer dropped his torch beside a leaking barrel. Pow!" He fanned his fingers out. "There was nothin' left of him when they stamped out the flames. It gave the king an idea. He had folks start makin' traps for the beastmen—at least, that's what Dram tells me. Soldiers can bait beastmen into pools that go up in flames and..."

He abandoned his story, for the colors had distracted Auralia. It seemed she was listening to them, waiting for them to tell her where she could employ them. He felt a strange pride to see her so engaged.

"You be careful then," she said at last, blinking, returning to the moment. "Colors can be dangerous. They play by invisible rules."

"Fire doesn't scare me," he said again. As long as she looked into the colors, he found he could speak freely.

And so it was there he told the story, as much to himself as to her, the lake, and the lights. He was not even aware of the words as they spilled out of him. He remembered the cradle burning around him as the house became a furnace.

The shadows all around, covering him. A giant reaching through the fire and carrying him away into cold air and darkness, and then down, down, down into the Underkeep. He saw himself there, swallowing the broth offered by an old woman who smelled like apples—or rather, as he grew up, apples smelled like her. Men stood in hushed conferences, discussing him and his future, something he recognized even if he could not yet understand their words. Then there were the years of learning to walk along the paths of black earth and across the rope bridges over the deep, expanding spaces of the Underkeep. Lessons in the brewers' discipline. *Ale boy. Ale boy.*

As he slowly surfaced from the memories, he became aware of Auralia's intense concentration. It was unsettling to be the focus of someone's attention. And it was good. What it must be like to be the king! How could a man such as that, so closely watched, not burst?

He leaned forward and blew out the flames with one steady breath. In the darkness, the story told, he was exhausted. "I like to be near the flames. It's…where I came from. I'm not afraid. It's the only way I can be close to *them.*"

"To them?"

"To my mother and father, whoever they were. And to whoever pulled me from the fire. No one knows."

Auralia pressed her hands to her face, and tears spilled over them.

"Maybe that's what the beastman is doing here. Maybe the colors are calling it."

She nodded, dabbing her cheeks with the edge of the blanket that still covered the boy. "You and me are lots the same. I stay near the water 'cause it's where I came from." She was looking out at the lake now. Or at something beneath it. "When I sleep near the water, I'm closer to the Keeper."

"You think he's actual?" The ale boy did not want to speak of this further, but he felt drawn toward the answer.

"As people grow up, they're embarrassed to think there's something out there they don't understand. It makes them feel small. Like maybe they're not in charge. Like they have to be careful." She released a whispered laugh.

"You don't know for certain, do you?" he whispered.

She turned away from him for a moment. But he saw her hands clench. When she turned back, her eyes had grown larger. She gazed up past the painted face of stone behind them to the overhang of vines and branches. "Once I climbed up there and almost fell asleep. I heard a beastman coming to attack me. I was so afraid, I kept my eyes closed. I did not have time to think who might hear my cry for help. But I called anyway. The beastman screamed. He fell into the water. And then..."

"You think the Keeper saved you?"

She smiled. "Do beastmen stumble over cliffs?"

There was a ripple in the water, and a shape suddenly slipped into their sight.

The ale boy jumped up and ran, his feet punching into the soft sand. "It's my raft! My raft is here! Quick! I've got to get to it!"

Auralia grabbed a long and twisted branch and dragged it after him into the shallows. Together they steered the branch to snag a corner of the raft and pull it in to shore.

He salvaged a wine bottle, which he had intended for the gatekeeper who would let him back into the house. He uncorked it and offered it to her.

"Thank you," he said, "for saving me from that...that stranger."

She blinked, stunned. She had forgotten.

She did not take the bottle, but she cupped her hands to him. He laughed, and poured the wine, which trickled through her fingers dark and gleaming. Her hair spilled around her hands as she sipped it carefully. When she lifted her head again, the wine had smoothed the creases in her face.

"Now *that*," he said, "is how to drink the king's wine." He glanced out at the sky over the lake. "Sun's gonna be up soon, and I'm gonna get an earful from the officers in charge of me."

Auralia stepped forward and threw her arms around him. Her neck smelled like smoke and honey. Her heartbeat fluttered against his face. She held him the way he'd always imagined his mother would.

Then he sneezed and made great apology as she let him go and laughed. He offered her the blanket she had draped around his shoulders. "You must take this. They'll never let me keep it."

"Come visit me again," she said, folding the cloth and holding it to her breast. "Oh, I wish I knew your name. What am I gonna call you? *Little brother?*"

"Just call me 'ale boy.' That's what they all do."

"But I know your real name," she laughed. "It's here. I just don't know how to pronounce it." Again she touched his forehead scar. "Promise me one thing. When I'm gone, will you play with your lights here, by the lake?"

"When you're gone?"

Nearby a fish jumped. Fluttering bats darted past and jittered out over the water.

"I can't stay here forever. I'll be caught and hauled into the house. Or someone will come and take over these caves. Or something." She broke off, bit her lower lip, and looked back at the dark stones where the colors slept until morning. "I'd feel better…it wouldn't be so sad…if I could finish my work and know that someone will come to watch over the colors."

He was still. Emotions surged in him like waves. The creature in her caves. The mysterious colors. The shadow in the lake. Abascar. She suddenly seemed vulnerable. "Be careful, 'Ralia."

Auralia sat on the stones as the ale boy shoved off with his oar, and the raft drifted back out into the water. They watched silently, until they could not see each other. It seemed to the ale boy that he was remaining still while the world turned and took her away, filling the space between them with deep water and traces of starlight.

The forest went on dreaming while Auralia folded her thoughts and set them aside for the night. She sat on the cliff edge, swinging her feet into space as if she might find a foothold and walk away on the air. She watched the lake, following the progress of that small speck of darkness drifting through reflected stars. This was a new feeling, something different from what she felt in the volatile company of Gatherers. She had a friend.

And there was something else puzzling her. The colors had drawn the attention of the beastly stranger yet again, this foul-smelling hulk of hair, claws, and teeth. She had been surprised at her own reluctance to call the visitor a beastman. With his deformity and crude intelligence, what else could he be? But he was drawn to her caves to stare into the colors, to sleep surrounded by the bowls of incense. This was still a mystery to her.

Uncomfortable with the thought of cooking or sleeping in her caves while such a shadow lurked nearby, Auralia had tiptoed around the slumbering creature, bundled patches of unfinished weave, and brought them up the corridor, deeper and deeper until she reached the hollows where a feeble mountain stream fell into a buried river. There she climbed a rugged, narrow stair that took her to the top of the cliffs. She emerged above her lakeside home and took shelter from the breeze beneath trees with warped and bristling branches. She spread the spans of faintly glowing cloth across a bed of brown, broad mushrooms. There she fingered the frayed edges of each piece, imagining what might join one to the other and bring order to their dissonance.

In the distance, she heard a faint trace of the Early Morning Verse. She did not sing along.

The waters of the lake grew restless, a white thread winding along the edge.

Whispering soft comfort to herself, she set the instruments of her craft before her—needles, leaf packets of dye, spools of various threads. She wove strands drawn from the stems of wild celery, stained her fingertips with dye, all crazy with colors of fireweed and swamp-muck green.

"Whenever I visit the Gatherers, they're talking about you," she repeated to herself. "You think I don't know what they say? Northchild. Dark secrets. A danger to them all. A spy." She twisted one red thread around her fingertips, drawing it taut to the snapping point.

BREAKING THE BLACKLODE

This deluge is a curse."

So ran the rumor down the line of Abascar diggers as they propped their shovels against the rugged wall of the tunnel and surrendered for the day.

"The philosophers of House Jenta would say our shovels have injured and angered the earth. And that the rain has come to stop us. That desert heat makes them crazy in Jenta. But…you have to wonder."

Submerging themselves in the strata of stone and soil and then returning with wheelbarrows full, these tunneling laborers found that even heavy storm-cloaks were not enough against such a determined storm. It pummeled them. It saturated the hours.

Three days the torrent battered their tents, two days' march northwest of House Abascar, in the valley between the northern edge of the Cragavar forest and the southern reaches of the deeper, darker Fraughtenwood. The two ancient forests regarded each other across the valley, indifferent to the efforts of the diggers.

The irony of it all—that the diggers, for want of an underground river to quench the thirst of Abascar, would all but drown in water from elsewhere—was not lost on any of them. But they did not laugh. Their capacity for humor had washed away on the second day of work. Here on the third, their willpower faltered. No one dared ask that the dig be suspended. They just worked, pressing on like mindless drones, gouging the earth and hauling boulders, dirt, and roots, dumping them into nearby ravines.

So when they hit a sudden stop, drills and shovels blunting against a vein of impenetrable, subterranean blacklode, they all but collapsed in relief. Their foreman, Blyn-dobed, had no choice but to announce the dig's suspension.

Errand-runners were sent to request new tools from the deep mining beneath House Abascar. Help would be five days coming.

Meanwhile, a musician, summoned from Abascar on the first day of the storm, had arrived with a royal escort who would ensure that she played properly inspiring music for the waiting diggers.

As her songs began, the foreman, more eager than anyone to see the work finished, paced from the deep tunnel to the spread of tents and back, trying to conjure a solution.

Under a sagging tarp supported by a feeble frame, fifty diggers sat on benches of fallen logs. They watched that grey, wavering light. They watched each other's grey faces. They watched the open maw of the ground, glad to be free of its stale breath.

A young man in an errand-runner's cloak stepped out from a tent where Yawny the Gatherer was preparing a meal. He carried a basket and moved up and down the rows of workers, distributing bread from a cloth bag. He spoke quietly with each one, glancing over his shoulder as if worried the foreman might notice.

"The foreman says it's just a matter of equipment," the young man said. "But what say you? Should the dig continue?"

The answers were a mix of bitter laughter and the occasional burst of determination and pride.

"The king's aim outdistances his reach," one weary man replied, his left arm in a sling.

"Abascar soldiers can't keep such a stretch secure," speculated a woman plagued by a perpetual shiver. "Cave-ins, corruption of the waters, pests, and vermin—such a river, if it should flow as directed, would require constant maintenance. And what if our enemies seek to poison us?"

Another scoffed. "What is a vein of blacklode against the might of Abascar? Ours is a house of accomplished miners. We will break through."

Yet another shook his head. "It's a bad situation. The king's judgment is to blame. If the grudgers do exist—and I'm not saying they do—this venture will give them more to protest."

That last comment caught the ear of the curious helper. "Grudgers? What do you know of grudgers?"

The digger—a white-bearded man with a broken nose—awakened from his sulk and fixed his listener with wild eyes. His pockmarked cheeks bulged as he puffed a cloud into the cold. "Oh, nobody's certain of anything as far as grudgers go. But if you listen for things that *aren't* spoken or watch for things that *aren't* there, you may wonder. Some of our beds were empty last night. Secret meetings going on. I reckon some of these folks aim to take action if things don't improve around here soon. Me, I'm too tired to do anything but complain."

"Complain? So you're not a grudger, but you *do* have complaints."

"Why are you askin' these things?" asked the whitebeard, grabbing the bread-giver by the edge of his hood. "Who are you anyway?"

"Moseli. Errand-runner. Just arrived." He held out a wedge of bread. "Sent with rations."

The digger hesitated, then took the bread and pressed it whole into his mouth, his rain-wet beard catching crumbs.

"And you?" the errand-runner asked. "What are you called?"

The digger snatched the bag and thrust his hand deep inside. "Who am I? I'm hungry. I'm tired. I'm forty-three years a miner for Abascar. Old enough to remember what the house once was. Old enough to resent what it's become. That's who I am." He pulled out another half loaf and stuffed it into a fold in his cloak. "And I'm called Marv. A miner assigned to a mudhole. This is not my trade. This is just a show of the king's ambition."

"Well, Marv, you are not the only one with complaints." The bread-giver gave the miner a bow, took back the bag, and moved on to the next digger.

Nearby, a separate tarp, patchworked with colors of privilege, protected the gold-clad musician and her instrument. She sat with the string-weave's span across her knees, sliding ring-jeweled fingers across its web. Notes sprang from the shelter like sparks from a fireplace, only to be caught in the rain and squelched. She sang a refrain, something about King Cal-marcus's youthful zeal and about how Abascar stood on the verge of a season of bounty.

The singer's stout, squinting escort, one of the king's officers of ceremony, wore a forced grin beneath a meticulously groomed mustache and waved his hands in the air as if conducting the singer, who refused to acknowledge him. Her corn-silk hair fell around a freckled face, and she plucked the strings vigorously as if trying to keep her fingers warm.

Increasingly distracted by the musician's aggravation, the bread-giver who had called himself Moseli emptied the crumbs from his bread sack and moved to the edge of the diggers' assembly. He whispered something to a small, aged figure in a soil-streaked labor cloak. Together, they broke off and trudged through the rain to the nearby row of boulder-burdened carts.

"I'd trade my vawn for a song about struggle and survival," said the young man to the old. "It pains me to hear Lesyl's talents wasted on such simplistic melodies. Those men don't want to hear cheery fabrications about their leader's greatness. No wonder the talk about grudgers is growing. Look at them, miserable in the rain."

"There's a saying in House Jenta," the old man whispered. "*The clouds weep for those afraid to cry.* From the looks of these clouds, those listeners must be in deep despair."

"And it's not just the music that vexes them." The younger leaned back against the cart, bowed his head, and let water stream off his hood and veil the world before him like a waterfall. "They've opened up more ground in the last few days than I would have believed possible. And what do they get for it? Abuse from the foreman. It's not their fault they ran into a blacklode ridge. We have good mappers, but they can hardly be expected to know what lies *beneath* the ground. May the Keeper protect those poor workers from their own superiors."

"May the Keeper protect them," agreed the old man, his words wisping about his cold lips. "But be careful how loudly you speak, boy. If the foreman hears you mention the Keeper, he'll give you a lashing of more than insults and curses." He shook his head. "Did I call you *boy* again? Forgive me. I haven't seen you in such a long time, and it's going to be tough to break old habits."

They watched the performer's sad mouth as she sang what she had been ordered to sing.

"Thank you," said the young man, "for inviting me to meet you here."

The old man pulled out a folded leaf, opened it and offered a mix of seeds to his companion. "You're getting better at finding my little hints. Someday I won't be able to hide from you even if I try."

"You've taught me to read everything I see closely." The younger tossed a seed to a mudbird, then ate the rest himself. "And speaking of looking closely, how long do you think it will take before the foreman notices he has two extra laborers?"

"Not long now. We'll keep this conversation short." The old man choked, his lungs full of debris from winter plagues. "*Kramm,* but I must get back to my storehouse for some herbs and lemon peelings. And liquor. Good liquor, not that poison the king drinks." He blew hot breath into his cupped hands, which were red and cracked from weather and work. "I've much to tell you, but first...tell me about the hunt. Did you catch the fangbear?"

"The bear eludes us. But I'm not bothered. Best we can hope for is to chase it out of the region. We don't have time for hunting bears. There are bigger problems afoot."

"Bigger problems! Wyrms?"

"Beastmen. Beastmen traveling in groups. We continue to find signs of ambushes against merchants and patrols, four beastmen working together. And this is happening farther north than beastmen have previously ventured."

"I've seen it too. The creatures of the forest are full of talk, and they tell me to beware. I wonder...has the curse of Cent Regus run its course? Perhaps the beastmen are collecting their scattered wits."

"You make it sound like good news," said the younger man, surprised.

"The end of a curse? Wouldn't that be good news?"

"Not if it allows the beastmen to grow smarter while their appetites still rage. I don't like it."

The old man stifled another cough as the foreman emerged from the throat of the dig, shovel in hand, to stand before the diggers. The workers sat still as their commander unleashed his latest diatribe. He held up the shovel and waved its bent, blunted tip in a digger's face, ranting about damage to equipment. Throwing the shovel down, he castigated another for laziness and another for moving too slowly with the wheelbarrow. Then he threatened to summon Captain Ark-robin to punish the mappers for leading them into such an obstacle.

The younger man started forward, but the old one grabbed his sleeve. "Wait. Look." He gestured down the long line of stone-laden carts.

A young woman wrapped in an elegant cloak sewn from grey green leaves scurried birdlike between the large wooden wheels and ducked under the carts. She clasped a chain of yellow bindweed, its long-stemmed strands punctuated with explosions of flowers, which she wound around and through the wheelspokes.

Watching her, their eyes awakened. She had been busy for a while. Among rain-wet boulders on several carts, certain rocks had become luminescent— ember red, flame blue, harvest gold. All along the haunches of the carthorses, she had inked spiraling tattoos, a script telling of strength, grace, and motion.

The young woman hesitated before the span of a wood-spoked wheel. She rummaged in a shoulder bag so full of cargo it nearly burst at the seams and withdrew a lump of chalk. In a sweeping motion, she dragged it along the edge of the wagon wheel until it gleamed as if plated with gold. Then she moved to the next wheel, laughing. Finally, she ducked out of sight to make more mischief behind the carts.

The younger man had already taken several steps toward the meddler when he heard his friend hiss a warning. The foreman had noticed them at last.

"Who do you two think you are?" The diggers' superior officer unleashed a barrage of expletives. "Think you can skulk around by the carts and excuse yourselves from my speech?" He sloshed through the mud toward them, spitting his words.

"We were about to empty these carts."

"Don't," his friend whispered in warning. "Don't provoke him."

"I commanded the force to assemble," said the foreman.

"The wheels will warp if you let the carts sit overloaded in the rain."

"Overloaded? Do you think you know more about this kind of work than I do?" the foreman said. "This is my dig site, not your backyard."

"In fact," remarked the younger man coolly, "it *is* my backyard."

"*Prince Cal-raven,*" whispered the old man so only he could hear. "Not now."

The foreman stopped in his tracks, notching new curses to the bow.

The prince was not about to stop what he had set in motion. "Isn't it interesting? You see my muddy raincloak and assume I'm one of your charges. But you were entrusted with *fifty* officers, Blyn-dobed. And I count fifty who were listening to you. I might be a Bel Amican spy in disguise. I might be a thief or a merchant come to lift what I can for a trade."

Frantic, the foreman scanned the faces of his now-attentive workers. Then fixing a firmer grip on the shovel, he faced his challenger.

The young man began to walk a wide circle around the foreman. "It's your job to secure this dig. But it appears to me that you think it's your job to shout at good workers who are exhausted from your demands. I think they're suffering enough from the weather, not to mention the abuse inflicted upon them by *that* one." Prince Cal-raven gestured to the musician's escort. "That one, who calls himself a royal authority on music. In the meantime..." The young man pulled back his hood to reveal his sharp brown eyes, his scraggle of beard, his wild braids of redbrown hair, and the emblem of royalty emblazoned on his tunic.

The foreman knelt. "Prince Cal-raven! I..."

"In the past few days, your diggers have made Abascar proud. And you reward remarkable progress with a lesson in cursing, accompanied by nursery rhymes."

"My lord, we were told you were off on a hunt," said the foreman, clearly shaken.

"If you had known I was coming, what would you have done?" Cal-raven stopped, standing between the foreman and his workers. "You'd have posted a guard at each corner. Emptied these carts. Someone would be helping poor Yawny prepare the meal. Instead the old Gatherer's in that tent trying to cook for fifty hungry laborers all by himself. Is it hard for you to guess, Blyn-dobed, why I sneak away from a hunt and enter your camp in disguise?" Cal-raven turned to the diggers. "I tire of people putting on airs of duty whenever I step into a room, knowing they're going to drop their guard as soon as my back is turned. I insist upon knowing the people of my house as they are. And I prefer to see Abascar's laborers treated with respect."

Cal-raven picked up the shovel. "You punish them for blunting shovels? Who is in charge of making sure they have the proper tools? You use this? For tunneling? It's about as flimsy as the song that poor Lesyl is being forced to sing."

"Sire," squeaked the musician's escort, his round head reddening in the rain. "Your own father approved these songs."

"Yes. He did approve them...for a formal occasion so many years ago that nobody can remember their purpose." Propelled by the same energy and pride that had made his mother famous, the prince marched toward the escort. "Songs are not meant to be used as blunt instruments, Snyde." He tossed the shovel down, splashing mud over the escort's polished boots. "They're supposed to lift us, dazzle us, rekindle our spirits. Oh, those are impressive honor stitches on your uniform, but you obviously didn't earn them for your understanding of music."

The singer covered her mouth with her hand and turned her head.

Cal-raven approached her, placed his hand on her shoulder. Flustered, she smiled at him. "Good morning, Lesyl," he said with a familiar wink. "I've heard rumors that you've composed some rather beautiful songs of your own. Let's hear one. The men have suffered enough."

"Sire!" shrieked her escort, who was now almost hysterical. "She does not have the authority to select music. The songs must be approved. These honors on my jacket represent my—"

"Snyde, those badges—which you *bought*—speak of nothing more than what you'll pay to convince us of your own imagined greatness."

The foreman spoke with just enough menace to draw back the prince's attention. "You are going too far, Cal-raven ker Cal-marcus."

Cal-raven met the foreman's steely gaze.

"You're right. I should have posted guards. Yes, I will correct my oversight. Now, if you're smart, you'll call your friend out of the tunnel. We have not secured it. And with so much rain, he might be buried in a cave-in."

"My friend?" The prince was startled to find that his companion had vanished. And then he saw the tracks, which led down the ramp and through the dig's gate.

One of the diggers gasped. "By the beard of Har-baron, look!" He pointed at the boulder carts. All the diggers came to their feet, agog, seeing for the first time the elaborate decoration of their equipment.

"Sabotage!" roared the musician's escort. "Foreman, your carts have been compromised. Somebody's defying the Proclamation."

"You see, Snyde?" said Cal-raven. "Imagination actually *offends* you."

"Foreman." It was Marv the digger who stepped forward. "Permission to examine the wheelbarrows, sir."

With a quick, nervous look at Cal-raven, Blyn-dobed nodded, and the diggers rushed, like excited children, to inspect the colors, designs, and ornaments festooning their equipment.

Lesyl began a new song, and the string-weave was transformed. The notes danced in light and shimmering tones. The more she played, the more confidence she gained, smiling at Cal-raven as if the song were emerging on its own, to her surprise and delight.

In that tense and temper-charged moment, the ground suddenly quaked.

All of them turned to the opening of the dig, where a cloud of dust swirled up and out into the rain.

Cal-raven's smile vanished.

The quake rattled the carts, and one of the wheels broke so that the cart tipped and dumped an avalanche of boulders into the puddles.

The prince sprang forward, yelling at the foreman not to follow him, despite the shouts of protest growing distant as he ran. He fought his way down the long ramp into a crooked, torch-lined corridor.

And there, where the tools were piled beside coal black stone, mounds of fresh rubble were settling. The wall of glittering blacklode had cracked, revealing a clear passage to the other side.

"Scharr ben Fray!" Cal-raven exclaimed. "Why didn't you wait? We were going to do this together. How do you expect me to learn stonemastery when you finish the job without me?" His words echoed in the breakage, and he listened to them fade. When he spoke again, it was in whisper. "Where have you—?"

Something struck him in the shoulder, and he sprawled onto cold shards of blacklode. Over him, a shadow loomed.

"You impudent child," the old man hissed.

"Teacher!"

"I've been counseling you since you were crawling. Haven't you learned anything?"

The prince scrambled backward on his hands, exasperated. "You taught me everything! Everything that matters…"

"I didn't teach you *that!*" The mage nodded toward the falling light. "Knowledge is one thing. Wisdom is another. Your arrogant tantrum out there… You may be right, but you're as guilty as the lot of them for the pride with which you say it." The old man gestured at the broken wall. "You've learned a thing or two about stonecrafting. But do you think that after a pompous show like that, which I'm sure has won you many admirers, I'm going to let you work some wonder and dazzle them all the more?"

"Most of the diggers will understand what I..."

"Here's what they now understand: Prince Cal-raven thinks their foreman is a buffoon. You've thrown fuel on the fires of resentment. This will fracture and trouble the dig. And if any of these beastmen that worry you should ambush? The men might not be ready to defend themselves."

"But that foreman...he's—"

"Blyn-dobed is a windbag. But he knows a few things about his job." The stonemaster stopped to listen.

The foreman's voice was raised again, demanding that the laborers repair the broken cart and lighten the load on the others.

"If his diggers don't fear his temper," Scharr ben Fray continued in haste, "then their own willfulness will stir up chaos. If you reprimand him in front of the workers, you hurt your father's mission. If you speak with him at all, speak to him with respect. Blyn-dobed might have actually learned something if you hadn't humiliated him. Now, you've only made him angry."

Cal-raven climbed slowly back to his feet. "Of course."

"You're the son of Queen Jaralaine, Cal-raven." Affection was returning to the mage's rasping voice. "Your mother's arrogance...it ruined her. It cost her everything. And it also cost your father. Never forget that." He grabbed Cal-raven by the shoulders. "Abascar will be yours someday, perhaps sooner than you expect. Be clever, but humble. Don't follow her example."

There were footsteps splashing down the ramp. Three diggers stopped, mere outlines in the dusty air. They were silent, staring in disbelief at the break in the blacklode. Then they ran back up the ramp, uttering selections from the foreman's book of expletives.

Scharr ben Fray watched them go. "We're out of time. We will meet again soon. Somewhere else. I wish to tell you what I've learned... Strange and incredible things."

"Does it concern your search for the Keeper?"

"Not exactly. But it does concern that troublemaking girl."

"When will you meet me again?"

"I will leave you a sign. You will find it. Don't worry about that. I'll place it right in your path. Look closely."

The foreman's pace slowed as he approached them through the dust.

A smile eased Scharr ben Fray's expression, and it was once again the gentle, gracious face that Cal-raven had grown to love. *"Look closely."*

And then he was gone through the gap.

"The blacklode!" Blyn-dobed walked a few steps into the new passage. "There is only one man in the Expanse who could even attempt such a display of power."

While the foreman stared into the darkness, Cal-raven stunned him further by unsheathing a dagger and handing it over, hilt first. It was a soldier's ceremonial gesture of surrender—a bit out of place, but clear in its intention. "I owe you an apology, foreman. I have dishonored you in front of your laborers. I will go and address them and praise your leadership. Forgive me. I spoke out of turn." He then exposed his forearm, an invitation for scarring.

Blyn-dobed reluctantly accepted the hilt of the dagger. Then he turned it and gave it back, quickly, as if it were hot to the touch. "Forgiven, of course," he said. And then, quietly, he added, "It is true, you have shaken my reputation with the diggers. Allow me to speak candidly, and keep my words to yourself. I respect your desire to see your people as they really are, Prince Cal-raven. Your father, whom I obey without exception, hides behind palace walls and sends orders with no sense of the cost. So hear this. Dissension is growing. There are men among these diggers who are not likely to swallow their frustrations much longer. Warn your father about the grudgers. Ask him to consider their complaints."

Cal-raven left Blyn-dobed to contemplate the magic of Scharr ben Fray. He climbed back out into a song of trouble and longing.

Lesyl's new song was reminding the men of all they loved back home. It gave shape to their loneliness, their weariness, and hunger. It awakened them.

Cal-raven listened, admiring the verse, while he searched for the meddling girl from the wild. He lifted his eyes toward home, up the western slopes to the northern edge of the Cragavar woods. And there she was—the small, mischievous stranger—slipping away. To his amazement, the girl sat astride a wild black viscorcat, holding the scruff of the predator's neck with the familiarity of a rider on her favorite horse.

"Auralia," he muttered, remembering the name at last.

10

A Day of Rain and Robbery

The viscorcat ran while Auralia clutched fistfuls of fur at the nape of his neck, his purr resonating through his throat. Woods opened before them, fields parted as they passed. They splashed up rainy inclines and flew down the opposite slopes.

As the wind streamed through Auralia's hair, the thickweave pouch at her side kept her warm. It warmed her for the hours of care she had spent crafting its cargo—a collection of inventions to lift the spirits of the Gatherers, to distract them from their troubles, to prompt their curiosity.

There was more, something unfinished folded beneath those packages. She carried with her everywhere the intricately woven threads of her finest work, an incomplete creation, a mystery. She kept it close in case she should find its missing piece, its final thread.

While the big cat ran, Auralia fell into a trance. The details of the landscape around her became a blur of color, which she sifted in search of some new hue.

At times a pattern or a shape would awaken her, and she would steer the cat to follow it, convinced there were tracks in the grass ahead, fresh impressions fading in the rain. But at other times she doubted, suspecting the trail was only a delusion born of wishing.

It was the way she lived each day—following a notion of the Keeper's progress. When she was very young, no one could tell her what was or wasn't, and she had been certain of finding the Keeper's tracks. But that was so long ago. Now, almost sixteen years among the Gatherers, Auralia's curiosity had taken a troublesome turn. For all her self-assurances, for all her claims, she had not seen evidence quite so convincing for months. In her darkest hours she challenged her own assumptions of what she had seen. If she could not find tracks to follow, she would feel lost and discouraged and wonder if she had ever walked in the Keeper's path.

Seeking such signs, her intuitions had led her to the Abascar dig. Decorating carts had been an unexpected joy, lifting her spirits whether she had been led there or not. Now she thrilled to the run, eager to reach the Gatherers before sunset, anxious to entertain them with her surprises.

As they crested that last thickly wooded hill before the descent into orchards and down to the shelters, the cat slowed. He stopped and pawed the air, spreading his toes with foreclaws extended to signal his delight.

But then he paused, an alarm rippling from his head to his toes, his tail bristling until it was as thick as the rest of his body. He stared at a mossy boulder, his tufted ears sharp and cupped. Auralia heard what had caught his attention—the nervous whispers of children hiding behind the stone.

"Isabel," Auralia scolded, "you and your cousins are not to climb this hill, and you know it! Now get back before I tell Dukas here to eat ya."

Screams—the sort that can warp a person's spine—seared the air, and a huddle of girls in berrystained tunics scampered through the edge of the trees and down, down the grassy hill to the orchards. The farther they ran, the more their screams thinned from knives to needles, but they cut Auralia's ears all the same, and the cat's purr soured into a whine of displeasure.

"Oh, be tough, Dukas." Auralia slid off the feline's back. She scratched his cheeks, where his whiskers were thick as spike-crawler spines, and his lips beaded with sparkling drool.

She drew from her shoulder bag an unfinished scarf—sky blue and cinnamon—and hung it around his neck. He smiled and pressed her shoulder with his cheek, gleaming green eyes clenched shut. Then he padded in circles before curling up on a bed of intoxicating madweed.

Auralia sighed and patted the grey stripes of his brow. "Thank you, Dukas. I'll be away for just a while. Rain or otherwise, I gotta make my deliveries."

She might have said anything. She might have insulted him and the litter into which he was born, but nothing would have disturbed the rumbling cat's sleep.

"Wish I was a wildspeaker. So much I'd ask you about. But that's just not my twist, is it?" She peered down through the trees at the rain-slicked grass and rippling mud. And then she opened her shoulder bag, taking a quick inventory.

She counted stockings for Lezeeka; a kite for Urchin; red reins for the vawn trainer; a shaving stone for Haggard's beard; and a pillow she had woven tight enough to repel water, a pillow for Radegan who never slept under a roof. "Those youngsters will have roused anybody left in the camp. It'll be tricky to sneak around and leave surprises if they're expecting me."

Something like a touch of wind gave her sudden pause, and she turned to glance over her shoulder. "Don't let no madweed keep you from watchin' out for hunters, Dukas. You hear me?"

She pulled the dark fur collar of her grey green cloak tighter around her neck against the rainy chill. A rainhound barked in the distance, and the sound drew her to the slope. She ducked behind a husktree and looked down past the orchard to the shelters. "When I go into House Abascar and make my pledge at the Rites, will they ever let me visit the Gatherers, Dukas?" She tilted her head. "That's odd. Something's missing down there."

⚬

As she headed toward the orchard, Auralia came upon a band of orphans. Some were swinging on rope swings or taking turns on a pair of crooked tree-branch stilts. A few had painted their faces with mud, and their eyes were white as teeth. But most were crawling on all fours and collecting stones before a line of scarecrows. A rainhound was scampering back and forth and barking at the handmade figures. When the children saw Auralia, all but the oldest boy dropped their stones and ran to gather in a dancing circle around her and to beg her to open her shoulder bag. They tugged at the edge of the leafy cape so that it fanned out around her.

"Show us what you brung!"

"No, no. It's for the Gatherers."

"Stop and play with us!"

"What's the game?"

"King's Lesson!" said Owen-mark, the scruffy boy who clearly believed he was in charge.

The scarecrows were as large as men, silhouettes in the evening light. Made from bundles of sticks, they stood with arms outstretched. The children had hollowed out heads of yellow squash and carved eyeholes and grins, then stuffed them with smoldering scraps of damp bark. Light and smoke emanated from their freakish features.

Auralia stepped closer and wrinkled her nose. "Howdaya play King's Lesson?"

"Simple." Owen-mark took a few steps back from the scarecrows and lifted a stone. "Ya take a rock, and ya throw it at this one. He's the king, ya see. And ya teach him a lesson." He clapped the stone into his palm. "First one to knock him down or break his head is called King of the Day. That's it. King's Lesson."

"So that one's the king?" Auralia walked toward the scarecrow in the center. It seemed to leer down at her. "Why does it have to be the king?"

"'Cause the king's a fool."

"Who are the rest of them?"

"Cal-raven, 'cause...well...he's the next king. And Ark-robin, 'cause he enforces the rules. And that one's a duty guard."

"Umm." Auralia fidgeted with the buttons on her shoulder bag. "I'm gonna suggest a different game."

The boy's face crumpled in disapproval, but the girls were intrigued.

"Sure, the king's got problems. But he guards us from beastmen. And he collects the harvest, so to feed us all. It don't do nobody any good to stand around throwin' rocks. How about you decorate 'em instead?"

The swings slowed. A boy climbed down from the stilts.

"Whaddaya mean?" Owen-mark put his hands on his hips.

Auralia unwound a purple scarf from her neck and flung it up and over the king-scarecrow's shoulder, then wandered around behind him, took the end, and tossed it back over the other shoulder. "You're all gonna make crowns. I'll be gone for just a while. But I'll come back through real soon. The best crown I see goes on the king's head. And I'll reward you with a surprise." A cheer went up from the girls, and she wiped the mud from a young orphan's face before kissing it.

The boy was not ready to surrender. "That's a stupid game," he growled. "I don't want to show no thanks to somebody who conspired against us."

"Conspired?" laughed Auralia. "Who's conspiring?"

"Haven't ya heard?" the boy mumbled. "They came and took away everything you gave us. Search all of our shelters—you'll find there's nothing left."

Auralia clutched her bag the way she had clung to the cat's fur, to keep from falling down as the world tipped and shook.

The gravity of the Gatherers' shelters took hold, and she turned to run into their trouble.

Like cartloads of crates that had tumbled from colliding wagons, the Gatherers' settlement seemed a scattering of half-wrecked structures. Passages ran between, under, and over them as erratic as threads of thought in a madman's mind. Patched together with pitch, tar, spikes, and curtains, the shelters had spread like wild mushrooms across this damp ground. The roofs were crooked as if they had been pelted with boulders by those who walked atop Abascar's looming walls.

Down the grass in skating steps, Auralia descended into welcome memories. How she'd savored the last summer painting walls and weaving welcome mats.

She glanced at the volunteer guards, Gatherers with bows and arrows who earned favor by marching along the perimeter and surveying the woods for predators and beastmen. As she ran in, they failed to respond with effusive enthusiasm and instead turned their eyes away.

"Greetings, Middle and Lop-head, Sam-jon, Lully, and Wil," she said in forced cheerfulness, skipping into the zigzagging avenue across rugged stones where the rainwater trickled into gutters.

The avenue was empty, as it should be. It was afternoon, and the Gatherers would not have returned yet from their tasks. No one would be around but the occasional wandering orphan or a few who remained behind to prepare simple meals for the returning laborers.

The structures leaned into one another, or backward and forward, like slouching drunkards and weary workers. An air of cold exhaustion hung stagnant in the air. And she did not see the flags…the banners she had crafted and distributed to so many, which they had displayed above their tents on all but the duty officers' inspection days. Nor did she see the colorful kites she had made for the corners of the pathways, kites that remained aloft even in the slightest wind. And while patches of the summertime paint resisted the rain, the curtains she had made were missing.

She went first, as always, to the black canvas tent where Krawg and Warney stayed. The tent shivered in the cold behind Yawny's cook-hut, leaning against the sturdy wooden wall of a storage shack. She was surprised to find smoke puffing up through the chimney shaft, and she ducked in through the back entry to surprise whoever was inside.

What she found quickly spoiled her playful ploy. Standing in the dim grey light, Warney was fussing over a firebox. In one hand he held the iron stoker, pushing the embers together to keep the flames rising, and with the other he cast herbs into the steam rising from the pot that rested atop the box. His good eye spied her, and he smiled sadly. He did not catch her up in his usual embrace.

Then she saw the reason for his busyness. Beneath a mountain of blankets, Krawg lay struggling for breath. His stone grey head lay heavy on a stuffed toy fangbear—a plaything she had crafted for an orphan who, at Krawg's surprising insistence, had traded it to him for a feathered hat. The old Gatherer lay there, head on the bear's belly, and blinked at her as if she had gone blurry.

"Wretched, his breathing," said Warney. "Since the burglary, Krawg's been ruined."

"Burglary?"

"Last night. Took everything. Everything you made."

"Krammed duty officers!" rasped Krawg, trying to lift his head. "Came in the rain and the storm."

"We didn't see or hear a thing," said Warney. "None of us."

"But you were thieves once," said Auralia. "Surely you should have heard them lurkin' about."

"These were trained and careful," said Warney. "Weasels and scurry-rats."

"They took the blue shoot-stalk curtain?" She went to the window they had cut in the canvas. "It was your favorite."

"Took Krawg's yellow scarf, they did. That's why he can't breathe." Warney spooned the herb soup into a half shell of a tree-melon.

"Oh, bother," said Auralia. "It was only a scarf. He can breathe just fine without it."

Krawg opened his mouth to disagree but was seized with a fit of coughing.

Warney put the bowl on an overturned apple crate beside the bed and then opened his hand to scatter shelled nuts and grapes alongside it. "He insists, Auralia. He insists your makings are more than color and heat. They fix what's broken."

"My work's just to brighten things," she protested, "and to show you all how to make stuff from nothin'." She went to the window and pushed Warney's words away. She did not want to know if her work did more than she intended. She did not want to think about all that could mean. "Now tell me," she said in a tease, "are ya sure you two didn't take it all when no one was lookin'? You sure this isn't some kinda trick? And you—"

Krawg surged upward, the blankets falling away, so that his frail old torso was grey and naked in the light. "Impudent girl!" he wheezed. "We done no such thing! We don't do us no thievin', and you know it right well."

Warney narrowed his eye. "Gotta 'gree with him there, 'Ralia."

Stunned, back against the wall, she was speechless, and her eyes spilled tears. Then she ran to embrace Krawg, and he spread his bony arms high and wide in surprise. She had never known him to be fond of embraces, but that would not stop her now. He awkwardly patted her head.

"Krawg isn't the only one, 'Ralia," said Warney. "Lotsa folk are stuck to their blankets today, sick from the loss of their treasures. It's like Abascar's robbed them all over again. With all your colors missin', well, the heart's gone outta the place."

And so he knelt beside her, his eye wet with the memory, and unfolded for her like a tapestry how the morning had dawned to outrage, how Gatherers emerged with tales of disappeared belongings, how panic and dismay had spread. The wind propeller. The name flags. The welcome mats.

By the time Krawg and Warney had finished telling their tale, a crowd had gathered at the door. Word had spread of Auralia's arrival, and they whispered in eager frustration, hoping she had brought them something new, some token to assure them that all they had lost would be restored.

Radegan, a clutch of arrows in his hand, stood red faced, fierce eyed, his jaw thrust forward. "We searched, we did," he seethed. "All up and through the settlement. All through the surrounding wood. But the rain washed out the tracks. Don't know which way they went."

Looming behind him as always, Haggard the giant blustered through his yellow beard, "When we find them that's done it, we'll knock their heads off their shoulders and set 'em on fire."

" 'Twas a conspiracy," said Radegan. "Came in from all sides. The colors are too precious in Abascar. Could be Housefolk got word of Auralia's doings and hired thieves to smuggle them inside the walls. Or it could be Ark-robin's thugs or duty officers who hope to win rewards. Or maybe they were sold to merchants."

"What'll you do, Auralia?" whined Lezeeka. "I want my leggings back. And Wenjee's got requests as well, but she got so upset about losin' her purple-gem slippers that she ate a whole basket of figs, and now she's...um...she's not too comfortable."

And so began the cry, the Gatherers appealing to the frightened girl to replace what they had lost. They had prepared a list and began to read it to her.

Auralia felt as if she were shrinking.

She pushed her way through the crowd and into the rain. "I can't replace them. They're not made by recipes and plans. They're each their own thing, come together in surprise and accident. There won't be no replacing." She glanced back down the lonely avenue and then up at the forest. "It's almost time for the Rites of the Privilege. I gotta go inside the walls and try to show them a thing or two."

Krawg had staggered out on a crutch, the blankets heaped over his shoulders, Warney propping him up. "You can't mean it," he coughed. "You can't mean you'll really go there."

"Don't tell me what I can't mean," she barked. "With all I've shown you, all you see are gifts. You don't get the how or the why of them. If you did, you might find them for yourselves. When will you try? You say the colors heal you? I don't see nothin' of the sort."

While their mouths opened and closed, while they looked around for someone to come to their rescue, Auralia hugged her shoulder bag. "And as for conspiracy...I can see colors on the fingers of the one who took it all. I see a thread from Krawg's yellow scarf snagged on a jacket. I know who took the curtains and rugs. Somebody's trying to make themselves a bargain. And that's just a shame, 'cause I made something particular for that one. And now it'll never see the light."

And then she turned and fled.

They scrambled after her, renewing their pleas. But she was through a narrow gap between two shacks, under a porch, through an empty tent, and gone.

Bursting through bracken and back to the scarecrows, she took off her shoulder bag, draped it over the prong of a broken branch, and marched up to the smoke-headed specters. The orphans, thunderstruck to see her again and in such a transformed state, stepped away.

Without hesitation, she scooped a handful of stones from the pile they had made and pitched them at the scarecrow in the middle. They rained down around its head, and one stuck neatly into an eye socket. Then she charged at the scarecrow, reached up to grab both ends of the purple scarf she had draped around its neck, and pulled the ends in opposite ways, tightening it until the stick neck snapped and the yellow sphere tumbled free and broke into clean halves on the ground. Spitting, smoldering bark sent tendrils of black smoke up into the rain.

"Why did you do that?" shrieked one of the girls, who held a bundle of flowers. "We was gonna dress him up like you said!"

Auralia, fire in her own eyes now, teeth clenched, did not say a word. She just knelt down to gather more stones.

A shrill cry rang out far away, falling like a bird call from the woods high above. No one flinched or bothered to wonder, save Auralia, who fell forward onto her knees as if struck from behind.

And then she stood, grabbed her shoulder bag, and was off again up the hillside.

As she returned to the patch of madweed, knees dripping with mud from her stumbles up the saturated slope, she fell forward, her hands touching ribbons of cold, bright red blood.

Dukas had been arrow-shot. Here the spray of the impact, and there... splashes of red trailing off into the trees...the signs of a desperate escape.

He would be miles away now, if he survived. And he would never return, not even with Auralia's persuasion.

Trembling, she began to follow the bloody line. It was not long before the crimson spots vanished and her feet sank into deep bootprints. Most likely a merchant scouting the edge of Abascar in hopes of bringing back something valuable for trade. She wiped her nose and dabbed her eyes. She uttered words she had heard angry Gatherers swear in frustration, until at last she shaped a solemn vow.

She declared to the air that she would not visit the Gatherer settlement again, for her gifts had only made them selfish. And then she vowed never to consent to the Rites of the Privilege. She would take her things and go far away, to a place where she could do her work alone.

There was a scent, not of fern or mushroom, not of bear piles or green needles or rain. Fish. She smelled fish suddenly, here and far from any pond. And then she smelled leather, like the sort used for bootmaking. Someone was near. Near and still. But beastmen did not bother much with fish or leather.

She glanced back into the approaching darkness beyond the shoulder-high ferns, where the trees guarded their secrets. "Keeper," she whispered quietly. "Keeper."

There was a commotion behind her, a swift approach. She saw the two figures in green hooded cloaks, the branches stripped bare in their hands, the decision—devoid of hate, devoid of feeling—in their eyes. She was halfway to her feet when the first one lifted his club and let it fall in a swift and easy swing. All colors vanished at once.

11

PROMONTORY

A growl rumbled like a drum in the belly of the hound-man while he paced in the wooden cage, sometimes stalking on all fours, sometimes striding upright.

From her vantage point high on the trunk of a tree that bowed out over the clearing, Auralia watched him, fascinated. She had run for hours to catch the thieves, delirious with pain and outrage. But now that she had caught up to them, she found herself stunned by the spectacle. She had never seen a beast-man in captivity.

The rest of the scene was familiar. A family of Abascar merchants were hard at work bargaining with Bel Amican traders, offering a mix of items they had purchased, stolen, or won at gambling. As so often happened in a conference of dishonest bargainers, things were going sour.

Auralia surveyed the menagerie displayed on the merchants' table. She recognized this family from her travels around House Abascar—the children, Wynn and Cortie, the parents, Joss and Juney. But she did not recognize anything they offered to sell. She did not see her stolen bag or any sign of its precious cargo—the unfinished cloak she had run all night to recapture. These were probably stashed in the saddlebags on the merchants' vawns...that is, if Joss and Juney were the guilty thieves. It had been a long night of pursuit through the wilderness, a throbbing headache of a night, and Auralia began to wonder if she had made a wrong turn following rain-blurred tracks.

She scratched at a ragged thumbnail and bit its jagged edge to keep herself awake while she watched the traders' faces. She hoped no one would bother to look up into the branches, for there was no concealing her cape with the rose petals woven along its hem, which hung in the breeze like a flag.

"Get back, Wynn!" Distracted from his presentation, Joss rose from the tree stump, his knees jostling the array of ornamental cutlery, arrowheads, and scissors on his rickety sellers' table. Wynn, his wide-eyed son, was caught in a cautious approach to the Bel Amican hunters' prize exhibit, the snarling beast-man. "That wicked dog might snap those bars and make a meal of you, boy!" Shaking his head, Joss muttered, "Children. They say you have 'em because you'll need 'em someday. But I swear by my mother's butter and cream that Wynn's curiosity will ruin us."

"Stop fretting, Abascar man." The blond-bearded Bel Amican, who had introduced himself as Sader, took another noisy bite of his carrot and then struck the cage bars with his polished walking stick. "The cage is unbreakable. Catching beastmen...that's what we do. When we get to Bel Amica, we'll earn a year's wage for this one. Hunters will outbid each other for the chance to turn him loose on an island and hunt him down for sport. Best game in the Expanse."

Juney jabbed her husband with an elbow. "Joss, let's go. We've got more sense than to keep company with folk that smell of beastmen." She and her daughter, Cortie, a tiny thing with a mop of tousled yellow hair, were already stuffing their cargo bags with the stoneware, the glittering ore, and the sturdy leather shoes they had spread out on blankets for the Bel Amicans to peruse.

Reluctantly Joss pushed his unsold wares off the table and into another bag, then yanked the wooden table legs from their sockets and bundled them together with a strap. He tucked the tabletop under his arm and lugged the pegs and the bags to the family's vawn and fastened them with the ropes and buckles.

Young Wynn, his frame knobby like twigs and roots, his hair a sooty confusion, stood five paces from the cage, growling back at the beastman, twirling a vawnwhip absently as if imagining a showdown with the monster.

Cackling, an old woman seated on a pallet of cushions on the Bel Ami-cans' wagon rocked from side to side. She surprised Auralia, who had not noticed her before. Wrapped in padded blankets like something breakable, only her face, carved in deep-cut lines, and her hands, fingers working at the air like spider legs arranging webs, revealed themselves to the cold mountain air. "My boys got no problem servin' up beastmen for those who want to bleed 'em and those who want to watch."

"You speak of what's worth watching, woman?" Joss laughed. "How would you know anything about that?"

"One more word about my mother's blindness, and you'll join her in the darkness," growled Sader, now holding a hunter's throw-arrow in each hand.

" 'Twas a beastman killed my boys' papa," the old woman shrieked, "and their little sister too. Then it spat in my face and burnt out my eyes." She spewed a string of obscenities so foul that little Cortie laughed and repeated the mysterious words quietly to herself. "Then Elyroth chopped off its tail, and Sader cut off its head."

Wynn looked up at his father. "Is that true, Pa?"

As if it understood, the beastman roared and pressed his face between the bars.

This set both of the Abascar merchants' whip-scarred vawns to scuffling in the muddy leaves and tugging nervously at their tree-bound tethers.

Auralia felt an urge to leap down, break the vawns' tethers, and chase them loose to freedom. But first she'd have to check those saddlebags.

"No use squabblin', Joss ker Harl." Juney bound up her goods and swung the heavy load over her shoulder. "We'd best make haste. Rains are starting up again. Wynn's been sneezing, and Cortie's lost her heavy cloak. Can't let 'em get soggy."

"Don't go just yet. We've one more thing to show you." Sader slid the arrows back into the sleeves of his green fleece-coat. "Wait until you see this prize. You'll want to offer all you have, maybe even the vawns."

"Sader, shut it," hissed his older brother. "They can't match the price we'll earn at home."

"Earn for what?" their old mother whispered. "What're you boys conspiring about?"

"May as well show these poor Abascar folk the kind of colors we can wear in Bel Amica." Sader walked to the wagon.

Cortie uttered one of the old woman's foul words, practicing, giggling at the sound of it. Juney cuffed the girl in the back of the head.

"What is it, Sader? What're you rummaging for?" The old woman rocked back and forth, legs imprisoned in her purple blanket wrap. "What are you hidin' from your mother?"

"Sader, keep that bag closed!" Elyroth seized his brother's arms. "Let's leave these wood folk."

Thunder set the mountain shuddering. Rain tapped the branches around Auralia and whispered on the fallen leaves below.

Sader declared that nothing would vex the merchants more than a glimpse of Bel Amican treasure. Conceding this point, Elyroth sulked, snatched stones from the path and tossed them at the cage. The beastman swatted the stones aside as if they were flies.

"Juney, untether the vawns." Joss turned his back to the Bel Amicans. "I'm tired of their taunts. And I don't want Wynn growing accustomed to the sight of a beastman."

Juney did not move. Sader dropped a bag to the mud, knelt behind it, and untied its leather binding. He drew a fold of cloth out and teased the air with it, wearing a gleeful grin.

Auralia sank her teeth into her thumb to stop herself from shouting. It was one of the stockings she had crafted for Lezeeka. She had not been attacked by Abascar merchants at all. Bel Amican hunters had ventured as far as the Gatherer huts. Elyroth and Sader had clubbed her and run off with her work.

"Brilliant!" laughed Cortie, clapping her hands. "It's brilliant!"

Her mother moved as if pulled by a powerful force, and Joss said, "Juney, you stay put!"

Sader pushed the cloth back into the bag and unsheathed a curved blade from the side of his boot. "Stop right there, Abascar woman. No closer. Not unless you're going to pay."

"What are you selling, you blasted mistake of a son?" shrieked the old woman, who had rocked herself dangerously close to the edge of their wagon. Her eyes, wide and milky white, blinked one at a time.

"Show it again," said Juney. "Show Joss what you just showed me."

Sader reached back into the bag and withdrew a fold of cloth that opened to become a vivid span, its edges frayed and incomplete. "You should see all we've collected."

Auralia felt a warm line of tears slide down her cheek.

"Ooooooooh." Cortie ran to embrace her mother's right leg. "Can I have those colors, mum? Could we make them into a dress?"

As the sun cut through the clouds and tried to part them, the cloth came alive in the shifting shafts of light. The weave resembled a bed of multicolored polished stones glittering in shallow water.

"Your mum can't afford the likes of this," Joss whispered.

Crouching over the luminous display, Sader whispered so his mother couldn't hear, "You don't, perchance, have anything special...anything we'd enjoy...to bargain with...do you, woman?"

Joss would have stepped between them, but Juney was so quick to whip the hidden saber from the folds of her skirt that the Bel Amican had barely finished his question before the tip of it pricked his throat. Sader seethed, head tipping backward slowly, sheathed his dagger, and then crawled backward on all fours, away from the blade. He took some Bel Amican hero's name in vain and glanced back at his brother for support.

"It's like I said, Sader," snarled Elyroth. "We're finished here. There's no more business to conduct."

"They're thieves, mum," yelped Wynn, jarring them all into a silence like a falling plate before it hits the floor. The Abascar boy aimed an accusing finger at Sader. He was angry. "These blasted Bel Amicans are thieves. Those colors belong to Auralia. And they stole them."

Auralia held her breath. Wynn remembered her.

"They've robbed who?" snapped Joss. "They've stolen what?"

"Thieves!" echoed Cortie excitedly. "Brilliant."

"We've seen her," said Wynn. "We've seen Auralia with the Gatherers. She wears colors just that wild. She's the one they stole it from. She's still a girl."

Joss's black-bearded jaw wagged as he groped for a reprimand. But the boldness of his son's fury astonished him.

Sader's throwing arrows were back in his hands, but he, too, was speechless.

"We don't rob children," laughed Elyroth. "We don't bother with Abascar folk, and Gatherers are the muck stuck to Abascar boots."

"Auralia's not a Gatherer," Wynn sneered. "She just brings them stuff. She's from somewhere else." He had picked up a stone, and his intentions were clear.

Auralia realized this was going to end badly. She pushed herself to her knees, poised on the leaning tree like a bird prepared to dive.

When Juney found her wits, she kept her saber aimed at Sader but informed her furious son they would sell him to the Bel Amicans if he didn't stop making things worse.

Meanwhile, the old, blind Bel Amican woman was turning against her own sons. "Take us out of here, Elyroth," she snapped. "We don't need to listen to insults from Abascar brats. If that was my runt making stupid claims, I'd knock him down."

"It could happen." Elyroth twirled his walking stick at his side, finding a good grip.

"Ah well, what do you expect?" Sader spat at Wynn. "Living in the wild with parents dumb as his, who do you think he takes after?"

Wynn lunged to dodge his father's grasp, drew back his arm to launch the stone.

"Wynn! Don't!"

Auralia jumped.

Her feet hit the ground beside Sader's stolen treasure and her cape settled around her shoulders so she appeared to be a pile of leaves and roses. She raised her hands, stood, and backed up, pushing Wynn away from the armed Bel Amican.

The merchants from both houses were open mouthed and silent, and Wynn glanced up as if waiting for more people to fall from the sky.

No doubt they were bewildered by what she wore and by her condition. Her bare arms and feet were caked with mud from her struggle up the mountainside. Fresh blood trickled again down her face from the wound inflicted by Sader's club. Her head pulsed with pain, and she blinked, trying to see through her right eye which was nearly swollen shut.

" 'Ralia!" It was Cortie who moved first, toddling to embrace her.

"Give me the stone, Wynn." Auralia held out her hand. "If you throw it, these men will bloody up your family."

The boy's arm fell to his side. "Did *they*..." He reached a trembling hand out as though to wipe the blood from her face. But then he looked down, seething, and shifted his attention to the tongue-tied Bel Amican brothers. *"Give her back what you stole."*

Auralia knelt down, seized Sader's bag of loot, and slung it over her shoulder. Sader clutched the cloth of the unfinished cloak and backed slowly away, delighted by this new turn of events. He teased her, as if baiting an animal with a strip of meat.

That twisted sneer had returned to Elyroth's face. "The boy says you made this...this thing...with your own hands. I say you stole it."

"Elyroth, did you take something from a defenseless girl?" demanded the old woman.

"If I'm wrong," said Elyroth to the girl, "please tell me. If you do indeed weave things like this, well...you're invited to join us on our journey back to House Bel Amica. You could craft whatever you like there. We would manage your work, find buyers."

"For a percentage, of course," said Sader.

Auralia was still scowling at Wynn. "Drop the stone, Wynn. Please. I'll be all right. And you will be too, if you forget about them and walk away."

"Does it...hurt? What they did to you?" Wynn said, voice quavering.

"Poor girl." Juney, speaking with more concern than she had shown for her own children all day, approached Auralia to enfold her in a motherly embrace. Auralia glanced at Cortie and saw wonder turn to jealousy. "We'll clean you up good. You can travel with us and weave anything you like. We'll protect you." Glaring back at Elyroth, she added, "And we'll report these trespassers to the duty officers. *Bel Amicans who beat Abascar orphans.*"

"I'm not an Abascar orphan," Auralia muttered under her breath. "And I don't use my colors to buy anything."

"Elyroth, I've a mind to turn this beastman loose so he can tear you apart." The Bel Amican woman had begun to unwrap the cloth that encased her. "What have you done to this Auralia girl? And what is it you stole?"

Auralia turned, pushed herself free from Juney's grasp. "Please," she said quietly, staring at Sader's muddy boots. "That cloth...it's not finished yet." She held out her hands. "Please. If any strand is broken...any strand at all...it will lose its colors."

"Not finished? What do you mean?" Sader lifted the piece of cloth, spread it over his head, and laughed in amazement as the sunlight, coursing through it, cast rays of changing color. "There's more?"

"Come and visit me. I have lots of other pieces. I'll make somethin' for you."

"What's your price then?" Joss glumly asked the Bel Amicans, humiliated that he had been brought so low as to bargain with them. "A vawn? The whole lot we've got?"

"You won't sell what you stole from me," said Auralia, stepping closer, "because Bel Amicans aren't thieves, are they?"

The old woman's brow furrowed over her sightless eyes. "My sons don't take what isn't theirs. I taught them right. They must have just found it in the wood. But if it's yours, they'll give it back. Won't you, Sader?"

"Sader, you scum," hissed Elyroth. "I told you to leave the bag closed."

Sader blinked again. He lowered his hand. "I'm a Bel Amican," he said to Auralia through clenched teeth, holding out the cloth to her. And he added in a whisper, "Taking your bag was my brother's idea."

Auralia took the cloth, cradling it as something fragile and alive.

"We'll be back to see the rest of what you've made," Elyroth promised, a note of menace in his voice. "You won't be harder to track than anything we've caught and strapped onto the wagon. But when you hear us coming, don't run. We might take you for a target and shoot you."

"I hope you bring your mother along." Auralia draped the cloth over her shoulder. And then, as every fiber in her screamed *run, run, run,* she glanced once more at the blind woman's deep-lined face and the flesh of her arms as fragile as parchment. "She has such beautiful skin." Auralia walked toward the wagon.

Instinctively, the old woman leaned forward, her large hands folding around Auralia's. She caressed the girl's wrists and arms, gasping in surprise. "You're...you're so young. You must be beautiful." She drew her softly forward and placed her hands on the girl's face. "Fourteen, I'd guess. Fifteen."

Auralia shuddered when those rough, weathered fingers brushed the swelling on her head. The woman cried out. "Who did this?" And then she screamed at her sons with words that made Auralia cower and pull away. But the woman's hand closed on Auralia's shoulder to hold her fast. "Oh, you're just the age my daughter was when..." She forgot the rest of her words, staring off into space. Her hand tightened over the fold of glimmering cloth and drew back as if from something hot. Then she took the fabric and gathered it into her hands.

"Oh."

The merchants and hunters watched as the woman gently explored the shining strands with her fingers. She choked and then clasped the cloth to her breast. "It's beautiful."

"Either that woman's losing her mind, or she's lyin' about her eyes," muttered Joss.

"I tell you," the old woman wept, pressing the cloth to her face. "I...*I can see this.* Just this. These colors...in my hands..." And then she let go, let the cloth fall back into Auralia's arms. "Take it," she whispered. "It's yours. And thank you. Thank you. What you've done...I could see it. I could see."

Auralia stepped away from the wagon, shaking her head. "There's just threads. It's just cloth. I didn't mean to..."

Sader brought his fist to his mouth and bit his knuckles. Elyroth laughed and walked to the edge of the wagon. "Mother...what did you see?"

"Blue. Deep blue, like streams of water." She smiled. "And then...gold. Flashes of gold. The colors, they were flowing into and out of each other." Her faced was pained with delight and yearning. "Son...what is happening? I think I see your outline. I think I see light. Shadows. Trees."

Auralia turned and ran, clutching the cloth. She took the path she had come by and left them all behind.

When the fear that snapped at her heels drove Auralia from the path, there was no longer any reason to run. She fought to break her momentum, but the slope was steep, and she plunged downward through the barbed branches gouging her legs, leaves of her fragile garment stripped away in pieces. She stumbled suddenly into open air and fought to keep her balance, staggering across a rocky jag that protruded from the mountainside. She reeled and stopped, the breath knocked from her lungs by the fierce light of the vast nothingness before her. For a moment she thought she had stepped to the world's edge.

Beacons of sunlight were falling through mist thick as cream. Standing on the stony promontory, Auralia was immersed in clouds that surged above, all about, and below. A sea of shining vapor seeped through the trees and billowed into space, veiling evidence of the land spread out beneath.

Her legs gave out, and she crumpled into a heap, shoulders shaking as she cried.

"Are you all right, Auralia?"

Wynn and Cortie, following just moments behind, stepped carefully out onto the stone. They sat beside her in solemn silence. Wynn patted her lightly on the back. She laughed a little. "I'm just scared."

"Scared of heights?" asked Cortie. "We're so high. We must be close to the moon!" She peered over the edge. "Look at the clouds, Wynn." She picked up a pebble and launched it into the whiteness.

"I don't know what the colors are doing," Auralia said to herself more than to Wynn. "I don't know what they're for. I just make them. I just love them. But I know that what I've started…it isn't finished. Something's missing."

"Just keep making the colors. No one else can," said Wynn.

"But why?"

"The blind woman. She—"

"Please." Auralia felt the claws of fear again. "Please. I don't want to think about that. Not now. Not yet." She tangled weeds around her hands and jerked their stubborn roots from cracks in the rock. "I have to go. I have to clean out the caves. I can't stay at the lake anymore. There are people searching for me. Duty officers, coming to seize me for the Rites of the Privilege. I can't go inside of Abascar, Wynn. I can't bear those people."

"You could come with us," he said.

Cortie was shocked. "Nuh-uh. No way! There's not enough food!"

"We'll buy more food, if Auralia helps us," Wynn replied in a measured tone Auralia recognized as his father's. "Mum and Pa, they could use the help. They're always sayin' they need somebody to watch over Cortie and me."

Pouting, Cortie turned and grabbed a handful of sharp-edged gravel. She cast it out, a spray of dots expanding and vanishing in the mist. "They wish they'd never had us," she mumbled. "And we don't have enough food." She fumbled with some of the old woman's curses and threw another stone.

The clouds frothed, moving in thick so Auralia could not even see the mountain behind her. Somewhere in the fog, Juney was shouting, her voice like the call of a sad, faraway bird.

"They're calling us to go back," Cortie whispered excitedly. "Shh." Wynn put his arms around his sister and held her close, his young face far too weary for one his age, dark patches deep as bruises under his bloodshot eyes. Cortie smiled with the mischief of hiding.

"They're who you belong to," Auralia finally sighed.

Wynn scowled. "Why go back to them when they treat us like they do?"

"They need you. They'll need you when they get old. When they realize they're not so strong as they think."

"Who do *you* belong to, 'Ralia?" asked Cortie.

She stared northward as if her gaze could penetrate the fog, reach to the mountains, and find an answer.

"I think you belong to Abascar," Cortie declared.

"I don't," Auralia snapped. "I'm leaving. They're just so...so blind."

"You mean, like the old Bel Amican woman?" Cortie asked.

The question hung in the air for a moment, then was carried away on the rushing mist.

"Let's go, Cortie. If Pa finds us out here, you know what he'll do." Wynn took Cortie's hand and led her off the promontory and up the slope to the path, the fog washing them from Auralia's vision.

Cortie laughed, "Look at me! I can't see a thing! I must be from Abascar!"

Alone in an ocean of gleaming pearl, Auralia wanted to vanish within it.

Far away, the beastman roared in its cage.

At that moment, the clouds released their hold on the mountain, slipping away from the world like a falling sheet. When Auralia opened her eyes, the Expanse was revealed before her.

She dug her fingers into the weeds on the edge of the rock to keep herself from falling. The whole world of colors—verdant fields, needled trees, the winding blue Throanscall River, the vast lake, the darker Abascar woods, the distant gleam of the palace towers, the rising rugged stonelands of the east, the dark line of the Forbidding Wall to the north—burst into vivid life before her. It was so much, so much to take in.

A winding line of birds unfurled from the trees at the base of the promontory, and she watched their serpentine progression. At first, they seemed to pursue the flying carpet of retreating clouds. But then she saw a strange white bird with a gleaming red tail at the head of the line. They were chasing it, trying to drive it away. Like a shooting star, it dropped in a wild downward spiral, circled back toward the mountain below her, and vanished.

And then the red-tailed bird was there, alighting on the edge of the promontory before her. It offered a hushed and inquiring chirp.

The bird's feathers were blindingly bright, reflecting something more than the sunlight. Tufts of blue feathers ruffled its collar. Its eyes were full of fierce intelligence. It cocked its head to one side, a small, round, black beak open and uttering that quiet word of question yet again. Slender talons gripped the rock. But it was the bird's tail feathers, which burst, curling dark and wild in a gratuitous flourish, that held her spellbound. Among those red feathers, a single shaft gleamed with a color deeper than red, a color she remembered but had never seen.

Auralia crawled slowly forward, breath fluttering, heart out of rhythm.

The bird waited, as if commanded to remain.

Auralia's fingers touched its tail cautiously. The feathers were hot, charged with the urgency of flight.

The bird shuddered slightly as its one otherworldly feather surrendered to Auralia's touch.

"Of course I remember you," she said. "On the windowsill. My mother laughed. A long, long time ago."

She looked back toward Abascar's palace, that point of darkness in the woods, like the pin in the center of the spinning world. She held up the feather, and its color, vivid in contrast, seemed to bleed into the air, igniting the surrounding green, gold, red, and blue in a violent conflagration. For a moment, all colors coalesced into a living whole, as if she could reach out and take them by the edge, drawing them around her like a blanket.

"This is why I'm here, isn't it?" she said. "This is what my colors are trying to become. The missing piece." Choking back emotion, she held the feather out to the bird. "Please. Please take it back. If I take this, then I must..."

The bird closed its eyes, sang a mournful note.

The river of furious mountain birds, catching up to their target, turned day into night, sweeping downward black and cruel across the promontory, buffeting Auralia backward. There was a sound, a scream. It might have been Auralia as she pressed herself against the stone to keep from being driven off the edge. It might have been the bird caught and carried away. The sound of wings and cries roared like a waterfall. And then they were gone.

The tail feather lay burning but whole in her hand. The Expanse lay before her.

Abascar waited, blind.

12

STRICIA'S VIEW

Suspended in a turret high above the ornamental wall around King Calmarcus's palace, the young woman who had been promised Jaralaine's crown leaned on the battlement and watched a gull soar down into the palace courtyard.

"They'll all come into the courtyard soon." Breathless from her climb up the steps of the tower, Stricia scanned the crowds for friends, for enemies, for people to impress. "They can't wait, you know. The Housefolk. Isn't it funny?"

Kar-balter, the watchman standing beside her, snorted but said nothing. Stricia could read his silence. *The Housefolk*, he must be thinking. *You're still one of the Housefolk.* He would not dare utter such thoughts aloud. Stricia was not part of the royal family yet, but she would soon have the power to give him orders. He would stifle his discontent and strive to impress her. All the officers would.

"They wonder what goes on inside the palace," she continued. "I'm glad my father is the captain. I get to see both sides of the wall."

"Do you find much of interest inside the palace wall?" the watchman asked.

She flinched, the question stinging like a fleck of dirt in her eye. This was a place of privilege, and she would climb higher soon. Anything close to a challenge, anything requiring her to question herself was just a disruption. She kept her back turned to her questioner.

But she knew the answer. As the wedding drew nearer, she found it more difficult to endure the company of Housefolk. Each day she stepped carefully, training herself to speak nothing but that which would flatter the king, to manifest perfect adherence to Abascar law. The sight of the palace wall from without gave her a strange sense of foreboding, as if she might misstep, might spoil the dream she had worked so hard to make real.

This wall of rugged stones and rippling crystal veins was the second barrier of the king's defense against attack, securing royalty, counselors, military, the king's stables and storehouses, and passage to the most protected chambers of the Underkeep. And the history scrolls confirmed that no assailant had ever reached the palace. But then no enemies had ever breached Abascar's outermost wall of ash grey brick either. Homes, schools, markets and mills, craft halls, training yards, gardens, stables and forges, dungeons and taverns—even in the days of war with the aggressive Cent Regus, these had been kept safe. It was unlikely any threat would ever encroach upon the palace itself, unless one were to rise from within. While no one would go so far as to call it unnecessary, this secondary stone curtain had become, at times, an object of derision, regarded among officers assigned to the watchtowers as merely a barrier shielding the king from bitter gusts of gossip.

But for Stricia, this vantage point was still a thrill. She might not live within the palace walls yet, but her father's status as captain of the guard earned her family the same palace access granted to the guards. Since her father had never restricted her from the palace wall, she seized the opportunity whenever she could. At first, the watchmen protested. She ignored them, keeping her distance. She busied herself with surveying the avenues below, hoping to catch Housefolk in acts of compromise or conspiracy.

This passion for surveillance troubled her mother. Say-ressa was a quiet woman, more attentive to symptoms of illness than evidence of misbehavior, and she inspired gratitude from those in her care. She had, for a time, sought to teach Stricia the fulfillment that came from offering comfort and help, but the girl was repulsed by the sight of injury or deformity. The inconvenience of suffering unnerved her.

Her father meanwhile inspired pageantry and allegiance. Wherever he went, Ark-robin's reputation preceded him, and he was received and honored for his power, experience, and the way he could compel obedience to the laws. To win Ark-robin's favor was to win freedom and respect from the king. And to win the king's respect…that would enable her to distance herself from the worries and trouble of ordinary Housefolk.

Once the king had chosen Stricia to marry Cal-raven, she saw the doors open to places that had enlivened her dreams for years. Here on the wall the watchmen had abruptly stifled their complaints and applied themselves to pleasing her.

This morning, enervated by the preparation for the day's prestigious event, Stricia wore one of her father's long raincloaks, more to remain inconspicuous than to shelter herself from the intermittent showers moving over Abascar. On most days she wanted to be seen, though she acted nonchalant and uninterested wandering along the wall. But today she was expected to be at her family's side while they prepared for the Rites of the Privilege. She did not want to endure such a fuss. She wanted to watch the Housefolk stream through the gate into the courtyard. She wanted to think about how many people would witness her grand entrance. She wanted to play out in her mind just how the pageant would proceed for the next big occasion—her wedding day.

As the gates opened between this watchtower and the next, Housefolk poured in beneath the entry arch and moved up the main avenue and spread across the broad green lawns toward the royal platform, which jutted like the prow of a boat into the courtyard. At the base of the stairs that descended from the stage, a circle paved with flagstones and ringed with torches marked the crux—the crucible where men and women would raise their pleas and learn their futures.

The Ring of Decision. She would never stand there.

While she fantasized, the two watchmen mumbled about their latest instructions. It was odd that there were two. It could only mean some possibility of trouble. Perhaps there was a conspiracy afoot, as rumors had implied.

"That dismal grey parade's going to trample the lawns," grumbled Kar-balter into the breeze. "And for what? Just to see a bunch of crooks plead for their lives and get sent back into the wild."

"You know why they're here." The metallic croak came from deep within the oversized helm of Em-emyt, his partner-in-watch. "They'll obey the summons so they can earn another honor stitch." He knocked on his armored chest. "They'll spend all day checking out how many stitches their neighbors have earned. And they'll boast to those who have fewer."

Stricia scowled at the portly old guard, who was slumped on a stone bench as though he had died during a previous shift.

"The only Abascar event that'll ever warm my blood is the day the king declares Abascar's Spring and gives us back the rights Queen Jaralaine took away." Em-emyt lifted the visor of his helmet to gouge a browning pear with the few teeth he had left.

"I've heard rumors about another rather momentous occasion," said Kar-balter, bowing to Stricia. "The Housefolk are chattering about some kind of wedding. Have you heard these rumors, my lady?"

Stricia did not like Kar-balter's vast forehead, his wiry bursts of greying hair, or his crooked teeth. She ignored his joke and turned back to survey the masses.

"We'll protect the wedding, don't you worry, future queen," said Kar-balter. "If the king has doubled the guard for this, you can bet he'll triple it for that grand occasion."

"He's doubled the guard," said Em-emyt, "because he's hearing rumors of the grudgers." With a sudden flick of his wrist, the officer sent the pear's core hard and fast into the belly of a black-feathered bird that had settled on the edge of the tower wall. Feathers spun in the air long after the bird was gone. "Hmm," he muttered. "That wasn't a gull. That was a mountain vulture. What's a mountain vulture doing here?"

Stricia watched a batch of young women pushing their way through the crowd, leaning into each other to gossip. She curled her hand into a fist. "There's Dynei," she said, not really caring if the watchmen listened. "Dynei's a stuck-up little brat. Calls herself a loyalist, but I've seen what she keeps under her blankets. She'll be losing some honor stitches soon if I have anything to say about it. And I will. Look at her. Charming the boys. Strutting and flirting. What has she done to deserve their attention? I'll put a stop to that behavior."

Kar-balter tweaked the medallion on the edge of his breastplate. "Humph. It was a good day when I traded in my honor stitches for a suit of armor. And now I've got a medal."

"I got four!" Em-emyt choked, spluttering juice, clinking his medals against his breastplate. "Blue level training. Yellow level training. Valor in battle. And archery. Heh...now that's the sort of honors that really make people stand up and notice."

"He says he has a medal for valor in battle," Kar-balter muttered to Stricia. "What battles have you ever seen, Em-emyt?"

"I earned that valor medal for killing two Cent Regus reptiles."

Kar-balter smirked. "I heard Prince Cal-raven held the beastmen off so poor Em-emyt could escape, running like a goose with his tail feathers on fire. Cal-raven recommended that medal just to silence those who laughed at Em-emyt."

A face emerged from the shadow of Em-emyt's oversized helmet, old and lumpish, like a tortoise waking. "I didn't run! I *withdrew*, you crusty old vawn nugget. I was injured!" The aging soldier's outrage almost brought him to his feet.

"If he starts stripping things off to show his battle scars," Stricia laughed, "I may just have to scream."

"I swear," Em-emyt continued, "it was the worst of beastmen that had at us that night. But what do you know about combat, you half-drowned drunk?"

"Look at that!" Kar-balter leaned out so far over the edge of the parapet, his partner could have ended their debate with an easy shove. "Look, Em-emyt!"

The stocky guard groaned. Using his sword as a crutch, he managed to stand and share the view. Curious, Stricia edged up beside them.

Looking south down the main market avenue, she could see across rows of tiled rooftops to Abascar's outer wall. The road was thronged with Housefolk. The noisy mass narrowed to push through the gates, where attendants quickly stitched a bright blue ribbon on each grey cloak for their voluntary attendance. Proud and pleased, they proceeded into the extravagant space where green grass grew, where striped flags flapped, to view the large stage with its swooping backdrop of red curtains and purple tapestries. They were elbows and shoulders against one another, crowding around the Ring of Decision like travelers warming to a fire.

Kar-balter turned his attention to one of the guarded Underkeep stairwells. "See him? See the ale boy?"

A child wearing an errand-runner's cap had emerged, holding a reflective silver tray aloft. He disappeared in the current of Housefolk, then reappeared near the platform. He spoke to no one and moved independently, swiftly, with purpose.

Stricia smiled. "I know him. Clumsy little orphan."

"He's got enough goblets on that ale tray to serve more than the usual number of magistrates. There must be guests with us today. King Cal-marcus is feeling generous." Kar-balter glanced at Stricia quizzically. "Shouldn't you be down there? To be seated with your family?"

"I suppose I should," she said, as if it were of little consequence. "Today is a kind of rehearsal for me, you see. Soon I'll be—"

Trumpets blared from a small platform to the right of the main stage. Drums thundered from a matching stand on the other side. On a smaller stage at the top of the crimson fall of curtains, a group of white-robed singers began a bold inaugural verse. The crowd roared approval. The music of the Rites of the Privilege had begun and would continue throughout the proceedings. This fanfare, a bombastic and ancient motif, would course for several rounds before settling into festive strains of strings.

The examination of orphans and Gatherers would take place at the front of the stage. Only those Housefolk standing near would hear the formal exchanges, and the rest would follow the progress by signal flags, musical cues, and the rapid ripples of gossip.

This was all according to tradition. But now the three observers could see what made this year's ceremony unusual.

From a doorway on one side of the courtyard, ascending from passages below ground, fourteen men and women emerged, proceeding in bright sky blue robes fringed with gold. Masks of similar blue concealed their faces, representing their roles as a unified force of law and guidance for Cal-marcus's house.

"I had better learn the names of all the magistrates," sighed Stricia.

These were followed by a company of tall, pale men and women in black uniforms and towering green headdresses.

"Bel Amican ambassadors." Stricia scowled. "Ugh. They look like insects. I cannot tolerate Bel Amicans. They're always looking down on people."

The magistrates and ambassadors walked to the platform through the crowd, moving in measured steps along a path that radiated from the stage and ascending the stairs on the left side.

They crossed the stage, pausing frequently before what appeared to be an array of kings and queens. Like ghosts undecided about this world or oblivion, wooden figures wearing robes and crowns stood posed to appear contemplative and watchful.

"What the kings and queens used to wear, back before the Proclamation..." Stricia did not bother to see if Kar-balter was impressed. "Someday I'm going to look through all the royal closets, see all the things they wore. The jewelry, the capes, the gowns."

"I like to imagine the food that was on their table," said Em-emyt.

"There he is! King Cal-marcus!" Stricia clasped her hands together.

Ascending from the back of the stage, Cal-marcus appeared among these standing tributes. He passed between the likenesses of his mother and father, their firstborn and thus the rightful heir, and took his place upon the throne, which brought a dutiful cheer from the Housefolk. The cheer would have been more vigorous, Stricia thought, had they not already received their honor stitches. What if the masses cheered for her more loudly than they did the king? It could trouble his temper.

As the musicians and singers raised their voices in bolder tones, Stricia wondered if they were trying to mask the halfhearted ovation.

"How much he expects them to forget," Em-emyt muttered, turning his attention from Cal-marcus to gaze upon the king's likeness that towered behind the musicians, a wooden sculpture carved from one enormous tree. Its eyes were level with the watchtower's parapet. The statue's right hand was raised, while the other hand clutched a scroll of laws. Its eyes were polished as smooth as eggshells. The lack of pupils, while a traditional style in Abascar art, had always bothered Stricia. It made the figure appear to be sleepwalking. Or blind.

The king's likeness dominated the left side of the platform. But the statue on the right had been covered with an elaborate drape of colors, a single rippling veil, as though the hues that had been taken from the Housefolk had been unraveled and woven into a single banner.

In spite of the pageantry, Kar-balter was still pointing to the progress of the ale boy and his tray of drinks. "Cal-marcus must be serving something from his best wine cellars. Probably some of the king's favorite drink there too." He sighed. "I'd serve a winter post here if I could just get me some of that wine."

Stricia thought for a moment, then gasped. "The bet!" She turned and seized Kar-balter's arm. "I bet that wicked girl Dynei that I would taste hajka before there was a crown upon my head."

"You're rather ambitious, aren't you?" Kar-balter squirmed, and Stricia could see that her charms were doing their work.

"Well, there's no law against it and no penalty for asking."

"No penalty but the king's temper if we're caught sipping a drink prepared for him. And it's no secret that hajka will punish the drinker with a judgment all its own. Aren't you a little young to be chasing dangers like that?"

"Oh, it's only a crime if I *drink* the stuff. I just want to *taste* it. Surely you can help me, watchman."

"How're you gonna prove you've tasted it?" croaked Em-emyt.

"If you can get it," Stricia continued, her voice losing its humor, "I will meet you at the gate after the Rites, and I'll bring a cup. Then Dynei can *watch* me take a sip. It'll be a barrel of laughs if we pull it off."

Kar-balter's smile faded. "My lady, perhaps we should wait for another occasion. It's going to be tough to get hold of anything served on the platform, especially once the ceremony begins. Watchmen can't be drinkers, so I'd best keep my hands clean. There are guards all over the courtyard."

"Watchman, I'm going to be queen. And as queen, I'll have the opportunity to grant favors to those who make extra efforts to please me. I need to know those I can count on to carry out orders quietly, even difficult assignments."

Color drained from Kar-balter's face.

"I do not yet have a crown. But should you happen to find a way to help me win this bet, I promise I will remember you."

"My lady, I..."

Playfully, she jumped at him, grabbed the hilt of the dagger strapped to his leg, and unsheathed it, just the way she often did when her father came home from a long day in the wild. He cried out in protest as she stepped away and the blade came free.

She had only meant to tease him. She had not anticipated that the dagger would have only half a blade. Nor could she have guessed that wine would spill from the open sheath.

She stood there, blinking in astonishment, while he knelt to wipe the red splash from his leg. "My lady, forgive me!"

Em-emyt was laughing now, holding his sides, until his laugh became a coughing fit. "You see, my lady," he chortled, "Kar-balter is a dangerous watchman. Nobody dares threaten this palace for fear he'll throw wine at them!"

"You'd best keep your hands clean, huh?" Stricia took a deep breath. She extended the half dagger back to Kar-balter, but she held it fast when he reached to take it from her.

"Please," he said, his voice trembling. "Don't mention this. The nights up here can be so long. I get thirsty."

"You smuggle wine to the watchtower without anyone the wiser," she said in a singsong way. "Surely you can wring some drops of hajka from a clumsy errand boy." She released the dagger.

"My lady." He dropped to his knees. "I'm just a tower watchman. I have no permission to approach the platform. And I—"

"You hear those horns?" Stricia ran to the wall again and looked down. "My father and mother are approaching. I'm supposed to be with them."

With that, she was through the opening in the tower floor and descending as fast as she could run, fighting her way free of her father's raincloak and lifting the skirts of her ceremonial dress to keep from stumbling. The hour had come when Abascar would look on her with new appreciation, and she would at last begin to enjoy all she had worked to receive.

Taking up the melody, two women drew a long arcbow across the rope-thick cords of the lynfr, the chief instrument of the event. Their solemn refrain quieted the crowd.

Housefolk drank in this view of painted spires and domes, shielding their eyes against the silver light that burnt through the sky's grey veils. Young men crossed their arms and strove to distract young women. Parents bent to scold talkative children. One toddler wailed, having stumbled, fresh blood on his knees, and his father, embarrassed, wiped it away. The congregated household pressed in close along the paths, while the celebrated families proceeded toward their reserved, slightly raised ground.

Cheers rose in scattered waves as army regiments entered in rhythmic pace behind the families, hands on hilts, jaws set.

There had been rumors. Whispers of revolt.

It would never happen, of course. No dissenter could muster enough strength and support to become a serious threat. They were sure of this. But still, under Ark-robin's strict orders, the soldiers were watchful.

The drummers provided an officious march for the officers as they took their posts about the yard. Vawns with jewel-studded saddles, carrying two riders each, were carefully guided, small eyes as expressionless as black coins. The children begged for rides, but the officers refused and sent them away with their heads full of sword fights. Some wanted to know Prince Cal-raven's whereabouts. He had been promoted from his rank as a troop leader to the station of house defender, second only to Ark-robin. The soldiers reminded them that the prince was away on a mission to protect Abascar's livestock, hunting a dangerous fangbear.

The families settled into a space between two massive stone fountains. These new marvels, currently dry, would one day spring to life as giant pumps beneath the surface blasted water into the air, where it would fall into bowls on the corners of the platform. These were certain to impress the Bel Amican ambassadors and set them to imagining the future when a river would course beneath this house. Smug as thieves, Abascar's Housefolk would drink, bathe, and water their gardens, never needing to venture forth from the walls again.

Some even said the water would bring Abascar's Spring.

As Ark-robin's family entered, a murmur rose, for here was Cal-marcus's chief strategist and captain of the guard. The captain's uniform jingled with medals. He waved his left hand to greet the people and kept his other hand concealed in a fold of his shirt. Two fingers, the tale was told, had been ripped off by the jaws of a beastman. Middle-aged women, struck dumb at the sight of him, yearned to meet his gaze, just as young ladies had when he was a new soldier.

His wife, Say-ressa, was in appearance his equal. Like him she was tall, smooth skinned, decorated in a seamless redbrown robe, as red as brown could be without crossing the forbidden line of Queen Jaralaine's proclamation. And while she kept her hands calmly folded, her elegant robes proclaimed her a formidable figure, the most regal and influential woman in the house, still shapely enough to distract the young men, if only for a moment, from her daughter.

To the eye, Stricia was the perfect balance of her parents, inheriting her mother's delicate complexion and grace, her father's piercing gaze and confidence. The observers hushed as Stricia waved, a gleaming circle around her wrist—the bracelet of King Cal-marcus's favor. This was the first public recognition of the royal choosing. The moment hung in the air as if the first firework of a royal festival had been launched. As the revelation swept through the congregation, they exploded into hurrahs. Even the musicians faltered, glancing up from their instruments to investigate the ruckus.

Permitted at last to discuss what they had already suspected, the Housefolk ventured their guesses as to the date of the wedding. Many nodded their approval that the king should bestow such an honor on Ark-robin's family.

Meanwhile, Stricia reached down to accept wildflowers from a young girl who rode atop her father's shoulders.

"She's come just to see you," the man shouted through the din. "You're the glory of our house. If only all our daughters could grow to be like you."

The captain's daughter pressed her face into the flowers. And when she emerged smiling, tears of gratitude were streaming down her face.

13

CUP, DAGGER, AND MASK

All the hysterical laudation for Ark-robin and his daughter made the ale boy want to smash his tray of wine-filled goblets. But he had watched the harvesters' labor, and he had seen the vintners perform their subtle arts. His respect gave him restraint; he bound up his bother and locked it away.

"Shoutin' and cheerin' for figments of your own imaginations," he said to no one who would listen.

While the procession pulled the crowd's attention, no one bothered to notice him. He was grateful for the invisibility, but it left him to shove and dodge, duck and scramble. Winding his way through their oblivious ovation, he shouted, "Delivery for the king!"

Nothing about Ark-robin's entrance or the celebration of Stricia's future inspired him. He wanted to scold anyone who planted hope in such shallow soil. The girl's arrogant laughter that had disturbed Deep Lake not so long ago seemed to go on echoing, a bad dream he could not shake. He could only imagine what she would become once she wore a crown.

Such a future only ensured that the ale boy would continue to cross Ark-robin's path. The memory of the captain berating Auralia still stung. While royalty, guards, soldiers, and magistrates seemed content to count the ale boy as a nuisance, a necessity, a paltry puff of dust, he could not imagine a day without the captain studying his steps. Try though he might during the noisy Underkeep night, curled beneath blankets made of reedweave, the boy still could not unearth an answer to solve this persistent puzzle.

A flask of the king's drink strapped to his belt, the ale boy retreated to the east wall of the courtyard. Obsidia Dram had told him Captain Ark-robin would give a signal when the king was thirsty. The boy would respond, proceeding to the stage to fill King Cal-marcus's cup and set goblets of wine on the pedestals alongside the assembled guests.

The ale boy would have preferred to spend the ceremony nearer to the gate, to see the Gatherers come in and the orphans in step just behind.

Would Auralia be among them?

Unable to sleep the night before, he imagined a hundred scenarios regarding Auralia's fate. She had purged her lakeside caves of their colors and slipped away from Abascar. Or she had stumbled into a duty officer's snare or crossed a summoner's path. That beastman who had crept into her caves—he might have eaten her alive. Perhaps she had gone to House Bel Amica or fled southward to House Jenta.

Even on tiptoes he could not distinguish one small figure from another as the orphans moved along the west side of the yard. Toughweed flutes accompanied their progress with a playful melody, this after a comical sawing of dissonant fiddles had mocked the stumbling Gatherers. Laughter scattered through the crowd. Though the potential for a pardon gave the Rites their fame and focus, Gatherers were still convicted criminals serving out their sentences, and the king was not about to object should people find amusement in their humble approach.

He watched Ark-robin's family settle on cushions in a prestigious place near the magistrates. Ark-robin bowed to his beloved Say-ressa, to Stricia next, to the gallery of magistrates, and the row of uncomfortable ambassadors. Then, beside the king's grand chair, the captain dropped to one knee and placed a golden-gloved hand on the hilt of his broadsword. There he would remain, a royal guard dog.

To a flourish of trumpets, officers escorted the first Gatherer into the torch-framed Ring of Decision.

In the shadow of the statue bearing his likeness, King Cal-marcus sat in his high-backed chair, elevated above the other guests. Nodding, he might have been numbering the subjects who would march up the redgold carpet to stand, make their plea, and await his judgment.

The Rites had become an annual festival of taunting and gambling. As Gatherers fought to maintain their composure, the magistrates sought to knock them off balance with unexpected questions. Some of these crooks reentered the house with a notion to take vengeance for the trouble they endured outside. The magistrates saw it as their duty to tighten the vise until they were satisfied (and even delighted). As a gesture of trust, they might even permit the Bel Amicans to interject a challenge.

Meanwhile, the Housefolk would bet stitches, rations, and favors on each decision.

And so it began. The first Gatherer, a woman in a bonnet and humble brown cloak, took her place in the circle, carrying a heavy clay bowl draped with a cloth.

This year it was Cal-marcus's chief advisor, Aug-anstern, who stood at the front point of the platform and cast the first sharp inquiries. The Gatherer unveiled her appeal—an array of rare flowers cultivated in the wild.

While the jury murmured, the captain clapped his gloves together, and the ale boy sprang forward as if prodded with a pitchfork. Careful to hold the goblet tray steady on one raised hand, he reached down with the other to ensure the flask of hajka was securely strapped to his belt, and then he moved along the edge of the crowd to the eastern processional ramp.

Hajka was the king's choice draught, and the ale boy had watched it carried up to the royal quarters in greater volume as the years went by, bringing the reign of Prince Cal-raven ever closer. Hajka first stung the eyes as the cup was raised, then burnt the tongue, scoured the throat, set fire to the belly, and rushed into the mind, raining fiery light. Surely it could bring no health to the body or the mind. The ale boy had sipped it once by accident, mistaking it for water. While he wept and shouted that Abascar was on fire, Obsidia held him and sighed.

The boy set down the tray, unclasped the hajka flask, and reached up to the king's chair, where his fingers closed around the goblet's narrow stem. He lifted it with effort—it had been carved from a heavy block of blacklode—and held it shakily while filling it with the colorless drink.

Ark-robin gave him an almost imperceptible nod of approval. But the routine dismissal did not come. The captain was distracted by a messenger at the edge of the platform.

The messenger's words carved creases across Ark-robin's forehead. He called for Aug-anstern, who turned the questioning over to the magistrates and joined the hushed consideration. The king dismissed the messenger, but only the messenger. The ale boy waited, worried he had been forgotten.

Aug-anstern's rings clattered as he rubbed his hands together. The ale boy heard him say, "Rumor or not, we have no choice but to mount a search. A grudge-bearing mage is not to be trifled with."

Ark-robin laughed quietly. "This ghost makes an appearance at every event. Scharr ben Fray has worked his way into Abascar's imagination. The more seriously we take such rumors, the more the people will look for him under every rock. I'm certain the grudgers start such gossip just to aggravate the king."

Their arguments made plain, the captain and the advisor watched the king ponder.

The magistrates continued slinging questions at the Gatherer. "Was the king justified in casting you out for your slander? Describe for us the proper show of honor toward an officer. How will the house benefit from your return? You approached us with a limp. What caused your injury? Have you heard any rumors of an uprising against our good king? Give us the names of the Gatherers you suspect to be most likely of rebellion."

It was unclear whether the king heard the woman's fumbling replies while he chewed on the messenger's report. Whatever the case, he raised his hand, closed it to a fist, and declared the Gatherer unfit to return to the Housefolk. The people approved. As if her legs were breaking beneath her, the woman staggered out of the circle. The ale boy thought of the king's private garden and how it had been closed off—fetid, weed racked, and colorless—for as long as he could remember. The king would not be moved by this Gatherer's flourish of flowers.

"Alert your officers, Captain," said Aug-anstern. "If one of them recognizes Scharr ben Fray amongst the crowd, he should raise his shield. Then move in for an arrest."

The captain's smile faded. "I have not heard the king's decision. Besides, how would you counsel my men to single out the exile in this throng?"

Aug-anstern leaned closer, like a vulture. "The more time we give him, the more young dreamers he'll lure into his web of lies and superstitions." The advisor shook his head. "Think about how deeply his teaching has damaged Prince Cal-raven."

Fast as a striking adder, King Cal-marcus grabbed the advisor's arm. "Do not speak so about my son," he growled.

"Cal-raven is our champion!" Aug-anstern screeched.

"*Damaged?* You think my son is *damaged?* Your future king is the apprentice to Captain Ark-robin, and he became such on his own merits. He ensures the safety of this house. What do you say about me, I wonder, when my back is turned?"

Releasing his grip, Cal-marcus seized his goblet, and for a moment the ale boy thought the king might splash hajka into his offender's face. "*Damaged.* That's what you'll be if my son finds out you harbor such impressions."

The ale boy wished he could make himself smaller and quieter until the king's temper cooled.

The exchange had drawn the Bel Amicans' attention, and they leaned in toward the king, a row of towering dark-robed figures in a crowded line like five fingers of a single black glove. Their wan faces watched unblinking, as if seeing more than anyone could guess.

The king slumped down in his throne, seeking to withdraw from their surveillance. "Search the crowd, Captain," he rasped. "Scharr ben Fray is still out there, and we should not take the threat of his return lightly. It's your concern now. I must return to the matter of 'pulling weeds.' "

Captain Ark-robin rose without protest. This was not a glamorous task, to leave the platform during a ceremony and comb the crowd for a criminal. And yet, he marched away, past his surprised family, and down the west ramp of the dais. There, he commanded a duty guard to take his place as the king's protector. He beckoned to officers posted at attention around the yards. They moved straight through the assemblage, their gazes sweeping across the heads of the hundreds as if anticipating their orders. As their shiny helms met in a bright gathering along the edge of the event, the courtyard gate closed with a resolute boom.

The musicians returned to the original theme to break the rising tension. Children danced again, but their parents, unsettled by the soldiers' activity, were anxious.

Another Gatherer was escorted by two duty officers into the stone circle at the foot of the dais. The ale boy recognized him—that gnarled thief called Krawg—and felt a pang of concern. He had never been fond of Krawg, but Auralia's obvious affection had impressed him. The boy whispered a wish that the Gatherer would be granted a pardon.

Krawg cringed in the crossfire of the Housefolk mockery, the captious judges, and Cal-marcus's unforgiving stare.

It pained the boy to see this, so while he waited for his dismissal, he preoccupied himself by surveying the crowd and wondering what the famous, exiled stonemaster looked like. He had heard so many stories about the man who could speak with the animals and sculpt stone with just a stroke of his hand.

But as he considered one face after another, his curiosity was quickly quenched. The realization of how many people could see him—his foolish cap, his wine red scar, his tattered trousers—set his bones to quaking. The ale boy's life was lived out of sight, out of hearing, a mouse in the wall, a beetle. As far as the palace honorables knew, bottles of drink arrived at their doorstep by magic. Outside of those who gave him orders, only the Gatherers knew him by face and a title. But here he felt as though he himself were on trial.

"Ale boy." It was the king.

"Sire!" the ale boy blurted, stunned.

"Did Captain Ark-robin forget to dismiss you?" Cal-marcus's narrow, chiseled face was as sullen as his eyes were sad. "Wearying, isn't it? Up here in front of so many eyes. But I'm glad you're here. We've been unfair to you."

The ale boy would not have been more surprised if the king had leapt up and embraced him.

Cal-marcus ker Har-baron tipped back his head and gulped the draught of hajka until it was gone. His eyes shut, one fist clenched, and his frame shuddered within the enormous robes. After a time, his expression softened. "Refill my cup," he wheezed. "And ensure that the magistrates and our guests have had their fill. Then you may go. And thank you, boy." The king turned his widening eyes skyward and murmured, "Is that a mountain vulture circling above me?"

After refilling the royal goblet, the ale boy walked in a daze behind the rows of magistrates and Bel Amicans, reaching to place goblets on the small pedestals between them. As he did, each magistrate gave him a curious glance. They had seen the king address him and were acknowledging his existence for the first time.

Unable to feel his feet, unsure how to respond, he hastily descended the west ramp, stumbling over familiar mysteries. What had earned him such an honor as to serve the king this way? What set him apart from the ordinary orphans outside the walls?

"We've been unfair to you."

When the ale boy reached the bottom of the dais, sinking into duty and obscurity once again, the only path open lay alongside Gatherers waiting their turn before the king. As he passed the line of hopeful criminals, they nodded in fond recognition. He answered with an almost imperceptible bow.

But as he scanned their faces, the last figure in the line stopped him in his tracks.

"Oh!"

And then fear compelled him to continue.

In the instant that he passed her, he saw a flicker of recognition in Auralia's eyes. Otherwise, her face seemed distorted, anguished, bruised.

Her eyes were dark, a tale of sleepless nights. Her lips were pressed together as if to stifle a cry. He would never forget her hair; it fell like wolf-spider webs around her face and shoulders, still decorated with fragments of leaves, a twist of thornbranch dust, a broken wispfly's wing—remnants of the home to which she might never return. Wrapped in a heavy earth-brown cape that dwarfed her frail frame, she hunched her shoulders against a chill. She stood still, but her shadow was restless as light flickered down between undecided thunderclouds. Among the Gatherers, she seemed alone in a forest of tall, windblown trees, swaying in currents of burdensome thought.

Each step he took became more difficult, as if Auralia had ensnared him with an invisible cord and was trying to draw him backward.

"When I'm gone...will you play with your lights here, by the lake?"

"When you're gone?" he had answered.

The ale boy stepped through a space of grass where children were casting wooden tokens into a pile, making bets on the king's judgments. A sudden fanfare announced Krawg's pardon, and some of the children cheered. The ale boy was tempted to seek a better view.

But Ark-robin was in front of him, speaking with one of his soldiers.

"No, no," Ark-robin was saying. "The man we're looking for has a round face, deeply carved. We must be thorough. Watch."

The captain marched boldly up behind a cluster of Housefolk. With a flick of his glove, he jerked back the hood of a bent old man. The nearby children screamed and then broke into laughter. The bewildered suspect reached up to shield his face with a bulbous, disfigured hand. He was merely concealing a deformity; it was as though a mass of flesh from his forehead had melted down over one of his eyes.

Ark-robin's officer smirked, but Ark-robin winced and stepped away, bowing in apology and flexing the glove of his own three-fingered hand.

The ale boy looked again at the ruined face. He had seen more alarming wounds in the Gatherers' camps, and he had enjoyed the company of Arec the Mute, One-Legged Jabber, and the Crab Lady many times, so this man's abnormality was hardly unfamiliar. As the children laughed and returned to their game, the ale boy's anger was rekindled.

The old man noticed him and approached. "Boy, what kind of drink you got there? Looks like just the stuff to make this ceremony tolerable."

The ale boy opened his mouth to respond, but bright horn blasts interrupted him, marking the pardon of yet another Gatherer. Polite applause rose from the multitude, not for the pardoned man but to show respect for the king's decision.

Auralia's test drew closer.

"Please," the misshapen man rasped, "could you spare an old-timer one sip?"

The boy felt a swell of pity. The audience was momentarily distracted. No one would notice if he made this small exception.

He offered the tray. With his one good hand, the stranger reached for the goblet.

Someone stepped between them and stole the tray away.

"Thank you, boy." It was Kar-balter, one of the tower watchmen, a soldier the ale boy had learned to avoid. Kar-balter held the tray up out of reach, smiling through the lifted visor of his ornamental helmet. Before the boy could respond, the watchman lunged forward and snatched the king's hajka flask as well. "Don't be alarmed," he laughed. "I've been sent to retrieve these. They need to be refilled."

"But...but that's *my* job!"

Kar-balter winked at the boy's confusion and grinned with teeth so crooked and eyes so wild that he might have been a clown. "Wait here. I'll be right back." The watchman stole away along the back of the crowd toward his watchtower.

"That thieving wyrm!" The boy started after him, but the old man grabbed his sleeve.

"Let him go. The king's in a foul temper. You don't want to cause any kind of disturbance."

The ale boy's temper had also run foul. Perhaps he was empowered by the king's recent attention. Perhaps he was spurred by feelings of helplessness as Auralia approached the Ring of Decision. Whatever the case, he was going to stop that watchman. He was going to right this one small wrong.

As Kar-balter reached the open door at the base of the watchtower, he realized this opportunity might never come again.

"A toast," he chuckled, "to me."

He lifted the hajka flask, pulled the cork out with his teeth, and spat it to the grass. "Let's find out what's so special about the king's drink."

He had pulled it off. He had met Stricia's challenge. She would taste the king's drink. He would win her favor. And what is more, he would take the medal from that lumpy old watchman who had never deserved it.

As he gulped down a long swig, his gaze traced the line of the looming tower all the way to the parapet in hopes that Em-emyt was looking down at this decisive moment.

And, yes, there was the other watchman leaning out and staring down. There he was, his arm extended, a weighty chunk of stone from the parapet falling from his grasp...

...down, down...to strike the edge of the silver ale tray with a clang.

The tone reverberated in the air like an alarm.

The tray jumped from Kar-balter's hand.

Launched in a high arc, the goblet flew, streaming red wine that splashed across the ale boy's tunic as he skidded to a stop.

The goblet fell into the boy's open hands before it could break on the ground.

Kar-balter grabbed at his throat, dropping the hajka flask and falling back over the first stair to sprawl in the open watchtower door.

❦

The ale boy stood up, wringing wine from his tunic, only to find two duty officers glowering down at him.

"Where is your tray, ale boy?"

The ale boy pointed timidly at the flailing watchman, who was coughing and spitting up hajka. "I think he's stealing it."

One of the officers stayed by the boy while the other approached the watchman.

Kar-balter, red faced, shouted and pointed back at the ale boy. "Arrest him!" he coughed, frantic. "He's wearing red in the presence of the king!"

"And you are not at your post, Kar-balter," said the officer, picking up the hajka flask and sniffing it. "You're choking up a drink that was meant for King Cal-marcus."

Kar-balter, no doubt suffering from the disorientation of the drink, waved his hands about. "No. I was just tasting it. I was supposed to give the rest to Ark-robin's daughter!"

"He steals wine from the cellars," the ale boy muttered. "I've watched him do it too."

The officers looked at each other, then at Kar-balter. The watchman, flummoxed, made a crucial mistake. He snatched his dagger from its sheath as if to defend himself from the accusation. The half-bladed weapon was dripping with crimson rivulets of wine.

Kar-balter's face grew as red as the drink. Before he could run, the officers seized him. A few steps toward the gate, he collapsed in their grip, slumping to the ground.

Retrieving his tray, the ale boy placed the goblet, still half full of wine, upright. His heart was quaking.

"What a day," he sighed. "What a terrible day."

In the tray's reflection, he watched thunderclouds conquer the sky, the only remaining sunlight smoldering around their edges. Exploratory raindrops plopped into the goblet, and the ale boy covered it with his hand. Then the tray revealed the face of the deformed old man.

The stranger's exposed eye gleamed, and he knelt, pretending to help the boy. A hand of thick, callused fingers took the cup. "Here, let me help you clean this up."

With a mischievous smile, he took a quick gulp and returned the goblet empty to the tray. "Ahh, that's good. It reminds me of the smell of the palace candles, the dark and smoky corridors." He touched his own eyebrow and nodded to the boy. "Your scar... I see you are acquainted with fire."

A roar from the crowd marked the denial of a Gatherer's hopes.

Auralia's almost to the Ring, thought the boy.

"Perhaps you should know," said the man in a whisper, "that I've heard tales about some rare and special people...people possessed of a powerful gift. Long ago they called them firewalkers. But they were so rare, most thought they were only fiction. In Abascar, superstition isn't welcome. There are people here, right here in this courtyard, who will never discover their own talents simply because they refuse to believe such things are possible." He tapped his forehead with a crooked thumb. "If you know the secret of passing through fire, there are many places only you can travel and a lot of things only you can know."

Rising, the stranger held out his swollen hand to help the boy to his feet. "Take that counsel, if you will, from what's left of this old brain...a brain that believes such crazy stories."

The ale boy cautiously accepted his hand.

The old man laughed, drew back, and the ale boy gasped.

The hand came free of the sleeve.

It was a false appendage—a hand sculpted of stone.

A stonemaster. The boy dropped the heavy sculpture and sat back on the ground.

"I have a gift myself." The stranger glanced about to ensure no one witnessed their exchange. "What others would call an obstacle, I consider an opportunity. What others call a barrier, I call that a door. In my hands, a pebble becomes a key that lets me walk where no one else can go."

The ale boy could now discern that the man's facial deformity was a stone mask, a thin shell concealing half his expression. "You're…the prince's teacher!"

A loud voice from the platform calling up the next appellant startled them, and Scharr ben Fray took back his false hand, drawing it into his sleeve. "Cal-marcus wants to shut me out of Abascar. But his walls are made of stone." He laughed. "I hate to trespass, but I pledged to protect House Abascar long before you were born. And I keep my promises, no matter how hard Abascar works to break me. Even if I have to wear a mask."

"Are you here to protect us from something?"

"Let's just say I've arrived at some troubling questions."

"Will you find the answers here?"

"No no, I'm pursuing something better than that." He leaned in close. "I'm pursuing an even bigger question, a question that might brush the others away. And her name, my boy, is Auralia."

"Is it?" The ale boy pulled up a fistful of grass.

"If we hurry, we'll see what she has planned for King Cal-marcus. They've called her into the Ring of Decision."

14

AURALIA'S COLORS

With every sharp challenge from Aug-anstern, Auralia flinched as from a barking dog.

In the Ring, the dancing flames of the torches stole her concentration. She could feel their heat, smell the sweat and the damp wool garments of the crowd that surrounded her. She traced the edges of the cold tiles with her bare, bruised feet.

When she closed her eyes, she dizzied in the gravity of sleep. How many days had she forced herself to stay awake?

Ever since her ordeal in the wild, she had braided, unbraided, spooled, and spun, worried that if she rested for a moment she might never wake again. The toil of weaving the last loose lines together had commanded all her strength and attention. She could not be sure if she had fastened them out of impatience, desperate to finish the work, or out of glad obedience to their subtle provocations. At times, the cloth in her hands had been heavy with tears.

From the moment the blind Bel Amican woman cried out and clutched at the colors, Auralia's day world and her dream life had become inseparable, no matter how she fought to unscramble them. It certainly seemed illusory when she staggered from the Cragavar trees to the gates of Abascar and ordered the guard to call for the summoner. For a few moments there, she felt herself drifting, pulling at strands that held her together, hovering like a kite above the scene, watching herself ask for something she felt no will to request. In that suspended state, she had glimpsed an audience around her, spectral and translucent figures, shy, curious, and close. *The Northchildren.*

"You do not know where you come from?" Aug-anstern was asking, his eyes red as cherries in a face of doughy flesh.

This was now. This was here. This was inside Abascar's walls. That was not a river of blood flowing beneath his feet toward her. "A crimson carpet," she whispered. "Crimson."

"You must know, you ridiculous girl. The Gatherers only care for orphans from within House Abascar. So tell me, are you a trespasser? A thief? Where is your true home?"

She replied, unsure if her voice was sounding. But the examiner's fingers flexed and grasped at the air, sharp black nails trying to catch and crush her words. What had she answered? Why did they laugh? Why were the people in the green headdresses clear and cruel in her vision, while everything else seemed pale?

"Never mind that for now. Something else offends me worse than your mumbling and your filthy brown cloak. You have seen summer and winter come and go sixteen times, and you have nothing in your hands. You bring no pledge of service to us. Did no one explain the ritual to you?" He gestured to those Gatherers pardoned in the Rites.

Her eyes found Krawg, who stood behind a ribbon that bounded the space reserved for the redeemed. He sat with his hood pulled over his head so she could see only the clouds of his breath on the cold breeze. His knob-knuckled hand gripped his picker-staff as if he might snap it in two.

"Stammer Cole carried a rake to us. Fudden Slopp brought a carving knife and a stone hammer. Krawg's too ill to be of much use, but as he has labored for years, he'll enjoy the safety of Abascar's walls for the remainder of his days. Each of these has earned an opportunity to make themselves useful to the house. But you... Your hands are empty."

Auralia opened her left hand, which held a strand of thread, the remainder of the string she had spun from the feather of that magnificent bird. The strand was such a deep, deep red...darker than blood, brighter than ruby.

This was the filament that fulfilled her quest, the key to the riddle of her work. She thought of the ale boy standing somewhere in the mass behind her, of how he loved to spark bursts of color for her delight. It was enough to give her a fleeting smile. She would give him one last surprise. She closed her hand over the strand, sure she felt the flame that burnt within it.

"We'll cast you back to the reach of beastmen until you learn something of use!" one of the magistrates bellowed. "What have you to say for yourself? Have you been sent to try the patience of King Cal-marcus ker Har-baron?"

A woman's voice, a whisper, reached her ear from the crowd. She knew the voice immediately—Ellocea, a Gatherer who had been pardoned two years ago. A Gatherer known for her ever-present crutch, but even more for her way with a paintbrush. "Be careful, Auralia," she was saying. "Do what they tell you to do."

Aug-anstern laughed and addressed the people. "Someone outside the walls has sent this wretched girl to entertain us, or perhaps to disrupt our honorable ceremony. She says she wishes to speak with the king, that she has come with something to show him."

Had she said that? Auralia thrust out her chin and faced her questioner, striving to muster some confidence.

Aug-anstern was enjoying all this attention as he pranced back and forth at the top of the stairs. "We know we have the respect of fair House Bel Amica. We know that House Jenta favors us, and we have never been troubled by spies from the south. So if she's a spy, she's been sent by a fool. And there is only one man who would dare to taunt his lordship in such a fashion. Perhaps..."

The advisor's jaw snapped shut as if he were a puppet responding to the will of his controller, and another voice—a roar—filled the courtyard.

The song stopped midverse, and the sky became a deeper grey. Auralia sent a pleading glance toward the musicians. But when the next question came in a different voice, resonant with menace, she looked up into the dissimilar eyes of King Cal-marcus—one green, one gold. There was something familiar about his face, as if she had seen him when he was a young man looking down upon her from a similar distance. Had she ever seen him ride a vawn? Surely not. She had not lived enough years to see him young. Another name came to her. *Cal-raven.*

"Have you been sent?" The king's question was pointed, full of accusation and anger. "Who sent you?"

Her eyelids fluttered, beaded with new raindrops. Even as she looked out at the world, she could see it reflected upside down and distorted. The storm was breaking. The gulls yelped and wrote invisible exclamations in the air, while the vultures above them maintained their slow, patient circles. The king waited. Gossip ceased. The world went still.

She watched the birds' hypnotic spirals, felt the wind brush back her hair, and then closed her eyes as a chance ray of sunlight broke through and warmed her face. It was as though the weather lifted her arms slowly above her head to embrace the light, to praise the storm, and in doing so she shrugged the heavy earth-brown cape from her shoulders. It was time to be free of its burden. And it fell away with ease.

Her dark cover dropped like a curtain, and the sunlight caught the second cloak that she had concealed—the cloak in which every strand had known her hands; every knot had been crafted once, twice, and again until right; every line of color had been teased, touched, and tightened until it found a perfect tension that would enhance the weave entire.

Auralia reached up, cold in the wind, and pinched the end of the loose red thread between her finger and her thumb, letting the strand rise and trace the wind. Then she nimbly tucked it through a loop at the collar point and wound it thrice around a bold black button of mountain lodestone.

The color of that last thread, like a drop of blood in water, dissipated and spread, transforming the extravagant whole.

The grey of the day might have been night in view of the brightness that flared up from the Ring of Decision. All the power of springtime had arrived in an instant.

The air, ablaze, filled with color the way wine fills a glass. Ripples of shimmering hues spread in expanding circles across the faces of the storm clouds.

The birds laughed, exultant.

Trapped by the thunderstruck crowd, the ale boy could not see Auralia. He stared upward instead, watching the light as it painted the sky.

Around him, children on their parents' shoulders silently pointed toward the Ring of Decision.

The adults remained as still as the towering wooden statue of the king, which was splashed with strange colors from the fountain of light far below.

Beside him, Scharr ben Fray reached into his hood to unfix the stone disguise, uncovering his face and a fall of tears while the mask fell to the grass. "All the colors of the Expanse and more," he whispered in reverence. "Colors... colors we've never seen." As if trying to find answers, the stonemaster turned to the north wall. "What does she know that we don't?"

The colors the ale boy saw in the sky—he remembered them. He had seen them before, softly flickering behind a curtain in Auralia's caves.

More birds were gathering—streamertails, greenfeet, blustercalls, bluebreasts, and the furious vultures. They rose and fell over the platform in waves, intent, trying to snatch the colors from the air.

There were so many things the ale boy wanted to be. To be strong, so he could push his way through the people pressed together before him. To be tall. To have authority. To be king. To be next to Auralia. To be elsewhere. To be free of this horde, of this role, free of his superiors.

But in that moment he remained small and thus unable to see. He remained weak. He was an errand boy, lost in a multitude, sent and expected. He teetered on tiptoe until his feet hurt. He strained for the voices of the king and the girl. But from his position on the trodden courtyard grass he could not see any piece of the event.

What he saw instead was the wet, windblown curtain opposite the king's statue, falling against all that it concealed—a statue of the lost queen. Her outline pressed through the cloth, a ghost raised by outrage, eyes empty and wide, mouth open in a protest, an ultimatum, a cry, her hands raised in a frozen gesture declaring this event an abomination.

Children broke the silence. They charged, climbed over each other, ran pell-mell between the legs of grownups, and pushed their way to the front, toward Auralia.

The ale boy prepared to move as well. But the mage caught him and lifted him. He stood on the old man's shoulders.

He gazed across the field of hoods, hats, and helmets—all of which revealed shifting, living colors—to the row of humble Gatherers, the clearing below the birds, and there, in the Ring of Decision, a bonfire of light.

For a moment, he feared they had set a torch to Auralia's garment.

But then, he saw that the fire *was* her garment—a cloak as elaborate as a tapestry, as magnificent as wings.

The ale boy understood now; she had indeed been weighed down but not with grief. This had been the vision compelling her from the day that first thread gleamed in her hands.

The magistrates leaned back as if scorched. The Bel Amican ambassadors covered their faces.

King Cal-marcus clutched his goblet in one hand, while he reached with the other to try and break a fall. He brought the cup to his lips and swallowed all it contained, a feat that (the ale boy was certain) would have knocked flat any other man in the house.

If a crowd looks upon the sea, they all see a different mass of water, for it casts color and light in all directions. In the same way, everyone saw Auralia's colors, but each saw a different flourish. Auralia's work played all the notes an orchestra can know. And more even than that. Such vision could only have come from someone who had been Elsewhere, seen Something Other, and focused all her energy into preserving the experience in a frame.

For all present in the courtyard, what was real and possible had been transformed. The eyes of their eyes were, for a moment, open to a world larger and more beautiful than they could have imagined, to the luminous presence of every man and woman, boy and girl.

Clouds moved again across the sun, and the glow of Auralia's colors softened, like a flame drawn down into a pulsing coal.

Auralia absently loosened the binding thread and pulled it free of the cloak, closing it up in her hand.

As she did, the lights diminished, and she stood before the king still radiant with the colors of what she had made. She heard the whispers.

"Who does she fancy she is?"

"Such colors..."

"The dungeon. Bound for the dungeon."

"Just a child."

"Now them Bel Amicans will have something to say when they go home."

"There's no queen rich enough to have somethin' like that."

The children surrounding Auralia reached forward to timidly poke and prod at the colors, hoping the hues might rub off on their hands. Auralia endured their gentle nudges and tried to remember Aug-anstern's questions. Moments later the guards stepped in, driving back her admirers with the butts of their spears to clear the Ring.

The king perched at the top of the stairs, his robes hanging around him like the wings of a predator bird. For a moment, many believed he would fall.

The torment in his face suggested that he was unsure if he had suffered a terrible symptom of the drink or if the world had been truly transfigured for a few breathtaking moments.

Auralia thought of the scarecrows, of the yellow-squash king whose head she had broken, of the smoke that escaped in a sigh.

"Who told you to come and taunt the king of Abascar?" barked Auganstern, twitching at the back of the platform.

"We already know the answer," said King Cal-marcus, finding his voice at last. The wooden stairs creaked beneath his boots as he descended toward his offender. "But I want to hear you say it, little girl."

"Scharr ben Fray," whispered the Housefolk behind her. "He's talking about the exiled mage."

"Tell me, Gatherer girl, who hides like a coward and sends a child to taunt me? Confess your master's name." Cal-marcus's voice rose to a commanding volume, even as it wavered under the influence of his turbulent drink. "Did he bewitch you the way he tried to cast spells on my son?"

Auralia watched the storm of birds. She thought of Dukas and how he would have purred at the sight of so many. She wondered if his dreams looked anything like this. Had she ever seen so many in the sky at one time? They did not make a sound, nor did they fight. They only circled, waiting.

"Did your master conjure that...that reckless magic?" the king asked. Auralia could smell the hajka on his breath. "Did he send you to insult me for allowing the Proclamation of the Colors? You foolish, gullible orphan. You are a wild, reckless wretch from the wilderness. You're a joke made at Jaralaine's expense."

The king looked back at the veiled statue of his lost queen. Then he lunged and seized Auralia by the wrist, pulling her forward. She stumbled and fell on her way up the stairs to the dais. Gasps and shouts burst from the crowd.

"Look out over the people." The king's voice trembled in his attempt to suppress his temper. "You'll recognize one who doesn't belong. Point out your master. Where is he?"

One of the reedflutists timidly sounded the ceremony's theme, coaxing the others halfheartedly to join him, but an order from the king silenced them.

Braver all the time, birds swooped low above the platform.

"Where is he?"

Auralia's answer would become engraved in each listener's memory as the boldest speech ever delivered before the king. Housefolk would try to reconstruct the words, inventing many and varied distortions. The people would argue and fuss over who remembered them best. But all would agree they were glad to have been alive that day to witness such a spectacle…that is, until the events set in motion during this ceremony would come to fruition and make the people of Abascar wish they could forget.

"You know where my master is," Auralia said, looking down at the tangle of thread in her hands. "When you're sleeping, he walks through your mind. But when you're awake, you have to look to find him. Right now, he's living in the lake. But tomorrow, who can tell? He might take to the sky or the forest. He's always moving about, but he likes to hide just to see who'll come seeking." She gestured to the northern horizon.

No one said a word, but their expressions confirmed what the Housefolk were thinking. To speak of the Keeper in the presence of the king was a flagrant violation of the law.

"What a curious creature," remarked a smiling Bel Amican. "If she was sent to taunt you, King of Abascar, then what an elaborate joke this is. Let us take her back to Bel Amica."

The king turned on his heel, seething.

But the Bel Amican continued. "Take no offense, King of Abascar. We seek to preserve the laws you have designed. We will take this trouble from your courtyard. Such an impressive exhibition will be welcome in *our* house."

Auralia heard the sharp crack before she felt the sting from the back of the king's hand. Her head snapped around, and whatever the king said next was lost in the ringing of her ears. It might have been "Foolish forest girl." Or "Reckless, worthless fool."

She collapsed to her knees.

A bitter cry from across the platform, a woman's voice, urged the king on in his anger.

A young woman—the one promised to the prince—was pointing at Auralia's cloak. "Take it away from her!" The young woman came forward, barely escaping her mother's anxious grasp. Auralia noticed the impressive colors of her gown. "Colors such as those belong only to the King of Abascar. They don't belong to…to her."

"Colors don't belong to me nor to the king." Auralia bowed her head. Small drops of blood spilled from the wound where the Bel Amican hunter had clubbed her.

"The Proclamation," Stricia hissed. "King Cal-marcus, don't forget about the Proclamation."

"I know the laws of my house." The king rasped, "Sit down, Stricia kai Ark-robin, and say no more."

Aug-anstern signaled to soldiers across the courtyard. They answered, marching toward the stairs.

The king turned to receive them. "Take this wicked girl away for questioning. We shall pry these lies from her head."

"What about *that*, my lord?" Ark-robin gestured to Auralia's cloak.

"Lock it away in the Underkeep like the rest of House Abascar's colors. There it will stay…until I announce Abascar's Spring has come."

At those words, the Housefolk exchanged uneasy glances.

Then someone from the back of the crowd responded with a spiteful *"Ha!"*

This inspired a rumble of discontent, one that rose in volume and turbulence. Others raised their voices, angry and bold. The young complained, and the old shouted their resentment.

Auralia felt the firm grip of a soldier's hands on her arm. She looked into his uncertain eyes. "Be careful," she said quietly. "If a single thread of my cloak is broken, the colors will disappear."

Ark-robin nodded, awestruck, and then lifted her and slung her like a sack across his shoulder. Auralia did not struggle. She just turned her face to the pardoned Gatherers.

Krawg had pulled his hood back, and tears ran off his crooked nose and whiskered chin. He reached out his hands as if to catch her in a fall. She tried to find a way to smile, but her face was so cold, so numb.

Objections to Auralia's seizure grew loud, and Aug-anstern shuffled up behind the king. "Grudgers, my lord," he whispered. And then, losing his composure in the noise, he shoved his nose out at the crowd, spittle flying as he jeered, "All of you! Grudgers! Disloyal to the king!"

The king slashed the air to silence his advisor, but it was too late. Like a plague, agitation spread across the yard. Cal-marcus backed toward his throne. As he did, he stepped on the edge of Aug-anstern's robe, and they both tumbled to the platform.

As if on cue, the crowd became a tidal wave of protest, surging toward the dais. Their colored honor stitches would not bind them to propriety any longer. Like a creature long caged suddenly set free, they would protest the Wintering. They would not let the soldiers carry Auralia away. Her arrest was a clear condemnation of their longings. Auralia had thrown open the gate of the past and unleashed their memories of glory.

The ale boy let Scharr ben Fray set him down. He felt that rough, callused hand take hold of his chin and wrest his attention from the crisis.

"If you are a friend of Auralia, when the time comes, help her." Scharr ben Fray was shouting to be heard above the riot. "You may be the only one who can."

The boy nodded, and yet he could barely grasp a thought in his spinning head.

"Listen, boy. I must go." The mage cast a glance toward the wall. "The king thinks I had something to do with this. But this is stranger stuff than even I have seen in all my journeys and years. We'll see each other again. When we do,

I want to hear the story of all that transpired here in the wake of my departure. Pay close attention. Understand?"

With that, Scharr ben Fray staggered crookedly back into the crowd, his false stone stump protruding useless, but convincing, from his sleeve.

The ale boy felt the nightmare rush toward its conclusion.

He had to find Auralia.

He pushed forward again, squirming, trying to break through the mob.

"*Help her*," the old man had said.

But he was pinned between a tall woman's pillowy hip and a short man's sharp elbow.

The people of Abascar joined in a shout of defiance, surprised to realize they could be a mighty force. Emotion turned to action. The ale boy was caught up in their momentum, lifted off his feet, and carried forward.

Then, as quickly as he had been carried up, he fell. The mob crushed his legs, smashed his knees, bruised his back, kicked his head.

The king was shouting.

Barking dogs joined the melee, turned loose by soldiers to break up the crowd and turn their anger to fear.

There was the rattle of armor, the shouting of orders, screams.

When he awoke, he sat alone in the debris-littered square.

The riot was over. The platform was empty.

Aggressive guards, their swords held high and gleaming, their dogs snarling, were shepherding the tumultuous Housefolk into lines and herding them like cattle through the gates of the courtyard.

Above him in the clearing sky, a thousand birds were going mad, their circles broken, reeling.

15

CAL-RAVEN COMES HOME

P rince Cal-raven returned with a trophy for his father, another set of wild eyes and bared fangs to join the gallery of ferocious faces that glowered in the king's library.

Shepherds, lamenting losses almost daily, had called for the hunt, showing officers the tracks in their bloodied fields and stables. Cal-raven's troop had pursued a fangbear that was easily persuaded to hunt for meals elsewhere.

But even as his officers chased the lumbering monster away, messengers reported that the slaughter had resumed. The bear had not been the only menace murdering woollies, chumps, and grazers. A snowcave wolf, big as any bear, had come down from the mountains—an unprecedented event—and evaded all of Abascar's bear traps. Drawing his troop back, the prince concealed them in the treetops around the pastures, and Tabor Jan, Cal-raven's guardsman, brought the she-wolf down with one precise arrow and then finished her with a spear.

It might take five or six years before the shepherds restored their herds and flocks, but that did not prevent them from sacrificing a few animals for the sake of a celebratory feast within the house. The threat had been removed.

Admirers filled the avenues from the main gates to the palace, enduring the rain so they could slow the line of vawns that bore the twelve hunters. All eyes were on the prince. The Housefolk learned to recognize him, despite his best efforts at anonymity. Unlike other high-ranking officers, Cal-raven did not announce himself by leading the procession, nor did he ride a vawn marked differently from those of his officers. The Housefolk identified him by his tightly braided hair, streaked with red, and by the way he always seemed preoccupied with the sky above the house. They loved him for that dull grey cloak, for they swore he chose it to show respect for the common folk. It seemed a gesture of defiance to the laws that kept the palace bedecked in color. They took this all as a hopeful sign that someday King Cal-raven would restore what they had lost.

He deflected their praise with a generous smile, directing their cheers forward to his guardsman. The crowd's enthusiasm only intensified at his humble gesture, shouting the names of two heroes instead of one. Tabor Jan frowned and muttered, spurring his vawn to splash faster up the slick avenue.

While this welcome was flattering indeed, Cal-raven was uneasy. A strange passion fueled this feverish display, as if his return brought relief from some burden, as if he suddenly represented more than he understood.

At the palace gates, the guards were strangely gruff. The prince tried to win the waiting stablehands' attention with details of how the great wolfskin across the back of his vawn had come to be their prize. They nodded dutifully but exchanged nervous glances.

Only guards awaited them in the palace courtyard. The prince calmly noted the condition of the lawns, which looked as if they had been plowed and tilled. The platform was bare, cleared of any clues that the Rites had taken place.

After the gates closed, cheers continued outside, cast up and over the wall, reaching through the tower windows so all within would know the favorite son of House Abascar had returned.

Cal-raven left his vawn with another officer and crossed the shredded yard, shoving Tabor Jan ahead of him. He tried to laugh and ignore the solemn, stagnant cloud blanketing the palace. They moved through an archway, pushed aside heavy purple curtains, and stepped into a fragrant golden corridor lined with glowing incense bowls.

He would customarily proceed to a receiving chamber where guards would offer him a formal robe. And then he would move into the royal court, where he would find the magistrates and the king himself waiting to receive him, eager for his report.

But the prince paused as if sensing a trap and decided not to follow the path prepared for him. He turned, parted curtains that lined the wall, and revealed a dark, descending stair. Today he would leave the magistrates to mutter and fume. He directed Tabor Jan down the stair, to pass beneath the Ceremony Hall, and then through quiet corridors where the air was heavy with dust and old echoes, leading them to a tower and, at last, up to the king's most private retreat—the library.

"There's something you're not telling me," Tabor Jan muttered, gruff and uncomfortable. "First you run away from the hunt for some secret conference with a man your father has condemned. And now you're rejecting the magistrates. Are you so determined to make enemies?"

"Something's happened. The people looked ready for a coronation, not a wedding. The courtyard—"

"Practically destroyed."

"And the guards—"

"Doubled, at every gate on our way in."

"And I'm—"

"Walking so fast you're getting ahead of yourself."

"Don't—"

"Interrupt you?"

"My father's in a foul mood. That's obvious. And when he's upset, he disdains all formal company. He'll be hiding from the magistrates too."

"Sometimes I admire his judgment."

Cal-raven slung his hunting bow over his shoulder and rubbed his hands together. "He'll be here, in his cave, drinking himself into a stupor."

"And you *want* to visit him in this ugly temper?"

"The angrier he is," the prince sighed, "the more honest he is. I don't like hearing bad news when it's been sweetened and stirred by a jury of false-faced, slick-tongued magistrates. I want to hear it from my father. If we catch him while he's bitter, we'll get a detailed rant about all that took place, without any flattery or foolishness."

With that, Cal-raven jumped ahead of his friend, ignored the bewildered guards who scrambled to their feet at his approach, and knocked open the heavy black doors of the fireside library so hard that they slammed against the inside walls. This shocked the quiet chamber.

Cal-raven was not one step through the door before he shouted, "A bottle! We've freed the flocks from a she-wolf with the help of Tabor Jan's arrows. We must raise a drink in his name!"

Startled, the king's small dog, Wilfry, bounded forward like a four-legged bundle of cotton, barking in panic and dismay. He yapped and snarled in a voice that would fail to frighten a housemouse, his pink eyes bulging and his pointed ears flattened back. The other dog, the ancient woodsnout called Hagah, merely lifted his head above his mountainous shoulders, layers of rolling flesh revealing the moist black nose that dwarfed the rest of his features, but not his eyes, which remained hidden by the flabby skin. His tail, heavy as the bough of a coil tree, lifted an inch above the floor and then thudded down, a rare note of enthusiasm from the elderly hunter.

Kicking back the annoying yapper, Cal-raven walked around the massive strategy table and snatched a bejeweled cup from the mantel. "Goblets of gratitude, Father. Let's warm his belly and dull his wits. Then we can send him off to endure the tedious flattery of the magistrates while I stay here with you."

Tabor Jan turned red—the prince could see that even in the firelight. The armored giant awkwardly bowed to the shadow-clad king, who was slumped in his chair before the hearth and staring into the flames.

The door guards looked around, nervous.

The king was unmoved by his son's humor. Cal-raven knew that once again he had guaranteed a scolding, for the king would find rebellion in the very fact that the guardsman, not the prince, had been given the honor of ending the hunt.

But such a prince was Cal-raven.

Feats of strength and violence did not appeal to him, unless they came in the form of a narrative he could dazzle an audience in telling. He took pleasure in praising others and peppered his stories with gratuitous details so nothing about them would fade.

While his father charted out his future as a soldier and king, the burden of Abascar's anticipation wearied Cal-raven. He had inherited the skills of a soldier, but as he rose in rank and dexterity, his boredom with competitive pursuits increased. He demonstrated more enthusiasm for chasing fugitive birds through the palace than for hunting beastmen. And he found himself increasingly nostalgic for those childhood hours playing alone in his mother's courtyard garden. Or for those long nights listening to Scharr ben Fray's fanciful tales. After his mother's disappearance and the exile of his father's aging advisor, the prince grew increasingly distracted by the wilderness, the woods, and the weather.

At home he groaned when magistrates sought to embroil him in debates about the law or win his favor for selfish gain. Much to their chagrin, he forgot their names and titles. He was more interested in the relationships, dramas, and secrets of his servants, whose names he did remember and whose histories he could recite with surprising accuracy. He was known to stay up all night telling stories to the dusty Housefolk children who swept the corridors and rearranged the tapestries. When advisors proudly paraded their decorated daughters through the palace, he shrugged and trudged to the sparring ring, where an exercise with ambitious swordswomen quickly became a flirtatious dance.

Rumors of Cal-raven's unpredictable affections ran rampant one scandalous season when he assigned himself to assist a young mosaicist, quietly observing as she meticulously designed a mural depicting Cal-marcus's battles with forest mercenaries. For days she was his only confidante. The king quickly arranged a year of formal dinners with families who had respectable daughters of marrying age.

When he wasn't whispering with those beneath his station, Cal-raven wandered alone, drawn more to the windows than the dining halls, more to the secluded libraries than the bustling court. Occasionally he would disappear entirely, prompting rumors that he had been living and working in disguise among the Housefolk. *A trick the exiled mage once taught him*—that was the popular speculation.

And so he had come home from another hunt without any boasting of his own. He tried to turn his father's attention to the courage of his guardsman, but the king was not particularly interested in *any* kind of report. Cal-Raven began to suspect that more troubling things were afoot than he had thought.

The prince approached the silhouette of the high-backed chair. His father's hands gripped the armrests, rings sparkling in the firelight. And then the king growled, though it seemed the voice came from the bared teeth of the wyrm head mounted above the hearth. "How generous of you to allow your friend to strike the killing blow."

Wilfry, suddenly noticing that Cal-raven had not come alone, turned and threw himself at Tabor Jan, barking in increasingly high-pitched squeaks.

Holding his bow as though it were a staff, Cal-raven knelt at his father's side, studied that narrow face, and felt the last sparks of his cheer go out. "I give Tabor Jan no charity. My arrows slew nothing but a few unfortunate trees. His shot was true. Had I some measure of his stealth and cunning, we would be rivals, not friends. I need his gifts on a hunt. Let's give gratitude where it is due…*overdue*. A bottle. Something special. Surprise us. We're thirsty. We'll drink anything."

The king's lips parted to reveal clenched teeth, and when he did glance at his son, Cal-raven knew immediately that trials had pierced through that toughened hide and struck bone.

"Wilfry!"

At the king's voice, the small dog crossed the room with a yelp to land at his feet and stare adoringly up into his face, tongue lolling out from an exaggerated smile. The king kicked at him with a wool-slippered foot, but the dog dodged and returned to the spot as if oblivious to the complaint. Hagah groaned—the sound of an old man whose patience had been beaten senseless—and turned his drooping jowls toward Cal-raven with a baleful sigh.

The long dormant anger that weakened the king was suddenly awake and hungry. Cal-raven could only assume there was more hajka in his father's belly than could fit in a bottle. He immediately regretted his request for drinks, but it was too late—his father lifted one of six small pegs in the arm of his chair, each of which bore a different bell, and let a cold, lonely tone ring through the library. The chime shimmered down a long corridor behind curtains in the corner, where it would reach the ears of a waiting attendant.

Cal-raven sneezed.

"Foul weather, this." King Cal-marcus gestured, as if fighting a cloud of insects, toward the tall window at the far end of the room. "You'd do well to curtain your window tonight. The season of plagues is upon us."

"Has the weather brought back your headaches?"

"Headaches? Where would you like me to start? How about the Rites of the Privilege, which you cleverly avoided? I might not be suffering so much had you been there."

Behind the chair, Cal-raven lifted a hand to caution Tabor Jan: *Do not come closer, but do not leave just yet.*

"We did not go riding for our own amusement, Father. The rain made the hunt a miserable bore. It slowed our progress. And the forest seemed…agitated. Those storm clouds, they did not move in the same direction as the wind. They were drawn toward Abascar as if tethered to flocks of birds. It seemed almost like an enchantment."

"Bristles and bracken, boy! I exiled Scharr ben Fray so I wouldn't have to listen to such nonsense."

This was the chamber where King Cal-marcus worried. This was the chair a younger Cal-raven had come to call "the Angry Throne." He learned to stand clear of it. Many attendants bore bruises from his father's sudden turns of temper. And he was still frightened by the way the firelight sculpted misery into Cal-marcus's features.

Cal-raven faced hideous beastmen in combat without flinching, but here he could not meet his father's turbulent gaze. Perhaps this was due to his fear of the day when he would inherit the throne and all his father's challenges. Perhaps it was his fear that Abascar's Wintering had buried his father's spirit in a freeze that would never thaw and that his faint pulse of life was beginning to falter. Cal-raven had lost the sleep of a hundred nights searching for a cure, hoping to chase off the memories that assailed Cal-marcus's heart. Many a time he had kept his father company, reading to him from the scrolls, but nothing from the library's cobwebbed shelves could fill the void in the king's empty heart.

"I am sorry I was not here to stand beside you. But that is not what boils your broth. Something has got its claws into you. I propose we wait until tomorrow to tell the tale of Tabor Jan's arrow."

Cal-raven had hoped to end the day by exaggerating tales of Tabor Jan's brilliance before admiring palace ladies. But he could not pursue such leisure now, not while his father was drowning in drink and in woe. He stood, carried his bow to the doorway, set it on a rack between two tapestries, and silently, with a furrowed brow of apology, dismissed Tabor Jan, wishing he could offer an explanation for the darkness here.

He knew his friend would be patient. The king's refusal to recognize the guardsman's accomplishment would soon fade. Tomorrow Cal-marcus ker Harbaron would rise ready to praise Tabor Jan and celebrate the hunt. But the guardsman would already be back on a wide patrol, preferring to move on rather than stand around and ruminate on past deeds.

As Tabor Jan retreated, the guards pulled the doors closed, and Cal-raven took a long, deep breath. He set a compassionate hand on his father's hard shoulder, then sat on the grand rug before the blazing arch of the fireplace. "It looks bad, this fever you're suffering. The Bel Amicans—have they given you some trouble?"

"I'm finished with them." The king, reaching down to massage the folds of Hagah's heavy head, seemed somewhat relieved by the change of subject. "These Bel Amican ambassadors—they call themselves 'seers'—are an untrustworthy sort. Do they really speak for the queen of House Bel Amica? Or are they planting the seeds of their own strategies? I fear Queen Thesere is just a plaything for meddling puppeteers. They flatter her, and her head swells too large for the crown, crushing her judgment. They are relentless bargainers. Everything is for sale, the way they look at things. And they have this ridiculous notion that we will help them build another fortress on the coast of some new land."

"You refused."

"I sent those ambassadors back empty-handed. I see no advantage in helping them. If Bel Amicans occupy a new kingdom in the islands, how will we know what they're up to? Must we double our efforts in training spies? Must we buy the loyalty of boatmen? They think they can put our fears at ease if they invite us to help. But I do not trust them."

"There was a time when you accepted Bel Amican bargains," said Cal-raven. "You even defended Queen Thesere against Mother's suspicions."

"And now your mother is gone. There are only two ways about it—either we were so vulnerable that our queen was stolen from us, or we were so disappointing that she left. Whichever is true, we are a joke to the rest of the world. Others are taking an interest now, trying to learn what it would cost to claim all that we've built. No amount of flattery can hide the Bel Amicans' desire for conquest. They would appear generous even as they invade, as though they could walk through *our* gates and offer *us* hospitality in our own rooms." He withdrew his hand from the hound's head and pounded a fist on the arm of his chair. "They should not have seen what they saw yesterday."

Cal-raven's pulse quickened. "What did the Bel Amicans see?"

King Cal-marcus rose, snatched a poker from the hearth, and paced a circle around his library throne, tapping its sooty tip on the floor while his worshipful white pet followed dutifully behind. "I...I worry when I hear reports that the only heir of Abascar has abandoned his troops to wander through the woods—especially as the forest is becoming more and more dangerous."

"I was not out for a stroll, Father. The beastmen are becoming more dangerous, yes. But if I am not attentive to the wild, investigating their schemes, how will I defend us against them?"

"I'm not talking about beastmen. There are dangerous men in the wild. Men who know our secrets. Men who seek to weaken us." He turned and pointed the poker at his son. "Men who lure my son into the open and then plant seeds of deceit in his mind."

Ah. Cal-raven felt an old, familiar anger stir within him. "You're talking about Scharr ben Fray." His father must have heard reports that the mage had appeared beside him at the dig. "You're talking about the good man who came to visit our troubled dig and cleared away the blacklode that could have cost us many days and resources. You're talking about *that* kind of threat to Abascar?"

Cal-marcus let the poker drop to the hearth, and Wilfry snarled at it and tried to drag it away.

The king fell back into his chair. "How far will that resentful old fool go for revenge? With what forces in the forest might he conspire?"

"Conspire?" It was all Cal-raven could do not to choke. "Revenge? Will a ghost you've conjured from worry and guilt distract you from real danger? The beastmen grow stronger every day. Their decline is over. They are rising again."

Cal-raven described the signs he had seen—marks of ambush, bloodshed, and the troubling image of bootprints alongside beastman scuffs. The thought of merchants, Gatherers, and Abascar traders being ambushed and dragged away alive to the Cent Regus dens—this should recalibrate the compass in his father's fractured heart. "I can show you these signs. And I can show you how we can take back the woods around House Abascar. But we must convince our merchants to be more vigilant. We will need trackers and rangers and, yes...mages too. If anyone hates the Cent Regus menace with the same passion as you and I, it is our old friend Scharr ben Fray."

Cal-raven stood, restless now, and watched his shadow stretch before him, leading him to the window. He was tempted to climb out. No, he could not surrender the evening, not like this. He was his father's son, and sleep would not come to either if he left these wounds open.

As he stepped to the history shelves, Cal-raven heard Hagah snuffle along behind him, surely picking up traces from the last several days of wilderness hunting. The poor old hound's senses were not what they had been in the days when he had run alongside King Cal-marcus's vawn and brought down merce- naries and beastmen. And yet he was still intent on solving the mysteries of unfamiliar scents.

The prince shuffled through the shelved scrolls, rubbed dust between his thorn-scraped palms. *Calm yourself. Hold back. Do not add fuel to this fire.* He drew in slow breaths, waiting until he could count a slackened pulse before he spoke again, just as Scharr ben Fray had taught him to do so many years ago.

"We are not ready," the king finally sighed. "We must build up our forces within the walls and prepare for a siege. It may come from the beastmen. But I am bracing for Bel Amica. And what of House Jenta, so silent and watchful? Who knows when they might advance and what shape such a siege might take? Scharr ben Fray was once one of them. Perhaps he is their spy."

"Who is feeding you these lies? Does this have something to do with what happened at the Rites?"

The king rang the bell again and cursed. "Hagah!" he shouted at the old hunting dog. "Fetch the attendant."

Hagah turned and looked at his old master, and his rump slowly thumped to the floor in front of the window.

"Go!" The king insisted, pointing at the corner where the curtains con- cealed the passage. "Fetch the attendant."

Wilfry looked at the king, yapped, and shoved his way under the curtain to bound away down the corridor.

"You old fool, Hagah," the king complained.

The hunting hound sighed again, extended his forepaws, and brought his chin down to the floor, his nose snuffling at Cal-raven's boots with interest.

"I will tell you what happened," the king finally conceded. "And since you speak of Scharr ben Fray's *concern,* I will match your evidence with my own. At the Rites of the Privilege, I was defied by a girl. A *Gatherer.*" He spat out the word like a scrap of gristle.

"Was she a grudger? Was she there to stir up a protest?"

"I don't think that was her motive, although it's certainly what she achieved. And, yes, the grudgers dropped their guises and started a riot. If we had arrested them all, we'd have to dig another dungeon. But no, this one…she has her own purposes. We don't have any record of her origins. But the Gatherers clearly adore her. There was one, a thief, Krawg—I granted him the pardon he has sought for many years. He is ailing and probably won't last another winter in the wild. But, *kramm* his spiteful heart, he stood up in her defense. I threw him back to the wilderness."

Cal-raven gazed out toward the distant wall and the secretive, moon-dusted woods. "Abascar's rejection has given them cause to grow their own society. They may be poor, but the Gatherers live freely, and some are even happy and well-behaved." He fought off another sneeze. "They feed us, meat to fruit, and yet you talk of them as if they spend their time relieving themselves on your tapestries. Why let a troublemaker stir you into this…this rage?"

"I am angry because of what she brought into our midst. She claims to have made it, this cloak she wore." The king made a tent with his fingers and stared into it, trapping the memory. "I do not believe it. I cannot believe it."

Cal-raven approached his father as he had when he was a boy, eager for fireside tales. He lay down beside the chair and stared at the image painted across the glass of the ceiling dome—a silhouette of the first king in the Expanse, Tammos Raak, from whom the ruling lineage of all four houses had branched.

The king grew quiet, eyes misty, and said in a strangely reverent tone, "It is magnificent."

"The cloak?"

"A cloak. A tapestry. A banner…something splendorous. All the colors of the realm and colors no one has ever seen. As vivid as a garden in bloom. I don't know much about the weaver's art, but…"

"Where is she now?" Cal-raven asked, caught off guard by tremors of memory. A girl, standing in a clearing, clad in a vibrant cloak of leaves. "I want to see this thing she made."

The king swatted at the air as if annoyed by a botherfly. "The cloak? It is a flagrant insult to our laws. She offended me in front of the magistrates, the guests, and the Housefolk!"

"It's only been law for twenty years." Cal-raven could not disguise the sadness in his voice. "I can remember when the Housefolk could fill the courtyard with color."

"I made a proclamation for the good of House Abascar!" The king was not speaking to Cal-raven, but to himself, or to whatever phantoms had been conjured by the drink. "Gah...where is that bottle?"

The prince bowed his head. "You say I am too...too sentimental. But what do you expect? We rule a colorless house and a people who await a day they suspect may never come."

"Abascar's Spring." The words were bitter in the king's mouth. "The very idea has made the Housefolk greedy. We have not yet prepared enough to repay them. And it's too late to turn back now. Treasures are scattered, woven into the textures of this palace. We cannot give back what we took away, or the house will be seized by a fever of selfishness. Remember what happened the last time one of the great houses was possessed by greed. Its people turned beastly and became a waking nightmare." The king rose and approached the dark, curtained corner. "We must be patient. When the River Throanscall flows through our house, we will have a new avenue of industry that can lift us up from where we have fallen."

Your last, desperate attempt to appease your people. Cal-raven swallowed his ready retort.

"Where is my drink?" the king roared and stood still facing the corner. Then he turned and gasped, as if frightened by a spook. It was only his image in the moon-shaped wall mirror. "We must defend our laws," he said to his haggard reflection. "If I surrender to the grudgers' demands and announce Abascar's Spring with no way to deliver it, I am declaring that my own Proclamation was a failure. What more can I do to show the world House Abascar's weakness? Yesterday we revealed too much."

"And where have you taken this disturber of the peace?"

"I have locked it away in the Underkeep. Our weavers will study it and learn...learn what it is made of."

"I wasn't talking about the cloak. The Gatherer, father...I would have thought you had thrown her back to the forest."

"She has been...temporarily arrested." The king pulled back the curtain as if he might hunt down the absent attendant. "Have we been compromised?" he whispered. "Are we vulnerable? My attendant does not answer."

"You've arrested her?" Cal-raven laughed incredulously. "Father, a suspension, maybe. Cast her back to the Gatherers, yes. But...the dungeon?"

Cal-marcus stormed back into the firelight, glowering down at his son. "Scharr ben Fray sent her as a taunt. The Bel Amican governors *laughed* at me, prince of House Abascar."

"That's impossible."

"I asked her, in front of all, who is your master? Who sent you to provoke me? I expected her to name that meddling mage. But he anticipated this. He convinced her to tell me that she was sent here by the Keeper. *The Keeper!* Now, tell me, oh sentimental apprentice of superstitious men, whose influence do you sense there?"

Cal-raven sat up, but he refused to rise and meet his father's challenge. His gaze strayed to the shadow cast by his father's chair, a wavering darkness like a sinister beast lurking on the edge of the firelight.

"That nonsense drove your mother to her wit's end, Cal-raven. Notions of the Keeper unsettled us all when we were young. Most of us learn to drive them away. But for your mother, they persisted as nightmares. Scharr ben Fray encouraged such delusions because he wanted to make us feel vulnerable and small. It's easier to manipulate people if they're living in fear. And when this wretch stood before me and declared she had been sent... Yes, she is a danger, and delusional as well."

"And so am I." The prince grappled to unfasten the straps of his muddied boots.

"Close your mouth!" snarled the king. "You are a bored, lazy, overgrown adolescent who would sooner heed a fool than his own father. Now the name *Auralia* is on everybody's lips, for she has made them anxious to be released from the restrictions, to revel in whatever expressions they please. I will hold her captive until we bait that traitor out of hiding. I will root out the grudgers. I will make my people loyal. And then, when the siege comes…however it comes…they will find us unbreakable and firm."

A fireplace log burst in two and crumbled into the coals, deep blue and red climbing the orange bricks and the sooty chimney. Shadows shifted around the room. For a moment it seemed to Cal-raven that a ghost passed between him and the fire, moving toward the window. As he tried to follow its progress, the vaporous outline faded, a wisp of wayward smoke.

"Ark-robin had to force the people from the courtyard. They should have gone back to their homes raving about your Promised, who was welcomed so warmly. Instead, they went away raving about a Gatherer girl. Such a clever taunt it was. We will recapture their attention on the wedding day, winning them with feasts and festivities." The king sighed. "Oh, you should have seen her, Cal-raven. Ark-robin's daughter is certainly eager to spend time in the palace." He made his best attempt to laugh, which triggered a fit of coughing. "She certainly revels in her good fortune. Prepare yourself for an enthusiastic bride. I have given her permission to wear a seven-colored gown. Knowing your opinion of my law, I thought that would please you."

Cal-raven kicked off his mud-caked boots so that they landed near the glow of the fire. "I have forgotten her name."

"How can you forget? What is wrong with you? I chose the daughter of Abascar's most faithful, decorated soldier. A woman of extravagant beauty and a passion for our laws. Stricia will be a leader, and she will appreciate her freedoms."

"Will *Stricia* walk in the woods or just entertain herself in the tower?"

"You should be glad she prefers the palace to the wild. The Cragavar woods had a hold on your mother, and she could never tear herself free. Even when she was queen, she had to wander. My father was right to warn me, and that's why I'm cautioning you. Stricia loves House Abascar, and she will uphold our laws. She will not take risks in the forest. And she will not run away."

"Mother loved her gardens because they were all that was left to her of the wild. I've told you this before. The palace made her lonely. It made her desperate and selfish." Cal-raven took out his dagger and scraped it against a brick on the hearth. "It's just as Scharr ben Fray believed—Mother slipped back into the behavior of a petulant merchant girl, and that jealousy...it possessed her. She did what any merchant girl would do when granted power and opportunity. She bargained. She bought herself a wilderness of riches, took them right out from under the Housefolk, and you fell for it."

"She is dead, Cal-raven," the king said, the deep freeze returning to his voice. "I've found a wife for you whom you will never have to mourn, who may live to bury you. And she will honor your memory and raise children to carry on our legacy."

You're trying to correct your mistakes by making my choices for me. Cal-raven stalked away from the chair, leaving Cal-marcus to scowl into the darkening ashes. "If my queen is going to be ignorant of the world outside these walls, then I will need an advisor who understands that the world is bigger than Abascar. Scharr ben Fray will be my—"

The king lifted something from the table and cast it across the floor. It broke into two pieces at Cal-raven's feet. A sculpture: an arm and a disfigured hand.

"What's this?"

"It was in the courtyard. It was part of the disguise that helped your blameless, law-abiding teacher trespass at our ceremony and escape our grasp."

Cal-raven knelt down to touch the cold, cracked hand. He felt a chill travel from his chest down the length of his arm. And then, that intensifying of feeling as the power the mage had taught him seduced the stone into surrender. He gave the hand a proper shape—an open palm.

The effort exhausted him. He rose to his feet with his head pounding. "I think...I think I've caught a fever, Father." He pressed his forearm to his brow and found it dry and hot.

In a triumphant explosion of yammering, Wilfry returned, running in circles around the king's chair and standing on his hind legs to dance for Cal-marcus's attention. A few paces behind, a small boy in a grey cap stepped trembling through the curtains. "My lord, I've been sent with the bottle you requested."

"Where have you been?" the king roared, grabbing up the fireplace poker again and waving it as he advanced upon the boy. "And where is my attendant?"

"Apologies, my lord," the boy whispered, bowing low and holding up the bottle. "Your attendant was harmed in the courtyard riot. No one noticed his post was empty until I found Wilfry running around in the kitchen. I will take up the post for the night. I brought you some new goblets." The ale boy cast a glance to Cal-raven. "For you both."

"Never mind the goblets," snarled the king. "The bottle will do."

Cal-raven pulled back one of the tapestries and pushed through a curtained door, all thoughts of raising cups in celebration left behind.

"Hagah, stay," said the king intently. "Hagah...*stay!*"

But the dog was already through the curtains, grumbling as if tracking something, nails tapping and scraping along the marbled floor. Cal-raven did not send him back.

As he moved down the corridor and up a winding stair, he lost all sense of time and space. His thoughts crumbled into each other like dying embers— wolves, cheers, whispers, flames, a hand of stone, a rumor of colors.

Back in his chamber, he watched Hagah amble to the windowsill, rest his chin there, and draw in deep breaths of the outside air. He fell into the blankets before an expansive window, still in his hunting garb.

The rulers of Abascar slept, their half dreams taking place in far separate worlds.

16

INQUISITORS

A muffled cannonade of vawn footfalls. Shouts of the king's errand-runners. The Early Morning Verse. The snap, creak, and jostle of market carts being assembled along the road.

These sounds clattered and echoed down to the dungeons, reminding the prisoners that the world went on undeterred without them.

Some captives were awake, stinging from the whiplash of their dreams, remembering deeds that had sent them to these small rooms of rock, reek, and reprimand. One by one they crawled to their barred cell doors in hope that something about the dreary scene would have changed—a freshly woven spider web, a new resident cursing in a cell.

In whispers, they passed along gossip as quietly as an underground stream. The prince was ill. His wolf hunt had been rainy and cold. A week of wedding preparations was postponed. The king's troops were interrogating Housefolk to find the masterminds of a grudger rebellion.

One by one they noticed the colors, the mysterious glow of a cell midway down the long corridor.

It was seven days ago they first heard the crying from that cell—a voice so young their hearts, though stony and cold, broke at the sound of it.

"She is bait," the guards had told them. "Bait for the exiled mage. He'll come and try to take her. And should you sound the alarm in time, you will be rewarded."

They tried to speak with the prisoner, but she had not shown her face.

They imagined the faces of past lovers, sisters, or mothers and believed her delicate and beautiful. While they would often grouse to one another that they had been framed for their crimes or complain about how justice had failed, in the presence of the young girl, as witnesses to her unwarranted punishment, they could not muster claims of their own innocence. Her cries were born of purest grief, not of indignation, contempt, or physical injury. Her voice was hollow with loss, without a hint of rage or shame. The world had gone wrong.

Mesmerized by the mysterious colors, they leaned against their bars and gazed into the glow as if sleeping in a field under the stars. Some compared the lights to an unsettling display called the Northern Lumination, when the night skies beyond the Forbidding Wall seemed splashed with vivid paint. It was a marvel thought by some to be the work of sorcery. But for most, the colors reminded them of times before the Proclamation.

Soon the river of whispers began to quietly speak her name—*Auralia, Auralia, Auralia, Gatherer girl who defied the king*—but she remained just out of reach.

Auralia could not distinguish the whispers from the trickles of water running along the walls or from the distracting itch of noise beyond the distant gate. She listened instead to the echoes of life proceeding as usual in the city and beyond that even in the Gatherers' camps. She longed for the sound of wind in trees, but no wind would ever lose its way so badly as to seep into these deep passages.

Outside the walls of Abascar, Auralia had survived by the sharpening of her senses, eyes attuned to the burnished gold of an apple among yellow leaves; nose keen for the rich, heavy spice that rises when walking on a bed of thyme; ears striving to recognize bats by their midnight chatter.

Here in the cell, she recalled the smell of a fallen tree near her cave, the one diggerbugs had ruined, rotten and soft. She was weary from the malodorous air, and her throat was raw and burning.

Silverblue lanternlight drifted stale and cold from the iron gate down the dungeon stairs, illuminating the edges of her dark corridor. These cells, shrouded in steam, were like the caves of the sleeping fangbears in winter, misty with the faint heat of bodies curled into cramped spaces. Those in bondage were kept out of the light's reach and revealed their presence by the occasional scrape of cold steel chains, link against link. Sometimes they would crawl to the bars and squint at her—haunted faces lined with longing. She was often awakened by their fits of coughing and obscenity. Occasionally one hummed the opening notes of a tune, but then all resolve failed, and silence returned, more unbearable than before. That was the worst of it...when someone tried to sing.

Weariness plunged her into half consciousness, cold water too shallow for drowning. She was out of place, left in this puddled stone box with only the cloak of her colors.

The cloak. It lay before her too vibrant to ignore, and yet it was a torment. It was not meant for this place. It was meant to shine, for everyone to see.

It had happened so fast. Not the way she had hoped.

The echoes of the king's ultimatum haunted her sleep. "Orphan! Outcast! Woods-girl! Runt! You would taunt me by appearing disguised as my lost queen? You have no place in such extravagance. Disown it. Surrender it to us willingly, and pledge yourself to the glorification of Abascar. Give it up to us to be unraveled and studied. Then you can walk free!"

They left her. No one took the cloak, although they all had in their own ways betrayed a secret desire.

At first she was surprised. But every time she thought of daylight or release, Cal-marcus's challenge returned to her with piercing clarity. The king's pride was wounded too deeply, his authority tested before his people. She could have offered him his dreams, and he would have refused them to avoid the appearance of weakness, to escape a confession that there were things beyond the wall worth having, things he could not control.

Auralia's journey from the ceremony to the cell was a short one.

In a locked, bare-walled room, she had climbed onto one of two wooden stools at a round, stone table. She was careful to keep the luminescent bundle from trailing across the filth, and she pulled her feet up and away from red smudges on the floor. There were fingerprints in those crimson scribbles. The heavy shackles, anchored to the wall with chains, were too large to bind her tiny wrists. But she felt shackled all the same, for this room was so small, its ceiling so low, without windows or views or decoration.

This would be where Abascar would assert its control and test her.

Casting the cloak across the table, she examined it for tears or snags. As if on cue, the door burst open, and a woman entered, grey as the mantle she wore. Her fading hair, pinned high, almost grazed the ceiling. She waved her hands in protest, then snatched the cloak as if it were a soiled rag and cast it into the corner.

"What a fragile, feeble weave you've made. Take a tug at this." Her sleeve was thick and woolen. "Simple, tough. That's what Housefolk wear. Useful for all manner of work. What could you find in the wild that will last as long as this?"

Auralia cocked her head like a curious bird. "Bones, I s'pose."

With a scowl, this towering woman closed the door, and Auralia heard a heavy wooden beam slam into the latch. She counted the corners of the room nervously. "Such a small space," she said to the woman. "Makes people seem enormous. In the woods, everybody's properly small."

The woman seated herself across from Auralia and began her tirade, grasping the edges of the table as though she might lift it and slam it down. Auralia sat with head bowed, chin barely above the table's edge, hands clasped tightly in her lap.

The questions stung like slaps. Years had weathered the woman's voice. She sounded like an old huskbird, raspy and rude, and the sounds reverberated in the closed room.

There were no surprises in the questioning. No, Auralia answered, she did not believe the people should rise up in violence against the king.

No, she had not been sent by an angry mage.

No, she knew nothing more of her beginnings than the Gatherers could tell of Krawg and Warney's discovery by the river.

No, she did not recognize the likeness of an old man sculpted in clay—she had never seen him in the wild.

No, she had never been to Bel Amica, and, no, she had never been offered wealth or treasure, nor had she been threatened or commanded.

Tell them how to find her caves? She could not explain it. There was no map. She only knew how to find them by going there.

When the old woman rose and announced that this confirmed her worst fears about the Gatherer children—that they were indeed no more than insolent liars—Auralia thought it was finished, and she would be cast out of Abascar.

But perhaps the trials had only begun?

When the beam slammed down to bar the door again, a man dressed in the bland greens of a Gatherer put his elbows on the table, rested his scruffy chin in his callused hands, and smiled as if to put her at ease.

"They needn't bar the door," Auralia sighed. "It's too heavy for me to budge. And I wouldn't know where to run."

The man launched into a practiced speech, a story about his days as a Gatherer, how he had earned his way into the house. He'd deserved to be left for the beastmen, and yet King Cal-marcus, in his mercy, had granted him another chance.

Auralia knew that these rags and rough vernacular were a charade. And when she asked him what his offense had been, his memory faltered, and he fumbled as if searching for a missing page. She asked him which camp had been his home, and he shrugged and said they were all the same. She would not meet his pompous, leering, lying eyes.

"Them colors you done wove together, they'd make a fabulous flag for the king. Take a look at this—what if you and me, we took a bad situation and turned it to good?" He pulled a fold of golden cloth from his pocket and held it high like a prize. "This here's a patch marked with a rune, a symbol representing King Cal-marcus ker Har-baron's royal line. Try stitchin' this patch, why don't you, in the center of your weaving?"

Auralia laughed, thinking this was a joke. "It's finished. It's done. There's no more stitching to do. And it doesn't belong to the king. It's not about the king." She lifted the cloak, spread it out like a banner, and draped it over the shackle pegs pinned to the wall. Standing before it, she was entranced anew, and the red thread was restless in her hand. She longed to unleash its glory again.

"What does it mean then? That thing you've made." The impostor crumpled his patch, which suddenly seemed so flimsy and plain. "What is it for?"

Auralia squinted into the colors and shrugged. "Can't say what it means. It's not a riddle. It's not somethin' you solve. It's more like a window. Look through it for a while."

This was not the answer the impostor wanted. He smacked the patch down on the table again. "This is the king's rune. It must be marked on any approved work of color. As you can see, it's rather dull. But you could change it. Make it shine, like the colors you've put in the cloak."

"It doesn't have shine in it," she explained with a sigh. "It's just a gold square, and no special gold. It's got no surprise. It's got no problem. It's just a stamp. Anybody could make another one just like it."

"There are many others, on the flags and the banners. It's the sign of his approval. It's the sign that something belongs to Abascar." He nodded to her cloak. "Like what you've brought."

"It's not for him to own," she said, exasperated and weary. "It's for him to *see.*" She picked up the patch. "Look at this. Nothing to wonder about. Nothing alive." She tugged at its corners. "I could pull it apart. We could tangle the threads with others, and then it might become something to look at."

He grabbed the patch, muttered something about having been warned, and banged at the door until the beam was lifted.

No one explained. No one apologized. Not the Housefolk, the officers, or the magistrates who paid her visits. Instead they pinched and poked her skin, tugged and scrutinized her silverbrown hair, emptied her pockets of stones and shells and balls of yarn. They dug into her head, hunting for stories or revelations she did not have to offer.

One was obviously chosen for her motherly persuasiveness. She spoke sweetly, as if Auralia might answer to such a tone and be fooled into surrendering her work to the king.

Auralia stared into the colors of the cloak, watched the way the tremulous lanternlight sent fiery gleams rippling across it, and she strained to catch the perfumes of the threads, some scent of the woods.

In a comforting voice the motherly questioner asked if Auralia knew the tale of Queen Jaralaine. Wild things took root in her garden, she explained, barbs and poison thorns. The queen's mind was distorted, and her madness sent her ravenous into the woods. Auralia said the Gatherers' tales of Jaralaine were quite different. . .that she had gone mad from her confinement, returning to die in the wild she had once known.

"Confinement? This is safety, unless you refuse to surrender what you have done and said. The magistrates want to send you to jail. I've heard that the jailer. . ." The woman stopped short of saying his name or what he would do.

Auralia was not listening. She was watching the woman's hands as they strayed across the textures of the cloak, which glittered like jewels at the bottom of a clear pond.

"How do you make new colors? Show me how it's done."

"Like I keep sayin'," Auralia laughed, incredulous, "I didn't make nothin' that's new. I *found* the colors. They're everywhere."

"How, then, did you find them?"

"By accident, mostly. I'd be looking for the Keeper, and I'd come across something new. A bird. A stone. Wildflowers with roots trailing in a hidden stream. Sometimes, you don't see a color until you've looked at something a long time, and then you see it's been there all along. After that you see it everywhere." She took the woman's hands, pointing to a bold blue vein. "See? See how much is in your hands?" Auralia's spirits rose as her thoughts returned her to the forest.

The woman folded her hand and drew it away. "We can show you all the treasure of Abascar, Auralia," she said, returning to her orders. "You can use any colors you like from wonders in the Underkeep, if you pledge yourself to craft what Cal-marcus requests. You'll be so much happier here with the Housefolk, where the wilderness can't corrupt you. You…" She stopped, a curious new question in her face.

"I know. You can smell the forest, can't you?"

She pulled the colors to her face, caressed her cheek. "Fernblossom. The river. Herbs. Wild honey. And something darker here. This. You wouldn't, per-haps, let me have this patch…just the smallest piece…would you?" She spoke with a hint of mischief. "Of course you mustn't tell anyone. It would just be a secret between you and me."

Auralia answered, "You're not the first to ask me that." She reached into her pockets, drew out a bundle of golden strands. "You can take these threads. Something to help you remember."

The woman held the threads up to the lanternlight. "Beautiful. Like autumn. Like honey. What are they?"

"I made them from long and bristly hair I pulled from a beastman's mane while he was sleeping."

The woman flung the threads aside and choked and staggered backward, her face purpling with revulsion and rage. "Insolence!" She hissed through clenched teeth, "You've touched an abomination!" She gestured to the tapestry. "Are there…are there curses and poisons woven here too?" She wiped her hand on the edge of her cloak, shuddering as if stained with something vile. "Now I see how reckless you are. Nothing good can come from wandering beyond the lands Abascar has tamed. A purging of poisons, that's what you need." She leaned against the door. "You touched my hand. What have you done to me?" She scratched at her wrist. "The jailer…he'll beat the darkness from you."

Alone again, Auralia watched the lanterns dim, their oil burning low. The air grew stale and cold. Was this what it was like for the blind Bel Amican woman?

Then the last inquisitor arrived. She was a servant girl, much younger than Auralia, with gaps between her teeth and carrot red hair under a grey hood. She peered warily at Auralia in the darkening room, as though sent to comfort someone diseased or disfigured. She pulled something from the fold of her cloak and set it on the floor—a white-furred house cat, which took to sniffing at the floor's dark smudges and creeping about in the corners.

"That's Ghosty," she said proudly. "You could have a kitty too if you came to live with us."

"I live out by the lake," said Auralia sadly. "I play with cats all the time. Big cats and little cats. They're everywhere. You should come and visit."

Jealousy flickered in the girl's green eyes. She spoke mechanically, pacing through the words she had rehearsed to find her way back to her assignment.

"See my honor stitches?" The girl pointed to braided ribbons of blue, orange, and green pinned to the shoulder of her ash grey cloak. "I got 'em 'cause I learned the right answers to all the questions that there are. I can teach you."

"All the questions?" Auralia laughed. "You don't believe that, do you?"

"What questions do you have? If I don't know the answer, I know who does."

Auralia smiled suspiciously. "Okay. This sounds like a game. What are the Northchildren, and why do they lurk in the shadows? And the Keeper? Where does he come from, and why is he here?"

"Easy," the child said sternly. "There's no such thing as Northchildren. They're just a lie made up to scare folks. And there's no such thing as the Keeper. It's just a bad dream that'll go away when I grow big like my mum."

Auralia's smile faded. The room was growing strangely warm. "Where did Abascar come from?"

"We came down from the mountains to the north a long, long time ago to get away from the darkness and the storms. We got stronger and smarter. And now we're the envy of the land."

"Do you even know what *envy* means?"

The little girl blinked. "Umm. I suppose it means we're leaders. Or the best. Or the smartest…or something."

"It's what they told you to say."

"It means Abascar's the best house in the Expanse. We're safe from the badness beyond these walls." As she spoke, her eyes strayed to the cloak spread across the table. "These colors…they're against the rules."

The child's words, an empty chant, made Auralia recoil. A sudden fear swept over her, and she climbed off the stool, dragging the cape toward the questioner as if to save her from a chill. "Nobody owns the colors. Can't you see? They're free. They're what trees do. They're what water and sky do. Fields. Hills. Mountains. No matter how much you give them away, there'll always be more."

The house cat jumped onto the sliding cloth and buried his nose in the folds of the colors, his resonant purr vibrating from whiskers and fur.

"It's better to keep treasure locked away, so no one gets jealous," the child said, searching her library of answers. "Better to put them away, where they'll be guarded and safe."

"I want to go back *outside* the walls!" Auralia cried.

"But it's scary there, Auralia." The dutiful girl walked slowly around the table, ignoring the stains beneath her bare feet, reaching for Auralia with her small, pale hand. "Stay here. Be safe. Safe from the monsters in the woods."

"I've seen the monsters in the woods," Auralia whispered. "It's you that scares me."

This took the girl by surprise. "You've…*seen* the monsters in the woods? But they'd have killed you."

Auralia smiled. "Yes. And much more besides." She lifted a corner of her radiant weave. "You see these threads? They're applecat whiskers. And these here dark strands? Vulture feathers. Bats have fur this color. And I even have hair from a beastman's mane. Look at the goldness. Look at the shine. This pearly white, it's grasshopper blood, and this intricate glisten, their wings."

Curious, the child touched a spread of silky blue. "And this?"

"I call it Evening Lakewater. The color of waves when the sun's just gone down. It's made from peacock feathers."

A few minutes later impatient guards burst in. Ghosty, who had settled on Auralia's shoulder, vanished out the door. The servant girl—Auralia had coaxed out her name, *Jarlet*—realized she had strayed from her task. She began to shake and cry, and the guards had to pry Auralia's colors from the little girl's hands. "I want one!" she ranted as they pulled her away. "I want to have one for my own. Auralia, make one for me!"

Another guard grabbed Auralia by the hair. She clutched the colors to her and was hauled out of the room, her face contorted as hair ripped from her scalp. She stumbled and found her feet, and they let her walk ahead of them up the corridor.

Auralia draped the weave over her head like a hood. She walked not like a punished child, but like a weary queen, victorious when tested, her promises kept, bringing light unspoiled wherever she walked.

Even to the dungeons.

Auralia had always loved how a cave could echo, how tunnels could whisper on their way into mystery. She could sit for hours in her caves and stare out at the world, pretending she was hiding in the Keeper's eye. She loved the exhilaration of bursting into the open in the morning as if being born anew.

But this cell was not like any of her caves. It was cramped, wet, and crooked, with walls of rugged earth. A door of heavy iron bars drew stark lines across the pale light, and there was no view but the filthy corridor and more bars across the passage with a tormented shadow beyond.

Her hours of waiting had begun, and Auralia lost track of day and night. When she closed her eyes, the lifeless blue of the prison transformed into the royal blue bud of a queen's cup surrounded by broad green leaves. She knew that where queen's cup grew, she would also find yellow ankle bushes, and among those bushes she would see white-winged grasshoppers that traveled in grand triangular formations like little herds of deer, bounding and soaring. And where there were grasshoppers, she was sure to find black ravens and red lynx that pursued and ate them.

The colors and memories of her wild home folded around her in the cloak, and she slept, a hot ember in a cold sea.

17

RADEGAN'S GAMBLE

Shards of marrowwood shot past Radegan's head as the ax found its mark. Releasing the haft, he stepped back, stared at the cleanly split stump, and smiled. This afternoon's work, done in secret, had earned him a stack of firewood that would bring a good price in trade among the Gatherers.

Marrowwood burnt hotter and lasted longer than any other fuel. Marrowwood trees rarely grew in this part of the forest, and when they did, the king's woodcutters guarded them and sparingly cut branches for the palace fireplaces. When Radegan had found this tree—its ancient boughs unmoving in the wind, deep red leaves filtering sunlight to drench the glade in purple—he'd vowed to make it his own.

With malicious delight, he tossed a rude gesture back toward House Abascar. This woodpile was nothing compared to his famous Underkeep robberies, but nevertheless, he was pleased to get away with something like this behind the duty officers' backs.

Inside he had been "The Fox," a masked visitor to Housefolk, trading everything from royal ale and desserts to garments, lamps, jewelry, and even pipes. That was, until he had been snared by Captain Ark-robin himself. The strategist had cleverly and famously captured him in an actual fox trap, just so he could gloat in the arrest. That blasted girl Stricia had lured him to the snare with kisses and overtures. She was the only thief cleverer than he—that became clearer every day.

If only House Abascar could learn how much she had enjoyed playing the bait.

Now he was called the Dog, thrown to the Gatherers with a jagged scar as his reward. Many asked why he had not been thrown into the dungeon. But a big man, with more muscle than three ordinary men, might prove a formidable soldier should his heart ever prove malleable. Prince Cal-raven was willing to give him that chance.

"How's that, Cal-marcus, O wise and mighty judge of men? When I trade what's left of this grandpappy of the woods, I'll have what I need for my journey to Bel Amica. You wanted to teach me a lesson, and there it is. I'm gone."

It unnerved him the way the forest could seem aware, alive, perhaps already grieving the loss of the marrowwood. He was not a man inclined to waste time worrying about consequences; he preferred to live life as if fleeing pursuers in a mad downhill dash, just thrilled at the speed.

He frowned, piling brush to disguise the even lines of marrowwood logs and hide them from the officers and Gatherers who would love to steal his treasure.

He was covering the last of them when three Gatherer women appeared suddenly. The trees were dense here; people could stumble into each other without noticing their approach. The women laughed and whispered, watching the bare-chested giant catch his breath.

The golden-haired woman wore a smart smile. She carried a bowsnapper with an arrow nocked to the string. These were dangerous woods.

The others cradled pouches bulging with fresh harvest. One watched him through a frame of ragged red hair much like his own, the other through a fall of black curls. In the evening sun, their eyes glittered.

"M'ladies! Evenin'!" He made a sweeping bow, all the better to flaunt his shoulders.

The first gestured to the cloth pouches carried by the others. "Streamertail eggs there, in Tarlyn's pouch. And in Merya's, red goose eggs and berries. It's been a rewarding day."

"And what have *you* been doin', Valla Rey, while they've been stealin' eggs? Wardin' off the beastmen?"

The archer playfully aimed her arrow at him.

"I might have something to offer in trade for some of those eggs."

"In a mood to bargain, Dog?" said Valla Rey. "Bring some of that marrowwood you're trying to steal for yourself." She flashed a lascivious grin and turned to strut into the trees. The others laughed and veered to follow, secure in the sharpness of Valla Rey's arrows.

Radegan reached and grabbed Tarlyn's sleeve. She complained, but she was smiling. A streamertail's purple egg spilled from her harvesting pouch. He caught it an inch above the ground. She was too distracted by his nearness to notice he only pretended to return it to her pouch. "Tarlyn, my sweet, can I borrow your friend Merya for a bit?"

Disappointed, Tarlyn bit her lower lip. Merya took a step back.

"I caught some news this afternoon," he continued. "Merya's husband has fallen sick. Let me escort her to the medicine tent." He turned a compassionate gaze to Merya, who bowed her head and trembled. White cottonwood strands were caught in her hair, giving her the appearance of more than her thirty years. "Sorry to have to tell you this, Merya. But Corvah's drinking has cost him his health."

"You'd better be tellin' the truth, Dog." Tarlyn spoke bitterly without looking at Merya. "Have you forgotten why Merya and her husband are being punished? Corvah punched an officer. He'll punch a Gatherer too, if he sees one making a move for his woman. You should consider more...available options."

"We've got a long way to go," Valla Rey called, barely visible through the trees. "Night's coming, and I'm your protection."

"Tarlyn, that necklace..." It had caught Radegan's eye the moment she stepped through the trees. He would have it by tomorrow evening, something else to trade for something better. "Are those riverstones?"

She blushed. "Auralia collected them for me. I was wearing this when the rest of her gifts were stolen."

"Pfft...Auralia never gave me anything," Radegan scoffed, "so I had nothing to lose. I asked her to make me a pillow once upon a time." He winked at Merya, who was watching him still. "I told her to make the pillow big enough for two."

Placing a hand on Tarlyn's shoulder, he grinned a crooked grin. "It's almost time for beastmen to lurk 'round here. Better catch up to Valla Rey."

As Tarlyn reluctantly left them behind, Radegan grasped Merya's free hand. "Not much time before sundown. Come on. I'll take you to the medicine tent." He leaned close and whispered. "And I want to let you in on a secret."

"A secret?"

"Yes. A secret plan."

They stood together, still and silent, while Tarlyn and Valla Rey's footsteps faded into the woods. "And if my plan works," Radegan then continued, "you'll never have to worry again about that drunkard who thinks he owns you. We'll get enough to buy our way into House Bel Amica. We'll pose as traders."

"But you said my husband is..."

"Corvah's not sick. I made it up just to get rid of your bodyguards. But I'd bet all this marrowwood that your cantankerous husband is already drunk. He won't notice if you're late gettin' home."

Radegan led her down corridors of peelbarks to a glade of gigantic shrug trees, which grew skyward from serpentine foundations of unearthed roots. She held her harvest pouch close, startling when shadows shifted in the trees around them. He ignored her worries, reaching into the tangled roots until he found the hidden lever.

"Cal-marcus's soldiers once used this tree as a highwatch." There was a snap, and a heavy wooden plank descended on two ropes, bringing a shower of leaves from the dense ceiling of boughs. The plank stopped shy of the ground and swung there as the leaves settled around it.

Merya pushed aside her hair, and her inquisitive, soft white face emerged, amazed. He gestured for her to sit on the swing as it twisted and swayed. She laid the pouch of eggs and berries against the base of the trunk and sat down with the hint of a smile.

He reached into the roots again. There was a sharp snap. She shrieked in surprise. He sprang to join her, his feet on the plank and his hands grasping the ropes. The swing shot upward, swift as a bird taking flight, and carried them up through an open square in a wooden platform. Radegan and Merya came to a stop with their heads above the leafy canopy in the light of the setting sun. Around them, a watchman's perch spread across the crowns of several trees.

Merya stepped nervously onto the platform to take in the dizzying view. From such a height the Expanse looked like a different world—rolling hills carpeted with leaves of red, gold, and green. She sank to her knees.

Radegan reclined beside her, gleefully watching the awe in her eyes. "Like my little hideaway? Go ahead and laugh. Shout. Sing the Early Evening Verse! Nobody can hear us." He ran his fingertip gently across her wrinkled forehead, up over her crown of black hair, then slowly down her back until she closed her eyes and trembled at his audacity.

An hour later, when the day was but a stroke of distant purple, Merya found herself wrapped in Radegan's embrace. She clung to her thin gown and felt the evening chill. Her heavier work garments lay in a heap beside her. The platform creaked and shifted with the swaying of the trees.

It had been many years since a man, even her husband, had held her like this. Her eyes followed a pair of red geese as they pursued the setting sun.

"This isn't your hideaway, young man," she said. "It belongs to soldiers."

"Don't you think I know? Highwatches help them send messages across the forest."

"Someday they'll find you here. Then what will you do?"

"We'll be long gone soon. Listen to me."

She leaned into him, keeping an eye on the swinglift that had carried them here. She wondered how it worked, how she might make an escape. "I'm not supposed to be up here with you," she said, for the third or fourth time. "If my husband hears about this..."

"Merya, your days of fearin' Corvah's tantrums are over. Both of us can get out from under Abascar's shadow for good. After what they've done to Auralia, how can the Gatherers bear it? Poor girl's trapped in a dungeon cell. All she did was play with colors from the forest. You can't make laws against that. Rules are supposed to protect us."

"Not all rules are bad," she murmured. "We're breaking some of the good ones right here."

Radegan grasped her small shoulders, lifted her as though she were a cat, and set her in his lap to face him. "The king's got what don't belong to him. He takes Auralia. He takes the colors. He takes the best of everything and says he's lookin' out for us. He took away your freedom to love any man you choose. Your parents forced you to marry old Corvah. And they call me a thief?"

"You're always grabbin' what doesn't belong to you," she protested.

"But there's a difference. I'm going to do something good with what I've taken."

She cocked her head. "Liar."

"I'm going to buy us a way out of here. You and me, we're going to House Bel Amica."

"How?" She tried to pull away, but he held her fast. "They'll never let us in."

"I've made a bargain, Merya. You won't believe it when I tell you." He leaned in close, his forehead touching hers, but she refused to meet his gaze. She looked instead at his powerful arms.

"What am I doing?" she whispered. "I need a responsible man. Not an overgrown pickpocket."

She pretended not to notice that his fingers were wandering from her lips to her chin and slowly down her neck. She was trembling again, and it angered her to be so easily manipulated. She knew Radegan's every move was calculated. Yet she remained still.

"You'll never know passion," Radegan said softly, "if you follow the king's orders. You can't deny your heart anymore."

She playfully pounded on his shoulder with her fist. "But my heart's a mess, and yours is reckless. If we're true to ourselves, we're in trouble. That's what promises are for, like the promise Corvah made me." She looked into the shadows of the trees. "They give you something to bind yourself to, so you don't get carried off on a whim."

The strength of her conviction awakened the will to strike back against Radegan's wiles. She pushed him away and staggered to her feet, careful to keep an eye on the edge of the platform. "If we go to Bel Amica, you'll run off after some new conquest. You just follow your appetite like an animal."

"Maybe that's because Abascar treats me like one," he snarled. "But I don't have to stay here. I'm going to get respectable among respectable people. Forget Abascar."

"Bel Amica won't let you in."

"They will if I make a good bargain. Listen, Merya, I've made a deal. I found something that will persuade the summoner to let me back into the Underkeep. I can collect enough treasure for us to buy our way into Bel Amica. *That's* a promise."

She shook her head laughing. "Nothing will buy a summoner's favor, Radegan. What did you promise *her*?"

Then she gasped and covered her mouth. She sank to her knees. "No, you didn't. Tell me you didn't, Radegan. Tell me you aren't the one who stole Auralia's beautiful gifts."

"The summoner's taken a liking to me. She's easily persuaded if you give her pretty things. I had to promise her something she wanted so she would let me into the Underkeep."

"You broke the Gatherers' hearts. You lied to Auralia's face!"

"Here's the trick, Merya—I *borrowed* Auralia's gifts. I told the summoner I'd steal them for her. So I had to take them, or she wouldn't believe me."

"I can't imagine why."

"But I'm not going to deliver them to her. My instructions will lead her off down some crazy path. By the time she realizes that, you and I will already be out of reach, living it up in Bel Amica. We'll eventually send a message to the Gatherers so they can find the hiding place. They'll get every piece back."

He began to crawl toward her. "When the sun rises, Merya, the summoner is going to smuggle me into the caves beneath the palace."

"What if you're caught robbing the Underkeep? Captain Ark-robin will kill you!"

"He won't catch me. As far as he knows, the game is over, and he won."

She shook her head. She had to get off this platform. She had to run...now. "You're insane."

"Here's what I think is insane, Merya. Tryin' to raise a child in the wilderness with a drunkard for a papa."

Merya could not hide her astonishment, nor could she keep herself from pressing her hands to her belly. How could he know?

"Why do you think I'm inviting you to Bel Amica with me, Merya? Because that child needs a home. A good home. And Bel Amica's the place. This is your chance. I'm giving it to you. What is *Corvah* doing to give you that chance?"

Far away, the Evening Verse rang down from Abascar's wall. The voice was faint and distant, but it made the lateness of the hour clear. Merya looked toward the house. Her ears rang; her pulse rushed.

Radegan stood up, moved a hand behind her head, drew her face near to his. She closed her eyes, afraid. But he only whispered through clenched teeth. "In a few days, Merya, you'll like me even better. You'll know what I'm made of." Before she could answer, he kissed her forcefully. And then again. And again, just enough to redden her cheeks, weaken her resolve, and take more that did not belong to him.

When they made their silent descent after moonrise, Merya found the shreds of her harvesting pouch at the foot of the tree. Fragments of wet eggshell, stark white and scattered, were all that remained of her day's work. She looked around and saw a fox peering at her through brambles with berry-stains on his muzzle. She could have sworn he wore a gloating smile.

18

THE DREAMERS

Cal-raven stood over a washbasin with a razor, scraping at his face. The golden beard that had grown during the days of his fever was gone.

"I don't know you, woman," he said, pretending to address his Promised. "And you don't yet know me. But you've spread the word that you prefer a clean-shaven man, and I'm expected to bend to your will."

"Ark-robin's daughter has a lash to your back already, Cal-raven?" came the voice from the next room.

"A razor to my face anyway. I'll remember this, many years from now, when I insist she shave her *own* beard." He glanced at the trimmings in the washbasin. "I should collect these and send them to her. A token of my *lack* of affection."

This contagion had knocked him flat for six days of coughing and fever. Back on his feet, he was eager to appear obedient, at least until he could find a way to escape this marriage plan. The news that his Promised had a preference for hairless chins made him wish his blond beard had grown down to his knees. But for now, he would do his best to play along.

He glanced briefly at the table in the adjoining chamber—his personal strategy room—where Irimus Rain, one of Captain Ark-robin's assistants, gestured anxiously at an unfurled map.

The prince put down the razor and rubbed his chin. He felt more like himself. The beard had reminded him too much of how his father had looked before his mother left.

Irimus Rain could not hide the sneer inside his bristling mustache, but he was clearly trying. "Prince Cal-raven, you appear...much like your younger self." He tugged at his own winding grey beard. "However, some would say a beard is a sign of maturity and wisdom."

"I'm not so fond of being grown up. Not when I have to spend evenings bent over maps." Cal-raven drew his grey and brown mantle over his shoulders. Irimus smirked in disgust. "Don't," the prince warned him. "You're a strategist, not a tailor. Believe me, on the day I marry Stricia, you'll see me dressed in funeral attire." He sat down at the table and frowned at the elaborate map.

The ale boy entered with a tray. A goblet, a bowl, and a plate rattled against the silver as he stepped cautiously to the table. Cal-raven took the plate of bread and oil and the bowl of stew, then instructed the ale boy to place the goblet atop the scroll shelves beside his bed. He would not take his wine until he had survived this late meeting with the advisor. It was a lesson he had learned from observing his father—keep your senses sharp so as not to be persuaded into folly. He looked down at the map, where Irimus demonstrated that the dig from the Underkeep to the Throanscall was steering too far to the north.

"Irimus," Cal-raven groaned, "I understand the dig has strayed from the prescribed course. But it will still reach the river as planned. If we insist they undo the last few days of work, just to correct their direction, it will add four days to the project. The diggers are exhausted. And they're almost to the river. We can't ruin their spirits *again.*"

"The current course, Cal-raven," Irimus insisted, "will steer the tunnel too close to the Fraughtenwood. You know the Fraughtenwood. Wyrms prowl there. Do you want them swimming into our underground river?"

"If the problem is that severe, Irimus, why can't the foreman make the change? Why bother bringing this to me? If I give the order, I'll become the target of their complaints. And this will embolden the grudgers."

"My lord, the foreman is nervous about making changes without royal consent. He specifically appealed for your support."

So, Cal-raven thought, *Blyn-dobed asked for this. He wants to correct their course, but he doesn't want to become a target for his grumbling workers. He knows I feel guilty for offending him. He assumes I'll willingly accept the burden.*

Cal-raven had ordered that a battalion be sent to guard the diggers. A transitory tower—a portable fort with a watchtower—would give them some refuge if they were attacked. The tower was a leftover from the war days of King Har-baron, but it would not provide enough security to protect all the men. They were still vulnerable.

"By my honor stitches," Irimus smirked, pointing to the carpet.

"Ale boy, your shoes," the prince shouted. "You're leaving a trail."

The ale boy, who was looking about for a footstool, flinched. "Sorry, Prince Cal-raven. I was just called in from the Gatherer camps to serve you."

"Of course. I spoke too harshly. But as you see, I have Irimus here for the sole purpose of pointing out matters that might bother me."

Irimus drew back from the table, indignant. But Cal-raven knew the advisor would not dare to disagree with him. Not while his request was still on the table.

"Go on, Irimus. Redirect the dig. But only if they agree to certain conditions. The Fraughtenwood is a terrible place, but we have to stay on schedule. I've never known the beastmen to attack such an organized endeavor, but they have surprised me lately. We need to finish the project and get out of there. They will have to work day and night in shifts. Make sure they understand that I command this for their own protection."

"Of course."

"Also, tell the diggers I am making arrangements to work alongside them and to double their pay. That is how much I desire to see this through. And if the foreman and his workers apply themselves appropriately, I will personally commend them, one by one, before my father."

Irimus needed no encouragement to leave.

Prince Cal-raven ker Cal-marcus collapsed, his forehead on the tabletop, his arms outstretched, and his hands flat against the map. He was too tired for any more strategy tonight.

These last several days he had been sprawled in his blankets with cold, wet towels wrapped around his head. His illness had postponed the hunters' victory celebration, but he wished they would go ahead with their frivolity. He needed time alone beyond the walls where he could find some peace, think about his future, track the endeavors of beastmen, and practice stonemastery.

When he opened his eyes, the boy was still trying to place the goblet on the top of the scroll rack by stepping onto a low shelf.

"You say you were with the Gatherers, boy? Do you spend a lot of time outside the walls?"

The ale boy answered, "Yes, sir, I suppose I do."

"Do you prefer working in the woods to working in the palace?"

"I...I like working in both places, sir. Inside and outside. But not one without the other."

"What a clever answer. But aren't you afraid of the Cent Regus beastmen?"

"Yes, sir. Nasty folk, Cent Regus. I'm careful to stay close to the duty officers."

"I could have you reassigned, if you like."

"Oh no, sir. I'd never want to be shut inside all the time. I'd miss too many things. The woods are beautiful."

"You sound like my old teacher." Cal-raven looked at his own shoes, polished, worn maybe once before, like all his shoes. He looked through a round window at the faint violet brushstrokes left in the sky. "Have you heard of the mage my father exiled...Scharr ben Fray?"

At Cal-raven's question, the ale boy lost his balance and fell, dragging the goblet tray with him, which swiped across the shelf and knocked a menagerie of the prince's belongings down to the floor with it. The boy landed amidst the tumbling debris.

Wine darkened the carpet.

The prince leapt to help him, shouting, "Of all the clumsy—" He snatched a towel from beside his washbasin and threw it across the spill.

The ale boy muttered, "Sorry, sir. You just startled me. I'll clean it up."

"Forgive me." Cal-raven was laughing now. "I shouldn't scold you for an accident. Once, when I was a child, I pulled a whole rack of scroll shelves down on top of myself. My mother was not very pleased."

The ale boy was not listening. He sat staring in sudden amazement at the array of fallen objects scattered across the floor. Among them, he discovered tiny sculptures, figures carved from glassy blackstone.

Cal-raven picked up a tiny stone figurine. "These are just toys. Figures my teacher made, mostly. I made some of them too. Do you like them?"

"Sorry, sir. I've just...I've never seen anything like 'em before, sir."

Cal-raven scooped up a handful of the small figures and held them out for the boy to see. The disparate pieces were no bigger than the prince's thumb. A black bear, crouched to defend its territory. A stag, crowned with intricate antlers like a king of the forest. Warriors in combat poses. A woman in trailing robes, running, looking back over her shoulder. A giant king with a strange walking stick and gems for eyes.

"This one is Tammos Raak, the great leader who brought people down into the Expanse from the curse of Inius Throan...you know the old story?" The boy nodded. "And this one looks like a row of teeth, but hold it up to the light, and see? It casts a shadow that matches the jagged line of the Forbidding Wall."

"Sir, the floor. Shouldn't we finish sopping up the wine before it stains?"

"And these two, ravens. Wait, no, this one's a silverhawk. This one's a redhawk. He can talk to them, you know—Scharr ben Fray. He's a stonemaster, *and* he speaks with animals. These, I forget what they are called, beasts from the remote south. Can kill a vawn with one lash of their tails. *Grounders*, that's it. Here, I'll show you more."

He reached beneath the heavy bed mats and withdrew a polished wooden box. "We made these together when he took me exploring in the Blackstone Caves, southeast of Abascar. The stones there are sharp as razors, but they shape beautifully if you have the gift."

He withdrew a small, crude map, one he had probably drawn as a child, and opened it. He traced a line from the X that marked House Abascar down to a region southeast of the Cragavar forest. "Right there. You should see them, boy, the Blackstone Caves. A different world, a labyrinth. That's where I first learned stonemastery. A whole houseful of people could live there."

He lifted another handful of figures. They clattered together like shells. At the sight of these, the boy forgot about the wine.

"You like these? They're my favorites. Things that aren't real. Things Scharr ben Fray saw in his dreams and things he gathered from children's stories. Dragons. The dreaded two-headed wolfsnake. Look, he even made some Northchildren." Cal-raven set the figures in a line on the floor. They were lumps of grey clay—hooded people, tall and short, skinny and stout, bent as though haunted or running from something awful. The ale boy took the largest piece from Cal-raven's open hand and held it up, wide eyed.

"Yes, you've found the very best. That one is extraordinary." Cal-raven took it away quickly. "You know what it is, don't you? So you know why I keep it hidden."

The ale boy nodded and bit his lower lip.

"Don't be afraid. You can speak freely here. This emerjade ring I made when I was a child, it has the very same outline."

"The king lets you wear the Keeper on your hand?" the boy whispered in disbelief. "But it's forbidden to even talk about the Keeper."

"And my father would like to throw this ring into the Underkeep's abyss. Princes in Abascar have always been given royal rings of trust. Some say Tammos Raak gave rings to all his children and that Abascar is the only house that honors this tradition. Whoever wears the ring of royal trust is protected from harm. The king must show favor and mercy to anyone who wears it, and I am free to give it to anyone I please."

He put the ring against his eye and stared through it. "They say that only children dream of the Keeper," Cal-raven whispered. "But it's not true. The Keeper's in everybody's dreams. And when we try to shake that memory, the dreams turn to nightmares. We're meant to dream about it. I'm sure of this."

Cal-raven saw recognition in the boy's expression. "Whenever Scharr ben Fray talked about this common dream, he would become very serious and squint his eyes like he was looking into a bright light." Cal-raven mimicked a deep, raspy voice, shook a finger at the ale boy and growled, *"They are fools that deny their dreams."* He leaned forward. "I'll tell you a secret, boy. I'll tell you something I've told no one else. I have seen prints in the forest. Footprints that don't match any known beast."

"I know somebody," blurted the ale boy. "Somebody who says that the Keeper saved her life."

Cal-raven's smile lingered a moment, then faded. "What?"

"A beastman tried to attack her, and she called for the Keeper's help. It threw the beastman into the lake."

"You know someone who says she saw the Keeper...*outside* her dreams?" He was skeptical. "The Gatherers eat a lot of mushrooms, don't they?"

"No. Not a Gatherer. An orphan. Some say she's a Northchild."

The prince folded his fingers as though to hide the ring. "A Northchild?"

"Well, nobody knows. She's not wicked or a thief. I don't think she's cold and cruel. Her name's 'Ralia." When he spoke the name, he suddenly turned away, as if realizing a mistake.

Cal-raven stood, eyes wide, then winced as his heel came down on one of the figures. "Rescued by the Keeper. Interesting."

The Evening Verse, sung sharply and officiously, drew the prince's attention to the window.

"It's late, and I still have a great deal to accomplish." His tone was again that of a prince addressing a servant. "Thank you for the wine, boy. You are dismissed."

The ale boy responded automatically, bowing as was proper. "Sir, I have yet to clean up the mess I've made. I'll fetch some rags and water."

"Good, but bring something else as well."

"Sir?"

"Bring me an attendant's cape. I must go out. In secret."

The ale boy's eyes widened, and he smiled at the privilege of the confidence.

"I am going to visit this friend of yours. There are some questions I suspect her interrogators overlooked. Is there any message you would like me to pass along?"

Cal-raven was quite unprepared for the torrent of messages, questions, and promises the ale boy produced.

Behind them, the wine sank indelibly into the floor.

19

THE RING OF TRUST

Her hands cupped beneath the shallows of the lake, Auralia drew out colors.

With a rush, the ale boy rose from the waters, a chalice in his hand. The cup was cast in resin the silverblue of evening water. Its stem rose from a base of tangled roots to shape a great and winding tree with four branches that held the cup's bowl. And in the bowl—fire.

"The fire doesn't harm me," the ale boy said, offering the chalice. A question marked his face. The cup was cool against her hands, like water from the lake. She lifted it and drank.

The flames tasted like colors. They ran into her blood, poured out through her eyes as fiery tears.

The silhouette of the ale boy had been replaced by a young woman standing in the water. She laughed, reached forward, pulled the cup free, and threw it at Auralia's feet. Flames engulfed her, but she did not feel pain.

A heavy hand touched Auralia's shoulder. She turned, watched herself retrieve the chalice from the fire and give it to a tall shadow whose face she could not see. "Pass this on," she said, and she kissed his hand, his ring. The colors staining her lips set the ring ablaze.

The stranger turned as though distracted. A roar came from House Abascar, the sound of a thousand voices calling for help, the sound of trees falling. She felt the lakewater rush about her legs as it overflowed its banks.

Auralia opened her mouth to warn her friends who could not see the flood, but then the waters became a tide of arms and hands, grasping at her, clinging to her, an ocean of desperation.

She called out, asking the tall shadow to help, as she was dragged into the mob. But he was engaged in a battle with a beastman. Their blades clashed, blasting bolts of lightning, and a dark shape swept across them all.

The mysterious warrior, knocking the beastman aside, turned and threw his sword skyward, piercing the shape's dark belly.

"No," Auralia said.

The desperate hands pulled her back down to the floor of her prison cell.

Auralia rubbed her eyes with scabbed knuckles, breathing quickly, wet with sweat and shivering as the thick blankets of sleep fell away. She got to her knees, fell forward into a puddle, and drew back. Prying her soiled cape up from the gluey ground, she buried her face in its abrasive folds.

Footsteps. The creak of the gate. The hushed voices of three men, perhaps four. One came nearer, cautious in his steps.

Gasps burst from the barred hollows along the walls, followed by a potent, awed silence. He was not the jailer. He was a tall man wrapped in the cape of a common errand-runner.

He stopped, as if waiting for his eyes to adjust to the darkness. And then he lunged toward her, gripping the bars.

She cowered, clutching her stained and dripping colors. A long, taut silence sharpened her senses. An exquisite ring glinted on the first finger of his right hand.

He was silent for a while, the faint lights from Auralia's cloak illuminating his hands. His attention frightened her. She rose slowly to her feet, lifted and unfolded the cloak, and then held it high, hiding behind it.

"So it's true." The man sounded younger than she had thought, like a Gatherer boy enthralled. "To know how colors knit together in this way, you must have seen the Cragavar forest from a very high place."

Uncertain whether to respond, she shrank back a step and drew the cloak around herself, utterly ashamed of her bruised and shivering form, her legs and feet stained with ink-dark soil.

"Stay. Stay in the light, Auralia."

She shuffled her feet, her head bowed, and waited, as if he might proclaim some judgment. He looked at her, it seemed, for as much time as he had marveled at the colors.

She braved another look. He crouched down, his eyes level now with hers, and leaned in close. She searched his glinting gaze, found only awe and questions.

"Where do you come from, that you can weave such wonders?"

"I don't know," she said abruptly, so very weary of questions.

"What inspired you to craft this?"

"I told them, and they threw me into this hole." There was defeat in her voice, something she had never heard before. "The king didn't like my answer."

"The king is angry. But I...I am not angry, Auralia. On the contrary, I wish to protect the colors."

She chanced another look into his face, which the colors had touched with a soft glow. "I haven't remembered where I'm from," she answered. "But I will, I think. Sometimes I can almost say it. I recognized a northern bird. And I dream of the Keeper. But you know that, don't you?" She staggered slightly, realizing now how hungry she was. "Nobody believes me when I talk about him."

"Some of us might," said the shadow cautiously.

His voice seemed so familiar. She had heard it in the forest. A high-ranking servant of the king? One of Ark-robin's riders? Someone who had heard rumors and come to see for himself? She stepped closer, and as the faint silver lantern-light touched her cape, even she was surprised by its eagerness to shine.

"Give me more light," the man whispered, staring up the corridor. To her astonishment, he gazed into her eyes. "You will not remain imprisoned. You will go free. You will be the blow that shakes this house. Now that you have shown them this, nothing can remain the same. We have no more excuses. That is Abascar's future you hold in your hands."

His hands smelled of leather, incense, and wine. Was this a conspirator? A rescuer? He spoke as though afraid of being overheard, whispers strange and faltering.

She marveled at his intricately sculptured ring. This was a man of influence.

"Who sent you here?" he asked her.

She laughed bitterly. "You wouldn't believe me. Who sent *you?*"

"You won't believe me either." He cupped a hand to his mouth and whispered, "An ale boy."

She gasped. "Really? Is he..."

"He is in no danger. He is safe. And you will be safe soon. But you'll have to be patient. My father is afraid to admit how wrong he was. Afraid to admit many things. He cannot bear the responsibility. I will need some time."

Something stirred in her memories. A vawn, a rider. *"Why do you always run from me?"*

And then she spoke, barely a whisper. "It's calling me to come back." She clutched at the cloak.

"The forest?"

"No. The Keeper."

"The Keeper." His forehead was against the bars. His hair was like fire and gold, twisted in strange and hasty braids. It made her want to laugh. He reached through the bars to touch a corner of the cloak, a patch of lavender. The stranger's fingers teased the golden fringe along the edge, and then he drew back as though burnt. "This ale boy, he says the Keeper saved you from a beastman." She could smell his sweat and his fear.

She liked his face. Clean-shaven. Boyish, but burdened, lines deepening between his brows and at the corners of his lips. One eye was gold, one green as the emerjade around his finger. They were honest eyes.

"Do you hear it at night?" she asked.

"I do not hear it, no. But I seek it. When I was very young, I found a footprint on the bank of the Throanscall."

At the sound of a rustling at the gate, he leaned back, listened. And then he urgently beckoned her. She could feel his words as he whispered in her ear. "You mustn't speak of these things. Not here. Not yet." There was a burgeoning anger beneath those words. "I'm going to help you get out of here. Don't despair. You'll live with us in the palace, if that's what you…" He paused, then laughed. "Listen to us. A prince and a Gatherer. Whispering like old friends in the dark."

His laughter triggered a rising tide of sound, and specters rose behind the bars on the opposite side of the corridor—naked, wretched prisoners drawn to observe this hushed rendezvous. Bony white fingers curled around prison bars. Pale visages of emaciated captives who had suffered long enough to absorb the cold, the corrosive air, passed in and out of sight like dead fish bobbing in dark water.

The prince swallowed, shivered. "You'll be safe. Nobody will take away what is yours."

"Mine?" Auralia's smooth small brow wrinkled. "This isn't mine really."

"Lordship?" gasped one of the prisoners. "Prince Cal-raven ker Cal-marcus?"

Suddenly the whole corridor erupted with the voices of convicts. One by one, they cried their innocence, confessed sins, rattled bars, and begged for mercy and release. The walls seemed to grow hundreds of thrashing limbs as they reached for him in desperate appeal. The commotion pummeled the prince like a hard rain. He reached through the bars, gently grabbed Auralia's cloak where she held it closed at her collar, and pulled her near with both hands. She surrendered, pressed against the bars. He brushed her silverbrown hair from her face, touched his lips to her tiny ear, and said, "I will bring you whatever you need. Name it, and it is yours."

"It's not me, m'lord, that needs your help. It's Abascar. That's why I came. The house needs these colors. Somehow, they will help. Somebody here needs 'em. Is it you?" Her cold hand curled into his rough grasp. As it did, she realized she was holding the crimson threads. *Of course*, she thought. *Now.*

The prince pulled his hand away, let go of the cloak. She tumbled back into it. He stood up.

The voices around him were a storm. Guards came through the gate.

In a sudden impulse, Cal-raven knelt once more before Auralia's cell. "Take this." He twisted the green ring free of his finger. "If you wear this ring of trust, you show all of House Abascar that I demand your protection. Only my father can say otherwise. He will not. Do you understand?" He took her hand, pressed the ring into her palm. "Do you know who I am?"

Closing her fingers over the ring, she felt heat coursing from his hands into hers. "I know who you are. But. . ." She closed her eyes, touched an echo of the dream, the shadow turning from his duel with the beastman to throw his sword into the sky. "But not what you will be."

He drew away, stung.

Auralia took the ring, put it on her finger. It was too loose, for her hands were as small as a child's. She slipped it around her thumb. Her mouth fell open. The band like a curled tail, the ornament like the body of a great animal—the essence of horse, eagle, behemoth—was the image of the Keeper. Simple, but unmistakable.

She took the colors in her hands. "They're for you. I don't need them anymore."

But he was gone.

She fumbled with the threads and then wound them around the button at her collar.

Knocking the prisoners to the backs of their cells and casting Cal-raven to the ground, color exploded like daybreak through the tunnels under the earth.

20

BLOOD TIDINGS

Unable to return to the palace after what he had seen in the dungeon, Calraven wandered out beyond Abascar's wall. He needed to think. And for thoughts of this nature, he could not tolerate walls. He needed open sky.

Deep in the forest, a concealed swinglift carried him to a platform above the trees, where he gazed northward to the Forbidding Wall. The dark forest rippled, swaths of night-shrouded green, murmuring with mystery, not unlike Auralia's cloak.

In that cell choked with darkness, the prisoner's prize had been like a light beneath a door, and when the door was opened, memory poured forth. He had wanted to move back down the corridor to look at her again, but the colors were too strong.

This is a woman who might walk with the Keeper.

He lay down on the mossy wooden planks, which made a damp and clumpish cushion. But the discomfort was small payment for the view of stars and passing clouds soaked in moonlight.

There, in the woods, he could still remember the colors and the scents rising from that cloak. And somehow, he was convinced he could map many of the paths Auralia had walked.

The scents—wild grasses, strands spun from the fur of long-haired bearmice, the spines of green streamertail feathers—teased his appetite for trails and the many ways to leave them. He was climbing on the Cliffs of Barnashum; lying on the smoothed, washed pebbles beside quiet waters; breathing the cold reviving air of a field of vibrant bellpetals. There was a heavy, ancient aroma of everstout trees that grew on the far side of the lake. Then a wind seemed to rise, and he was caught in a wave of golden dust from firestalks in bloom.

Could Auralia have ventured so far at such a young age? Few would have seen, or cared to see, so much. And no one would have observed so intently in order to appreciate such a wild array of life. No one. But Auralia had.

Asleep on that secret platform, just as he had slept as a boy in a tree house, Cal-raven let his dreams take him across the entire Expanse, from the parched, desolate land of House Jenta, up through the Cragavar forest past House Abascar, past Deep Lake, to the dense dangerous Fraughtenwood of the Fearblind, then farther north along the sparkling blue line of the River Throanscall, to the jagged mountain ridge of the Forbidding Wall where he was engulfed in cloud, drowning in the sound of an invisible waterfall.

A hint of delirium flowers on the air pulled Cal-raven's dream on another path, one familiar but long forgotten: a winding trail that became a stair descending into a small, walled courtyard—his mother's garden.

In her days of failing health, Queen Jaralaine had found her only joy in tending the lush and aromatic flower beds in a hidden, guarded arboretum. She had never spoken much, nor had she given small Cal-raven anything of herself but color. Her gowns, linens, loom, and her private garden. Only her son and her husband could pass through the ivy-crowned garden gate or walk on the thread-mad floor of her weaving chambers. Even there she would accompany them, protective, smiling, shy, yet watching their every move.

"It's mine," she would say. "My sisters will never walk here. My father and mother will never take it away from me."

It troubled him when she spoke this way, as if these people she hated were haunting the palace and making cruel threats. Once, in the garden, he had cleared his throat, reached for his mother's hand, planted his feet, and declared, "When I'm all grown, I'll fight to defend this place. It's the jewel of the Expanse." She had laughed until she dropped a bowl of seeds and wiped away tears with her wrist, her smile the most vivid treasure of all.

He was grateful for the memory, the only clear image he had of his mother beyond the disintegration of her beauty. All about her had gone grey—the gold hair, the orange eyes, the redbrown skin of a woman who had grown up in the woods.

And now, many years without her, he found these colors deep in the dungeon, a resurrection of the queen's gift. But as his eyes followed the spiraling patterns, Cal-raven had seen the face it framed.

This was no painted competitor for his affections, no groveling daughter of a proud soldier. Auralia did not seek to impress him. Further, she had not asked to be released. She sought only to offer what she had. In her face there was a terrible loneliness. Her hair was lined with silver, wispy as cobwebs, as if she were an ancient wise woman made young through enchantment. He saw hunger and pain in her movement, yet she seemed oblivious to her fragility, more intent upon him than he was upon her.

A dull grey blur took on definition—a winged squirrel on the edge of the platform, paralyzed, wide eyed, as stunned to see Cal-raven as the prince was to see the animal. Then, without a glimmer of forethought, the squirrel cast itself into the open air and vanished.

Cal-raven wiped a thin layer of mist from his face, groaning with the cold, bruised ache of a night on unforgiving wooden planks.

Clinging to the lift ropes, he plunged down through the branches before dashing off the trails for a quicker route to the gates, where bewildered guards saluted their leafy, twig-littered master.

Cal-raven clenched his fists and marched up the lane toward the palace, blinking into the brilliant daylight.

Everything was a blur.

Pulling webs and burrs from his hair, he reached the stairway that would take him to the map rooms. There were things he had to say. His father was probably being pestered by advisors, hearing reports from night patrols. He was sure of his convictions but uncertain how to begin.

Auralia has crafted the wonder of Abascar, Father. And not just of Abascar, but of all the houses of the Expanse. There was something to that. And *If she can do this, then imagine. . . Imagine what Bel Amica would say if we now declared Abascar's Spring. Auralia could guide us into blessing the house with radiant colors. We would at last be the very house Mother wanted. . .the envy of the Expanse.*

The cloak stretched like a banner over all he was thinking, colors rivering in his mind, Auralia's face the sun at the center.

But before he could ascend, his father appeared above, still dressed in his nightrobe and flanked by soldiers in full battle armor.

"Cal-raven!" The king hurried down the stairs and seized the prince by the shoulders. "Son, where have you been? There is urgent news! We summoned you earlier." He was clearly piqued by the prince's appearance. "You look like a pile of wildbrush. Someone might think you slept in a treetop!"

"I did."

Palace servants were sidetracked by the sight and began to congregate behind the prince, stirred up and muttering at the rare appearance of both leaders in the same place...and in the portentous company of combat-ready soldiers. Whatever was about to unfold could fill their hours over hot stoves and steaming basins with stories for the rest of the day.

"I was wrong to think so little of your warnings."

"What is it? What's happened?"

"A band of beastmen has overwhelmed the tower at the Throanscall dig."

"How..." Cal-raven's mouth went dry.

"I am sending out the first troop straightaway. And as much as my heart breaks to think of it, you must ride at their head. If those savages succeed in overpowering our defense, we could lose this project."

Irimus Rain caught the prince's gaze for a moment. They both understood that if the tower was indeed overwhelmed, severe damage had already been done.

"That's not all we'll lose." Cal-raven spoke so the people would not hear. "There are a lot of good laborers out there. Blyn-dobed, the foreman. Cama-roth. Arven Parks. And Nav Ballash."

"Do you think I am a fool? Of course we'll lose good laborers! We've received reports from Gatherers harvesting near the site. They saw the smoke and heard an uproar. A morning patrol reached the river project and found some of our men fallen, broken bodies nailed to the trees, severed heads hung by the hair from branches."

Cal-raven spat bile. He reached for the sword he had not yet put on. "An organized assault, Father. The beastmen *planned* this."

"Differing reports. Some said twenty beastmen, but one said four."

"Four of those pigs couldn't besiege a transitory tower!" Cal-raven had often slept inside the cramped quarters of just such a military structure. Designed to house twelve soldiers, these towers were defended by archers above and swordsmen below. Four beastmen would have been shot full of arrows. No, this was something larger.

"Nevertheless, the reports all confirm the tower has been taken," the king said.

"Where is Captain Ark-robin? Where are his riders?"

"Ark-robin will stay to secure Abascar's perimeter and to make sure no beastmen have made it into the tunnels. If they have, they could run from the dig all the way to the Underkeep. It's up to you to recover the dig and the tower. Move now, Cal-raven, and we shall salvage what we can. Tabor Jan is preparing riders for you. You'll find your armor ready with your vawn."

Cal-raven nodded. There was a pang in his head, a thought he had been carrying and then suddenly lost. "Father."

The king smiled, leaned close to him, and said intently, "This could be important Cal-raven. Think of what it could mean. Remember how I cleansed the woods of those barbarians years ago. That story is told again and again. It made me beloved in the minds of the people. It made them eager to crown me king."

The people are ready for me, Cal-raven almost said aloud. *Only you lack faith in my abilities.* Instead, he closed his eyes and said, "I must consider the matter at hand, not any future glory."

"I will arrange an enthusiastic reception for you upon your return. Old Har-baron did the same for me once. There is no better time to address the people, to be generous to them, than in a moment of victory. You could make a prince's proclamation. Commission a monument celebrating the victory. Or call for a commemorative day of rest. Whatever you wish. I will make sure your Promised is there."

There was an unfamiliar tone in his father's voice, a sort of hysteria, an unraveling. "You are writing the end of a story that has not yet been told, Father."

Cal-raven walked alone toward the stables while he listened to his father address the gathering observers. Looking up at the tower, at the library windows, he knew suddenly what he could hear in his father's voice. Cal-marcus was inviting the people to see this as the end of his kingship. He wanted to surrender. He could bear his burdens no longer. And here the stage was being set for Cal-raven to establish himself and make the people forget their grudges.

After a few isolated cheers of support, the Housefolk scrambled to the main avenue, hoping to be the first to describe the bloody news to friends and family. A great lament began—cries and unanswerable questions from those who knew people at the site of the dig.

The king was catching up to him now, flanked by Aug-anstern and Irimus Rain and followed by his guards and twelve armored warriors carrying spears and shields. Sunlight flashed off polished breastplates and helmets.

Cal-raven walked through the high wooden gates of the royal stables and pushed through thick and musty air—the dank smell of the vawns' grub-sludge, the earthy scent of fresh hay, the heavy, dark aroma of animal dung.

Tabor Jan waited by the vawn troughs looking like a hound anxious to be released. He presented Cal-raven with armor and weapons. "I'll plant a hundred arrows in those beasts if you will ride behind me and chop off their heads," he said.

With that, the guardsman planted a boot in the stirrup and climbed astride the scaly back of his great green vawn. He grabbed the thick black hair and reached forward to scratch it behind its ears. The vawn squealed through its nostrils and ground the teeth within its snout. "Easy, Jetaka," said the rider to his mount. "We'll be running soon."

"You're a musician with your bow, Tabor Jan," said Cal-raven. "Let it sing."

"And you're a soldier, not a poet. Get on that vawn."

He accepted the flag from a stablehand, a warning banner that would declare the urgency of their mission, a signal to merchants and other passersby not to detain or follow them. It was also an invitation for passing patrols to join the charge.

His black vawn stamped its gigantic feet. Pacing in small circles, it lashed its scaly tail.

The king stilled the vawn with a whistle. "Time is short. You must surprise the beastmen." He lifted the polished helm up to the rider.

"We will slaughter them. And upon my return, I will do as you suggest. I will make a proclamation." He pulled the helm down over his head.

"Indeed? Good. *Very* good. Assert yourself as a leader and a man of vision. Best to ride into battle with eyes fixed firmly on the days that lie ahead." Cal-marcus reached up to tighten the buckles of the vawn saddle and playfully punched Cal-raven's shin, like a father celebrating a small boy's first ride. "And what shape shall your proclamation take, my visionary boy?"

Cal-raven lifted the visor of his helm, reached down, and caught his father by the forearm. "I will call for the pardon of Auralia."

The king broke his son's hold. He seemed to lose his balance for a moment. "Will you?" he replied coldly. The joy in his face had cracked like a broken mask, revealing the furious wraith Cal-raven had seen in the library several nights earlier.

Tabor Jan cleared his throat. "I'll just...I'll let the two of you finish your farewells. And take the troop to the gate."

"I will call for Auralia's pardon and propose that we name her Abascar's Lady of Colors," Cal-raven continued without flinching. "I would have Auralia oversee the advent of Abascar's Spring on the day I inherit the throne. Unless, of course, you still intend to declare these things within your own reign, an event I would be the first to celebrate."

"Your impudence would extend so far!" It was Aug-anstern, tiptoeing warily across the hay-strewn floor. He stepped boldly to the king' shoulder and hovered there. "Upon taking the crown, your defining gesture would be to defy your father and cast down his legacy?"

"Not to defy him, you old vulture. But to give him an honorable escape from a trouble of his own making. It's either that or wait for the grudgers to rise. In this, the king can revive the people's pride and grant them what is rightfully theirs."

"And what does Abascar have to grant them?" laughed Aug-anstern. "Nothing, I say."

"You're wrong. We can restore the freedoms we've taken away." The prince prodded his vawn forward toward the advisor, bringing the animal's seething snout up to nudge the man's chest. "And we can begin by granting Auralia her proper reward."

"How shall I find peace, Cal-raven," Cal-marcus hissed bitterly, "knowing your words here will spread like a contagion? Would you write into history that you stood up and saved House Abascar from your father's cruel judgment, you arrogant son of a Gatherer?"

There was no time to resolve this conversation. Cal-raven sensed, with rising panic, that he had somehow put Auralia in greater danger. "You accuse me of lack of love for you? Even as I ride at your command to defend you? Do you wish me to stumble in my charge?" He could hear his old teacher's reprimand echoing from their trouble at the dig. *Not here. Not in front of the people.* There were too many witnesses. "Grant me this," he said, leaning down to whisper, "that I can dismiss my mother's ghost and let her rest at last. Let Abascar have something more to celebrate than the carcasses of beastmen!"

The silence, the unflinching hatred on the advisor's face was enough to tell Cal-raven that, no matter how strong this appeal, the king would be quickly overwhelmed by relentless pleas to the contrary.

King Cal-marcus's face purpled as though he were sick.

"Showing such favor to this prisoner," the king hissed, "you risk offending your Promised."

"Then perhaps we should postpone the wedding until these matters are resolved."

With that, he turned his vawn and fell in behind the departing troop. Fearing what he would see on his father's face, knowing such images should not haunt the mind of a soldier heading into battle, he did not look back. Reconciliation would have to wait.

And yet his father's fury did haunt him like a fever as he rode, and it was all he could do to turn the fires of anger and fear into fuel for the blows he would strike against the enemy.

Just inside the main gate, the king acknowledged another wave of cheers. His people would assume he was outraged by the attack. They would take comfort in his rage. They would not understand what had brought his temper to a boil.

Wilfry bounded down the lane to throw himself at the king's shins with a volley of affectionate yips. Cal-marcus kicked him away.

"If the prince's first appeal was bold," Aug-anstern muttered in King Cal-marcus's ear, "that last one borders on treason."

"Treason, Aug-anstern?" Cal-marcus bowed his head. He looked at the black gloves Cal-raven had given him in exchange for the riding gloves. They were gloves for rangers and trackers. He slipped his own hands inside. They were still warm. He had not worn gloves like these in many years, since before Jaralaine fled the house. "It was *reason* that I heard."

His heartbeat stumbled out of step, and he clutched at his chest, staggering forward. Irimus Rain, who had snatched the complaining dog back from the king's boots, pushed Aug-anstern aside and stepped in to offer Cal-marcus his arm. The king steadied himself, his heartbeat stable again, and fought to recover his dignity while Irimus brushed stable dust from his cape.

"You are the king of Abascar, son of Har-baron," Irimus said. "Your tale is not finished, however impetuous your son has become." He smiled kindly through his silver beard. "Were we not so audacious ourselves, you and I, when we routed the barbarians, when we made the Cragavar forest safe? My, how times return to the same refrain."

"I should never have told Cal-raven about that meddlesome girl." Cal-marcus tightened his fists. "Too young for prison. Wild and brave. Beautiful. I should have known he would get curious. He *saw* her, you know. It is my fault, and it must not happen again."

"May I suggest some quiet and some counsel?" Irimus handed the wriggling white dog to the king, clearly hoping the animal's affections would ease his temper. "Let us retreat to the library."

Cradling Wilfry in the crook of his arm, Cal-marcus turned his attention to what had once been the queen's tower. "Not again. This Gatherer girl will not cloud my son's vision the way Jaralaine clouded mine."

The rumble of the charge faded in the distance as the king raised a hand to decline the royal litter. He would not be carried. He would walk the long path back to his chambers. He would kindle a fire. He would call for his drink. He would wrap himself in the fireglow and find himself a space to think.

Startled and gossiping Housefolk gathered at every corner, watching the king, his advisors, and his guards. Stablecleaners shuffled in the streets, swinging brooms to rid the road of refuse and vawn tracks. Somewhere a woman wailed in despair. Bad news could spread like wildfire in Abascar.

Mustering what dignity he could, Cal-marcus ran his gloved hand across his forehead as if to smooth the furrows carved by regret. When Wilfry licked his face, he grimaced and passed the dog to Aug-anstern. "I'm in no mood for his maniacal affection," he said, "and I'm likely to smash him if he gets in my way again. Take him away, and stuff him somewhere I can't hear his—"

He stopped so suddenly that Aug-anstern proceeded several paces past him. "Of course," he said to himself.

And then he turned abruptly, informed his entourage that he wished to visit the dungeons. And he quickened his pace to outrun any second thoughts.

He would pardon Auralia. That would please his son.

He would take the cloak she had made, to show that he appreciated her gift. That, too, would please his son.

And he would explain that Auralia had asked for an escort to take her to an undisclosed location, her secret home. Captain Ark-robin would choose riders who could carry her far into the north, to a place where she would be lost. Surely she would never find her way back and never be found.

The problem would be removed from the house. Scharr ben Fray would not have a chance to rescue his meddling agent. And best of all—Cal-raven would never see Auralia again.

21

A Thief in the Underkeep

I n the moment that Radegan the Fox saw Captain Ark-robin turn toward him, the thief had the advantage of surprise. He knew it, and he used it.

Abascar's stone foundations were a complicated maze. Housefolk were forbidden from access to maps revealing its intricate secrets. Even the Underkeep's busy, burrowing laborers were given specific circuits and were arrested if they strayed. Only the king and his closest advisors had complete diagrams of its passages and dens. Radegan knew obtaining such sketches was as dangerous a gamble as stealing the Underkeep's guarded treasures.

Thus, when his guesswork led him not only to the richest pickings of his career but also to an occasion for vengeance, he felt as though he had fallen into a fantastic joke. How in the vast anatomy of the king's underground fortress could he have become such a champion of chance?

He reached to the hilt of the weapon he had stolen. He stepped forward and laughed, triumphant. Recognition—the first paralyzing blow—stunned the king's chief strategist.

It was over in a few frantic moments.

For hundreds of years House Abascar rested on a great stone plateau, looking out in all directions at the rich woods, hills, and rivers of the Expanse. At first the Underkeep was merely a subterranean treasure room, a burrow for the king's secrets.

House Abascar's wealth had grown when Prince Cal-raven's grandfather Har-baron broke deeper ground to mine valuable elements in the stone and clay of the palace's foundation. By the reign of King Cal-marcus, the labyrinth had spread outward, honeycombing the plateau. Tunnels spread deep beneath the homes of the Housefolk. At major crossroads on the surface, guards monitored Underkeep stations, accepting wares and harvests and sending them down on ropes and pulleys to those who would sort, distribute, and prepare them for their best use. Each passageway below had its guard and its purpose.

Any ambitious burglar hoping to steal from the king's hoard would have thought to find a way into the Underkeep by way of one of these stations. Crossroad stations were heavily guarded, but some thieves managed to smuggle themselves down in the crates of contribution. A few smaller shafts opened within privileged officers' homes, allowing them easy access, and if a thief could enter those quarters unobserved, he might manage a clever descent.

Radegan's plan, however, depended on penetrating the highly guarded hoard of Housefolk treasures directly beneath the palace. Even though his most famous thefts had convinced the people he could pass through walls, he had never dared venture within the palace boundary; he could never have hoped to reach those well-secured Underkeep stations.

But the summoner who fancied him happened to serve a regular shift guarding one of those stations. When Radegan promised to hand over a secret hoard of Auralia's inventions, he persuaded her to take a sizable gamble. Out in the forest, she bundled him into a harvest bag and carried him in on the back of her vawn.

Inside the dark Underkeep station—a wooden silo with a rope-and-pulley apparatus rigged within its high, conical ceiling—she lectured him on how long she would wait while he went on his looting spree.

"I will not defend you if you are caught," she insisted. "I will point to evidence revealing that Gatherers smuggled you in on a harvest cart. And you will not be the only one who suffers."

He smiled at her best attempts to appear stern. He knew she could not resist him, and even in the thin lines of sunlight, he could see the rapid pulse along her neck, the flutter in her eyelids. "And who would you sentence to unjust punishments on my account?" he asked.

"I have not been idle during the days since we made our deal," she said. "There's a certain Gatherer woman, married, one with long black curls..."

"You would not meddle with that poor girl," he scoffed. "Merya's a mess."

"Oh yes, I would. You think you can win my trust while you're romancing other women in the wilderness?"

"I have to play certain games to stay a step ahead of fools," he laughed. "When I get to Bel Amica, I'll establish a place there where you and I can revel and relax. I'll come for you within the next six seasons if my strategy plays out. And Abascar will never see you again."

"You'll know I trust you when I tell you my name." She kissed him then, taking off her officer's helm and tossing it aside, running her fingers through his ragged hair and pressing him back against the pulley crank so that the chains clattered and the ropes swayed. "Now," she said, breathless, "where did you hide Auralia's inventions?"

He detailed a path to the stash of marrowwood and explained how many steps to walk south, how many birch trees to count, and where to find the boulder that emerged from the ground like the prow of a sinking boat. "At the base of the stone is a cross thatch of evergreen. You'll find Auralia's bounty beneath it. Then you'll trust me."

He watched her turn the heavy crank, and the platform on which he stood descended. He sank into the musty air of the Underkeep. And he called into the bright, shrinking rectangle, "Farewell, *Brynna.*"

Her head appeared in the light, stark as the pupil in the white of an eye staring down at him. He caught the curse she dropped and laughed quietly, satisfied.

He arrived in a storeroom fragrant with new-mown hay, buckets of apples and globefruit, piles of rocknuts, twinseed, and berries.

A pink, hairless cavecat with enormous ears stared at him. The animal's eyes were so wide, round, and white they looked ready to drop from their sockets. Then it crouched, shoved its head beneath a harvest cart, and slunk out of sight.

Just across the adjoining corridor, a curtained closet of military woodscloaks, waiting for soldiers and duty officers to suit up for patrol.

"Captain Ark-robin," he muttered, drawing back the curtain, "the Fox has slipped its trap and is back in the chicken pen."

He would survive here only in the guise of a soldier and only if he appeared to know where he was going. Somewhere he would have to overcome a patrolling guard. This was risky enough to give him pause...pause to determine a variety of ways to noiselessly end the guard's life.

He chose a long and soiled woodscloak and shook it free of dust. When he did, a shadow slumped to the floor. Radegan jumped back with a shout.

The shape beat leathery wings against the floor. Then from beneath that spiny span, legs, one after the other, emerged—jointed and striped. Clusters of oily eyes emerged and stared at him over fangs that seemed carved from obsidian.

A spiderbat.

Radegan pulled the cloak around himself and shuddered. He had never seen the famous menace of the Underkeep, the plague loosed by the opening of the abyss.

Abascar's miners had broken through, once upon a time, to a chasm that seemed to stretch on forever. Some of the diggers had fallen through, swallowed by an ancient silence. A slightly more fortunate few managed to catch a hold on the chasm walls and remain there screaming until rescuers could pull them back up. They spent the rest of their lives locked in rooms wrestling with a powerful madness. Even those who merely guarded the abyss were seized by weeks of excruciating dizziness. Eventually the king commanded that no one, not even patrolmen, could go near the abyss. Gates were installed. The king ordered the soldiers to secrecy.

But nothing could silence the rumors, and soon there were many and varied stories about what lurked behind those gates, what wafted through the tunnels with sickening groans. Some spoke of an invisible terror, a cruel wind with a will of its own that sent its prey into panic and confusion. Another menace was easier to prove—a storm of eight-legged bats had reportedly emerged, flapping and crawling about in the recesses of the Underkeep. One prick from their venomous fangs, and a victim would swell like bread in an oven; a few days later the poison would lay siege to the mind and memory.

And here was that terrible proof, clutching at the floor like a massive, hairy hand. The bloodthirsty abomination flexed its legs as if preparing for a leap, raising and stretching its fanlike wings.

Radegan stepped back into the corridor and closed the curtain. In that instant, he felt the weight of the creature as it struck at the curtain. Its claws scratched and slid down the cloth.

He stepped aside and waited, gasping. He saw the legs protrude from beneath the dark veil. One moment more, and its head was through. Radegan brought down his heavy boot and smashed it against the floor. Bruised, spluttering foam, the spiderbat thrashed, pounding against the dirt, clinging to the curtain and pulling itself around onto its back. Radegan struck again, the heel of his boot snapping its neck and crushing its bristly black head like an egg. The wings flapped in spasms, the legs clutched at his ankles and pricked at his shins. And then it went still.

He heard a hiss behind him and turned to find the cavecat standing, back arched and fangs bared.

"It's dead," he said. "Let's go."

Radegan broke into a run down the corridor. He had made too much noise and would need more than a woodscloak to avoid drawing attention.

A commotion echoed ahead of him. He stepped sideways into a small cell-like room.

They were unfriendly voices, one unmistakably the complaint of an inebriated man in great distress.

Radegan's eyes adjusted in the dim light to another kind of horror. Shackles were fixed to the wall where a man could be chained at the wrists, arms stretched. Stains lined with hair smeared the floor. A bench ran along the opposite wall for whoever would decide the prisoner's fate. And in the far corner was an empty wooden crate.

When the guards and their prisoner entered, Radegan was curled in the box below the reeking, heavy woodscloak, holding his breath, listening intently for a clue he could work to his advantage.

The drunken prisoner must have been a guard or a soldier himself. He cursed like one as he was shackled to the wall. That would explain the clang of a helmet hitting the floor, the clatter of armor cast aside.

"Kar-balter ker Keven-lor, you are stripped of your title as an officer of House Abascar. Your medals are retracted. And you are sentenced to five years among the Gatherers for stealing ales from the king's distilleries. In addition, you are accused of recklessly endangering those who dwell and work in the distilleries by entering their storehouses in a state of unruly drunkenness with a forbidden and unshielded torch." The officer clucked his tongue and muttered, "What are you, some kind of goatbrain? That's like throwing a match into a tank of lamp oil. For this, an additional year is added to your sentence."

Shackles were fastened with forceful clacks. Kar-balter's weeping increased Radegan's anxiety—plainly, the reprimand would entail more than the reading of the captive's misdeeds.

The initial physical punishment did not last long. After suffering several dull blows, Kar-balter's protests ceased. Guards and others talked in a hush. One, Em-emyt, was praised for cleverness in setting the trap for Kar-balter's theft. And then heavy boots clumped across the cell to the door.

Radegan smiled, pulled back the woodscloak...and was struck in the head by the prisoner's armor, which the last of the departing soldiers had tossed into the box.

He lay there, holding his breath, his skull ringing like a bell, blood spilling into his eyes. "Fantastic," he almost said aloud. "Another scar."

When the throbbing of his bruised forehead subsided, Radegan looked at the helmet, armor, and boots. And he laughed.

As he pulled on the soldier's boots, he stopped to salute Kar-balter, who hung by his wrists, naked, blood splattered, and drooling. "What a tired old lesson you are," Radegan whispered, finding the boots a bit large. "Like a moth to a lantern, eh, Kar-balter? It's a miserable life, serving King Cal-marcus. Could drive a man to drink."

Putting on the armored breastplate, he smiled at the prisoner's attempts to reach the floor with his feet. "You should never drink before stealing. It clouds your judgment." He strapped a curtain of chain mail around his waist. "My father was a drunkard. Taught me a great deal about how not to live my life."

He slapped the senseless convict's face and then pulled the helmet onto his own head. "This is just too easy. Now I'm off to take a thing or two that never belonged to the king. Thank you for the armor and weapons. They'll come in handy."

Leaning close, he added, "Here's a tip. Don't develop desires you can't control. That's what makes men slaves. I may have been cast out. But today they're going to learn what a man can do when he's sharp, quick, and free."

All that Kar-balter could manage was a moan.

A few moments later Radegan was running swiftly down the hall, noisily—Kar-balter's armor was a loose fit. He paused to remind himself of the turns he had made. If he could not find his way back to the right lift, he would have no sure way out.

He was straightening his weapons belt, guessing at the passages that would take him to the storerooms, when a company of soldiers surged toward him. He thought of retreating, but that would look most suspicious of all. He stopped, pulled the visor of the helmet down over his eyes, and decided to stand his ground.

No one seemed surprised to see a soldier alone in the corridor. He turned and stood flat against the wall, allowing them to pass. That's when he noticed these officers were clustered around none other than King Cal-marcus ker Harbaron himself.

"My lord, how shall I explain this to the people?" It was Irimus Rain who leaned against the king. "The riot is still fresh in their minds. When they hear you have sentenced Auralia to the Hole, it will spark another uprising."

The king stopped, just three strides past Radegan, his robes billowing dramatically about him as he rose to his full height and stared at his sniveling advisor. "I went to the dungeons to pardon her, Irimus. I went to fulfill Cal-raven's wish. I would have sent her far from Abascar. But you saw what she had done."

"I did, yes."

"She's a witch, I tell you. Did you see that corridor? The stones in the wall...stones don't *shine*. And the prisoners, they were claiming she had come to save House Abascar. As if we needed saving. Powers like those will make her dangerous anywhere we take her."

"Yes, my lord, but..."

"How can I proceed with Cal-raven's wedding when rumors are already spreading that a treasonous Gatherer is wearing his Ring of Trust?"

The Hole. Radegan felt a pang of panic. Auralia was to be left in the hands of the jailer, the abomination of the Underkeep. She was being sentenced to a fate far worse than he would ever have guessed. The Gatherers would be ruined. Nella Bye would walk, weeping, into the forest and go missing for days. Krawg was already at death's door, and this would break him.

It was easier to consider how others would respond than it was to imagine what Auralia would face.

Perhaps he could rescue her.

He remained still, at attention, every bit the dutiful soldier as the crowd waited for the king's temper to cool.

He glanced back down the corridor. If they had just come from the dungeon, then he could find it. He could pose as a jail guard, come to escort Auralia to the Hole, and then spirit her away. In her gratitude, she might even learn to think of him differently. Perhaps he could take Auralia away with him and leave Merya to deal with her husband.

And then Radegan had another surprise.

What he had assumed to be the glow of torches carried by the king's guards was in fact something glimmering in the king's own hands.

"She refuses to destroy this abomination," the king roared, shaking Auralia's cape in his advisor's face, "this open mockery of my Proclamation. I will have it plunged into a dye that will obliterate her work, then throw it back to her before she chokes on the jailer's tools!" Face red as a beet, the king looked ready to collapse in the corridor.

And then, as quickly as Cal-marcus had stopped, he started forward again like a charging vawn, the guards scrambling to keep up.

Radegan stepped away from the wall as the last man passed, his gaze following the king's crown in the dim torchlight.

He would take those colors. He would snatch them from the dye vats. It would be risky, but there was nothing more beautiful in all the world.

To steal the very thing the king had outlawed and to be rewarded for bestowing it upon Bel Amica... That would make Cal-marcus the greatest fool of the Expanse. This was better than staging Auralia's rescue. This would be his parting insult to House Abascar.

As the king and his company passed the room where Kar-balter hung bleeding, and then moved beyond the cloak closet, the last man in the procession slowed to a standstill, staring down at the sticky mass of smashed spiderbat.

Radegan laughed in spite of his peril, for he knew now what he would do. He had no choice.

The last man in the entourage was Captain Ark-robin himself.

Obeying his hatred, Radegan placed his hand on the hilt of the dagger he had taken from the captive officer. He advanced, just a few steps behind the soldiers, ready should the moment present itself to strike down his enemy, seize Abascar's prize, and leave this blasted house behind.

22

THE JAILER

Maugam was bald, and so broad and flat was his skullcap that sweat pooled there and became stagnant. With such vigor did he apply himself to his vocation that he did not bother to swipe the grime away when it finally spilled into his eyes nor as it continued falling like tears to soak his baggy trousers.

He was focused, committed to his responsibility—he considered it an art—and accustomed to the solitude of his macabre workshop. What did his unsightly mass or his reputation matter? The dungeon was a small corner of House Abascar, but it belonged to him.

Abascar's kings—Maugam had served three of them—detested him in every way. But they had each been forced to admit the benefit of keeping him close at hand as a silent threat to Abascar's criminal sort.

How Maugam stayed alive through the years, no one understood. Some said he was dead inside and moved only by the will of the darkness his deeds attracted. Others whispered of the shapeless menace that drove Underkeep miners mad, saying the jailer had embraced it.

Some proposed another possibility. Cursed with a repulsive appearance, Maugam found joy in spoiling those more beautiful than himself.

Maugam loved scars, if he could love anything at all. He was meticulous about inflicting them. Some people sculpted stone or clay. Maugam's medium was flesh. When Abascar deemed a criminal too loathsome for the Gatherers, the magistrates sent him to the dungeons, either to rot in Maugam's deliberate neglect or suffer as objects of his cruel arts.

He mastered his prisoners. He measured their respect for him in the silence that met his approach. He forged and mapped many and varied paths to confession, to supplication, to surrender. Some paths were efficient. But others were more interesting.

It was true that young Maugam, a sickly child, had been fond of verse before his training busied him with other skills. He had written volumes praising his young sister, whose beauty he worshiped. Here he would sometimes practice his talents on the guilty until they offered praise in the form of pleasing verse.

Few found enough wits under Maugam's punishments to compose any verse.

Maugam's scarmaking required a wide array of tools, one of which he held lightly in his hand, a good solid whip. Once in a while, when a prisoner survived with impressive scars, Maugam would loose him among the Gatherers to spread the testimony of his persuasive methods.

Razor stones were tied to each strand of the whip, and as it swished along the floor of slate tiles like a restless snake, they rattled and scraped. A white coal sizzled and hissed in the corner lantern.

"Maugam, be a good child and thank the prisoner," the jailer sighed. He was no longer able to acknowledge that this pulpy, ghost-fleshed creature was, in fact, himself. Thus he addressed himself with scorn, as if he were someone else. "You enjoyed this, Maugam. The prisoner cooperated so willingly, you had the chance to carve something that pleased you. The grudgers you carved yesterday, they were not so willing. Ah, well, you know you are not finished. It is time to take this good subject to the Hole."

He got quiet as he thought about that. He got this quiet at other times too. Like when he gazed admiringly at pieces of freshly carved roast streamertail or after setting a ripe pear on a board and slicing it into thin, sweet, precise wedges.

Blood dripped from the dangling prisoner's toes and into the pit over which he was strung.

"King Cal-marcus is sending someone special down to you, Maugam," the jailer said to himself. "Someone who must be taught a lesson. Treason, they say. Inciting riots among those same grudgers that you carved yesterday. You hope she's like a beastman, don't you, Maugam? Something unnatural. Those half animals, they bring out the worst in you. And they make such exquisite noise." The jailer yawned wistfully. "Save some strength, child. Prince Cal-raven is on the hunt. He will bring you beastmen soon."

He rubbed his forehead. Even when he was busy elsewhere, pacing the corridors, that vacuous black Hole gave him a headache. He rolled his head back and popped his vertebrae like a string of firecrackers.

The chains suspending the prisoner squeaked like dissonant fiddles.

The jailer sighed. "No cell time for this one, Maugam. Doesn't learn his lesson, the good captain said. Came back from outside the walls for revenge. Such audacity. Ark-robin's dogs, they helped, they did. They sniffed out the Underkeep station where someone had let him in. And they found the summoner, didn't they, Maugam? You wonder what the thief had promised her. You wonder, don't you?"

A faint sob escaped the prisoner.

"You're laughing, Maugam," the jailer said, scolding himself. "You're laughing at the prisoner's pain. Is it really so amusing that this disobedient fool drew a dagger to strike Captain Ark-robin and—so unlikely, yet it's true—the dagger had only *half a blade*?"

That inspired a rattle in the shackles, a surge in the prisoner's spirit.

"Ah, but this unruly burglar was wearing Kar-balter's armor. Yes. You've heard about Kar-balter, Maugam. It's a simple rule: examine your blade before you attack. And that's why a man is hanging here, getting stuck. Stuck with those dreadful, sharpened things. Stuck." Maugam liked that word. He said it again as he picked up an old spear, rusty from its years lying in the underground mud. "Stuck."

He gave the spear one more thrust into the back of the prisoner's knee, and the body seemed to come alive, a puppet flailing on strings. Maugam dropped the spear and walked to the wheel from which chains ran up to a ceiling pulley and down to the prisoner's wrists.

"Was that really necessary, Maugam?" he asked himself. "Now he may not survive the Hole."

He kicked the lever on the crankwheel, which spun and unwound a long clattering stream of chains, plunging the prisoner into the Hole. When the chains reached the end of their slack, the dungeons rang with an echoing bang.

The jailer withdrew a pear he had stuffed in his pocket for just such a moment and took a deep bite. As he held the juicy orb in one hand, he worked the crankwheel, muscles flexing.

The prisoner reappeared, a clutch of shredded rags. Maugam slid a large net across the top of the Hole and kicked the wheel's lever again, dropping the body into the net. Then he dragged it back to the floor. He knelt down and unlocked the shackles. Then he towed the prisoner by hand and hair to a corner for the guards to clean up like trash.

But the guards who arrived were not interested in what was left of Radegan.

There were two, and Maugam could see immediately they were new to this task. They eagerly tossed their burden into the cave and drew back, waiting to make sure he acknowledged their delivery.

She was a small and shuddering girl.

Maugam heard that officers had locked up a rebellious woman who had provoked the grudgers. But he had been too busy to visit her himself.

Never in all his days as jailer had he seen a prisoner so young, so vulnerable.

He quickly put down the whip and blinked mole eyes at the flinching guards. "No one with any sense would bring...*that*...to Maugam. No one."

One guard escaped without reply, but Maugam's words stopped the other. "Auralia refused to respect the Rites of the Privilege," he haltingly explained. "She is guilty of conspiring with an exiled advisor, an enemy of House Abascar. She is guilty not only of speaking deception but of inciting a treasonous riot. She has provoked the grudgers. And since she's arrived in the prison, she has made things worse. She has sought to deceive Prince Cal-raven and taunted the king by transforming the prisons through her strange powers." He glared at the shadows where the girl was almost visible. "It is…unfortunate."

"Unfortunate?" the jailer shrieked. "What do you mean, she *transformed* the prisons? Maugam rules the prisons."

"Her magic lit up the prison, Jailer, and enchanted the prisoners. She set the stones to shining. The place is full of color."

"But…" Maugam peered at Auralia out of one eye, then the other. "What Maugam will do to her she cannot endure. What is that she's holding?" Maugam reached for the girl, touched her trembling hand, and then recoiled as though stung. "Great bones of Tammos Raak! She wears the prince's Ring of Royal Trust! If Maugam were to proceed, he would be…he would be arrested and sent…to Maugam!" The jailer began to quake, confused and distraught.

"Command of the king, Jailer. It overrules the Ring of Trust."

"Why didn't the king take the ring off her finger?"

"He also…" The guard clearly found his own testimony implausible. "He also condemned the *ring*, Jailer. Childhood fancies, you see. It's crafted in the shape of the Keeper. He wants it to vanish. Into the Hole. With the girl."

"This…this little thing," Maugam murmured, unable to look at Auralia directly. "It might make Maugam remember. Things will not go well if he remembers." In this dark place, he had never seen a girl of such gentle, fragile beauty. His memory stirred against his will, the image of his precious little sister surfacing suddenly. The sweetness of the pear upon his tongue soured.

"Don't give her to Maugam," he shuddered. His hands fumbled about in the air as if searching for some response that would correct the situation. "Don't let him have her. For he cannot bear to see what will happen."

The guard fled, taking the orange torchlight with him.

In the feeble glow of the lamp, Maugam fixed his eyes on the hole in the floor, on the yawning darkness. Beside it lay the spear, the whip, and other spiked and blunt-ended instruments. He closed his eyes, clutched at his protruding belly.

"Maugam," he said to himself, "you must think this through. Why would you hurt her?"

It had become one of his favorite rants against prisoners, to torment them with memories of their childhood, to force them to search for the moment when their hearts went bad. Maugam enjoyed it when they found regret at last, when they wept for what they had become.

Now, hating himself instead of the criminal, he turned those questions inward.

He remembered the day his mother told him to drive away the serpents basking in the sun beneath a bush outside his sister's window. The snakes, she had said, would eventually be hungry, and they would try to steal eggs from a nest in the tree nearby. Or worse, they might bite his sister while she played in the grass.

The very thought of their predatory nature troubled young Maugam. He determined he would teach the snakes to fear him. He would punish them for even *thinking* of harming his sister.

So he tortured them. With sharp objects and with flame. He had felt a rush of virtue and a strange delight in seeing them feel the pain they might have caused others. Further, there was the thrill of secrecy, for nobody watched him. Nobody stopped him. How far could he go? What would it take to change the nature of a snake?

The next day tears had soaked his pillow. But when a troop of soldiers passed down the avenue, his dreams of riding among them flared, and he sprang to his feet. He felt ashamed of himself for crying, for if he was to be a soldier someday he would have to kill without tears. So, with his mind fixed upon strength and courage, he returned to the snake bush with a shovel, determined to dig them up. Determined to practice, and practice, and practice the art of hindering those who might work evil, who might threaten his precious and beautiful sister.

As these memories seized and shook him, he slumped to the ground and stared at Auralia's feet. They were so small, toes as perfect as peapods. She lay blinking, like his sister in her bed when he had run in to wake her.

For many months Maugam's mind had sought to tear itself free from his person. As if clinging to the ceiling and looking down with contempt, it had declared itself a separate thing, rejecting any relationship with what the body exercised upon its property. But now, here, it lost its grip and fell back.

"Enough. It's all gone on too long, too far. I want you to get out of here," Maugam said to the girl. "It is dangerous here. I want you to go."

The darkness of the Hole below the hanging chains...

On hands and knees, Maugam crawled toward his tools. He lifted a heavy, blood-caked spade. It was not so different from the shovel he had used to capture the snakes long, long ago.

He looked down into the Hole.

Auralia thought she had fallen asleep. There were no dreams, just darkness interrupted by the faint outline of a monstrous, pale, crawling shape.

But then she heard faint, feeble cries. She lifted her head and turned.

The eyes that caught the lamplight were colorless, blind. But she recognized him anyway.

Auralia pushed herself to her knees and crawled across the murky soil to the broken body of Radegan the thief. As she did, she felt her own tears flow for the first time since her imprisonment.

She leaned down and kissed his bloody cheek, and heard the faint rasping of his throat.

"I'm sorry, Auralia," he was saying. "I'm sorry."

"No," she said. "*They* should be sorry. Nobody, nobody deserves this."

"I'm sorry. I took all your gifts from the Gatherers."

She wept now, clutching her hands together, for she dared not touch his broken fingers.

"I've told no one. They are strung up in a basket, high in a tree. The tree with the hollow arm. Beside the old gorrel warren."

"I know the tree, Radegan."

"I'm sorry."

Auralia glanced over her shoulder. The strange white giant had disappeared into the pit. She did not know who he was or what he was doing.

Auralia began to push through piles of bones, tugging at loose shreds of cloth, fitfully tying and bundling them together. Whispering to Radegan, she described the beauty of the lake, of the ghostly shapes she saw on the shore. She feared to look about, for she could sense something listening, hearts beating close. She braided the strands and the shape in her hands began to grow. When Radegan's weeping softened to a faint and steady breath, she lifted his bloodied head and rested it upon the pillow she had made. Her tears fell like white jewels in the cold lamplight.

23

CAL-MARCUS TURNS

Agoblet of rare black crystal splintered the afternoon sunlight on the windowsill of the king's bedchamber, radiating bright and jagged lines throughout the room. Patches of light wavered on the walls as if exploring the tapestries. One of those woven murals illustrated King Gere-baron fighting Bel Amicans before the Truce of the Trade Routes. Another depicted Har-baron leading a charge against Cent Regus beastmen.

There was no tapestry bearing Cal-marcus's image, his story. Not yet.

Cal-marcus sat by the window and touched the goblet. The weight of all that had transpired held him fast to this chair. He had looked out upon Abascar for hours, watching the shadows turn about the towers like the dial of a compass. As those dark lines moved, the beauty of the change seemed to right what had been jarred askew. He could not explain it, nor could he even recognize it, but his thoughts had realigned, the dark haze of wrath and fear clearing as the perfumed wind washed over the windowsill. His world had come back into focus. No one counseled him. Nothing persuaded him. He just knew this was the moment—the time to decide what his own story would be. How would he be remembered? As the king who cleansed the woods of marauders? Or the man who drained the color from Abascar? Tomorrow the dye would have settled in the fabric, and no one would ever be able to wash it clean.

He watched the clear hajka swirling in its dark bowl. He traced the circle of the brim, surveying the view before him, west and north across the Expanse with all the attention of a watchtower guard. Cal-raven was out there somewhere, fighting beastmen, saving the laborers, risking his life for the glory of Abascar. No, not for the glory of Abascar. Cal-raven did things for those he loved. Today he fought to save his father from disgrace. He fought to save the lives of people he knew and cherished.

How would Cal-raven be rewarded upon his return?

To the west, the sun slid down into woods. To the north, its rays painted the fanged peaks of the Forbidding Wall.

The king looked away from the window, winced, and pushed the cup off the sill.

As if the gesture called on a curse, his hand began to shake. It would never stop shaking. It would shake until he died.

Frightened by the seizure, he stood and grasped the window ledge, looking down for the cup as if he might snatch it from the air.

He spied it lying in a tangle of long-dead rosebushes along the edge of the small, private garden.

"Dig up the garden." Even though he had not seen the meddling mage for years, the old man's counsel lingered. "Dig it up. Let it go. Do not dwell upon her ghost." It had been good advice. The garden was a graveyard now.

His cup lay among the dry, brittle thorns, the drink seeping through cracks in the crystal.

He wanted to feel relief. But he felt nothing. Nothing at all. He had cast away the danger, but the work had barely begun.

He collapsed into the chair and lifted a bell. It took no will to ring it. His hand was already shaking. The attendant came at once, ready for instruction.

⁂

One morning early in Jaralaine's reign, Scharr ben Fray had stood at this very window, sharing the view of the roses. "Your queen has quite a gift," the mage had said. "Her love for beauty gives the garden a magic. She could coax color from ash. A shame that she clutches such wonders to herself."

Cal-marcus understood the queen's compulsion to keep the garden private.

As she narrated her childhood memories to him while they lay awake, he was taken by how many of her stories found her wandering off into wildflowers. Her father had always dragged her back, tearing bouquets from her grasp. Here in this courtyard she could cultivate the scents, sights, and sounds she loved. Here Cal-marcus had given her what she needed. He had ensured her safety and given her peace.

Or so he had tried.

But what he had first thought of as scars were, he now realized, wounds that had never closed.

"People judge merchants," Jaralaine had told him when they met. "We made a trade, and they called us devious. We crafted our clothes from things in the wild, and they called us primitive. Even merchants judge merchants. We were totally alone."

When Jaralaine was born, the youngest of four, her arrival strained the family's meager resources, making things even worse. Her father despised her for increasing his burdens, and her mother could not meet her gaze. She never grew close to her brother, Jermin, for he mirrored his father's expression and disdain.

She had been left in the company of her older sisters, Jeriden and Jesimay, who were often humiliated at marketplaces and sometimes sought in trade. They hated their lives and hated that they were forced to work so hard along the road. Labor in the morning, danger in the day, bitter disputes over bargaining tables, shadows in the evening. Hunger. Injury. Snakes. Jeriden and Jesimay came to despise the judgmental people who lived within houses. And yet they tempted boys from the Abascar Housefolk in hopes of being seized and stolen away, escaping the road. Rejected at every turn, they were prone to fits of temper. Jaralaine was easy prey.

So she found her own paths, roads that led away from roads. She made friends among other living things—things that would not condemn her, things that wanted, even needed, her attention. She named herself the forest's gardener, and flourishing gardens sprang up in the woods.

Cal-marcus had been drawn to her enthrallment with the wilderness. He had lured her to follow him, just so he would not lose her, so he could escape his own responsibilities and play with her far from the harsh gaze of his father.

His life became dependent on her whims, a truth he carefully ignored. He convinced her to come and live among the Gatherers, just to keep her within his reach. He would steal away to visit her, his favor provoking further contempt from her new and jealous neighbors. "An exile among exiles," Jaralaine called herself in sighs.

But it was not merely to rescue her from the Gatherers that Cal-marcus chose to marry her. She was beautiful, and in the gown of a princess more beautiful still.

He took a sort of wicked pleasure in sitting beside her at the court banquets, for she would speak to no one but him, remaining a mystery to his father and the council. *His* mystery.

When he was king and she was queen, his was the only heart in her favor.

At one elaborate dinner, they sat at opposite ends of the feast. A wide red ribbon ran the length of the abundant table, decorated with glittering candles. As the somber counselors debated across their plates and glasses of wine, Jaralaine playfully pulled at the ribbon, drawing it down inch by inch into her lap. It slowly carried the candles, the vases of flowers, the bowls of seasoning and olives toward her until the magistrates were struck silent to find all the table's decorations clustered around her plate.

He had laughed with her, failing to see this as a portent of things to come.

Those had been different days before the death of Cal-marcus's own father and mother in a wasting winter plague. Too immature for the responsibility of the throne and frightened by a brush with the suffocating outbreak himself, he worked days and the nights, commanding his people to stay in their houses until the spread of disease had been halted.

Meanwhile, Jaralaine helped him master the kingship and prepare his house for an uncertain future. Flourishing where she had been planted, she would emerge from her garden with inspired ideas.

"The house, the forest, the river—they're ours," she said amongst pillows, drawing him toward her. "No one can take them."

"Careful, my love," he whispered, repeating words he remembered from a lesson with Scharr ben Fray. "Desire's a dangerous guide. He has no respect for borders. There are deeper laws we must respect."

"But who's to say any law is better than our will?" Her soft hands spidered up his back, her sharp nails dug into his shoulders. "We've seen the world, and more, we've learned what it can be. I was just a merchant's daughter, and now a king is in my arms. Do you see? Where your heart leads you...follow."

Indeed, where Jaralaine's heart led, the house soon followed. The magistrates were malleable, the captain and defender easily conquered. Cal-marcus had re-inforced the walls, ordered Housefolk to stay inside. Convinced that Gatherers were conspiring, he had heightened restrictions and doubled the guard.

While Jaralaine delighted in establishing new restrictions, she refused to respect any authority these laws might have over her. She continued to pass beyond the walls for long strolls along the winding River Throanscall, taking only one or two guards with her.

Once she returned to tell Cal-marcus she had seen a thief running away from the house. "He could have killed you," he grumbled. She ignored him; she defied him, in fact, wearing brilliant red and yellow dresses through the woods.

Among the king's disgruntled advisors, only Scharr ben Fray had been compassionate. But he had also spoken warnings that kept Cal-marcus awake. "You may not yet know what kind of flower you have plucked from the wilderness," the mage had murmured. "She is generous, in your experience. But think about why she chose you—a prince, one who could offer all she lacked."

Cal-marcus forbade the mage to advise him regarding Jaralaine again, but those words had already taken root. When he cautioned her again about wandering, she flew into a rage. "To keep me from danger, you would build me a jail?"

And that night she stole away without guards for the first time. She stayed out in the woods as the moon rose and had not yet returned when the king searched for her at daybreak.

That same day a few vagabonds made a vengeful strike, butchering a company of Gatherers harvesting seeds. When Jaralaine appeared the next evening, burrs and blood streaking her ragged gown, she clutched at her belly and fell to her knees, crying, "I won't go away again. Forgive me."

"I will give you whatever you need," he said again, now, engrossed in the memory. He stared out at the familiar darkness, but in his mind he still knelt before her.

"Cal-marcus," Jaralaine had said, surprising him with a smile, "I have brought you a gift. I have brought you an heir."

Reports of marauders increased. Even though the queen was now bedridden, caring for their son Cal-raven, Cal-marcus faithfully related to her all information he received on these strange attackers. Jaralaine's close call with danger should have convinced her to stay home. But Cal-marcus's attempts to frighten her brought his heart no assurance that she would not run away again.

He doubled the combat exercises for his army's swiftest riders and equipped them with the best weapons his forge could produce. He gave Tar-brona a charge and sent him out to canvass the woods. Tar-brona found marauders and fed them to the wolves.

Certain this triumph had earned them House Abascar's respect after years of unrest, Cal-marcus and Jaralaine had taken their place before the people. But the cheers praised only Captain Tar-brona and his king.

Then Jaralaine spoke the words that ruined him, confirming Scharr ben Fray's many warnings. "House Abascar treats me with reproach," she declared, leaving no room for argument. "I can never escape the dark cloud that followed me along the merchant roads. I will go to House Bel Amica, where the people call their queen beloved. And I will learn what it is that makes them love her. I will learn how to break this curse."

When Jaralaine returned in a jealous rage at what she had seen, she was already plotting ways to match, and even surpass, Queen Thesere's glory.

Scharr ben Fray was in a panic, declaring that the queen had bent Cal-marcus's will. But he was too late. And all was lost to the Proclamation of the Colors.

The king had disguised himself with confidence and pleasure as the house surrendered its colors, its treasures, its life, and its future. He presented his queen in a new gown, with a new crown, to inspire the love of the people. But they only applauded now because it earned them honor stitches and credit for loyalty.

King Cal-marcus ker Har-baron placed his hands on the mirror frame. *A jail indeed, this house. I raised walls within walls.*

Around the time of the Proclamation, as Cal-raven had begun to play with toy swords and declare himself a soldier, rumors spread of a great beast hiding in Deep Lake. The stories captured the boy's imagination.

"Pretend you are the Keeper, Papa!" the boy had laughed, jumping out from beneath the great map table and waving a wooden sword.

The king had dropped to all fours, playfully swiping at his son with imaginary claws. "I thought you said the Keeper protects you. Why would you run at me with a sword?"

"I want to protect the Keeper!" the boy had announced. "Protect it from fangbears and wolves!"

"Son," Jaralaine had whispered, "there is no such frightful thing walking in the forest." When the king suggested that she should allow the boy such comforting fantasies, her reply was sharp. "I saw what remained of my family after the savages struck. There was no one to help them. Nothing came to save them. The dreams are wishful thinking, a childish comfort for the weak. We must learn to save ourselves."

At that moment Cal-marcus began to suspect that Jaralaine ventured out not to force him to respect her will but to challenge the darkness in the woods, to overpower it, to prove to everyone the Expanse belonged to her.

As Jaralaine stepped beyond the reach of law, Scharr ben Fray dared to say, "I've changed my mind, good king. I will not goad you to restrain her anymore."

"At last you've understood. She cannot be bound."

"No. And that is why you must let her go. There are boundaries across which we cannot step, Cal-marcus. Perhaps she will only learn when she steps across them."

That step had come so quickly.

Less than a month later he woke to find her gone. Her resplendent gown of colors, woven from threads stripped from the finest Housefolk treasures, was missing.

All the palace heard his cries. "Thieves! Invaders! She is taken! She is gone!" It took three guards and Scharr ben Fray's potions to quiet him.

In her garden, flowers drooped, once-green leaves curling, ashen. It was never replanted.

He wanted to believe Jaralaine had been kidnapped, numbing his heart to any doubt. Not long after, he banished Scharr ben Fray, for despite the mage's counsel, Cal-marcus had lost his queen.

The voice he heard in his memory crying out for the lost queen had been so like the voice that had sounded in the dungeons only a few hours ago. Could it have been only this morning?

The mirror rattled against the wall in the hold of his trembling hand. Everything he touched, he broke.

A voice at the door broke his grasp. "My lord, the Lady Stricia, Prince Cal-raven's Promised, is here. You called for her?"

"Did her summoner deliver the gift of the pearls?"

"Yes, master. She's wearing them."

"Thank you. Send her in."

He did not turn to look at Stricia. He continued to stare down at the dead garden.

"I must make haste. So listen carefully," he said.

Even now—with this hopeful, ambitious, beautiful woman waiting behind him. He would crush her too.

"I have sent for you, captain's daughter, that I might save you. My son is all I have left. He minds not anything I say of you. His heart is all in knots. The wedding plan was a mistake. I would force him to follow the leading of my heart. But what is my heart? How dare I depend on such a misguided instrument? What kind of wonders might I have seen in this world if I had listened before I spoke, observed before I seized, hesitated before I proclaimed? I am king, laying claim to all I see from this window. And yet nothing gives itself to me. Nothing but beauty. And the love of my son." He gestured to the north, his shaking hand appearing to grasp at the last flaring diamond of sunlight behind the mountains. "He is all I have left of the world you and I once knew."

You and I.

"I'm sorry, my lady. I was thinking of my dear lost queen. Her pearls. It is right that you should have them. And the royal apparel you so desire." He gestured to the marrowwood closet. "I give it all to you. You may wear anything you find within it without fear of punishment. That is my offering to you. For all that I have destroyed stands beside me. I cannot let Cal-raven join that line of resentful ghosts. He is to be king, after all."

He glanced backward and sighed. "Thank you for accepting this."

She stood there, wavering in a splendid gown of white and gold. Already arrogant in her assurance of a royal wedding and a throne, she had come to him in illegal colors.

But she was not alone. Wraiths slipped past her, crowding into the room, shadows with pale, mournful faces. She did not see them, and he was not surprised.

"Ah, they have come for me." He spread his arms in welcome. "I have always wondered if they were conjured by the drink. But here they are again, come to watch and wait. And this time, at last, I do not loathe their gaze." Was there comfort in the hands of Northchildren? Were they perhaps not so malevolent as the stories said?

Stricia, looking around but seeing nothing, sucked in a shuddering breath. "*Why?* Why take back what you proclaimed?"

He stepped forward to touch the pearls that glistened around her neck. She flinched.

Stricia cautiously approached and took his hand. "Do not make any hasty decisions today."

"You will always ask me why, captain's daughter. Perhaps someday you will find something beautiful has grown around *your* question. I've made nothing from my questions. I've only caused more pain. I have nothing beautiful to give. Nothing but these. Just empty garments, frail skins the queen shed."

She stood beside him, a young Jaralaine distracted by her jewelry. Together they were like giants of history, statues for the stage at the Rites, gold in the torchlight. Stricia clutched at the pearls. Did she understand?

The king sighed. "Perhaps where I have failed, Cal-raven will succeed. I won't hinder his journey anymore. You want a gift from the king? Hear this: if you allow Abascar freedom, some people will choose what they shouldn't." He took hold of her shoulder, speaking with urgency. "But take away that freedom, and *no one* has opportunity to choose what they should."

He was speaking nonsense, his trembling hand shaking her shoulder. She wrested away, and he was filled with despair. The Northchildren crowded around him. They said nothing, but their touch was comforting, not cold as he had feared.

Could Stricia not see these shadows?

He fought on, determined not to falter in this final proclamation. "We thought we loved each other, Jaralaine and I. Maybe we did." He spoke with difficulty, struggling to translate from a foreign script. He managed a soft smile. "You resemble her, captain's daughter. But you still have time to choose. And so does my son." He turned from her to the window. "Do not hate him. Punish me instead."

"But you are the king," Stricia said desperately. "Your will—not Cal-raven's—must be done."

"My son is too kind to insist upon his own will. No, he is finding the path of some greater will. I think I used to know that path." He looked to the window, but the world was dark now. "There is something familiar about his spirit."

He heard the pearls hit the floor as Stricia ran from the room. He winced, but remained still, waiting for an answer to an unspoken question.

The answer came, for she ran back into the room, snatched the necklace, and then departed, never to return.

"Come away." The whisper was gentle. "It is finished."

The shadow dissolved under his gaze. "No," he whispered, "not yet. I have one last wrong to right." He drew back the curtain and called with newfound strength for an escort to take him to the dungeon.

"Please," he growled as he leaned on the bewildered guard and staggered down the stairs. "Please let me reach her in time."

Roselinda had just returned from a conference with the tailors and weavers who would outfit the wedding party and the jewelers who were crafting kingly rings and queenly bracelets. It had been her task since Jaralaine's time to gather the finest artists in the house and direct them in weaving all manner of cloth. The royal marriage was still many days away, but there was much to do, and if Roselinda had learned anything in her years as royal seamstress, it was the value of working ahead of schedule.

Today, however, she had immersed herself in the wedding plans, delaying the task that lay waiting in the washroom.

Roselinda leaned with one heavy hand on the edge of the deep washbasin. It seemed cruel, what she had been ordered to do. She turned on the water, reached to the shelf above the tub. The jar of dye powder seemed small in her hand, but when she lifted the lid to see it was full, she knew well what its contents could do.

She set the jar beside the basin.

Auralia's colors lay draped over the drying rack, shimmering in the cold white light.

Roselinda pulled in a deep breath, patted her bosom in dismay, and then, gritting her teeth, grasped Auralia's weaving by the edges and lifted it over the basin, ever so careful not to knock the dye into the water prematurely. Perfumes flowered in the air, and she drew her face into its folds, where a sob escaped. The colors smelled like a forest in the morning after a rain.

"Never," she had whispered to the tailors and jewelers, "never has there been anything so beautiful."

As Roselinda placed the cape slowly in the water, she glared at the dye jar, wondering what accident might cause the powder to disappear, at least until the king saw reason and withdrew his instructions.

The cloth sank into the water and began to twist and fold and turn like a living thing, the water glittering with its light.

On impulse, she put a safe distance between her and the basin. "Maybe I'll just tease loose some of those stitches before it's destroyed. I should store those mysterious threads for safekeeping."

Relieved that the deed was yet to be done, Roselinda rushed from the washroom and back up the stairs to search for her scissors. Along the way she was interrupted and drawn back into the wedding plans.

24

THE PROMISE BROKEN

Stricia moved as if sleepwalking through the dark door of her family's seven-structure home.

As she did, she remembered that she had been the first to step through this door into the most coveted lodging outside of Abascar's palace, on a day of inauguration after her father had been promoted to the role of chief strategist and captain of the guard. A host of soldiers pulled carts with the family's belongings up the path through the brandberry bushes. A wreath of roses decorated the door. As Aug-anstern delivered a speech, she had jumped from her chair, dodged her mother's grasp, and run up the front path, plunging into the house which smelled of marrowwood, incense, and newly woven grass rugs.

She had run through every room in search of her own, the youngest woman in House Abascar to have a chamber all to herself. When she found it, she immediately realized that some of the laborers had huts smaller than her room. This pleased her immensely.

Behind her, the Housefolk had laughed, but she was not embarrassed. This place belonged to her.

She never hurried through the front door again. She liked to be seen going in, liked to linger and greet the stone-carved wyrms that guarded the door. She liked to salute the guard, who ensured their privacy and patrolled the perimeter of the adjoining structures on a nightly fire watch.

But this evening...

The nature of her conference with the king was clear to anyone who saw her walk from the palace past the guards without so much as a nod or a blink, past servants hurrying home and dusty grey-clad children being told the time for roadball games was past.

The servant woman busying herself within the house nearly dropped an armload of towels as she dodged the captain's daughter. Stricia went straight to the tapestry above the fireplace, a reward to their house from the king, granted because she had turned in several young Underkeep thieves. Without hesitation, she tore it free, knocking cold candles from the mantel, which shattered into waxy crumbs. She bundled the tapestry against her as if squeezing the life from something within it, wrapped it into a tangled ball, and thrust it into the piles of ash in the fireplace.

With that, she rushed down the corridor. The servant woman, now carrying a broom, had to jump again to stay out of her way.

As Stricia stepped into her mother's chamber, a sudden movement caught her eye. She turned to behold herself in the full-length mirror. Her face was fixed in the pale horror that had possessed her ever since she had faced the king. She straightened and regarded her proper stance. The pearls about her neck were large, exquisite.

In the reflection she saw her mother's dresser. On it stood a clay sculpture dressed like the king, a figure she had made as a gift for her father years before. Muttering, she turned and smashed it against the edge of the dresser. The head broke off and rolled across the floor, and its crown of dried flowers disintegrated. She dropped what remained, and it shattered.

Falling back against the bed and trembling, she was horrified at what she had done. The statue lay broken in jagged shards, sharp as the knowledge piercing her. A piece of the king's face, eyes sightless, looked up at her.

She turned her eyes away from the king's broken head, remembering that she had seen another broken face in recent days. Her father had confiscated evidence from the courtyard after the Rites. The stone-sculpted arm and hand—those he had turned over to the king. But the face, the mask of Scharr ben Fray—that he had kept as a souvenir.

"I did it all properly!" she said to the ruin of the king. "It's not my fault! I followed all the rules."

She wished her mother were home. But Say-ressa was at the medicine house, tending to those who had been injured in the riots. Did her mother know already? The whole city might already know. They might have known before she ever received the summons.

She sat up straight like a queen, closed her eyes, and said to the servant who was carrying a cat out of her father's chamber, "It's all just a misunderstanding." She touched the line about her neck. "You see. These are pearls for a bride. They were the queen's. He gave them to me."

"I'm sure they will make you very happy," said the housemaid. The cat wriggled and yowled, and she shook her head and walked away. Stricia would have asked her to come back. She wanted the company. But she did not know the woman's name.

Descending the long stair, in the rising thunder of her pulse and panic, she had heard the king's distant voice echo down a command. He would go to the prisons. He would release Auralia.

Which meant the afternoon rumors were true. Cal-raven had mentioned Auralia to his father in a favorable fashion, and now everyone was caught up in a mad scandal.

She heard the sound of the Underkeep hatch creaking open and then a resentful hiss as the housemaid turned the crank and lowered the troublesome cat into the tunnels on the delivery pallet. She heard a distant, bitter growl as the hatch slammed shut.

Stricia stood, pulling the necklace over her head, and paced into her father's room. The servant woman scowled. "Blasted animal." She pushed past Stricia with a hint of contempt in her voice and did not stop when the girl turned to ask her name.

The shields and helm Ark-robin had worn in his days serving Captain Tar-brona were hung on an armor stand in the corner, oil-lamp flames scrawling silver lines across their polished angles. At the edge of Stricia's vision, the empty figure of the soldier seemed a ghost from her childhood.

"You promised me."

Tears sped from her cheeks to her chin, trailed down her neck. Too ridiculous to wear, these jewels. *Rocks from inside some sea creature's shell.* She hated them. But if she didn't wear them, someone else would, so she could not bear to throw them aside.

Into the shadows she said, "What will become of me?" She approached her father's helmet, touched her forehead, knelt in the first salute they had ever taught her.

She had hoped that someday others would kneel for her.

Somewhere far below this house, Say-ressa's serving women had prepared the first gown of many colors since the Proclamation. Even if the king allowed her to wear them, they would be worthless, signifying no superiority, no privilege. People would look at her and be reminded of Auralia, and their thoughts would wander to the moment color had filled the courtyard.

"Witch. Weed-puller. Deceiver."

What if that enchantress had claimed the prince's affection?

Stricia looked at the distorted outline reflected in a tarnished boot. She saw the hilt of the dagger in the scabbard. Glancing back over her shoulder to ensure she was alone, the captain's daughter unbuckled the sheath and then pulled up the train of her elegant gown and tightened the knife strap around her thigh. She needed a way to make herself dangerous. She needed someone to accuse, someone to punish.

The rushroof above wheezed and rustled. She glanced up, imagining the king's spies would break through and take back the pearls.

They would come for the pearls and the gown and everything else. She was sure of it. They would give it all to Auralia.

Dropping to her knees on the wide circle rug, she peeled back the edge to uncover the door in the floor. Her father never locked their Underkeep hatch, for no one sought to open it except the servants who sent down deliveries...and cats apparently.

With a sound like a gasp, the hatch opened easily.

Light from the oil lamps reached through the swirling dust, revealing the ropes, the pulley, the pallet. She stepped onto the pallet. With a hand on the rope, she released the catch, and descended into the shaft.

In a storage room only the servants had seen, Stricia searched for signs of the treasures prepared for her. A filthy owl launched, circled twice, and disappeared down the patrol corridor, feathertufts tracing its passage and twirling slowly down. She wandered absently about, feathers settling lightly on her head and shoulders.

There, the mask her father had stored away, the half face of Scharr ben Fray, on the shelf beside a bundle of scrolls. She picked it up, then ran her hand across the scrolls with affection. Those were the parchments on which she had learned to write out Abascar's laws.

She stepped into the corridor, and there, swaying slightly on a rack the same height as Stricia, was the gown.

Stricia gathered it and pressed it to her face. She cried into the fabric, trying to breathe in the colors.

So this is how it feels to stray beyond the law, she thought.

"No," she decided. She had worked too hard. The law would not disappoint her. This was not transgression. It was just a way to bring things back into alignment, to patch where the law had been torn.

She wrapped the mage's mask in the wedding gown. She would hide it somewhere deep within the Underkeep. Someone would find it and draw clear conclusions—the exiled advisor had been plotting all along to strip the Promised of her wedding.

"Today," she said, "I must be the law."

Just inside the heavy portcullis that barred the dungeon gateroom, four sleepy guards sat fingering their game chips, casting them clumsily into concentric circles drawn in the dust.

"Oh, hey, I remember now," muttered the oldest, who had done time in these prisons himself. "This is how it goes: *A man of Abascar was thrown in the Hole and tortured for penning a letter of praise to the king. Why was he punished?*"

The other three looked at each other, weary with the old man's riddles. One of them tossed in a chip. It struck the edge of another, rolled, and disappeared down the steep incline to the cells below. "Ballyworms. There goes another one."

"No guesses? *A man of Abascar. Goes to the Hole. For penning a letter of praise to the king.*"

"We give up," they chorused and not for the first time. "Why was he punished?"

"Open up!" came a voice from the avenue outside.

The four dungeon guards fumbled to tighten their buckles, stuff their feet back into boots, and hide the bottle they'd been passing around. Jostling each other at the gate, they finally determined which of them carried the portcullis key. *Clack!* The latch released, and one on each side of the entry turned stubborn cranks to lift the heavy barrier.

Before the gate was fully open, King Cal-marcus ker Har-baron strode into the impenetrable darkness of the descending tunnel, a bottomless throat of dead earth. As he lifted his torch, his three personal guards did the same. They walked briskly, descending into the prisons of the Underkeep.

Behind them the prison guards muttered to each other, amazed at this, the second royal visit of the day. The king rarely made appearances here, and never had he done so with such a small guard and no advisor at his shoulder.

The old guard leaned forward, still preoccupied with his riddle, and grinned. "The letter...it was *read.*"

Down in the corridor, at the edge of the dungeon's dark chill, Maugam emerged, white as a maggot, slow as a snail. Cal-marcus detested that flabulous form—a pale mound of bare body that looked as though it had not grown but rather had been poured, slowly, like porridge from a bowl.

Cal-marcus knew that Maugam considered him a disappointing remnant of a once-great royal line. The jailer preferred to wallow in memories marinated in the blood of King Gere-baron's madness. But that sluggish survivor would never do anything less than cower before someone who could take away his power and his place.

Still, the king was unprepared for the shaken, sniveling sight that met him there.

"Maugam is among the greatest of fools, master," said the jailer.

The king laughed. "Indeed you are, Maugam. You are among the greatest of fools—and I *am* he. I have changed my mind. Go and find Auralia. Bring her to me. I have something to announce."

Aug-anstern's voice, loud and sharp at Cal-marcus's ear, surprised him. "I don't have to tell you, sire, what the other prisoners will do if you…"

"How is it you are here?" The king's tone darkened, like blood spilling into water. "Did I request your presence?" Cal-marcus did not even turn his head. There would be the flaring judgment of reason, of law, in that old man's hard face.

This was not an hour for reason or law.

After a long silence, Aug-anstern backed slowly away from the king. He said clearly, so all could hear, "Very well. Your servant, your trusted advisor, takes his leave. On *this* weighty matter you clearly require no counsel."

The implications would be clear to all present. The words seemed to shake Cal-marcus's confidence, for he appeared to be sinking into the floor.

And then the king unsheathed his ornamental sword.

The guards stepped back. No advisor had ever provoked such a gesture.

It felt strange, the weight of the weapon in his hand. He had not grasped a hilt since the days when he himself had fought the beastmen. It felt good. He wanted to smite something and defeat this encroaching sense of helplessness.

But Aug-anstern, having struck his verbal blow, turned and ran, vanishing beyond the reach of the torchlight. When the king spoke again, it was clear the situation was slipping from his grasp. "What is wrong, Jailer? I commanded you to go and wake Auralia."

"Master..." The immense man fell to one knee and hung his head. "Maugam's calls are met with silence. There is no answer from the Hole."

The king jabbed the tip of the sword into the ground. "What do you mean?"

The muscles on the jailer's neck flexed and tightened as he opened and closed his jaw with no words.

The king tapped the sword against the stone path—*tak, tak, tak.* "You were too harsh on her, perhaps. She is unconscious. Or perhaps she fainted."

"Maugam should be dropped into the hole," groaned the jailer. "For he was a foolish, reckless child. He was weak and could not follow orders. You told Maugam to torture the prisoner. But he could not bring himself to do so. He was not strong enough. He decided to end her suffering. He used a shovel, master, deep down in the dungeon's Hole. And now she is gone."

"A shovel? You...you did what? What are you saying, Maugam? I told you to punish her, not destroy her. Pull her up out of the Hole!"

Maugam's hands were open and empty. "Maugam sent her on her way, master. He took a shovel into the pit, and now there is no prisoner to bring back. She's somewhere else now. Punish the jailer, king of Abascar."

"There has been enough punishment in these dungeons." Cal-marcus didn't understand. He heard something about the Hole, something about the shovel, and something about the end of the poor girl's suffering. He had heard enough stories about the jailer's perverted preoccupations. Fear kept him from daring to ask for any more details.

"Maugam must be punished," the jailer was insisting. "The Hole is for snakes, not for little sisters. But it is too late. She is gone."

"You will not raise her up for us, Jailer?"

"Master, there is nothing left to raise." The fat man turned, still on one knee, crawled a few steps, then heaved himself to his feet with the sob of a man walking to his execution. "Will you not punish Maugam? He has sent her on her way."

Tak, tak, tak.

The darkness ahead offered no redemption, no answer.

The king slowly turned his back on the prison.

"Sire?" one guard said quizzically. "The jailer..."

"Is it midnight?" The king blinked up at the pale gateway as if he was lost. "Are we finished here?" He slid the sword back into its sheath for the last time.

25

LAUGHTER IN CHAINS

Soon after Maugam shackled her and dropped her down the narrow shaft of the Hole, Auralia felt the burning in her wrists and shoulders fade. Her arms became numb, bloodless. Her body, from her head to the throbbing bruises of her heels, seemed a burden, a weight, and she longed to slip free of it and fall.

The coal in the lantern high above looked like a star dancing in a slow, circular path.

She was not afraid.

For as Radegan had fallen into a deep, restful sleep, and as she curled on the damp floor next to him, she had seen the Northchildren come. They sang to her in whispers, like the ripples of Deep Lake. And she had fallen asleep.

The dream that waited there was quite different from the nightmare she had suffered in her cell.

In this dream, the Northchildren carried her to the lakeside, coaxed her to sit by the water, brought her cloak back into her eager embrace, and then took their places around her. In their company at last, she saw they were not all as small as children, but they played and whispered together like the Gatherers' orphans. They were fascinated by the driftwood, enthralled by the shapes of stones. They pointed out stars and sometimes whispered about Auralia herself.

But when it happened, they went silent, unified in awe.

Like a dark curtain flung across the moon, the creature's wings spread above her in the sky, and something drew her to her feet. She took the cloak of colors, draped it over her shoulders.

Like a great heron, the creature soared down to the lake. It bent its powerful legs and descended, tail touching the water first, and then crashed into the glassy surface, sending spray up on both sides and driving waves onto the beach, where they rushed up to Auralia's knees.

As the Keeper folded in its wings like translucent tents, gigantic shoulders eclipsed the light of a whole red moon. Its massive head was maned and muscular like that of a wild horse, and it arched a neck of glittering black scales to bring its forehead down close to Auralia. Wide nostrils flared, puffing wind against her face.

It could have swallowed her.

Her feet were rooted to the ground. The Keeper investigated the magical disturbance of the colors. It nudged the cape with its snout, bumping her elbow, breathing deeply the perfumes of the threads. Auralia stared into the globed, liquid eyes.

Her mouth moved, searching to name that creature, that force of water, wind, or fire the presence so clearly resembled. But after a timeless moment, she knew—it reminded her of everything. Or maybe, as she looked at the forest and the sky, everything reminded her of the Keeper. All things in the landscape seemed to yearn, leaning toward the creature the way flowers lean toward the sun. *Through* the Keeper, all things seemed to draw color and vigor. And *for* the Keeper, waves splashed, trees swayed, stones protected knowledge, and wind waited for orders. In its scales, she saw millions of colors, and she felt deeply ashamed for how few of them she recognized.

"You don't come from here," she whispered. And then, half-surprised at herself, "I don't think I do either."

Like a whip lashing, its neck jerked back. The creature rose from the water to clasp the shore, sinuous legs ending not in hooves or cold shiny claws but in fingered feet that reminded Auralia of Krawg's large, rough, and gentle hands. Feet that, while heavy, left subtle, delicate prints. Head high, the Keeper inhaled two passing clouds and puffed them forth from its lips. Lightning crackled through its mane. Auralia was sure the creature would leap skyward in a cataclysm of water, but instead, slippery as a fish, it relaxed back into the waves. That grand, strange face came in close, large eyes blinking.

The Keeper was looking at her.

The earth shuddered, for its voice came not from its throat but from all it touched. A deep rumbling began like a purr. Auralia sensed the creature's pleasure as it gazed down on the soft glow of the cloak. And then she noticed something about the sunflare of the irises circling the black slits of its eyes: they were like her own, glints of emerald green radiating through rings of blood-dark red. The Keeper was as fearsome in size and strength as told in all the tales, yet it was also familiar.

"You brought me here. We traveled down an underground river, came up into the world through a secret spring."

The Keeper was looking at its tail as fish leapt over it playfully, back and forth.

"I must look like one of those dumb wrigglers," Auralia laughed. "They see my shadow, but they've only ever known their world of water. They have no idea what my world is like. And they don't know how I love to swim with them."

Purring still, the Keeper scratched its chin against the stones. With a trembling hand, she reached out and pulled rubble from the cords of its beard, warm and bristly spines like a thick bundle of riverside reeds. In the dark deep spaces beneath the Keeper's thick lashes, the stars reflected in pinpoints of fire. Auralia thought she saw them move, as if constellations lived within the Keeper's eyes.

"Your eyes are so full. How can I know what you see?"

Then the Keeper reared up, and a roar came from the trees above as if they had split from their trunks to their crowns. But it was not a challenge, nor was it a threat. It was a roar of affirmation, of completion. She could not comprehend it, nor could she translate it into words. But she had been given an answer, one that dissolved all her fears, leaving only laughter.

Her name was in the music of that voice. She was part of its secretive scheme. It would not forget her, had never forgotten her.

The Keeper stepped backward, watching her intently, sinking into the water until only the tips of its wings remained in the air, like the sails of a boat that could travel beneath the waves. The waters closed over it, whirling in thousands of sparkling circles. And after it was gone, the trees all around her hummed, struck by the hammer of the Keeper's mighty laugh, resonating like strings.

Even here, as she dangled, chained, that laughter rang in her ears. She laughed into the darkness of the Hole. She laughed in hopes that Radegan might hear and that the sound would ease his passing.

In this dungeon, nothing had gone so wrong that it could evade the sound of that laughter.

She tried to clap her shackled hands together, and the cuffs clanged like cold, dissonant bells. She began to sing the Morning Verse.

The cuffs of these bindings had been made for men, not children. And as she rang the shackles to measure the meter of the song, she felt their grip slipping.

She was free.

She fell.

She fingered the emerjade ring about her thumb. Something tangible and true.

This was still House Abascar. Auralia had not fallen out of the world.

Nothing was finished. Not yet.

She sat among muck, gore, and bones. Even if she could find the strength to climb, she would never reach the dangling chains. The walls were smooth and slick, offering no hold.

There were whispers at the top of the Hole, shadows staring down at her.

"Come away," they said.

"Not yet," she replied, for she was staring through an opening someone had dug in the wall.

And then she remembered.

Before Maugam had bound her hands and lifted her high by the chains, he had emerged from the Hole himself, climbing on a knotted rope. The noise he made had awakened her, and she had whispered to Radegan, "Don't be afraid."

As the jailer collapsed, exhausted, beside the maw of the pit, she saw the shovel in his hands. He was wheezing and talking to himself, mumbling something about his "biggest mistake."

But she had been humming a quiet song, too distracted to care. She had been holding Radegan's large, broken hands until she felt the faint pulse vanish and the heat fade from his skin.

Then Maugam had lifted her to her feet and walked her to the chains, whispering what must have been his best attempt at comfort. He had coaxed her to the edge of the Hole, locking the shackles about her wrists.

And now she could see what Maugam had done.

He had provided her with a chance. Unable to find the courage to carry her to freedom, he managed a gamble that would allow for a possibility. It was the closest thing to kindness he could muster.

She seized the opportunity and pushed herself through the opening.

For a while she pondered if she felt more like a rat or a worm, wriggling her way through the earth. But she soon pulled herself through into a chamber. And there she laughed again.

Auralia stood in a pen lined with bars. It was piled high with bundles of yarn. Red. Green. Purple.

She looked up, and she saw, far, far above her, lanternglow falling through a grate and a pallet suspended by ropes. But there was no way to climb up to it, and she felt unsure about shouting for help. Instead, she climbed out between the bars, but not without snatching some bundles of yarn.

"Better not get lost," she said.

As she wandered through a maze of long and empty corridors, she unspooled the yarn behind her so she wouldn't wander in circles and just in case she might need to find her way back.

With the string unwinding she walked, numb with cold and nearly naked, into the Underkeep.

It was just as the Gatherers had described it. She had often stared at the cliffs of Abascar's stone foundation, amazed to think that people were traveling within it. She thought of the colors hidden here, the life burgeoning below ground.

She walked past row after row of cages piled high with garments and linens and carpets and curtains. Some were labeled with names and contents. The past. Childhoods. Mountains of color. Souvenirs of lives. These were the inner linings of hearts ripped out. Her tiny arms slipped between the bars, and she felt these clothes, wrapped the colors around her, breathed in their musty patterns. These things were as lonely as their makers, dry, miserable, and yearning for light.

When the yarn ran out, she borrowed treasures from these forgotten bins. She tied them end to end and left them strewn along the floor behind her.

26

THE UNDERKEEP OPENS

Once, on a day of great occasion, the king had tousled Stricia's hair. He had dropped to one knee and smiled at her. No doubt his favor shone upon her because of something her father had accomplished. She didn't remember the details; it was the honor that impressed her.

"Your father," Cal-marcus had said, "is as fine a man as there is. No doubt his daughter is made of the same stuff. Serve the law, Stricia kai Ark-robin, and the law will serve you. The secrets of the palace could be yours someday."

She was ten years old then, speechless in the attention of this giant. Laughing, her father had hoisted her up with his arm, the last time he would lift her like a child, and they had all remarked on her wide-eyed awe. As she had looked down from his shoulders, she had glimpsed her life's true purpose.

But here, she was caught in the thrall of a darker revelation. She had served the law. It had served her, but only so far. Not far enough.

Silently, the invisible beast—that nameless Underkeep menace—rose from the ground and coiled about her. She felt its cold, unnatural presence. For a moment she was terrified. But then she felt something else. A strange and compelling strength. A tantalizing confidence.

She could pass unseen, plant the lie, and let it take root.

She took a deep breath and ran, surprised that she felt no fear. At the end of the corridor that opened onto an immeasurable chasm, across which she could see myriad paths, stairways, and bridges, she stood in plain view, and no one took notice. She was invisible to them. Whatever she had consented to receive was hiding her from guards who stood at every entrance and from workers who moved across bridges and scuttled like beetles down long, winding staircases.

Even the guard standing beside her failed to see her, although she jumped and shied away when she saw him. He was lost in some daydream, smoking a pipe that smelled of cinnamon.

She tiptoed past him and hurried down a rugged stair, taking care not to step too close to the edge or to look down into the whispering void. She passed three entryways, felt drawn into the fourth, and ran down a long tunnel lit by golden lanterns, her footsteps muffled by the soft grass spread across the floor.

It was coming back to her now, a memory of her father giving her a tour. "And here," he had said, "is where we keep our family's history, the things we have surrendered for the glory of the palace."

Beside one of the sparking lanterns, a den was carved into the clay. Within it, piles of garments—capes, dresses, shawls, stockings. Her mother had commissioned an entire wardrobe for her future as a princess. There were older things, faded treasures. A man's red tunics, rich burgundy and green capes, smart blue trousers. She could see these sleeping colors by the wavering light of the wall lantern, a glimmering sacrifice sealed away in the name of honor and obedience. She wanted to touch them all.

A gate, barred and locked, refused her, holding these things almost out of reach.

Almost.

She set the wedding gown down in the dry grass. She would not try it on. There was no time. But why not take one of those long, dark, elegant robes? Silken and slight, they had the allure of scandalous rumors, dark magnetism.

She shed the white gown she had worn into the palace and let it fall. Naked, she paused, pinching the flesh on her arms and wrists, puzzled by a strange deadness, as if she might shed her skin.

Shivering, she reached through the cage door and groped, grinding her teeth, her fingers almost stretching out of their joints. The metal cut into her shoulder. One fingernail hooked the edge of a nightgown; she carefully worked it into her grasp. When she had drawn it out, she wrapped it around her neck and breathed through it, soaking up tears she hadn't known she was crying. Then she drew it over her head and let it fall weightless around her. The corridor seemed to darken as she was draped in its silky shadows. This pleased her, although she found it difficult to move. How would a woman walk with such a long, clinging dress trailing about her feet? It did not matter. This was what it felt like to be a queen.

Through her tears, she saw a shadow cross the corridor down an adjoining trail, momentarily eclipsing light from a distant lantern.

She froze. A soldier. Coming to light the torches or check for burglars. She would be found out. It was over.

But as her eyes discerned the shadow, she saw a small person in rags, oblivious to her, staggering through the illuminated crossing. The figure stopped and looked directly at her but did not see her. The sensation thrilled Stricia. Then the shape turned down another branch of the forking tunnels. Behind it trailed a rope made of knotted stretches of cloth.

A thief?

Stricia was drawn to the train of color. Even as the frail shadow passed from view, the winding line of garments shifted, rolled, and writhed along the floor. She picked up the wedding gown, pinched it to ensure Scharr ben Fray's mask was still folded within it, and then followed.

The trail of bound cloth stretched out of sight in one direction and then fell over the edge of an opening in the floor. The wanderer had descended a ladder to the next level.

Fascinated, Stricia moved to the edge, stared down, felt the shudder of strength beyond her own—the strength of that dark wraith that had somehow fused with her anger and grief.

Like a flutterbird snatched by a hound, Merya shrieked, clutching at the hand that dragged her by the hair, kicking so defiantly that her feet dug through the damp to drier ground and scuffed dust into the torchlight.

Ark-robin ignored the shouts of protest from the other Gatherers, who had been on their way home from the day's labor. He blinked as his captive flung dirt across his face. Then he calmly turned, released the woman, and clubbed her on the back of the head with a bonewood stick the size of his forearm.

Merya slumped to the dirt and went still.

The captain looped the strap of his club back into his belt, then removed long leather strands from a pocket inside the folds of his dramatic blue cape. He lifted Merya from where she had fallen, pressed her forehead against the bark of the tree, and lashed her wrists together behind her back. Then he hauled Merya up by the back of her grassweave gown and showed her limp form to the glowering gallery of observers.

"This woman was named by one of your own as an accomplice in a planned desertion. That man, Radegan the Dog, now lies in the Underkeep after attempting to steal from King Cal-marcus's treasure. Fortunately for the rest of you," he shouted, his gaze sweeping across the Gatherers, "Radegan named no one else. Merya will serve time in the dungeon. But as she has a husband here, she shall eventually be returned to you. If he is a husband of any merit, I expect he will have his own punishment to deliver upon their reunion."

Corvah was not present among the Gatherers here, but the worried glances they exchanged confirmed he would not be pleased.

The captain cleared his throat and threw Merya over his shoulder. "You have been sentenced to hard labor outside the protection of Abascar's walls for a reason. To learn something. And until you learn it, you will not come back inside. Radegan did not learn."

"You speak of him as though he's a thing of the past," came a disgruntled voice.

Ark-robin smiled, searching their faces. "Ahh. A good listener. Excellent. Then I have your attention." His gaze connected with one whose broad shoulders were hunched forward as though he was poised for a charge. Haggard, the captain remembered—simpleminded, fond of drink, and a bully when his temper was kindled.

Ark-robin moved toward him, unblinking, until he could smell the faint trace of the evening's indulgence on the man's bristling mustache. "Now," he continued, challenging that fiery stare, "any self-respecting creature, animal or man, will keep his mouth shut until my officers and I have hauled this wench into the dungeons."

He turned and tossed Merya across the back of his silver-scaled vawn. The long black curtain of her hair hung down by a stirrup. The vawn raised its tubular snout from the mud, cast a baleful look back at its master, and then returned to snuffle at the soil for beetles. *The worst is over,* Ark-robin sighed, climbing back into his saddle. *The evening can only get better from here.*

Though there were three duty officers on vawnback monitoring the laborers, Ark-robin was glad of the eight soldiers he had brought, keenly aware of the agitated mood among the Gatherers. Since the riot, he had known the possibility of an uprising was too dangerous to ignore.

So when old, crooked Warney stalked forward like an angry crow, Ark-robin feigned indifference, but his hand hung loosely beside his sheath.

"Get back in line!" barked a nervous duty officer. "Old man, stand back!"

Ark-robin smiled and cautioned the officer to allow the confrontation. But all Warney managed to do was open his trembling, sticky lips, shake a gnarled fist, and glare from the one good eye inside his hood. "Radegan was a thief and liar. But why do you hold Auralia, who knew no better than to play like a child? Bring her back to live with those who have cared for her. We're not plotting against anyone. So why spoil our spirits and answer our efforts with cruelty? Krawg's sick as a rat and can hardly climb out of bed. If Auralia comes back, he'll get well again. But the king must show us fairness, or..."

"Or what?" Ark-robin signaled with a turn of his hand. The soldier next to him closed his fingers around a club. If Warney's next words were in any way vulgar, the old fool would pay.

Warney backed away. "I'm gonna climb up on the roof of my hut and call down great-grandfather's most powerful curse! I'm gonna knock Abascar's walls right down, I tell you!"

"And you can bet I'll be sittin' there beside him," rasped a voice. It was Krawg, leaning heavily on a crutch, hobbling from the trees to stand by Warney's side.

Ark-robin shook his head. "Very well. For your treasonous remarks, I hereby—"

A shower of leaves and then a broken branch fell from the boughs above. Ark-robin and the Gatherers jumped back, and the vawns clomped several steps away. A man fell from the sky, standing on a plank of wood suspended by two ropes. A duty officer in green concealment garb. He stepped down off the lift, straight and officious, and bowed to the captain.

"Signal from northwest," he said without hesitation.

Ark-robin growled, shifting his attention from the Gatherers' disturbance to the interruption. "What is it, Everin?" He had not grown used to the presence of Cal-raven's highwatches, but they had been a useful invention. With watchmen on these platforms, simple news could be relayed across the forest with efficiency and clarity. "What is the news?"

"It's Cal-raven, sir. He's reporting from the trouble at the dig. His riders intercepted a company of beastmen that were on their way to the battle. Twenty, maybe thirty of the monsters. His riders are driving them away, and they've changed course. The beastmen are fleeing in this direction. The riders are going to steer them *toward* Abascar's western wall, trusting you to set an ambush."

"We will trap them against the wall."

"Cal-raven calls for an alarm to draw all Gatherers back into their camps. These beastmen will probably try to pass right by Abascar. But I suspect they're in too much of a hurry to stop and make any mischief. They'll head for their dens to the south."

"Captain, we've done what we came to do." Wolftooth, Ark-robin's second in command, could not conceal his excitement. "Let's set an ambush for those bushpigs."

Ark-robin held up his hand for silence. He looked back at Wolftooth, as though listening. The leaves rustled.

"What will you do, sir?" the duty officer asked.

Ark-robin drummed his fingers on Merya's back. "Tell them to drive the beastmen between the ridge and Abascar's western wall. We'll wait on the ridge. When we descend upon them, they'll have no choice but to fight us on one side or be picked off by arrows from the wall on the other. If Cal-raven's pursuit is strong, we will not lose. We can make something memorable here."

He turned and pointed at Warney. "Why don't you try using your great-grandfather's curse on something that deserves it. And while you're at it, you're responsible to lead these wretches back to the camp."

Then the captain turned and pointed to a cowering figure hiding behind the Gatherers' harvest barrel. "Ale boy! Shouldn't you be inside the walls? The Evening Verse is about to be sung."

Ark-robin lifted the unconscious Merya from the vawn's back and tossed her as though she were a folded blanket. Haggard caught her. "I'll be back for her," Ark-robin warned, wiping his gloved hands against the neck of his vawn as though he had just touched a diseased rodent. "And she'd better not myste-riously disappear before my return, or you'll all end up in the dungeons."

He seized the startled ale boy and lifted him onto the mount. "No time to take you back to the gates, boy. I guess you're going to experience your first ambush. Just hang on to the vawn's mane. Don't let go. And don't worry. If a beastman gets close enough for you to see his eyes, he'll already be dead at the end of my sword."

As though to spread their own rumors about the beastmen, the trees moaned with sudden wind, bending. Birds flitted through the clearing with calls of alarm and disappeared. Ark-robin watched them and scratched his thick beard with his three-fingered hand. *What a marvelous evening,* he thought.

The captain of the guard drove his company eastward from the woods by

Deep Lake and up the rising ground. At the top of a deeply forested ridge, they could look down the slope and up again to the long line of House Abascar's sun-painted wall.

To the east, the edge of darkness approached on the backs of the massing nightbirds.

Auralia walked from cage to cage, yearning for the buried colors, wanting to gather them into her arms like abandoned children. Every time she reached a cage of forbidden, castoff belongings, she wanted to unlock it. She wanted to climb ropes and chains and open the doors above to let in daylight, to give the Housefolk back what belonged to them.

Auralia smiled to see the long line of garments she had managed to pull from the cages. Perhaps they would instead lead someone to find her, lost in the labyrinth. The prince had vowed her protection. Surely he would come to the prison and discover she was missing. Surely he would find her here.

She could not stay underground. It was difficult to breathe here, so unlike her caves beside the lake, which opened to water, starlight, and the voice of the woods. This maze did not end. It circled back upon itself. With no sun, moon, or stars, time became meaningless.

What was left for her to do without the colors she had brought to this house?

"I'm not a Northchild. I'm a Gatherer," she repeated to herself. The word *Gatherer* spoken here seemed a comfort. She closed her eyes, struggled to remember. "Nella Bye. Haggard. Krawg. Warney." She laughed. "Wenjee." Perhaps she could find her way to them. She had paid the price for what she had done. Now she could enjoy a return to the small things. The simple gifts.

She resumed her pursuit of a mystery, passing over a narrow stone bridge, leaving the long rows of cages and caves. Her hands worked busily with a bundle of sheets and scarves, knotting them together into a record of her journey. The walls fell away, the ceiling disappeared into the dark, and an immeasurable mine shaft yawned beneath the bridge. She inched forward, with a strange sense that her steps had been laid for her.

Something with wings flapped past her head.

On the other side of the bridge, she entered a huge cavern where rows of stacked barrels, six high, stretched into invisibility. There were no lanterns here, only mirrors that caught and cast light from lanterns somewhere else. There was just enough light to continue, and as she did, the air turned thick and sweet.

"Ale boy?" She turned suddenly.

But she was still alone, standing in the distilleries, the ale boy's fragrant home.

She gazed about with new understanding. These would be the chambers where he worked every day. The king's breweries, the cellars of liquors, ales, wine, hajka. Perhaps the boy was near. Perhaps he could help.

With one hand, she leaned against a barrel; with the other, she clutched the end of her garment-rope.

Suddenly the mirrors flashed and brightened. Someone was approaching with light and color. A flare of red behind her. A lantern. She turned, almost calling Cal-raven's name.

At first Auralia thought the figure stepping across the bridge was a ghost. She smiled and whispered, "Beautiful." The woman was dressed like a queen, wearing a dark and elegant nightgown. She held the lantern in one hand and clutched a colorful bundle of cloth with the other.

Auralia squinted into the lanternlight, trying to discern the face of her visitor. As she did, dizziness swept over her.

"Who are you?" came a small, angry voice.

Auralia remembered now that she was an escapee, a fugitive. Perhaps this one had come to drag her back to the Hole. But dressed like this? Unlikely.

She slumped against a barrel, pulled her dirty, scratched knees up to her chin. She sighed once, opened her hands, let go of the cord of colors. "I'm Auralia," she answered.

Auralia's path at last converged with the journey of the captain's daughter.

Above them, Housefolk slept, exhausted from their work, troubled without hope of a better day ahead.

Above the weary Housefolk, a despairing and defeated king climbed the steps of his tower slowly, as though he might not reach his chamber.

Beyond thick walls of stone, along the edges of the woods, Gatherers hurried to their camps, worried about beastmen. They could not sleep. Some of them wished for the return of that vivid girl from the riverbank.

Miles away through the forest a prince unsheathed his sword and felled monsters, shouting the name of his father, his house, his teacher, and then a name new to his lips, that of a young woman, a woman who had confirmed his wildest suspicions about the life of mystery within the Expanse.

That prince's teacher stood in the woods far to the south, shaping stone with magic, careful to replicate what details he could remember of the design in Auralia's colors so he could contemplate the work.

There were so many more, a world of people whose lives were strangely changed by this frail girl huddled against a liquor barrel backed up to a massive column of stone and earth in the cellars of House Abascar.

Stricia stood still. She looked at this little creature in rags, this ugly girl who had just spoken the name she had come to despise.

She felt wounded, as though in her weakest moment this one whom she hated had appeared in calculated malice.

And yet the chill prickled beneath her skin, and a possibility flowered in her mind. She could give the gown and mask to Auralia. She could bring all the threads of blame together.

"Auralia," Stricia laughed. "Of course, dear little Gatherer girl. The prince...he speaks so highly of you."

"Prince Cal-raven?"

"And he would want you to have this." Stricia lifted the wedding gown and held it into the lamplight.

But as Auralia reached out to receive the gift, Stricia glimpsed an emerjade ring circling her thumb.

She recognized it and staggered back. Her feet tangled in the train of the wedding gown, wresting it from her hands as she fell to the ground.

The lantern flew out of her hand and smashed into jagged shards across the stony ground, its oil pouring out, shocked into flame.

Auralia stared into the dance of brilliant color. "Where is the ale boy?" she asked.

"You?" Stricia asked, shivering. "The prince has given you his ring of protection?"

Around her, sparks flared and rose high toward the chasm's distant ceilings. She thought to run. But the wraith that had its claws in her whispered a different idea—a solution to all her woes.

Stricia was surprised at the absence of emotion as she considered this possibility.

Sparks from the burning oil settled along the damp ground like constellations. She watched, as some of the flames spread in crooked lines, consuming droplets and puddles of the powerful liquors that had leaked down the corridors. Here and there it caught at strands of dry grass. The flames licked hungrily at Auralia's cord of garments. The fire coiled about the strand, sank into it, swelled and intensified. It paused as though awaiting permission and then surged, eagerly working its way in both directions along the bound line.

Stricia did not watch the fire traveling up the corridor the way Auralia had come, nor did she see it leap in a line like a shooting star across the bridge, sparks spraying outward and falling away.

She was transfixed, hypnotized by the growing flames that gathered in a half circle around the strange, dazed girl.

Auralia showed no signs of pain at the rising heat. She seemed asleep, almost thankful, fingering the prince's stone ring around her thumb. Smiling, she said, "I think it's time at last to sing the Evening Verse." And she began, indeed, to sing it.

Stricia could not reach Auralia. The heat had become searing. She was at once horrified by what was about to happen and yet unwilling to interfere. The heaving breath of the Underkeep seethed within her. As if to defend herself from darkness and flame, she reached into her skirt and unsheathed her father's dagger.

There was a sudden roar as the dry wood of an old marrowwood ladder propped against the wall caught fire and became a pillar of flame.

Panic shattered her trance. She turned to flee and screamed. Her escape was cut off. She looked down the long row of barrels. Smoke blackened the air around her.

She cried out for her father.

Stricia looked at Auralia, a shadow now behind a wall of flame. She held out a hand, timidly approaching, but the heat repelled her. There was nothing she could do but shout. "The fire! Auralia, quick! Get up! That's hajka in those barrels. We've got to find a way out."

Without waiting, Stricia stepped onto a precarious ledge that led to a lower level of the Underkeep. The chasm opened out, dark and measureless. She would be safer the deeper she went.

Before descending, she looked back once more.

Translucent shapes moved in a crowd through the smoke, encircling Auralia while the tunnel filled with heat and light. The barrel behind Auralia caught fire, its top bursting open in a rush of flame. And then the one next to it exploded. Behind it, the massive pillar of stone, twenty trees wide, cracked, split, groaned as a wedge-shaped section crumbled into rubble and dust. It leaned toward the abyss, breaking under the weight of the ground above.

In rapid succession, the remaining barrels blasted fire at all that surrounded them, erasing walls, collapsing ceilings, tearing open earth, and destroying the central supports that held the foundation for Abascar's palace.

Maugam was faint from blood loss. For breaking the law and freeing a prisoner, he had condemned himself to shame. For digging an escape and making sure her shackles were loose, he cursed himself as a criminal.

But the king had not condemned him. The king had demanded he bring Auralia back from the Hole.

"I used a shovel," Maugam admitted again. "I have ended her suffering. And sent her on her way."

He had gathered his sharpened tools about him. He had made a message out of arms and legs, ears and eyes, crafting himself into a testament for the next jailer. The demands of justice were satisfied. His name would be remembered. Maugam: the artist of the dungeons.

In the shifting tides of pain from his self-inflicted punishments, he watched the world waver before him, illusory.

The strand of hanging chains began to rattle and squeak inside the pit nearby.

Had Auralia slipped free of her chains? Had she found the tunnel he had opened for her?

Suddenly he had to know.

Burying all fear, he leaned over the edge of the pit and reached to grab the chains.

They swung lightly, freely, clanking against each other. He felt relief, and he smiled. "Very good. You are free."

But now the ground shook beneath him. Dust and rubble began to rain down. The chains writhed in his hands like snakes.

The explosion flaming through the Underkeep was so sudden and so great, he did not have time to move before the fire rushed up through the Hole, reducing him to wisps of smoke driven by the rising flames.

27

THE QUAKE

Taut as the strings on their ready arrowcasters, invisible as held breath, the Abascar troop waited in the thick stand of high trees. Their captain gazed eastward over the orchard slope, across the wildgrass span, to the stone foundation and Abascar's long and winding wall, to the bold towers beyond.

The towers. High, golden, encircled by grand balconies. Soon, the wedding would open them, and Ark-robin would escort his wife up and away from their past to chambers that had once belonged to the queen. They would wake to see the sunrise bathing the mountainous stonelands of the east in colors brighter than the tedious sights of labor and law. The wind would course through the windows, carrying the sounds of birdsong rather than the grumble of vawns, the snarl of dogs, the Housefolk chatter, the markets.

He wondered if Say-ressa had lit the bedcandles. She was probably sipping redtwig tea and surrendering to the scratch of the cat at the door. She would begin her yearly conference with the palace doctors soon and probably teach them a thing or two. Had Stricia ever fallen ill under her mother's care?

The ale boy slid from side to side on the vawn, not nearly old enough to sit comfortably for hours on such a large animal. Ark-robin smiled, watching him tangle and untangle his fingers in the black mane in search of a firm grip.

The captain had often promised himself he would someday teach a boy of his own. It occurred to him, and not for the first time, that he might at last revise this promise—grandsons. Royal grandsons. Princes. Ark-robin would see his dreams walking the corridors of the palace, and they would have famous names and reputations. They would be so much more fit for service than this orphan, who had inherited so little of his father's strength and stature.

"Must be quite a thrill for you, ale boy. Better than collecting berries, eh? Just think, now you're a part of something important."

The boy turned and stunned the captain with a scowl born of something deeper than displeasure. The boy did not like him. Did not even seem to admire him.

The captain frowned, tightened his own grip on the reins. Radegan, Auganstern, the Gatherers… He was surrounded by animosity these days.

But Ark-robin had no chance to pursue the matter. For there, winging low from north to south, barely visible as night's flood rose to pool over the wildgrass, were three black birds, gliding without a single stroke of their wings, cruising expertly together as though joined at the wingtips and steered by kitestrings. Which they were, in a sense.

"Brascles," Wolftooth remarked to his comrades. "Navigating for the monsters that run beneath them."

"The birds are not looking for us," Ark-robin added. "They have no reason to suspect we're here."

"Won't the birds see us coming?"

"When they do, it will be too late. The beastmen can't climb the wall. If they turn back, they'll run into Cal-raven's riders. Ready?"

The sound of a stamp from each vawn signaled that the men were prepared.

Ark-robin leaned forward. "Hang on, ale boy. You will thank me when this is over."

He dug in his heels and clicked his tongue, and the vawns were off as one body.

Once they entered the orchards, the wide boughs of the fruit trees dimmed the evening light. The riders bent low, occasionally sliding off the saddles to grasp the sides of their mounts and duck beneath branches that would have otherwise beheaded them.

Directed by an almost imperceptible whistle from the captain, the vawns entered an open field and turned with impossible precision to become a single-file parade, flanking the unseen foes.

The beastmen would soon burst out into the open, running like wildcats, down on all fours.

Ark-robin put his hand to his sword hilt, pulled his vawn ahead of the rest of the company, and leaned forward. "Here we go," he growled into the ale boy's ear.

And then something altogether unplanned happened.

The earth moved like an ocean wave.

It caught and raised the orchard. Then brought it down again.

Trees twisted, broke, and fell against each other in a deafening clamor.

Vawns lost their footing and stumbled on the heaving ground. Trees, uprooted by an impossible force, crashed down the slope toward and around them. Ark-robin's vawn bellowed, unable to dodge the tree that was crashing toward them.

Ark-robin wrapped his arms around the ale boy, and both were flung into the air. A branch struck the side of his helmet. He landed on his back and felt the impact cast the boy away. He was in the air again and came down hard on his belly, lights flashing through his head, blood in his throat.

In the next several moments, or hours—he was not certain—the world was a strange and dreamlike cloud. As pain racked his body inside and out, he thought the beastmen were upon him with whips and clubs. He could not distinguish the sound of dying men from the roars of trees splitting, stones cracking, and earth tearing.

He found himself staggering around the tree-blasted landscape in the dulling blue dusk, climbing across the twisted carcasses of trees toward the ale boy who was crawling in a patch of tangled wildgrass. The boy was so blackened by earth that he resembled an unfinished sculpture. The vawn's body, or a good part of it, lay behind the boy. The rest of it hung suspended on the sharp stump of a broken tree.

Sorcery.

Ark-robin tried to speak, but his speech slurred. In the fall, his breastplate had been shoved upward, the edge nearly shattering his jaw, smashing his teeth together. He spat a gob of blood against a fallen tree.

"Wizardry!" came a voice nearby, and he thought it might be his own. But it was Wolftooth, crawling forward and out from under a tree. "What in the name of Great Tammos Raak—"

"Kramm, the whole land's exploded," came an answering cry.

"I see that, you sheepskull." All about him pieces of the hillside rose and fell, as though a giant had thrown fistfuls of forest upon them. Small birds flung from the trees in the quake settled on the broken ground, pecking at grubs that had been thrust into the air. He trembled. "Beastmen don't have the power to rain trees down upon us!"

"Then what does?" asked Wolftooth, gripping his sword as a walking stick, his face twisted by the snarl that uncannily suited his name.

"I smell smoke," the ale boy groaned.

Two of the three duty officers were in sight, alive, one of them still sitting unfazed on his vawn. But two of his men lay to the side impaled by the same blade. The strangest fates men found...to die in the midst of certain victory by chancing to fall upon one's own sword. Six men climbed over the husks of trees leaning askew all about. One wept.

"Wait."

He looked toward Abascar's wall.

There was no wall.

Ark-robin turned a slow circle, checked his direction. He saw only sky.

Wolftooth realized the same thing. "Are we off course?"

"The mage." Ark-robin pulled his helmet off and wiped the blood that was spilling down his face. "That kramming mage. He's done this. He's besieged the house..."

"Captain! Fire!" One of the surviving officers was waving, frantic and terrified, pointing toward the house. "And the wall has come down!"

It was not night that had plunged the world into darkness. It was smoke. Black, billowing smoke.

"The ale boy's right." Captain Ark-robin grabbed the branches of a fallen cloudgrasper and pulled himself up onto its trunk to try to get a glimpse of the palace.

Ruination.

Parts of the palace wall were standing, but they were broken or crooked, their foundations tilting, gleaming domes blackening as flames stormed upward. Many things were missing, most noticeably. . .the palace itself. A massive column of cloud had replaced the towers, looming high enough to catch the red glow of sunset. The earth was swallowing Abascar.

"The Underkeep's caved in."

The words made a terrible kind of sense, but he regretted saying them because they robbed him of any focus for his rage.

"Sir," murmured Wolftooth. "The beastmen."

"What about them?"

"I don't see them here."

Ark-robin reached for the hilt of his sword. It was there, as it should be, but that brought little relief. "We'll go in," he choked, holding his throat. "Beastmen. They've probably gone in." Was the earth still shifting beneath his feet? "It is my duty to find and defend the king." He brushed tufts of grass from the edges of his leg guards. Poise. Posture. He needed to regain his composure.

But only three of his men and the ale boy remained. The others were running, either away from the destruction or into it. Two who stayed with him were fine archers but only passable swordsmen. The third, a stolid, stalwart fellow, could fight with the best.

With Abascar collapsing, there would be no refuge. There would be only the run, the race to salvage what one could. Perhaps he could save his wife. Or his daughter. Or the king.

It had begun with tremors, then the full quake, quickly followed by claims that the Underkeep was burning. Chaos spread through House Abascar.

Flames had rushed through the breweries, and burning debris had plunged down through layers of the labyrinth until they found the dark, slumbering inventions of war that Kings Gere-baron and Har-baron had hidden away. When touched by the fire, these barrels of strange oils and concentrated poison turned volcanic. Calamitous fires raged, thundered through the Underkeep, sending jets of light and smoke up through the floors of the Housefolk homes.

King Cal-marcus had seen this, standing at his window, staring out at his quaking house, watching smoke rise from all around.

As he gripped the empty bottle of hajka, his blurred reason convinced him this was a vision, a prophecy or punishment set before him as his own mind caved in.

Housefolk homes burnt like haystacks, one after the other. The sound of his name rang through the streets in panic. Somehow this was his doing.

"Come away." A touch on his shoulder. "Come away. It's beginning."

Earlier, the news had been good—Cal-raven had sent a large number of beastmen scrambling south toward an ambush and certain defeat. But then, not an hour later, another message. The dig had fallen. Cent Regus monsters were in the tunnels. Tunnels that would lead them to the Underkeep.

Cal-marcus had felt his heartbeat stumble out of step, and in that very moment, a quake had shaken his chamber.

Now the tower tilted with the moving earth, and his view of the forest became a view of the night sky. Smoke billowed and soared in the air like ink in water.

And yet the shadow had shape and purpose, a looming figure like a fallen piece of moon, soaring over the house, watchful and intent. He saw all this and knew, as sparks caught in the curtains framing his window.

"Now?" he asked.

The shadows prodded him, found loose threads, unstitched him.

Buffeted by wind, the curtains flared into brilliant colors, fell, wrapped themselves around his remnant, and embered in his ashes.

Krawg and Warney coughed dust. Warney had a gash just below his eye patch; half his face was a mask of streaming blood. He crawled out from under the heavy hut wall. Krawg helped him up, and they clung to each other's sleeves, walking slowly away from their ruined shelter, through tangles of trees, past their fellow Gatherers weeping, wounded, and afraid. As though he had spread his arms wide to catch it, Haggard lay crushed beneath a tree, motionless.

Krawg's eyes were wide, and his mouth hung open. He had been inside the hut, snarling at the ceiling, calling for Warney to come down off the roof. His furious friend stood there in the dusk, chanting curses he had learned from his grandfather, determined to break a hole in the palace wall.

First there had been a shudder. That brought Krawg to his feet. Then cracks spread like lines of spilled wine across the walls. And then the ground had lurched. Krawg grabbed his crutch and got outside in time to watch huge sections of Abascar's wall tumbling down.

"My great-grandfather's curse," Warney whispered after he had fallen. "Bally-worms, but I didn't mean for it to be that bad."

Krawg, for perhaps the first time, didn't know what to say. He turned a slow circle, staring from the horizon of smoke, sound, and fury to the forest where night settled, indifferent, into the wild.

Warney shook his head. "Krawg, what's become of 'Ralia?"

28

At the Edge of the Fearblind North

C al-raven steered his vawn through a tangled patch of snaregrass, his bones jarred by each forceful stride. As he shouted, the forest stole his voice, twisted it, and thrust it back at him. The echoes sounded like distant, muffled cries.

His troop had routed a wave of beastmen advancing on the river dig. Those monsters had turned tail and run, and half of Cal-raven's troop had pursued them.

But he had yet to reach the dig, where more of these bloodthirsty creatures had carried out this unprecedented attack. So he had circled back, leading the rest of his battle-eager soldiers.

As Cal-raven crested the last hill above the valley of the dig, he saw, to his dismay, the gutted remains of the transitory tower gushing black smoke. Men with tusks and snouts like boars, heads and arms bristling with black, wiry hair, clustered at a ramp that led down into the tunnel.

Brascles beat the air and ascended from their carrion along the edge of the trees, shrieking and reeling.

As the Abascar vawns charged down the hill, the air rang with shouts, and half the company bore down upon the guards of the hole, forming a ring around the crouching, cursing, spear-wielding beasts.

The rest of the riders circled the smoking tower. Cal-raven rode close enough to see, in the failing light, that heavy axes had hacked through the walls, opening the wooden refuge for torches that had quickly found fuel. Obscenities like nothing the men had ever heard from their prince echoed in the clearing but diminished into silence as he noticed his vawn was stepping around contorted, smoldering corpses. They were too late, far too late.

The prince tried to ignore the scattered, bloodied shields and cloven helms. He drove his mount over smoking foliage where fire volleys from tower archers had fallen short.

The tunnel workers would by now have abandoned their massive, wheeled digging machines, forgotten the goal of reaching the Throanscall's flow. They would be fighting for their lives in the crowded passageway.

Cal-raven and his men reinforced the advancing ring around the gaping earthen gate, shields steady, closing in. Three beastmen guarding the mouth of the dig spat, feinted, and withdrew, trapped and desperate. The creatures were not accustomed to working together; their self-interested wills were still too abrasive for such cooperation.

Distracting the beastmen with threatening lunges, the inner circle of guards dropped to their knees to let the outer circle unleash a storm of arrows.

Writhing, the beastmen pulled at the arrows, but the shafts were barbed. Cal-raven urged his men past. As they went, he felt a throb of fear. There were so few beastmen here. How many more were down in the dig? Had they ventured through the tunnels toward Abascar?

Vawns craned their necks to glare at their riders, but the whips were convincing, and they lumbered forward, down the sloping ramp into the underground corridor, growling.

He had to get to a highwatch in the woods and flag a signal to warn Abascar.

"Prince Cal-raven!" came a cry from below ground. "You had better see this!"

In the broad, low-ceilinged cave, bodies lay twisted, entwined in combat, blades still in hand, the shapes of men and beastmen paralyzed across the floor.

But something was not right.

"Master, they've lost their legs. All of them."

"No," said Cal-raven slowly. "No, they haven't. Something happened. Something. . .*melted the floor.* They sank into it."

Someone, he thought. *Someone melted the floor.* He waved his torch around, bewildered and afraid.

Along an open swath of floor, he found what he had suspected. Long, frantic lines of script carved into the rock. He knelt over them and traced them with his fingertips.

"Sir?" The dizzy, horror-stricken soldiers climbed from their vawns and walked with blades unsheathed, prodding at the corpses half-encased in the ground. "What happened here?"

"Oh no." Cal-raven stood, turned, and walked toward two of the half-sunk combatants. The armored Abascar body was Blyn-dobed, the dig's foreman, dead in the arms of a corpse with broad and bristling shoulders. The prince reached down, grabbed the scruff of the monster's neck, and jerked it back.

The disguise slipped away in his hand. It was not a beastman at all but an Abascar laborer, his face caked in dark paint.

"Grudgers." Cal-raven sobbed. "Grudgers attacked the guards." He looked toward the ramp. "This was not a beastman attack. The beastmen have just come for the spoils."

"Grudgers struck their own tower," seethed Tabor Jan.

Cal-raven picked up the crude, bloodied disguise. He prodded the grudger's paint-smudged face with his boot. "They disguised themselves as beastmen to spread panic, to turn the guards' attention outward while they struck from within." His arms shaking, he dropped the disguise. "Abascar is turning against my father." He looked toward the tunnel.

"No, master," said Tabor Jan. "Only a few misguided fools. But their resentment made them angry and strong. We'll go back and find the rest of them. We'll draw them out of the house by their roots."

"Cal-raven," cried one of the shaken soldiers, "those were beastmen we filled with arrows, yes? Those are beastmen that your riders are pursuing southward. We saw them running. No grudgers move like that."

"Those were beastmen, yes," Tabor Jan shouted. "They moved in like vultures, smelling trouble."

Cal-raven stared into the dark tunnel, the passage intended to someday carry a river. "I've got to flag a warning to Abascar. Grudgers may be plotting something back at the house. And even if I'm wrong, it's likely that some of the beastmen have run into the tunnel. That will lead them back home."

"Prince," said one of the soldiers, "these men, these...grudgers. They're up to their ribs in stone."

Cal-raven glanced at Tabor Jan. "Scharr ben Fray did this," the prince explained.

"The *monster*," gasped Tabor Jan. "He killed both the grudgers *and* those who struggled with them?"

"Perhaps he had no choice. Perhaps he froze them in their fight, preserved them for us to find and judge. If he had not, we might never have known what happened. We would have thought—"

"That beastmen did it all."

A rasping voice suddenly burst from the half-buried grudger, who lunged and grasped Cal-raven's arm. The prince fell and fought to pull away. But then he saw the face of the man who had hold of him. It was Marv, the bearded digger who had warned him of the grudgers' growing discontent.

"*Tell them*," the man hissed, his blood-caked nails digging into Cal-raven's arm. "*Tell them at Abascar.*"

"What?" Cal-raven pried his arm away, brought his sword around, and pressed it to the grudger's neck. "You want me to send a grudger's message? I'll be doing what I can to write your name in the book of the condemned."

"Tell them..." Marv was staring blankly at the cave ceiling, his vision already faded. "Tell the people of Abascar..." He fought for breath, clutching at his chest. "They were so obsessed with what others might think...that they forgot who we really are."

"And who are we?" asked Cal-raven.

The man grasped at the floor. He released his grip; he released his breath.

When Cal-raven and Tabor Jan emerged from the tunnel, the quiet around them seemed unnatural.

"This storm," said Cal-raven.

"It still has thunder in it."

"I suspect so."

Tabor Jan cursed and steered his vawn around the sprawled body of a beastman. "What will you do?"

"I must get to a highwatch."

"To send warnings back to your father? Good."

"And to call for another troop. We need soldiers to protect the dig until the tunnels can be collapsed. Unless my father persists with his plan. And you. You should—"

"Comb the surrounding wood." Tabor Jan unbelted his alarm horn and sounded three quick notes. Vawns and riders moved inward from the edges of the battlefield.

"The dig is lost," said Cal-raven. "If there are survivors, they are scattered, and the grudgers—"

"They will have run."

"If you find beastmen—"

"Kill them."

"And if you find grudgers—"

"Kill them as well."

"No." Cal-raven frowned at his guardsman. "Seize them if you can. Kill only if you must. We need answers."

They gazed into the woods, gathering their bewildered wits. Cal-raven posted several swordsmen at the mouth of the dig tunnel, instructing them to watch for beastmen until he returned with new orders.

"Cal-raven," Tabor Jan quietly asked, "do you suppose your father will think this through? Or is it too late for him to change how he governs?"

Cal-raven shook his head. "We can only hope."

Tabor Jan sighed. "It will be a long ride back."

"And a tough winter ahead."

"Do you remember where the highwatch is hidden?"

Cal-raven tried to force a smile. "Of course. Keep your horn at the ready. I'll sound my own when the signal is sent."

"Cal-raven."

"Yes?

"If you see any Northchildren—"

"Don't follow them."

The prince spurred his vawn southward, up the steep hill toward the trees of the Cragavar. He thought about his arrival back home and how it would not inspire the celebration his father had predicted. Instead it would worsen a season of trouble. He wondered where Scharr ben Fray had gone.

Back in the woods, he found the giant cloudgrasper tree, reached into a tangle of roots, and threw a hidden lever.

Ropes fell, fastened to a small wooden step. Without looking back, he threw the lever again, jumped for the step, and caught it. The lift carried him up swiftly through the air, coming to rest deep in the broad canopy of needled boughs.

The hatch slammed shut, and he stepped off the swing to the platform.

As the sun surrendered, it singed the horizon, like a gleam of firelight along an edge of polished steel. Mist began to rise from the treetops.

That was when he saw the smoke roiling from House Abascar. That was when he saw its ruined silhouette.

His father's tower no longer speared the sky.

The platform seemed to tip and slide away beneath his feet. He had the sensation of falling. But the platform was steady. His right hand curled around the hilt of his sword and drew it out; his left unbelted his alarm horn, but he knew no signal to suggest the horrors on the horizon.

"Besieged," he gasped. "We are besieged at Abascar."

Thunder in his head. A crushing band of thorns around his heart. Aiming the horn northward to the dig, he blew with such force that he knew Tabor Jan would bring a company to his aid. All Abascar soldiers within hearing would converge upon this place.

He dropped the horn, stooped, and snatched the signal flag. He flashed it to any watchmen who might be left, to tell them that he saw, that he knew, that he was alive.

It was all he could think to do. Summon all powers under his command and send them charging back to the house.

"Help me on this dark day!" he whispered to the air. Grief had hold of his throat.

He stood alone between earth and sky, vulnerable and afraid. He had never been in such distress, never felt so helpless. And he had never had reason to fear that the kingship would pass to him before his father became old.

But he knew, somehow, it had.

29

A Storm of Remembering

While silver ribbons gleamed in the calm night water, the raft had drifted to Auralia's shores as though directed by an invisible navigator. And as the ale boy watched it arrive, while he and Auralia crouched by the water's edge playing with color and fire, he had sensed it—a great change approaching. All the signs were present, the echoes of his first days in the world—fire, trembling, and change.

The night the queen disappeared, he was in the motherly embrace of an old woman in the breweries. Men with torches had searched the whole house for Jaralaine's hiding place. Fire, trembling, and change.

The day Auralia walked into Abascar, bearing the burden of her labors: fire, trembling, and change.

And now again he walked through a world out of balance. Change. Fire. Kneel and tremble.

Incredulous but unharmed, he parted the smoke. He passed beneath the anxious gazes of dizzy, bleary-eyed survivors. He was a wraith in a nightmare, cloaked in ash, waiting for the quavering world to grow still again.

His first impulse had been to flee, to return to Auralia's caves. But she would not be there, and he feared the grief would overwhelm him. It was the one thing he wanted to do, to see her again. In this cataclysm, the dungeons might well have collapsed. But he had to know. Perhaps she had survived. Perhaps somewhere she sat in a cell, frightened, trapped, pressing her cloak to her face so she could breathe.

He found himself stumbling in pursuit of the soldiers. The ruin of the main gate, the wreckage of the principal avenue, the houses made of flame…he witnessed wonders and horrors. When Ark-robin turned to urge them on, his teeth were bared through the bristling beard, his eyes gone crimson. It struck the boy as strange that he had spent his life trying to dodge the soldier's frown, and now he was compelled to follow, if only because that formidable silhouette was the only familiar sight in this spectacle. Or perhaps it was because Ark-robin, unlike the others scrambling all around them, was running *toward* the fire. The ale boy knew he must follow. *Into* the fire.

The fire held the answers to his questions.

There were people everywhere, running, injured, crying, dying, or dead. Fleeing destruction and danger, clinging to each other, searching for belongings or family. Outlines in the dust, smoke, and falling night, traces of fear and desperation. Staggering toward the palace. Trudging outward, dragging lumpish bags of salvage. One shouldered a tall, golden candlestand. One clutched her silent, naked infant. One held another's hand, but there was no person attached to it.

Ash fell in a torrent, settling into patches of sunken earth and smoking craters. Fire licked at the edges of chasms, worsening the closer they came to the wall that had guarded the palace. The ale boy marveled as they passed the top of the palace watchtower, which had toppled outward. Along its length, the ale boy twice saw an arm protruding from piles of crushed stone.

Eventually they reached the gate that had stood at the foot of the toppled tower. In some surreal act of defiance or ignorance, the gate still stood.

Ark-robin attempted to shoulder it open. It did not budge. But the ground had fallen in on both sides of the gate, and he could climb down on an accidental stair of spilled stones and move around it. He did and commanded his three soldiers to help the ale boy down and through the deep crevasses. The soldiers obeyed, but he could see in their increasing hesitation that questions were rising.

Behind the gate, things were far worse.

The ground was open before them, a great canyon, jagged about the edges as though the earth had been merely an eggshell, and something had hatched. Below, distant rumbles—a subterranean thunderstorm. Fires were scattered through the turbulent cauldron of smoke, burning at dizzying depths through the chambers of King Cal-marcus's hollowed house. He recognized the color of marrowwood flame chewing at props that supported a few spans of the Underkeep ceiling. He recognized a different kind of fire burning curtains and garments and ropes. And yet another, a yellow fire, burning the oil from fallen lanterns.

The ale boy could guess what had happened. He had spent a great deal of his short life below, wondering how the ceiling stayed up. The elaborate network of supporting columns always seemed a pending doom. All for the sake of hoarding and hiding treasure, for the secrecy of forging weapons, for the ability to move beneath the city and spy upon people in their homes. But something had upset the central braces.

Colors like those he had shown Auralia by the lake were leaping into the sky, not from cups, but from fissures and collapsed buildings. The force of such a fire…he was weak-kneed for imagining. It would have moved swiftly. It would have smashed ceilings, melted floors, and ripped stone walls. As rooms above descended into rooms below, the burden would have increased…more fuel for the hungry fire.

In rare moments when a breeze cleared the death clouds, Abascar looked like a shattered anthill. People rushed madly about through broken tunnels, but paths that had been passageways led to sheer drops. Deranged survivors clung to walls or crawled along what was left of the floors staring into a fire-sculpted abyss. Some tested their weight on the ragged walls, fumbling for a firm hold. A tunnel would collapse nearby, shaking the earth and stripping their grasp. He saw a solid wall of soil; arms and legs reached out in clusters as though pinned there in some sickening gallery.

There were voices in that canyon as well, sounds he had never heard from human throats.

In desperation, he scanned the darkness for something unscathed, something that had not been consumed by this ravenous and bottomless appetite. All he saw was Ark-robin's drive to save what could not be saved, a boldness to go forward and risk his life to save another's. He had not noticed this color in the captain before. But now he realized it had always been there, winding through the arrogance and the cruelty; once dormant, now awakening in the heat.

Seizing upon the captain's quest, the ale boy surfaced from his strange meditation and, gasping in the immediate details of his circumstance, remembered the closeness of the precipice, the sound of beastmen in a murderous rage below. He tasted the bitterness of ash between his tongue and his teeth.

Two of Ark-robin's soldiers unfastened their bows, set their jaws, and unsheathed a fistful of arrows.

"Like wolves hunting injured prey," growled Ark-robin. "The beastmen don't ask how Abascar's been hurt. They just pounce."

"What do they want here, Captain?"

"Don't be dense, Wolftooth. Their poison has given them a taste for little more than murder and pillage."

He turned with a shuddering breath and looked back into what had been the neighborhoods of Housefolk, and the ale boy could read the creases on his brow. Somewhere the captain's wife and daughter were lost in all of this.

As the captain marched into the dark clouds below, the ale boy followed, descending a crooked path to one of the few remaining bridges that crossed a great cavern from one Underkeep station to another. For a while they were engulfed by smoke, as if moving through a storm of black-robed ghosts, the gleam on Ark-robin's sword just another light in the sea of Abascar's myriad fires. The soldiers followed him, arrows readied.

The ale boy took one last look up at the sky, one last glance back at the gate.

An old woman, so frail and small it seemed impossible she had survived at all, passed them on the path. She ignored the captain when he tried to stop her. In one hand she carried a torch, and with the other she pulled a long bundle of multicolored garments from the Underkeep, their vivid hues smudged with soot. Ark-robin would have pursued her had he not been silenced by what followed: two children dragging a much different sort of burden—a man, probably their own father, still and lifeless. The smaller child, a girl, looked at the ale boy with sad, frightened eyes, her hair wretched with dust and debris. For a moment he thought it was Auralia. But no; Auralia would be much further down, much deeper.

In the dungeons.

Still they descended, walking on a thin arch of stone and earth that spanned the canyon, reaching into the space that had once been the palace cellars.

He pressed his sleeve to his face, stepping lightly for fear too heavy a footfall would snap the arch. How to get to the dungeons from here, he could not imagine.

And then—the strangest sensation—an evening wind gusted through the chasms, brushing aside the black clouds. The sight before them was spectacular and terrible.

The palace lay ahead, tilted, like a sinking ship, one side buried in earth, the other suspended toward the sky. The domes were broken, dissolving into ash. The towers had snapped at their bases. The windows were curtained with flame. Scars of soot and soil marred its once pristine surfaces. Walls had fallen in here and there, leaving hollows like open wounds.

"No!" Ark-robin roared, running down to the place where the bridge met the earth. The boy knew where Ark-robin was heading; there was a crooked window not far above the place where palace merged with earth. The captain was going in to find the king.

The gust of wind faded, the smoke returned, and Ark-robin and his men disappeared. The ale boy followed, slowly, gingerly, hanging on to the edges of the bridge. A few steps later the span broadened, and he pressed his hands to the wall of earth. The glow of the window high above him was faint through the smoke.

Ark-robin and the others had climbed in.

He was too scared to climb and was about to start back across the bridge when three hulking shadows emerged, stalking like predators. "Beastmen," he said, and a strong hand grasped him by the back of his collar and dragged him up, up, up into a golden corridor.

Ark-robin set the boy down, grasped his shoulders, and said gravely, "Stay with me. Stay close. Do you understand?"

"Why, sir?"

"It's…it's complicated."

Ark-robin led the boy by the hand, slipping on the tilted floor of the smoky chamber.

They found an adjoining corridor where the ground was almost level. The three soldiers wore blank expressions, moving with mechanical precision as if these rehearsed maneuvers were lifelines to sanity. The archers knelt behind shields, arrows to bows; behind them a swordsman crouched with blades catching and casting light.

Ark-robin strode into the stifling smoke and began to roar like a bear in full attack. The ale boy sensed that something in the captain was dying as he left his men behind to face the beastmen. In any other circumstance Ark-robin would have stood with them and fought, but his duty to the king overruled his emotions. Behind them, the twang of a bowstring sang, answered almost instantly by a shriek, a piercing horror that went on and on, soon matched by others in a sickening dissonance.

"My life," the captain muttered. "My life, protecting this house. And now this."

Ark-robin suddenly lurched as if struck from behind. He fell upon the ale boy. Rocks gouged the boy's cheeks, just inches from a curtain of roaring fire.

He pulled himself away, the ground burning his hands and knees. A moment later he found himself crawling over the captain, who was closing his hands around an arrow hewn from something black and porous like bone. It had entered his leg just below the knee and protruded behind with a jagged metal barb. He choked on airborne debris and let a sob break free, watching as the captain snapped off the forked tip and pulled out the arrowshaft.

"Will you die?"

"Not from this," spat the captain, as if commanding his own body to obey. He pulled off his cape, breastplate, and shoulderguards and ripped his tunic free. The boy could see that the captain had suffered many other wounds; his chest was painted with darkening blood. "What sort of bad dream is this, a house so heavy that it sinks into the earth? Curse this Underkeep and all it contains." Suddenly Ark-robin was laughing. "There you are, wretched Queen Jaralaine. Your house *will* be talked about in Bel Amica and remembered in House Jenta. Your monument will be seen all across the Expanse."

"We can escape," the boy said, feeling a mysterious urge to comfort the captain. "I can get us out."

"The map has changed a bit, boy." The captain wrapped the strips around his leg and knotted them tightly, clenching his teeth until they looked as if they might shatter. "This is it. This is the test."

"Test, sir?"

The captain seemed to be repeating things he had heard many times before. "Here's a soldier's lesson for you, boy: Every man lives for a moment of testing, a moment when you have nothing but your own resources. In that moment you discover either you have what it takes or you don't." Ark-robin gave the boy a strange, suspicious look. "But that's a shame, isn't it? We're all going to fail. We don't have resources enough. Unless...unless we all have the help you had once upon a time."

The ale boy was suddenly afraid of something else, something looming behind the captain's words.

"If you know something, boy, anything else that can help us here, tell me now." He had the fierce gaze of an interrogator, but he seemed to be looking through the boy into some other time and place.

"Do you mean about the Underkeep?"

"I mean about your mysterious guardians. Where are they this time?"

"Guardians, sir?"

The second archer's voice rose in agony, stuttering cries of pain from the corridor behind them and then stopping short.

"Stand up, Wolftooth," Ark-robin muttered. He wrapped another strip of torn tunic around his wound. "Oh, I am feeling the lateness of things."

The ale boy watched a burst of darkness and sparks in the center of the flames as a piece of the corridor fell away.

"Don't you find it strange," the captain continued gravely, "that we are here again, you and I, surrounded by flames and shadows?"

Again, that mysterious terror.

"The king agreed to cover up that I was anywhere near that fire. It's never good to be second in command when the first in command goes down. Every-body suspects you. Some thought I murdered your parents. You probably don't remember. But your father, Tar-brona, was my mentor. I tried to save him. I failed."

The ale boy, on his hands and knees, blinked and shook his head.

"You were only a day or two old. There were gifts all over your house. A thief came through the window. Bumped the lantern." Ark-robin pushed him-self to his knees. Sweat ran in streams through his wild hair and dripped to the ground. He pulled his armor back on, pressed his helm back onto his head.

"I was the house defender, second only to your father. We often met at night to discuss plans. I was on my way when I heard screams. I saw the thief and tried to catch him. Radegan…that blasted Radegan. If he didn't die in Maugam's pit, he's burning now. At last, a fitting punishment." Ark-robin choked on bitter laughter and smoke. "Is that what this is? Punishment?"

The ale boy wanted to ask the question that wavered there. And then he didn't want to know.

The answer came anyway. "I heard your parents calling your name. They couldn't get through to you." Ark-robin forced himself to stand, weakened by the withering heat of the furnace a few steps behind them.

Still, nothing came through the smoke at the tunnel's entrance, nothing but a scuffling sound and something like a wild dog's growl.

"I tried, but I could not save Tar-brona or your mother," the towering soldier said, looking down at the kneeling boy. "I gave up and ran. But then I heard your cry. I could not leave empty-handed. I wanted to save something. Your cradle was blazing, but something was draped across you. A dark, glittering sheet. You were shielded by... I was never going to speak of this! All huddled about your bed...they wore strange robes. The fire didn't burn them."

Northchildren. The ale boy felt the urge to run into the fire. Ark-robin's story entered him like a phantom clutching keys and moving to a door he had locked. He did not want to know what came next.

"They stepped aside when I approached. I thought I was going mad. Smoke in my lungs, delirious. But I reached through and lost two fingers in the fire. The strangers formed two lines and cleared a path for me through the fire. And I carried you out." He flexed his three-fingered hand. "Told everybody I'd lost those fingers to a beastman."

Ark-robin held out his bare hand.

As he stared at the captain's hand, the ale boy could also see the hand of that nameless phantom reaching through time, clutching those fiery keys. He remained still, paralyzed. And then, moved by a need greater than his fear, he lunged forward and gripped Ark-robin's scarred hand with both of his own.

Relief swept through him, carrying away the ache.

Another howl pierced the thunder. It was the last of Ark-robin's swordsmen. The ale boy had heard men die at the claws of beastmen before. They always cried like children.

Captain Ark-robin pulled his hand away, carefully planted his feet, wincing through what must have been unbearable pain. "Your guardians, boy. If you know how to call them, *this* is the time. You've got to get out of here."

"I don't think the guardians are coming," the ale boy said, not knowing why. "I can take us through. I can get you out, Captain."

Ark-robin, turning to consider this, gestured to the flames. "The king is in there. It's my duty to defend him. If you know a way to get out, then go. This is my place. This is my thread, right to the end. Never had a son, alas. But my daughter, my magnificent daughter." He took two impressive strides forward, his wounds seemingly forgotten. "She would have been queen. She would have been queen."

My thread. The ale boy was startled by the words. They reminded him of something. He looked back into the flames. *Auralia.*

"Why?" he asked in a rush. "Why didn't you tell me who I was? Why didn't you tell anybody?"

"Cal-marcus's advisors. . .some of them were eager to find evidence that I set the fire. They wanted to replace me with someone they could control. I told the brewers I pulled you from a burning barn. I mentioned fire, you see. To explain your scar. Nobody asked any questions."

And then he put a hand on the child's soot-dusted, tangled hair and stood there for a long moment. "Tar-brona," he said, his voice strangely weakened, "was so proud the day you were born. I sometimes wish that I'd. . ." He stopped abruptly, shook his head, and cleared his throat. Before turning to meet the advancing threat, he reached to his breast, took the band of medallions that measured the achievements of his career, pulled the pin free, and fastened the band to the ale boy's tunic.

And then he drew his long blue cape around the ale boy's shoulders. "Pull this over yourself, lie flat, and perhaps the monsters won't notice you." He walked forward into the smoke, and the ale boy heard him mutter to himself, "What I would have given. A room in the tower. A view of the woods."

Fire. Trembling. Change.

The scar on the ale boy's forehead was burning. He reached for Ark-robin's cape as he had been told to do, but the scar blazed even hotter, as though suddenly alive. He touched it, and it scorched his fingertips. He felt faint, drowning in heat. And yet he was not afraid. He had known he would fall into fire again.

Through the blazing haze traveling down the tunnel after the captain of the guard, the ale boy saw a flash of memory—the exiled mage in disguise, Scharr ben Fray.

"If you know the secret of passing through fire," the mage had said, *"there are many places only you can travel and a lot of things only you can know."*

The ale boy turned and stared into the blinding corridor.

As Ark-robin's sword met the blades of the approaching beastmen, the sound was like the peal of a massive bell.

The ale boy could not bear to wait any longer. He plunged into the fire.

The phantom met him there. Vivid images rushed through his mind; he was seeing that fire again from so many years ago.

White. Blue. Gold. He sees nothing but light and color.

There is pain, but it is a distant thing, like a dull ache sensed through a heavy blanket of sleep.

There are echoes. Shouts. A man's voice, panic and fear. A woman's voice, anguish. A name cried out over and over.

A hand seizes him, pulls him up out of his blankets and his cradle, up through the fire. A man in gleaming armor, a large man with a beard, a man screaming, fierce. The stench of burning flesh. Pressed to the breastplate of the great armored man, the boy clenches his tiny newborn fists. He wails into the fire.

But as they push forward, he sees them. High walls of flame, pressed back to open a path. The soldier shouting as blood pulses from his red and blistered hand.

And then the memories dissipate.

He falls, or rather is *caught* by something like a net and then set on his feet.

There is a darkness ahead of him. It is not a door. It is a shape. It moves. It parts the flames, creating a path. He is pulled along in its wake. He has seen this shape before, underwater, deep in the lake, as he struggled to the surface toward moonlight.

He is in a great, charred space. All around, metal racks emanating smoke. He recognizes these bending, melting metal structures. This used to be the distillery. The smell he knows…blackening sugars, burnt liquors. The fire has devoured its fill.

He sees on the floor before him a twisted mass of ash, bone, and hair. He recoils, his eyes settling on a strange detail amidst the remains. An open jaw. Small hands, finger bones still curled into fists. A strand of pearls.

He lifts the jewels and stuffs them into his pocket.

There are tears in his eyes as he sees this first death by fire. He looks about for comfort. He finds only strange, blurred footsteps in the ashes.

A sound like drums and heartbeats draws his attention to a distant corner across the tilting floor to a huddled mass of quivering shapes. He remembers them. And he can see through them to the fallen woman with the silverbrown hair.

The figures kneel, gingerly touching the body. When they withdraw their hands, he sees they have taken hold of strange and shimmering threads. As they gather those threads, the body surrenders. Knots are undone. They drape a dark shroud across her. The shroud gathers a fullness and rises, joining them in a series of embraces. But the body of the young woman lies, smaller now, hollowed.

He approaches in his own cloud of smoke, offers a soot-smeared hand. It pierces the shroud of the newly robed figure, and he feels a warm, smooth, familiar hand grasp his. It is Auralia's hand, though he sees her lying curled on the ground, like a child asleep.

The Northchildren draw back, watching, but he does not look at them. She opens her eyes, and they mirror the fire above her in the ceiling and beyond.

Her voice comes through the strange, shadowed shroud, as quiet and calming as it had been on the shore of the lake. "It's you," she laughs. "I shoulda known. You rowed 'cross the water to find me. And now you've come through fire."

The shroud becomes more translucent as he stares, until he does not see a shroud at all. He sees Auralia. Her skin is full of the color he has only seen in her weaving, the color that contains all colors.

He lets go of her hand. As it slides free of the shroud, it is clean, all ashes wiped away.

"The Northchildren. They remember you. They came to gather you before, to unstitch your skin and smuggle you away. But someone snatched you from their grasp."

"You're alive?" he says to convince himself. "Everything's exploded. And who is that, the one lying there?"

She rises to her feet, glowing. "I'm done with that skin. It's just not strong enough. That's what the Northchildren say. I remember now how it goes. I'm remembering a lot all of a sudden. What my home's like and how to get there."

He allows himself another view of her folded, ash-dusted form—a shed skin, hair singed and blackened, bones.

"You're...you're different than the rest of us," he says. "You come from somewhere else, don't you?"

"I was brought from somewhere else. But all the four houses...they *all* came from somewhere else, ale boy. A long, long time ago. But they've forgotten. A fifth house. I woulda told them, but I forgot too. I was just a baby when Krawg and Warney found me."

"Is that where the colors come from? Take me with you, Auralia."

"I can't take you. Not yet."

"Then tell me how to get there."

"Nobody can take you. You gotta make your own journey when *you* find the tracks. And you can't see them unless you remember how to look. They can be anywhere. On the road or off it. Even in dungeons. They're different for Gatherers than for kings and different for anyone in between. Even a beastman can find them, I suspect. They might take you on a long journey. Or it might be just a few steps." She shrugs and then yawns in sudden weariness. "Anyway, I've come to the threshold. Northchildren are unlocking the door. But don't worry, ale boy. I think you're already remembering how to find the tracks."

He startles as she reaches through the shroud to tousle his hair. "Fire boy," she sadly whispers, "you look like you've been in Yawny's oven."

He feels his tears coming now. "Auralia. The house. It's fallen to pieces. It's all burning. And Auralia, my mother. My mother and my father. They—"

"I know." She reaches for him, and he falls into her embrace. As her strange, glittering veil wraps around him, he remembers its stinging texture. This cloth was laid across him once, when he rested in the cradle. It tugs at something inside him. It shields him from heat and pain. He wants to draw it around him. Auralia holds him as he cries.

Tears are in her eyes now too. "They are not suffering, ale boy. That's long past. It's time to look to what's ahead."

"Auralia." He pulls free of her embrace, and suddenly he smiles. "When I was in the fire. My parents. I heard them calling me. From a long time ago."

"Yes."

"And I remembered. *My name.* They said it over and over."

"The remembering. It's slow and ever so strange. But when it comes, it's all so clear. I've done what I came to do. I brought the colors to try and remind folks." Her voice falters, choked on feelings. "But I guess it takes more than just showing. They've gotta be willing to see. Their remembering will be long and painful." She stares into the distance where flames twirl like dancers, a thousand writhing strands. "When I think of Cal-raven...it hurts."

She is different indeed. Queenlike. No longer afraid or timid. "I've got to get home before I become forgetful again. When you reach the end of the steps meant for you, don't linger, ale boy. The Expanse...it can do that to you. Distract you. Make you forget. Make you think you're home and that it's all you need. But you know it isn't. You want so much more."

She slowly descends to one knee again, until her gaze is even with his. Her face is still so small, shimmering, as it had been on the lakeshore under the moon. Tears spill down her face, and when she bows her head, they fall into strands of her hair.

The glow of the firelight behind him goes out, and a sudden shadow stretches across the floor to ascend the walls. The drums have stopped. The Northchildren are bowed low. Auralia looks up at what casts that shadow, the presence looming behind the ale boy. He can hear its breath, like waves sighing against the edges of the lake. He does not turn, but he knows what is there, what has come.

And then she laughs. "Oh, I am remembering it all. That beautiful language. The light. Oh, the light."

He glances at the Northchildren. Here, in the presence of the Keeper, at the edge of death's barrier, they seem more substantial, more real. He sees faces through their dark veils, hears murmurs as though through a wall. They seem familiar.

Auralia kisses his forehead scar, cooling it. So many mysteries here in one place. She smiles. "Well? Will you tell me?"

"My lady?"

"Never call me anything but Auralia. Promise? And I will never call you anything but your own name. So hurry up and tell me what it is."

"My name?"

"Your name. How can I tell the ones back home all about my brave friend if I do not know what to call him?"

He looks down at his blistered, soot-blackened feet. "You will not tell me where you are going?"

She gives him that playful smile he first saw when he met her among the Gatherers—when she protected him from Radegan's temper. "I'm not allowed to say, ale boy. And I'm not sure yet myself."

He loses his control and weeps. "If you're not tellin' me where I can find you, then I'm not gonna tell you my name!"

She embraces him. Her face is cool against his as she whispers, "Let me tell you something else instead." She tells him where the thief concealed all her gifts to the Gatherers. "Go and find what's been stolen. Take it to those who need it. While I'm gone, I cannot help House Abascar as I have. You, ale boy. You will be my hands."

She turns then and passes behind him. He listens to her go. A powerful wind rushes about his feet, rising, lifting the great shadow up through the turbulent cavern toward escape. The Northchildren flicker and fade, like candles in the gale. The ale boy glances over his shoulder.

He sees Auralia, for just one instant, carried up into the shadow like an autumn leaf into a thunderstorm, the prince's ring on her thumb glinting in the firelight.

He awoke, but he did not know how much time had passed.

And he lay still, remembering and weeping in the ashes.

30

THE REMNANT OF ABASCAR

B lack coral geese soared stark and sudden in a straight line, appearing from a continent of burdened clouds, crossing a river of grey, disappearing into a dark, miasmic island in the sky. The storms were winter's harbingers, burdened with bad tidings.

Cal-raven watched them as he walked briskly among the silent, sniffing hounds. They found nothing, these surviving twelve dogs from the great hunting host of Abascar. But this breed knew nothing of surrender—only the moment and the hunger.

Cal-raven admired their unyielding hope. For him, surrender was dangerously appealing.

Each day the Abascar survivors became more desperate, contending with cloudbursts, sleet, bearcats, fatigue, nightmares, despair. They could appeal to House Bel Amica and hope that they might be taken in as refugees. They could flee to the deep south, to offer their services to the quiet, sedulous mages of House Jenta. Cal-raven had sent messengers prepared with appeals, but perhaps the survivors would be more persuasive if they arrived on a doorstep all at once.

Tabor Jan, leading the company on his large vawn, did not look at the migrating birds. Silent as slumber, his arrowcaster at the ready in his hands, the guardsman never turned his gaze from the path ahead.

Cal-raven sensed that even here, in this ragged multitude, he was alone.

Behind them marched the hard truth, the survivors. No one voiced hopes or plans. Not yet. They spoke of food and weather, of changing bandages, or taking a turn astride a vawn to rest their weary feet. Of immediate need. Of refuge.

Some, especially the children, collected fallen leaves, berries, and stones along the way, souvenirs of lands they'd never seen before. Late autumn offered strange comfort, for the Housefolk had not seen such a conflagration of color in their years of compliance with Cal-marcus's code. They had pictured a world snarled with thorns and putrid swamps.

There were seventeen vawns for one hundred and forty travelers; all Abascar's horses had either died or run wild. Sixteen soldiers patrolled the path before and behind, and a few moved through the trees alongside.

Tabor Jan had trained the hounds to refrain from howling in this stealthy journey. Still, he knew their restraint would eventually give way as they grew too hungry to resist barking at the hint of prey.

But there was no prey. They found no sign of rabbit, goom, groundbelly, or flightless birds. Either the increasing numbers of beastmen had driven the wildlife from this region or the animals anticipated a winter more severe than any in recent memory.

Occasionally a patrol would drift wordlessly back to the company with a man or a woman or a child who had been found wandering alone in the trees, and there would be fresh tears, embraces.

The company swelled to nearly two hundred. Each newcomer carried the names of many more who had not been found or had been found slain. Having left others behind to die, some were prone to stumbling and glancing over their shoulders.

Cal-raven tried to assemble words to assure them they had done the right thing by leaving the ruined house behind. But others spoke his thoughts before he could muster the courage.

"We could have stayed there, fought the beastmen, and tried to salvage our home, but the ground in Abascar is not safe."

"Disease will spread quickly there."

"With the walls down, we'd be vulnerable. Cent Regus won't relent in their attacks."

"Help may come from House Bel Amica, but it may not. And if it does come, it'll be too late."

"Soon snows and plagues'll be dangerous as beastmen."

"But where will we go?"

"We will journey to the Blackstone Caves," Cal-raven said, finding his voice at last. "The Blackstone Caves are above the Cliffs of Barnashum, and we must reach them before the full freeze arrives. There we can burrow deep. Barnashum conceals a world of underground waterfalls. We can stake out a defensible hideaway, tend to the injured, and make a plan."

The Caves, Cal-raven had thought. *The Caves where I once ran to be alone or to walk with my teacher and learn the slow and silent work of shaping stone. Now I bring my house with me. Now I make it a place of hiding and, inevitably, survival.*

As he spoke, the people quieted, and those far behind hurried to catch up. He could see the scowls and the suspicion, but he expected nothing more. He would have to earn their trust.

He turned, cleared his throat, and sought for a speech. He hated speeches, and he knew the people had learned to distrust them.

As if anticipating Cal-raven's intent, Tabor Jan suddenly steered his vawn around to stand beside the prince and delivered a speech of his own.

"You look at Cal-raven as if you're seeing the ghost of King Cal-marcus. Know this—Prince Cal-raven is as weary and worried as you. Each loss you suffer, he suffers with you. You are angry. And I assure you, your anger is but a spark. Cal-raven's is a bonfire."

Cal-raven had never heard his guardsman speak so many words at one time.

"Muster what strength and courage you have, and I swear to you, Cal-raven will match you—day for day, risk for risk, breath for breath."

Let's not get ahead of ourselves, Cal-raven said to himself, but he was not about to interrupt this surge of zeal. Tabor Jan had stunned the survivors into an attentive silence.

"I am Cal-raven's guardsman. But I will stumble from time to time. Pick me up, for Cal-raven's sake. And he, too, will grow weary. Encourage him. We give for one another's good, and no one will give more than Cal-raven. Try to prove me wrong. Try to give more than he will. You won't manage."

Their eyes shifted from the guardsman to the prince, and he knew that he appeared pale and pathetic.

Tabor Jan placed his hand over his heart. "It is fair to say that too many words from Abascar's throne have given you reason to worry. But Cal-raven does not sit on a throne or make himself separate from you. I have fought alongside him, and I can you tell you: he will not leave your side. He presses on for one reason only—to make right what has gone wrong in Abascar. Walls do not shape a house. For Cal-raven, *you* are House Abascar. He is the king we need. And if you are true to him, as I am, together we will become the wonder of the Expanse."

What followed was far less than a cheer, but some of the people nodded, and the scowls softened.

Tabor Jan turned and fixed his friend with an expression of ferocious threat. "You'd better not make me a liar," he whispered.

Cal-raven cleared his throat. With the sensation of stepping out onto a frozen lake, he began to speak, moving gingerly into the reverent silence his guardsman had prepared.

There was no coronation. But from that day on, the people addressed Cal-raven as their king.

The survivors' journey wound down into hilly lowlands, through branches of the Cragavar woods, but the survivors felt as though they struggled up a steep incline.

The Housefolk whispered among themselves, refusing to treat Gatherers as equals. But the Gatherers' coats of hair, bark, and rags became the uniforms of knowledge and experience. The children soon revered them as mysterious teachers.

Tabor Jan had successfully delegated tasks during the rude awakening of the journey's start. It was with a mix of astonishment and fear that Gatherers like Krawg and Warney heard their names called to teach others how to construct makeshift tents, how to find edible roots from patterns of leaves, and how to discern poison's disguises. The respect brought Krawg strength and humor, and soon he threw his crutch away.

The caravan's greatest burden was the salvation of those who could not sleep. Once she had exhausted a substantial reservoir of tears, Wenjee—who tired easily even when riding a vawn—found enough voice to raise the walls of Abascar behind the closed eyes of her listeners. She took pride in preserving Abascar's legacy for the Housefolk, even if the histories she described bore little resemblance to the house they had known. For most of them, Wenjee's bizarre imagination provided a welcome escape from heartache.

One night Wenjee's story grew raspy and faint, and in the morning they found her still and cold, her tongue swollen, her throat clenched, as if the tales had grown too large and squelched her voice. The remnant of Abascar gathered around as the soldiers hoisted her onto a pallet of sturdy boughs and carried her in a solemn procession, to bury her out of sight and scent of predatory hunters.

"Stories must be heavy," a little girl had said.

When carried by the vawn, Cal-raven clattered small blackstones together in his hands, unable to find enough peace to sculpt them as Scharr ben Fray had taught him.

"Move into the eye of your storm," the mage had said, "where you cannot hear the world about you, where your fears cannot reach you. Let your thumb move across the stone until it finds the shape within the stone, the image waiting to be revealed."

Here there was no escape from fears. That magic remained frozen.

He was wary of the forest, as though a new menace were prowling there. Scharr ben Fray was fond of saying, "Hasn't our experience taught us that there are more things at work in the world than our experience can teach us?" Cal-raven concluded he had not experienced enough—not yet—to name the trouble he sensed. Sometimes he became suspicious of the ground beneath his feet. Without the solace he found in molding stones, Cal-raven sought other ways of giving shape to the rising fury within him.

At night he armed guards with alarm horns and then took others out on their vawns, patrolling the area, riding hard and fast as though pursuing nightmares to trample underfoot. More than once they surprised a beastman. More than once they tore into their foes with swords, arrows, and spears until there was nothing left but the stains of blood on their flesh in the morning.

"This does not help me feel better," Tabor Jan muttered.

"I'm not interested in feeling better," he answered. "I'm interested in sending a message. We can be dangerous too."

For the soldiers, the burden of the people's dependence was excruciating. They quickly tired of the constant inquiries about their destination, and they wondered if they could trust the maps Cal-raven sketched from memory.

So there was great relief in Tabor Jan's voice when he laughed out loud and said, "The calling geese! Their cries have an echo. The Cliffs of Barnashum must be just ahead."

He moved to the fore to speak with Cal-raven, who had become so quiet and remote that he seemed a ghost.

"I know how much you wish to reach the Blackstone Caves, but I have the snow chill in my bones. The hounds know it too. They sleep pressed together, and one is always watching the sky. There are old bear caves in the cliffs. Surely we can defend those for a while, even if we have to split into groups for a time."

Cal-raven did not hesitate. "We will camp here then," he said in a voice like a shred of fog, "until we see clear sky. But we'll have to move on to the Blackstone Caves before winter. Our spirits will choke if we stay in these bear caves for long. We need room to move about, to develop relationships, to store food. We need a new house. But you are right. Snow's coming. And the bear caves are better than traveling in wet and freezing rags. We will trust the weather to break soon."

The weather proved untrustworthy.

They stared out from the bear caves down the rocky slopes, through whirlwinds of snow, to the forest as it slowly turned white. Above them loomed a massive plateau that seemed to be turning from stone into ice, and it revealed no passage or further retreat. It was as though they had come to the end of the world, to a wall that could not be breached.

When a hint of smoke reached the caves one night, Tabor Jan disappeared to investigate. Cal-raven, furious with his friend for heading out alone and on foot, could only pace, wait, and stare out at the starlit snow. Eventually he fell asleep in the mouth of the cave.

He awoke to find an Abascar officer singing the Verse of the Passing of Midnight, a low, steady, murmuring melody like the quickening of spring beneath the blankets of winter.

Slowly the world came back into view.

One of the guards, Brevolo kai Galarand, smiled to see that her brave impulse was, indeed, calming the quakes that had shaken the sleeping leader.

Cal-raven propped himself up on an elbow, his cape over him like a blanket. "I could kill you for singing of home...while we die here in these caves," he wheezed.

The officer abruptly ended her song.

"But it did calm me in a dark dream."

"Perhaps," ventured Brevolo, "we should keep that tradition, my lord, when we have a new house at last."

It was the first time anyone but Tabor Jan had addressed him directly in days. He let the words swirl in his head for a long moment. *"When?"* he finally said. "When we have a new house? You still permit yourself to dream?"

"Not as vividly, sire, as it seems you do," said the officer, whose forwardness left the other guard gaping. Brevolo smiled like a child testing limits. "If you'll pardon my saying so, sire, it was difficult to ignore your shouts. We thought that some music might calm—"

"I was shouting?"

"I hope you're as strong against the winter as you were against whatever monster threatened you in your dream."

He looked suddenly out at the night, his pulse quickening. "Forget about dreams. We are threatened now!"

Yes, there was something. Footfalls on the rocky ground below. Heavy. Growing closer.

"Silence. Stand back," he whispered hoarsely, fumbling for his bow. "Arrows!"

He crouched low as the guards pulled back. He quickly and quietly readied his bow, waiting for the first glimmer of a presence.

Those sounded like vawn hooves.

"Tabor Jan took no vawn," he whispered. "We are discovered."

The steps went silent. Then they heard the thud of riders dismounting.

Cal-raven cursed. He had only one arrow. Brevolo was a good archer, better than he, but she was not a trustworthy swordbearer. If these visitors bore ill will and came too close for arrows...

And then, the Verse of the Passing of Midnight, rising again. A woman's voice.

Even as the singer's face emerged from Cal-raven's memory, he heard another familiar voice calling up to him. "Bless those singers!" Tabor Jan emerged from the dark, his voice low and tired. "These caves are tough to locate under a moonless sky. Don't shoot, Cal-raven. I know you're angry, but you're also tired, and you'd probably strike my companions."

"I'll fill you so full of arrows, Tabor Jan, that you'll make a fine cloakrack." Cal-raven rose, lowering his bow. "You deserve it for scaring us half to death. And that vawn deserves even worse for the racket it made. I should—"

A shape leapt from the shadows, struck him full in the chest, and knocked him backward.

"Hagah!"

King Cal-marcus's hunting hound pinned Cal-raven to the ground with his front paws and pressed his wet nose to Cal-raven's cheek, plastering his face with his thick, wet tongue. The ancient dog set everyone to laughing with his ecstatic howls and yips, and then he bounded about, trying to knock everyone down with his forepaws and shoving his nose between the guards' legs. Cal-raven stood, wiped off his face, and then brushed away unexpected tears as he embraced the guardsman.

Over Tabor Jan's shoulder, he saw two more figures.

The taller woman, familiar in her tattered white cloak, was weary and sad in her crooked stride. "It is good to find that the prince is still capable of laughter." She stepped into the torchlight. "Maybe I'll laugh again someday."

"Say-ressa! Good healer. My lady, you live." Cal-raven dropped to one knee, a reaction that startled her.

And then she knelt too, facing him. He took her hands and kissed them. "My king," she said to him, "I am your servant as I was your father's."

"Tell me that your brave husband, the valiant captain, will return to us as well. And oh…your daughter…" He had forgotten the girl's name again, and he sharply regretted all the disrespect he had voiced to his father in the past. "Hear this," he whispered. "It is time for us to offer you what you have so faithfully given us. We will bring you healing."

"Wounds like these don't heal, my king." Her laughter was bitter. "But that does not mean I cannot find comfort. Music helps, as this one has taught me."

Suddenly recognizing the younger woman as she knelt in respect, Cal-raven laughed and took her up in his arms and spun them both in a circle while she cried onto his shoulder. "You'll write a song, Lesyl!" he shouted.

"Perhaps there is a song of your own that will find its way onto my strings, my king," she said, and he observed that she seemed different—audacious and free.

Tabor Jan grasped his arm and pulled him away. "There are more alive, Cal-raven. Maybe two hundred more."

Cal-raven looked back to Ark-robin's widow.

"In the Blackstone Caves," Say-ressa said. "We lit a fire tonight, a rare thing, to warm the caves for some who have caught a chill."

"Two hundred more...reached the Blackstone Caves?" Cal-raven asked.

"The boy led us. The boy who saved us from the fires."

"The boy? What boy?"

"I swear I will only have the strength to tell our story once more." She pressed a hand to her forehead, stroked back her tousled hair.

Cal-raven slumped to the ground. Hagah returned to nudge him happily, then rolled onto his back to present his snow-flecked belly for a scratch. "Only a few even know how to find those caves..."

"Apparently you told an ale boy, my lord," said Tabor Jan.

Say-ressa picked up the tale. "You showed him some small stone figures that you carved in the Blackstone Caves. And then you showed him a map. This is what he told us."

"The ale boy. Of course."

"He is full of secrets, this boy," said Lesyl. "He said you still believe in the Keeper. That you still have dreams about it."

Say-ressa looked to Tabor Jan, a question on her face. He laughed.

"You may speak of these things," Cal-raven assured the singer, "so long as I am king. In our house, it will not be a crime to admit our dreams. We'll need them, especially during the winter. But how... You say he led you out of the fires?"

"There was fire everywhere," said the singer. "He knew the way out, some-how. There were so many of us trapped there."

"I'll think of some reward for him."

"I wish you could. But the boy went back to Abascar to search for others. More did come to us, following his directions, but the boy has not returned." Lesyl bowed her head. "Perhaps my song should remind us of him."

"This is stranger than dreams." Cal-raven looked out into the night. "The poor child."

"Missing, like so many." Say-ressa's shoulders shook, and Cal-raven rose to embrace her again.

He held her, overcome by the unfathomable loss. He would have welcomed his Promised again, even with all her failures and flaws. He would have welcomed those in the dungeons who had earned their judgments. He would have welcomed any if he could draw them from the earth.

"We will not forget," he said as he held her. "Your brave husband. Your beautiful daughter. We will honor them in our new house. And you shall remain our chief healer. Many have asked for you in their fevers."

"My lord," said Tabor Jan, holding out a small gift.

A cold stone fell into Cal-raven's outstretched hand.

"I told you if I found any Northchildren, I'd drag them back with me."

His touch recognized it before he could lift it into the light.

"The children were so afraid, but when the ale boy gave them these figures and told them they belonged to Prince Cal-raven, they stopped crying. He told them they would be like rings of trust, and they would protect them from all danger along their way to a new and better home."

"And so he was right," said Cal-raven quietly. He remembered the boy now. That smudged and timid boy who marveled at the sculptures, who had been so glad to hear that the prince dreamt of the Keeper. The boy who had told him of Auralia, who had seen the Keeper in the woods. It seemed another lifetime, ages and ages ago.

Cal-raven closed his hand over the figure. "We will leave these caves tomorrow and join you in those corridors of Blackstone. Perhaps some of the children will have the gift for stonecarving." He looked into the bear caves, thought of the names and faces he knew so well, of the hundreds more he soon would know. "The Expanse will be our house for now."

"I might ask," Lesyl ventured in a sad and urgent whisper, "if we are to be a house, my lord...perhaps we should give it a new name, one we can speak without trouble."

A name came to mind. One name clearly, and he touched the finger that had borne his ring of royal trust.

But they remained House Abascar in memory of those they had lost and in loyalty to a kingdom that had fought so hard for some measure of honor. It was a history fraught with error, greed, and weakness, but that history was far from over.

The days of heavy snow at the Blackstone Caves seemed endless, so the people of Abascar spoke often of their dreams.

One of those dreams, burning in Cal-raven's mind both day and night, came true on the first morning of open skies, as sunlight caught the forest by surprise and stunned sleepy birds into a frenzy of chatter. As he walked cautiously out of the silent canyons and into the ice-barked trees, dawn broke within his heart as well. He turned a familiar corner on a trail he remembered from childhood ventures with his mentor. Hagah, bounding about and sniffing at trees, suddenly barked and bared his teeth. A human figure loomed in the path ahead, hand raised in greeting.

It was a statue, carved from blacklode, manifesting such a lifelike form, yet so simple of features, that it seemed haunted. Half-alive.

Cal-raven knew that such masterful art came from only one set of hands. He recognized the clearing. Here Scharr ben Fray had taught him how to know direction when no stars were visible. And now here stood the very likeness of the mage, pointing the way to a mystery.

"Did he know I would come here, Hagah?" Cal-raven asked the hound, who was cautiously sniffing the statue.

The familiarity of that face, round as the moon and scribbled with age, brought tears to Cal-raven's eyes for the first time since the reunion in the Blackstone Caves. But he laughed in spite of them, for he could see that Scharr ben Fray still imagined himself a handsome man.

He solemnly read aloud the script etched along the edge of the figure's stone scarf, a script he, being Abascar royalty, could read. "North. Hurry. Fifteen passages of the stag. Twelfth new moon. Between old cloudgrasper and tall pine. Midnight. Wait."

He smiled, drawing his sword and chipping at the icicles that hung from the figure's raised arm. "Of course I'll be there," he said, turning in the direction of the mage's pointing finger. "We'll talk about dreams again. And we won't have to whisper."

Hagah stiffened and barked at something through the trees to the north. "Have your senses come back to you, Hagah? That's good. We have tracks to follow."

On a second thought, he touched the elaborate textures carved into the scarf and recognized them.

The mage had seen her after all. Scharr ben Fray had watched those colors unfurl. He had wondered at Auralia's mysteries and pondered the part she was playing in the story of the Expanse.

Cal-raven did not realize it at first, but somewhere along the path back to the caves he began to sing the Morning Verse. He was distracted, looking for the textures and colors of Auralia's work reflected in the wild woods around him while the snow melted and the season changed.

EPILOGUE

W hen the scent of dust and death from Abascar's fall reached Cent Regus dens, the half men swarmed into the Cragavar woods. Most were dragged along by their powerful appetites. They smelled smoke, trouble, blood. Into the fray they charged, all claws and jaws, killing and feasting wherever they could.

But some possessed a sense of restraint, having trained themselves to conspire for a greater reward. They prowled through the charred and crumbling ground, ensnaring those who fled and gathering treasures for their chieftain.

Beastmen were short-lived creatures unless they drank from the source of the power that had changed them. That secret reservoir, which in reverent whispers they spoke of as the Essence, was their wellspring. The chieftain controlled the Essence and determined who deserved to drink of it.

So they strove to please the chieftain in order to win more life, more power. He gave them deep draughts that numbed the pain of their grotesque evolution, even as it fueled far greater distortion.

Like all house leaders, he had ambitions and appetites of his own. Abascar's fall affirmed his conviction that House Cent Regus was gaining an advantage. It had become his strategy: since the beastmen by their nature could not ascend, perhaps they could make the other houses fall.

His minions might have lost the advantages of wit and wisdom, beauty and order, but they had lost *desire* for those virtues as well. They wanted only to grow stronger, to seize and devour. And now Abascar's survivors were his slaves.

Every day his doglike drones prodded a line of prisoners through the throne room before driving them to their humiliating chores. Torchlight cast shadows across the captives' features, which were hollowed with grief, hunger, and fear.

It was no secret that the chieftain despised the company of the uncursed. He brought them into his throne room only to mock, disfigure, and destroy them. While he could not imagine surrendering the Essence, even so there was a subtlety and a purity to the people of the other houses that maddened him.

But there was one prisoner, one trophy, he kept close at hand, ready to flaunt her at new captives.

He savored their responses if they recognized her. Some trembled, called her name, and wept. Some reddened with rage and spewed bitter words of blame.

He paid careful attention, as much as a beastman could, to what her survival required. Bread. Water. Meat. A barred chamber where she could sleep on furs and skins. But his urge to make her drink the Essence—that urge he had resisted so the prisoners would recognize her.

And on this day, as he felt the ground about his branches and roots forget winter's cruelty, a sniveling, cowering guardbeast approached him.

The chieftain sat high on a magnificent throne carved into the trunk of a black and twisted tree. The tree's roots, bulging with blue veins, crossed the dais and disappeared into the floor. Its boughs spread wide and pressed against the ceiling far above, shoving into the stone there and worming their way toward the surface. In the ground above these dens, the branches spread like wild ivy. Their barbed limbs wove through the soil, ready to ensnare any living thing, trapping animals for predators and travelers for enslavement. This was the chieftain's growing influence. This was his plan.

His body was in many ways that of a man—or rather, a corpse—from his common size to his pale flesh. But the curse was plainly evident in his shriveled legs and decaying feet, which hung useless before him. And in his doubled jaw, one very human mouth spoke in a child's pinched voice, while the other grinned broadly below with a hundred interlocking teeth. His skin adhered to the throne with gluey secretions through which he absorbed unnatural nourishment. The roots of his throne-tree tapped deep into the Essence far below, which pumped through his veins, increasing his subversive powers.

He beckoned with a long and curling claw. "Closer."

The messenger hesitated. While Abascar prisoners were passing through the room, the chieftain was agitated, excited, bloodthirsty. On a whim, he might devour his own trembling servants.

The chieftain could see that this simpering guardbeast was afraid to make his report. Since the creature had come from the cell of the chieftain's favorite prisoner, it could only be bad news.

"Master of Expanse," the guardbeast whimpered like a dog who awaits a beating, "your favorite, she is weakening, master. Sick with fever. We feed her; it does not help. We carry in water from beyond the wood; it does not help."

The chieftain blinked, absent for a moment. One of the long, bulbous roots coiled around the guardbeast's waist and lifted him up, carrying him close to the chieftain's lidless eyes.

"Keep her alive," said the beastman on the throne.

"H-h-how?"

"Make her think of Abascar." The chieftain waved the guardbeast around as his mind fumbled for an idea. "Give her…Abascar things. Spoils. Toys. Trinkets. Make her remember that she is Abascar's queen. Make her feel important. It is what she likes."

As a guardbeast slammed the two-wheeled cart into the bars of her cage, the clamor summoned the prisoner from sleep. Again he rammed the cart into the bars.

She made her way to investigate, her chains snaking along behind her. She reached through the bars and began to draw the clutter of remnants into the cell, pausing to examine each piece as if searching for its name. Two copper cauldrons. A jewel box. A humble clay cup. Three musical instruments she did not know how to play—a lynfr scorched with smoke, a karyn with a broken key, and a perys with only half its strings. A child's hand puppet, limp and missing one of its eggshell white eyes. A rusty pair of garden shears, which she held for a long time in her trembling hand.

And then she reached for the fabric that lay beneath it all. And when she touched it, it emanated a faint light as if she had shaken loose a cloud of golden dust.

"Yes," sneered the rodent-faced creature, "I find this...in barrel of water. Fire did not burn it. You see?" The beast reached into the strange glow and unfurled it before her, a cloak, a weaving so radiant that Jaralaine felt both fear and desire.

Someone had worn this in Abascar. Either Cal-marcus had lifted the Proclamation of the Colors, or...he had taken another queen.

The possibility had never crossed her mind. She had never considered that someone else might take her place.

The guardbeast threw the cloak into her cell. "Take. Keep. Feel better. Chieftain...he needs you to be well."

She regarded it with dread as the guardbeast wheeled the clunking cart back up the winding path.

For days she walked in a torment of hauntings, rejecting the cloak and all it suggested. Whatever had become of Abascar, she was free of it. She was subject to no one, a thread floating on a current of wind, true to her heart, denying the chains around her wrists and her feet.

While she slept, other voices rose in sharp contradiction, leaving her helpless and wanting.

She saw a multitude meandering in wonder through a pageant of color and life, their threads spread across the land in a tapestry. Each participant was distinct and bold. And yet they were interconnected and thus stronger and brighter, gathered together in glory. They were coaxed and guided by luminous hands, which bound weaker threads to sturdy cords, connecting them in an enduring design that ran off the map and into the source of all colors. She lay to the side, faded, forgotten, powerless to draw any eye, having detached herself.

She might have turned to dust there in that cruel despair.

When she woke, her hands were clenched around the rusty shears. All about her, spread like sunflares, lay her long, tangled hair. Fire and gold. She placed her hard, cold hands against her bare crown and wept.

That hands of mercy might unlock this prison or eyes might see her kindly in this wretched state, she never dared to hope.

For comfort, she groped for the colorful cloak, lifted it, and drew it about her shoulders. As she did, a strand of thread came free of the cloak and floated in the air before her.

It was a dark thread, deeper than red. It had not been woven into the cloak, she decided, for she could find no broken strands, no frayed seams. Having bound so many cloaks at the collar in just this fashion, she reached to the shiny stone clasp at her throat and laced the thread around to bind it.

And so it was that Jaralaine's open eyes opened, and she basked in the mysterious ways of Auralia's colors.

This is the end of *The Red Strand in the Auralia Thread.*

The story will continue in *The Blue Strand in the Auralia Thread—Cyndere's Midnight*—in which a Cent Regus beastman, haunted by the memory of Auralia's colors, follows the tracks of the Keeper into an unlikely adventure with a woman from House Bel Amica. What happens between them will change the course of their lives, weaving them together with the threads of the ale boy, Cal-raven, Scharr ben Fray, and the remnant of Abascar.

About the Author

Jeffrey Overstreet composed his first fantasy novel on a black Royal typewriter when he was seven years old, and he's been writing stories for all ages ever since. Since 1996, his film reviews, music reviews, and interviews have been regularly posted at his Web site, LookingCloser.org. His perspectives are frequently published on *Christianity Today's* Web site and in many other periodicals, including *Paste, Image: A Journal of the Arts and Religion,* and *Risen.* His "travelogue of dangerous moviegoing," *Through a Screen Darkly,* was published by Regal Books in February 2007.

Jeffrey and his wife, a poet and freelance editor named Anne, spend time writing in the coffee shops of Shoreline, Washington, every week. He works as a contributing editor for Seattle Pacific University's *Response* magazine. And now he is hard at work on many new stories, including three more strands of The Auralia Thread.

To learn more about WaterBrook Press and view
our catalog of products, log on to our Web site:
www.waterbrookpress.com